Roger Taylor was born in Heywood, Lancashire, and qualified as a civil and structural engineer. Having successfully sold his two daughters, he lives with his wife in the Wirral, Merseyside. He is a pistol shooter and a student of traditional aikido. He is the author of the four Chronicles of Hawklan (*The Call of the Sword*, *The Fall of Fyorlund*, *The Waking of Orthlund* and *Into Narsindal*) and the epic fantasies *Dream Finder*, *Farnor*, *Valderen*, *Whistler* and *Ibryen*, also available from Headline Feature.

'A classic effort which deserves to sell well' *Bookshelf*

'A delightful fantasy . . . easy to read, with a strong plot' *Norwich Evening News*

'Easy story-teller's style . . . a rip-roaring climax' *Chorley Guardian*

Arash-Felloren

Roger Taylor

First published in 1996
by HEADLINE BOOK PUBLISHING

First published in paperback in 1997
by HEADLINE BOOK PUBLISHING

A HEADLINE FEATURE paperback

10 9 8 7 6 5 4 3 2 1

ISBN 0 7472 5404 4

Typeset by CBS, Felixstowe, Suffolk

Printed and bound in Great Britain by
Cox & Wyman Ltd, Reading, Berks

HEADLINE BOOK PUBLISHING
A division of Hodder Headline PLC
338 Euston Road
London NW1 3BH

For my wife and children.
And Joan.

Chapter 1

THE WYNDERING

The door opened, creaking noisily. As the sound faded into the miasma of stale ale that pervaded the gloomy interior of the inn it was followed by that of a glass being knocked over and hastily retrieved. The innkeeper had started violently out of his drowsing vigil at the crude wooden counter. He swore, a little too loudly, and gazed around angrily, to indicate to such as might be watching that he had not been asleep but vigorously alert.

His charade evoked no response from the six customers in the drinking room. Two of them were slumped inelegantly across their tables, having succumbed either to the poor ale that was the inn's speciality, or to the heat that had been oppressing the region for the past weeks. The other four, with varying degrees of suspicion and concern, were doing what the innkeeper was now doing – staring at the figure of a man silhouetted in the doorway, stark and still against the red sky.

For a moment, the figure seemed to the innkeeper to be emerging from a glowing fire; despite the heat in the room, he shivered. A quick and unnecessary rearrangement of several glasses and bottles disguised the reaction.

When he looked up again, the man had not moved though there was an inclination of his head which indicated that he was perhaps examining the interior of the inn before deciding to enter.

The action reassured the innkeeper. Not normally given to thinking about anything other than his own immediate needs, the sudden intrusion of his imagination into his thoughts had unsettled him far more than he would have admitted – not least to himself.

1

Now, however, the surly normality of his life was reasserting itself. The new arrival was exhibiting one of the signs which were typical of a traveller in this area: caution.

Mercenary? the innkeeper thought. Trader? Labourer? Artisan? Miner? It was a game he played whenever a stranger arrived and he flattered himself that he could identify the calling of any newcomer at the merest glance, though he usually announced his success at this retrospectively with a knowing nod to his cronies and, 'Saw it, as soon as he came in,' or something similar.

Studiously turning his attention away from the door, he returned to his normal position, leaning heavily forward on the counter as though keeping his clientéle under revue. It was an unremarkable posture and only his regular customers knew that his brawny arms were so arranged that his right hand would be hanging near a weighted cudgel strategically placed on two makeshift brackets behind the counter: a cudgel that he could wield with a speed and accuracy quite at odds with the lumbering pace that his overweight frame imposed on most of his actions. They knew too, that his small, peevish eyes were not in fact watching them, but maintaining a close, sidelong observation of the newcomer.

The figure stepped forward. The red evening sky behind him appeared to flare, as if suddenly released. He had scarcely taken one step when the innkeeper's eyes came sharply forward like those of a dog avoiding the gaze of its pack leader. The hand near the cudgel softly curled and eased away from it, as if even its hidden proximity to the weapon might antagonize. The actions were instinctive and he could not have accounted for them even if he had realized what he was doing. Habit, however, overrode this response and straightened him up to receive his new customer.

Whatever ominous presence the newcomer had seemed to exude on his first appearance vanished as the door closed, and the dim light of the inn dressed him in a long, travel-stained coat and a wide-brimmed and equally stained hat. His right hand was wound around the strap of a pack hanging from his shoulder. He looked about him as he walked through the silence, then he reached up and removed his hat to reveal a lean weather-beaten face.

The innkeeper found himself looking into deep-set eyes. They were heavily shaded in the poor light and he could thus read nothing in them, though a fleeting glint from the depths unnerved him momentarily. Uncertain of his voice, he raised his eyebrows in insolent inquiry.

'Do you have a room where I can stay?'

The ordinariness of the question aided the innkeeper's recovery. He frowned, though it was not at the request, but at the man's accent, which he could not place immediately. Still, that would have to wait. First things first.

'Got any money?' he demanded.

The man nodded slightly. 'How much is the room?'

The innkeeper told him, increasing the normal price by a half and adding, 'In advance.'

Unexpectedly, the man did not quibble and his left hand dropped two coins on the counter. 'Three nights,' he said quietly.

The innkeeper swept them up a little too eagerly, then, remembering himself, examined them carefully. They were local and they were good. 'Three nights,' he confirmed, stoically keeping a gleam from his eyes.

'I'll put my horse in the stable,' the man said, turning away.

Fully himself again now, the innkeeper jingled the two coins significantly. The man paused, then placed a smaller coin on the counter. 'This will feed us both.'

The innkeeper opened his mouth to remonstrate, but though the voice had been soft and unprovocative, the statement was categorical and he found himself disinclined to barter. The coins in his bulbous fist weighed heavily and he nodded in agreement. The man turned and left. As the door opened and closed, the red light washed briefly into the inn again.

'Gave me a start when he came in, that one, Ghreel. Thought he was one of Barran's men.'

The speaker was a rat-faced individual. He scraped his chair back and sidled up to the counter. Ghreel jingled the coins again, then grunted. He was speculating urgently about who the newcomer might be but he had no intention of exposing his confusion to the likes of ale-swilling flotsam such as Riever here.

Nevertheless, his position as supreme authority in such matters

3

had to be maintained. He pursed his lips knowingly and tossed the coins casually into his apron pocket. 'Not one of Barran's,' he said decisively. Little risk in that. Barran's men didn't wander about alone, out here, didn't pay for anything if they could afford it, and had no need for rooms at an inn. Further, though his entrance had been oddly disconcerting, he did not have the presence of a fighter of any kind, least of all one of Barran's. From the hang of his coat he wore a sword, but that signified nothing.

Curiosity suddenly got the better of him – and greed. The man hadn't haggled, so obviously he wasn't short of money. Either that or he was simple. 'Better see what he's up to,' he said, propelling himself away from the counter. The room shook under the impact of his heavy footfalls as he rolled across to the door. Riever took half a step after him, then changed his mind and returned to his table.

Outside, the setting sun, made almost blood-red by the day's dust hanging in the air, flooded the landscape and turned the inn's untidy yard into a patchwork of unfamiliar shadows. Ghreel screwed up his eyes then grimaced as a warm and dank breeze wound itself about him like a clinging blanket. He unearthed a soiled kerchief from a deep pocket and ran it over his face as he made an undulating progress toward the open stable door.

As the various parts of Ghreel came to an unsteady standstill in the doorway, the stranger was rubbing water over the muzzle of his horse. He turned to face the panting innkeeper. Despite the heat, he had replaced his hat and Ghreel felt himself the object of an intense scrutiny even though he could not see the man's eyes.

'Got everything you need?' The words blustered out of him.

The man led his horse to a stall and whispered to it before turning back to Ghreel.

'Yes, thank you,' he said, hitching his pack on to his shoulder and picking up two saddlebags. 'Could you show me my room?'

Once again, the soft voice and quiet manner left Ghreel at a loss, throwing him, untypically, into politeness. 'Are you travelling on, or looking for work hereabouts?' he asked as he motioned the man back to the inn.

4

'Both,' came the reply. 'I'll need to work for a little while until I've enough money to move on.'

It gave Ghreel the opportunity he had been waiting for. 'What's your trade?' he asked.

'I'm a teacher.'

'Teacher!' Ghreel exclaimed. He wobbled to a halt and looked at his companion with a combination of disbelief and distaste. 'Teacher!' He was in his element now – he hated 'clever' people. His inadvertent politeness vanished. 'What do you think you're going to teach around here?' He waved a dismissive hand and set off again.

'Whatever people want to learn.' The answer showed no sign of irritation at the innkeeper's manner which soured further as a consequence.

'That's precisely nothing,' Ghreel retorted, with a sneer. 'Or at least nothing that comes out of a book. All anyone wants to know here is what they can use – who's got money they can steal, where they can get a woman, and who's got the cheapest ale.' He patted himself on the chest.

He expected some argument, especially from a know-it-all like this one. The man obviously had no idea what the real world was like. He'd be lucky if he didn't end up in a ditch with his head stoved in. Even experienced travellers went on their ways wiser after passing through here. Wiser – and poorer.

'Perhaps I should just move on, then.'

The reply brought Ghreel to another halt. In his enthusiasm to persecute this newcomer he had nearly stepped over the mark. His hands involuntarily closed around the coins in his apron pocket and he gave the man a quick, narrow-eyed glance. The hat and the low sun combined to prevent him from reading anything in the shadowed face, but with an effort he forced himself to look concerned. 'Your horse looks as if it could do with a rest,' he said. 'As do you.' He tried to make his expression fatherly, but it became a yellow-toothed leer. 'There'll probably be something for you.' A fat thumb flicked towards the setting sun. 'There's the city. And the Lowe Towns. Not to mention more than a few farms.' The leer nodded to the east. 'Then there's the mines in the Thlosgaral and

5

the Wilde Ports on the other side.' He was unable to resist a final jibe. 'Providing you don't mind doing *real* work, of course.'

Once again, to Ghreel's annoyance, the man did not respond, and they entered the inn in silence.

'What is the city?' the man asked as the stagnant dimness of the drinking room embraced them. He took off his hat. Ghreel blinked to clear his vision, then looked at him with a mixture of disbelief and suspicion. There was no sign of mockery in the face however.

'What do you mean, what's the city?'

'What's it called?'

The innkeeper pondered the question, testing it carefully, still suspicious. 'Arash-Felloren,' he said eventually, speaking warily, as if to a treacherous child. 'You can't not have heard about Arash-Felloren, surely?'

The man gave a self-deprecating shrug. 'I live far away.'

Like a hunting animal returning to its lair, Ghreel scuttled back behind the counter, and into his natural condition. He addressed the room. 'Hear that, lads? Man here's a teacher.' He lingered on the word. 'But he's never heard of Arash-Felloren. You must have come from a very long way away, that's all I can say. And it must have been a quiet place.' Unfriendly laughter greeted this but the man just turned and acknowledged it with a smile.

'I have, and it was,' he said. 'But I'll take your advice. I'll stay a while. Perhaps try the city tomorrow.' He met Ghreel's taunting gaze squarely. 'I'd like to rest now, if you don't mind.'

Ghreel scowled. This man's lack of response was increasingly irritating but it also gave him no excuse for picking a quarrel. 'Never heard of Arash-Felloren,' he growled, loath to let the topic pass. 'Biggest city in the world, lad.' He was about to indulge in a scornful tirade about the stranger's chances of surviving there when the coins in his apron reminded him that they might have cousins nearby. He contended himself with a laboured shake of his head as he indicated a door at the far end of the room.

The wooden stairs creaked unhappily as Ghreel made his way up them. It was not until he had reached the top that the stranger followed him, apparently anxious not to be trapped in this timber-sided ravine with Ghreel's mountainous bulk lurching above him. The stairway led directly on to a wide, unevenly boarded balcony lined with doors and shuttered windows. Ghreel kicked open the nearest door.

'Here you are,' he said brusquely. He was about to turn away when a spasm of proprietorial pride seized him and he followed the stranger into the room. 'Shutters are a bit stiff,' he said, giving them a powerful slap. 'But you'll not be wanting them open too long, what with the flies and dust and all.' The tour moved to the bed. 'Mattress was given a good beating only last week.' And thence to a stone sink. The pride became incongruously visible. 'And water.' He pumped a handle energetically and, after some peevish coughing, a desultory trickle of water spluttered irritably into the sink. 'Only inn round here with that,' he announced. 'You'll be lucky with most of them if you've got a pump in the yard and a bucket that doesn't leak.'

The stranger raised his eyebrows and nodded an acknowledgement to indicate his appreciation at finding this haven. 'Only here,' Ghreel repeated. 'Only at The Wyndering. Anyone'll tell you.' Then he was gone, the floor shaking rhythmically to his departure.

The stranger put his saddlebags on the floor and laid his pack on the bed. He left the door open and, after a brief struggle, managed to open the various shutters – one on to the balcony and one overlooking the inn yard. The brilliant redness of the setting sun was fading to a dusty ruddiness, though there seemed to be no lessening of the day's heat. He took off his hat and the long coat and laid them carefully on the room's one chair. Then he unbuckled his belt and, carefully placing his sword by his side, lay down on the bed, his hands behind his head.

His eyes moved slowly and methodically about the room, noting the old workmanship and the scars of many years of usage. The room, like The Wyndering as a whole, had the air of a fine old gentleman fallen upon hard times but now revelling in it. His study was punctuated by occasional sounds from the yard and the drinking room below.

'What's it to be tomorrow?' said his companion. 'Arash-Felloren, or the Wilde Ports?'

7

Chapter 2

Gasping for breath, but made even more vigorous and fleet than usual by the angry cries following him, Pinnatte ran frantically along the crowded street.

He had made a mistake – a serious one – but it was not until after he had snatched the man's purse that he realized he had been one of the Kyrosdyn. Worse, the wretch had been a full Brother too, perhaps even a Higher Brother, judging by the quality of the crystals marking out the emblem on his purse, and the size of the guard who appeared from nowhere at his master's cry.

Pinnatte swung round a corner.

And that cry had been another thing – it was still ringing in his head – that peculiar blend of fury, disbelief and throat-wrenching petulance. It had confirmed the man as a Kyrosdyn even as Pinnatte was registering the emblem and its implications for his immediate future.

He cursed silently. Damn the man, wandering the streets looking just like any other person. How was an honest thief supposed to know? Why the devil hadn't he been wearing his robes or at least carrying his staff? Pinnatte did not debate the questions, however. Instead he twitched his head as the memory returned of his victim's guard looming ahead of him, massive hands outstretched, eyes full of malevolent focus. His head had twitched thus while his mouth had been gaping, his mind teetering on the edge of panic and, having saved him then, it seemed to be locked into him now, as if every time he did it, he might suddenly find himself free.

Passers-by moved hastily out of his way, some nervously, others angrily, swearing after him or aiming a blow. One or two, sensing reward, tried to grab hold of him, but he was moving too quickly, and the one individual who did succeed, found himself a victim of Pinnatte's momentum, ending his attempted seizure by spinning round incongruously and tottering into the path of a passing carriage.

The resultant din brought vividly to Pinnatte the realization that his headlong flight was leaving a trail for his pursuers as clear as footprints in the snow. He must slow down! If he didn't he could well set off the Cry, then, if he survived that, he'd find his fellow thieves after him as well.

But he was not fully in command of his legs. The Kyrosdyn were terrifying. Steal crystals from most people and you could certainly look for a more vigorous pursuit than if you had stolen coin or any other jewellery. But steal one from a Kyrosdyn and you could look to run as far as the Wilde Ports, then a long swim, if you hoped to escape. Kyrosdyn obsession with crystals was legendary. It was one of the great 'Do Nots' of the Guild of Thieves – 'Stole a crystal from a Kyrosdyn,' was the knowing way of saying, 'He's a dead man.'

That was why he had thrown the purse in the guard's face almost immediately – as if the action would absolve him from all blame. But the Kyrosdyn were more than just obsessive about their crystals, they had a lust for them that was almost religious, and to touch them without respect, still less, without permission, was to bring down that unreasoned and self-righteous wrath on the perpetrator's head that only the religious can aspire to.

And strange things happened to those who were taken by the Kyrosdyn . . .

He must stop running! He must stop! The urgency of this inner demand was beginning to outweigh the urgency of the need to flee. Amongst the many skills that Pinnatte's years of thieving had given him was one which made him aware of the sound of the crowd even when he was not particularly listening to it. Sometimes it would tell him that he could almost stroll from pocket to pocket, shop to shop, and take whatever he wanted without creating even a stir. At others, seemingly no different, it said, 'No. Walk away. Leave it. It's too dangerous.' Whenever he had chosen to ignore this soft voice, he had suffered for it. Now, he could sense his erratic progress rebounding through the bustling chaos of the streets and leaving a wake that was not dissipating, but gathering in force. If he didn't stop soon, then the Cry would be called as sure as fate.

He changed direction abruptly and careened into a narrow alley. It was a dangerous thing to do, as he could be trapping himself there, where his manoeuvrability would be of little avail, but he needed a moment to force himself to stop and gather his scattered senses. As it was, it took him twenty paces before he could slow down to a walk, and a further twenty before he really began to take command of his thoughts – and stop his head from twitching. Belatedly checking that the alley was empty, he pulled off his jacket, turned it inside out and put it on again. A dirty yellow kerchief was dragged out of a pocket, wiped across his perspiring face then wrapped about his neck. Then his trousers were tugged out of his boots and, finally, his unkempt hair was swept into some semblance of tidiness. It was thus a markedly different Pinnatte who emerged from the other end of the alley and, with studied casualness, sauntered into the busy traffic.

It was as well he stopped his reckless career when he did, he realized. Even here he could feel a tension in the passers-by. Somewhere that screeching Kyrosdyn and his guard might still be looking for him – making more din than a mother looking for a lost child! He'd like to choke the creature on his damned crystals! He'd got them back, hadn't he?'

Then, for the first time ever, he wondered why the Kyrosdyn were the way they were. The crystals were valuable, some much more than others, with their many tints and hues, and valuable things made some people very strange. But why should the Kyrosdyn – to a man – have such fanatical regard for them?

It was rumoured that in the Vaskyros they had a great hoard, even of the most precious of all – those with that faint and subtle green glow at their heart. He had seen few worthwhile crystals in his life, and he had never seen one of those – very few had. Occasionally, in some drinking hole frequented by his own kind,

11

boastful tales would emerge of green crystals won and lost, but such stories were usually worth no more than the ale that was creating them. Only once had he felt himself on the edge of the truth when, in the middle of such a yarn, an old man, sullenly silent until then, had suddenly snarled out a drunken oath and accused the teller of being a fool and a liar. By way of emphasis, he slapped his hand down on the table, palm upwards. It was withered and dead and the fingers were curled into a painful grasp. 'That's green crystals for you, lad,' he said. 'That, and nightmares for the rest of your life.' He tapped his head and sneered. 'You've seen nothing. Still less touched.'

The outburst had won him only a measure of his length in the street, yet Pinnatte had never forgotten the despair and pain that had shone briefly through the old man's bleary eyes. The memory returned to him whenever green crystals were spoken of. It was with him now. And in a way he could not define, it chimed with the cry that the Kyrosdyn had uttered when his purse was snatched – there had been a fearful despair in it.

He shook his head to dispel these thoughts. This was no time to be daydreaming. He must pay attention to what was happening about him. Was he still being sought? Had his flight and the pursuit been sufficient to let loose the Cry?

He paused momentarily, ostensibly looking at the fruit on a roadside stall but, in reality, listening, and debating his next move. The street was noisy but the tension he had sensed when he emerged from the alley was no longer there. The pursuit had either ended or gone off in another direction. He let out a long, silent breath. He'd been lucky there. Luckier than he deserved. He resolved to be more careful in future – it was the third time that month he had made such a resolution. Even as he was reaffirming this oath however, he saw his hand about to slip an apple into his pocket. With an effort he stopped it and conspicuously replaced the apple on the stall. He'd have to steal something else, later.

'Don't maul 'em if you're not buying,' the stall-holder barked by way of acknowledgement. Pinnatte bit back a retort, but could not avoid curling his lip at the man as he rejoined the crowd.

Still a little unnerved by his escape he wandered aimlessly for some time. Although he was calmer now, scenes kept playing themselves through his head, showing him talking his way out of the clutches of the Kyrosdyn and his bodyguard with ingenious and quite convincing excuses, or somehow dashing them both aside and escaping with the purse to become the most famous of Arash-Felloren's thieves. In the wake of these came endless, wilder variations and, even though he tried to dismiss them as so much foolishness, Pinnatte could not help himself but rehearse each to a nicety.

Gradually, more prosaic needs began to impose themselves. The combination of terror and his frantic run through the afternoon's heat had made him thirsty – very thirsty. And, too, he would have to find something for his Den Master, Lassner, if he was to eat properly tonight. He dismissed this last concern for the moment. Unlike his fantasy about the Kyrosdyn, if the worst came to the worst he *could* talk his way around Lassner for at least one night's credit. Far more pressing now was his thirst.

He came to where several streets met, or rather collided, to form a wide and ragged square. Arash-Felloren was replete with charters, statutes, laws, by-laws, and all manner of rules and regulations dealing with the movement of goods and people, the conducting of business, marrying, burying, begging, borrowing, stealing, and every form of social and commercial intercourse in which waywardness of some kind had occurred since anyone had bothered to record such matters. Sadly, while they were both extensive and comprehensive, they were also, for the most part, either incomprehensible or mutually contradictory. They had one thing in common, however. They were almost universally ignored. True, there were several, large areas of the city where order and prosperity prevailed, but the greater part of it was subject only to one law – the oldest of laws – survival.

The square that Pinnatte now entered was a frenzy of confusion and disorder as faltering skeins of wagons, riders and walkers struggled to cross it, weaving around and through a random sprawl of stalls and tents and gaudy handcarts at its centre. The dust-filled air was thick with oaths and clamour as travellers and shifty-eyed traders each vied for attention.

Pinnatte entered the fray. The jostling and buffeting in a place like this made it ideal for snatching purses and picking pockets, especially working with a team of like-minded souls, but, apart from his thirst, his luck having turned so sour today, he was in no mood for it. A good yarn about today's events should serve to keep Lassner satisfied tonight, he decided. The old man was a realist, he'd do nothing impetuous because of one night's rent. Pinnatte took a perverse pride in his integrity as a thief – amongst his own kind, his word was good and he settled his debts promptly – he was a model Den-Mate.

Towards the middle of the square, where the traders outnumbered the travellers, was a raised fountain – a remnant of the time when the square had been more prosperous. The carved figures that formed it had long been mutilated – fine features rendered pugilistic by the breaking of noses and ears, stout stone shields and swords shattered and split, then weathered and decayed. But the water had always flowed. With its source far from the city, it was too good to be hazarded by the reckless damaging of its supply and outlet conduits, and a general awareness of its value by the locals had always protected it from complete destruction.

Pinnatte reached it with some relief. There were two or three groups of people, mainly men, lounging on the steps that led up to the fountain's basin. He stepped through them with a studied combination of assuredness and inoffensiveness that he had cultivated over the years, meeting gazes clearly where unavoidable, though without challenge.

At the top of the steps, he leaned over the low parapet to catch a handful of water tumbling from one of several spouts. As ever, it was as cold as the mountains it came from, quite unaffected by the weeks of humid heat that had been pervading the city. He drank noisily, relishing the chill that marked out a route inside him. When he was sated, he scooped both hands deep into the basin and splashed his face luxuriously. The strains of the day faded almost immediately. He began to practise his tale for Lassner. It would be a good one and, if he told it well, he might get more than one night rent-free. There could even be extra food – Lassner liked a good tale.

As the thought came to him, a powerful grip closed around his neck and plunged his head under the water.

Chapter 3

The same powerful grip that had thrust Pinnatte's head beneath the water eventually withdrew it but he was retching and struggling frantically for some time before he realized that it was air entering his lungs and not freezing water. For a moment he hung limply, then he made a desperate attempt to free himself. It was to no avail however, for though he was much stronger than his wiry frame indicated, the grip was unyielding and merely tightened painfully until he became still again.

Then the sound of laughter penetrated the booming in his ears and a vague shape formed through his blurred vision. Reaching up cautiously, for fear of antagonizing his captor, he wiped the water from his face until the shape became clearer.

It was the Kyrosdyn.

A chill filled Pinnatte that was far colder than the water he had just been immersed in and he began struggling again. The grip on his neck tightened mercilessly, making him cry out this time, and a stinging blow struck him across the face.

Ironically, the blow cleared his mind and once again he became very still. The grip eased slightly. Pinnatte glanced around rapidly to assess his predicament. He saw that the laughter was coming from a gathering crowd and that the Kyrosdyn's hand was raised to strike him again.

The crowd offered him a glimmer of hope. It was unlikely that they would intervene if he was about to receive a beating. He himself had stood by and watched while others had been beaten, even killed – interfering in such matters was rarely wise. But the Kyrosdyn were loved by no one and, with luck, the crowd might perhaps be swayed to his side.

If he got the opportunity to speak.

But whatever else happened, he must stay here, in public view. He was lost if the Kyrosdyn managed to take him to the Vaskyros.

'What did you do that for?' he spluttered, mustering all the injured innocence he could find.

The Kyrosdyn paused, tilted his head on one side, then brought his face close to Pinnatte's. 'I think you know,' he said softly. Pinnatte's insides tightened. It was as though the man's gaze was burning through him. He wanted desperately to look away, but the grip on his neck prevented him from moving and all he could do was screw up his eyes.

'No, I don't,' he managed to protest.

The Kyrosdyn moved a finger in front of his unblinking eyes. The strange gesture was made slowly and with a deliberateness that frightened Pinnatte far more than any angry fist-clenching could have done. He could do no other than focus on the man's hand, turning the staring eyes into a glinting blur in the background. As if in some way he might hide from what was happening, he found himself noting that the hand was long and delicate – like a woman's, almost – and it was clean. Very clean. However the Kyrosdyn practised their craft, it involved nothing that would coarsen and harden the hands.

'Look at me,' came the command. Pinnatte could not disobey and, once again, he was staring into the Kyrosdyn's eyes. The soft, high-pitched voice continued: 'We who study the crystals have a vision which you could not begin to imagine. We look into the very heart of all things.' The voice dropped almost to a whisper. 'Even into the worlds between and beyond. So when you sought to steal from us, your every line and shadow was etched into our mind on the instant. Your flight was a mere irritation – one which will worsen your punishment. It is not possible to hide from us – the echo of your stunted, shrivelled soul shone in the air itself. Nor is it possible to avoid the consequences that your desecration has set in train.'

The last three words were pronounced with great deliberation and each was accompanied by a slap across the face. Once again the blows served only to bring Pinnatte's mind into sharp focus.

Though the Brotherhood of the Kyrosdyn never seemed to vie for power over the city themselves, their influence was avidly sought by those factions that did, for it was a commonplace that they possessed dark and mysterious powers and whoever could win them to their side would prosper. The malign influence they had in the endless political manoeuvring that plagued the city had little or no effect on the lives of such as Pinnatte, and he affected to hold it in disdain. Yet he was well aware of its potency. Thus, suddenly finding himself confronted by one of these sinister manipulators, his reaction was coloured by the superstitious fear that street gossip had imbued in him. And each word the man spoke brought this fear closer and closer to the surface, until it threatened to unman him. Now, however, the blows to his face somehow reduced the Kyrosdyn. Now he was just another street bully. For an instant, Pinnatte experienced two opposing emotions – a sudden elation mingled with an unexpected and indefinable sense of loss. But he was freer now.

'I don't know what you're talking about,' he replied angrily. 'Are you touched in the head, or something? Half-drowning a man for just having a quiet drink. And let go of me, will you.' He swung a fist vaguely backwards but it bounced impotently off a solid, muscular frame. He appealed to the crowd. 'Get him off me,' he shouted, catching the eyes of as many people as he could. 'He's a lunatic. I've never seen him before and I certainly haven't stolen anything from him.'

The Kyrosdyn struck him again. Pinnatte reached up with both hands and managed to seize the wrist of his captor. Then, supporting himself on the extended arm, he kicked wildly with both feet at the Kyrosdyn. The man holding him tottered forward under this unexpected burden and Pinnatte used the movement to bounce his feet off the ground and kick again. None of the kicks found a target, but the Kyrosdyn was obliged to jump back hastily and the whole escapade was greeted by the crowd with a cheer. The second attack further disturbed the balance of the guard and Pinnatte tightened his awkward grip on the man's wrist, and began to struggle desperately. Abruptly he was on his knees and the man was tumbling over. Then the grip vanished and Pinnatte stood up.

19

Quite unaware of how he had achieved this, he turned round to see the Kyrosdyn's guard staggering down the steps of the fountain, his arms flailing to catch his balance. He was fully as large as Pinnatte remembered and now his face was alight with rage. Pinnatte reflected briefly that humiliating some ox of a mercenary in front of his employer was almost as bad as trying to rob the Kyrosdyn in the first place, but he did not dwell on the comparison. With the instinct of a fleeing animal and the cunning of a life-long street thief, he glanced round and, where others might have seen an impenetrable crowd, he saw a score of openings through which he could make an escape. He selected one that lay in the opposite direction to the Kyrosdyn and, scarcely hesitating, made for it.

'No!'

The Kyrosdyn's voice, penetrating and shrill, seemed to Pinnatte to wrap itself around him like the claws of innumerable tiny creatures and, abruptly, his legs stopped moving. The superstitious fear of the Kyrosdyn that had only just left him, returned in full force and burst openly into his mind, as he tried to continue his flight only to find that his legs would not respond. Several hands caught him as he tumbled forward.

'He's done something to my legs,' he heard himself saying in an echoing distance. 'I can't move them.'

'Bring him here,' the Kyrosdyn's voice raked through him again.

There was doubt in the supporting hands, some holding him protectively, others pushing him away anxiously, as though he were suddenly contaminated.

'Bring him here!' The command was repeated.

Part of Pinnatte was telling him that he should be trying to sway the crowd to his side, but it could make no headway against the torrent of fears breaking over him at the loss of the use of his legs.

Someone turned him round to face the Kyrosdyn. The man was standing with his hand extended towards him, the centre, Pinnatte thought, of a strange disturbance. For an instant he thought he saw something green and baleful, flickering on the man's hand, but he blinked, and it was gone. He screwed up his eyes but the disturbance

20

did not change. It was as though the air about the Kyrosdyn was dancing and twisting, and too, as though he was somehow standing by the fountain and, at the same time, somewhere else. Pinnatte felt a cold awfulness possess him at the sight. With each bursting heartbeat he felt movement leaving his limbs. He could do nothing. He *was* nothing. He was prey held captive by the gaze of a predator. All that remained now was a timeless time before he was no more.

But even as the thought formed, a faint cry of denial began to make itself heard through Pinnatte's terror. This was not his time. He would not fall to his miserable creature, who squealed like a pig just because his purse was snatched, and who needed a guard just to walk the streets. From somewhere, he found a voice. 'Help me,' he said faintly, forcing himself to look round at the crowd. 'He's doing something to me. He's killing me.'

The disturbance about the Kyrosdyn faltered a little and Pinnatte felt the bonds about him faltering in response. And his sense of the mood of the crowd began to return. It held hope. Where before there had merely been excited curiosity, now, mingling with it, was concern and alarm – and anger.

Pinnatte saw the guard move to his master's side as if in confirmation. The Kyrosdyn inclined his head as the man whispered something.

The disturbance was gone completely, and Pinnatte almost staggered as the use of his legs suddenly returned. 'He's doing something to me.' He shouted this time. 'I can't move.' He gave a brief stiff-jointed mime.

'He's nowhere near you.' It was the guard.

Mistake, thought Pinnatte. Too loud and too soon.

The Kyrosdyn thought so too, judging by the angry look he gave his defender.

'*Something* queer happened,' came a supporting voice behind Pinnatte. 'I felt it.' It was followed by an unsteady chorus of agreement.

'He's lying,' the Kyrosdyn cried.

The voice behind Pinnatte became an indignant figure at his side. 'Are you calling me a liar?'

'Kyroscreft!'

Coming from somewhere within the crowd, the word hissed through the air like an assassin's arrow. Pinnatte started and cursed himself for a fool. It was the cry he should have made from the first. It was the cry that represented all that was deemed to be the Kyrosdyn's true calling – the searching into the mysterious and dangerous powers that lay hidden in nature – forbidden powers – and for which their proclaimed craft of crystal-working was a mere façade. It was a word loaded with fear and hatred, and response to it was invariably unreasoned and primitive. In the past it had rung out loudly in rioting against the Kyrosdyn. Rioting that had resulted in many lives being lost but which, strangely, had left the Kyrosdyn, as innocent and injured parties, somehow further entrenched as a powerful force in the city's shifting and complex government.

Without hesitation, the guard drew his sword and, slowly moving around his charge, swung it in a wide, horizontal arc. It was an action that forestalled any sudden assault on the Kyrosdyn, and the watching circle widened immediately. Though several men laid hands on knives and swords, none were drawn. All knew that the first one to step forward in anger was likely to die and, Kyroscreft or no, nothing had happened here that was worth that. There were one or two cries from bolder sparks, standing safely at the back of the crowd, but they were quickly silenced.

The crowd began to break up, its excited mood dissipated. Pinnatte sidled backwards with his immediate neighbours. He caught the Kyrosdyn's eye and could not forebear a triumphant sneer. Unexpectedly, three long and furious strides brought the Kyrosdyn face to face with him, and a hand gripping the front of his jacket hoisted him up on to his toes. Pinnatte gaped, wide-eyed, taken aback by the speed of the man's response, and too, by the strength in that delicate hand.

'I meant you no offence, sir,' the Kyrosdyn was saying, his voice pleasant and apologetic. It took Pinnatte a moment to realize that he was talking to the man by his side who had protested at being called a liar. 'I was referring to this . . . wretch.' He shook Pinnatte. 'He's a thief and not worthy of your protection.'

Pinnatte looked round at the crowd again, but it was already much smaller, and the traffic around the fountain was re-establishing

22

itself. The Kyrosdyn's guard was sheathing his sword – the danger had passed. Pinnatte thought desperately. Whatever else happened now, he must not allow himself to be taken to the Vaskyros.

'I took nothing,' he said plaintively to his now solitary ally, catching hold of his arm urgently. 'You can search me.'

The man seemed anxious to be on his way, but the Kyrosdyn's soft apology and Pinnatte's appeal had placed him in the position of an arbiter. He looked from Pinnatte to the Kyrosdyn. 'Will that satisfy you, sir?' he said uncomfortably. 'I can call for the Weartans if you wish.' He pointed to a building some way down one of the streets that led into the square.

Pinnatte uttered a brief prayer of thanksgiving. It was highly unlikely that the Kyrosdyn would want anything to do with the Prefect's guards – the men and women nominally responsible for enforcing the law and maintaining order on the streets. No one walked away from an encounter with them other than poorer.

The Kyrosdyn tightened his grip about Pinnatte's jacket and his eyes narrowed savagely. Then, abruptly, he released him.

'No,' he replied, still polite. 'I don't think that will be necessary.'

Pinnatte wasted no time in thanking his inadvertent saviour, but turned to flee immediately. He had not taken one step however, when something struck his shins and sent him sprawling painfully on the cobbled road. It was no relief to him to note that this time it was not some strange power of the Kyrosdyn that had brought him down, but the guard's foot. Before he could recover himself, that same foot placed itself deliberately over his ankle, and pressed. He cried out in pain and tried to pull his foot away, but the guard merely smiled and increased the pressure. Such of the crowd as remained kept their distance and watched warily. Passers-by stepped around them nervously.

Then the Kyrosdyn was bending over Pinnatte. The pressure on his foot eased, but still held him fast. 'There will be another time, thief,' the Kyrosdyn said. He crouched down, untied the purse that Pinnatte had tried to snatch earlier, and held it out for him to inspect.

The leatherwork alone was worth more than Pinnatte could expect to earn in many weeks of good thieving and, while he was no expert in the value of crystals, those he could see inlaid there represented wealth he had only ever dreamed of. He looked stonily at the purse, knowing that if he had been lucky enough to escape with it, he would probably not have been able to dispose of it. In fact, he would almost certainly have been at as great a risk from other, more successful thieves as from the searching Kyrosdyn. He could even have found himself having to deal with Barran's men . . . He pushed the thought away.

He noticed that the Kyrosdyn's eyes were grey, as if all the colour had been drained from them.

'You've caused me grievous offence, thief,' the man was saying. 'And thus the Brotherhood. And though circumstances have conspired to protect you at the moment, I'll have your worthless soul before we're through.' He bared clenched teeth and, with a curiously delicate gesture, reached into the purse. When he withdrew it he was holding a clear crystal between his thumb and index finger. It glittered brightly – more brightly than it should have done in the hot and dust-filled light of the square, Pinnatte thought.

'I'll bind it in here. Hold it with bonds smaller and more powerful than you could believe.' He held it to his ear. 'I'll listen to its futile struggling as it flitters about the latticed cages of its new home. Reflecting and refracting endlessly, bouncing to and fro, echoing and resonating. Doing our bidding. Trapped. For ever.'

The crystal was gone, suddenly encased in the Kyrosdyn's hand. Pinnatte blinked. For a moment the square seemed to be much darker than it had been. Though the Kyrosdyn's words made no sense, they had been terrifying and his mouth and throat were dry with fear. 'I took nothing,' he managed to say hoarsely. 'You know that.'

The Kyrosdyn made no response but stood up and motioned the guard to release Pinnatte's foot. Then he started, as if he had seen something unexpected. Doubt and certainty, both equally terrible, began to vie for mastery of his face as he stared at Pinnatte, and his head canted to one side as though he were listening to something far away. A shaking hand drew something hesitantly from inside his jacket. Pinnatte watched him, wide-eyed.

Slowly – painfully, almost – the doubt faded into a tight-faced resolution, then, with an almost reckless swiftness, the Kyrosdyn took Pinnatte's right hand and pressed his thumb lightly on the back of it. As he did so, his eyes glazed and then closed. For a timeless moment, Pinnatte felt as though he was somewhere, something, else – a brightness, without form or place, beginning or end.

Then, abruptly, he was in the square again, snatching back a hand that was no longer being held. He began scrambling away from the two men over the rough cobbles. The Kyrosdyn made no movement to pursue him, and kept a restraining hand on the arm of his guard.

'Come to the Vaskyros when you are ready,' he said, his tone strange, almost respectful, then he turned and walked slowly into the busy crowd.

Pinnatte watched him go, unable to accept for a moment that nothing else was going to happen. His confidence began to return.

Lunatic! he thought witheringly as he limped back up the steps of the fountain.

Sitting down, he leaned back against the wall, and began massaging his bruised foot.

As he did so, he noticed a small blemish on the back of his right hand.

Chapter 4

THE THLOSGARAL

'It was in the time of the Final War, when the Great Lord sought to wrest His birthright from the usurper Estrith. So terrible was this War that from the depths of the ocean to the highest of the clouds, no haven was to be found, and no living thing escaped its bloody taint.

'And the Great Lord built a mighty Citadel to the south of Estrith's land so that His army might find rest and shelter there before they ventured forth, and so that His many aides could study and teach the ways of war.

'But Estrith's spies brought to him news of this place and he sent to it a great gathering of the cloud-lands, having deceived their peoples so that they denied the justice of the Great Lord's cause.

'From the east they came, in numbers the like of which there had never been before nor have been since, and all decked and dressed for battle. Black and terrible they were, darkening the Citadel and the land about it and bringing terror to His people.

'And as they gathered there was a strange silence. Then, the army of the Lord, which stood outside the Citadel heard the rushing of a wind and looked to see winged warriors, shadows within shadows, descending upon it, bearing missiles and fire. And great harm was done, for, being without true courage, it was the way of the cloud-land warriors to soar above the reach of arrow and spear.

'For many days the army stood fast, yet it seemed that it must be destroyed utterly, and great was the anger of His soldiers that they should perish thus, unable to strike a blow in their own defence.

'Then the Lord was with them, come suddenly and mysteriously from afar. He moved among His soldiers, brilliant, like a silver star in the false darkness that the cloud-lands had brought. And when He saw what had been wrought, such was His fury that He gathered His lieutenants about Him and, raising the Power that was His to command, struck at the darkest of the lowering cloud-lands. And so great was His Power that the cloud-land was rent in two, and the sky was filled with the cries of its dying people as their extremity gave them the vision to see now the truth of Estrith's deception.

'But there was no rejoicing from those in the Lord's Citadel, for it was seen that the stricken cloud-land would fall upon them. Seeing their plight, and spent though He was, the Lord sent forth the last of His Power so that the cloud-land fell to the east of the Citadel.

'Yet so awful was this fall that much of His army was destroyed, and not a building in the Citadel was not shaken to its foundations, many being tumbled into ruins.

'And the land upon which the cloud-land fell, once beautiful and prosperous, was broken and crushed, and made barren for ever. And it was named by the Lord, Thlosgaral, from an ancient tongue.

'And the Lord wept as He sought amongst the destruction for remnants of His army, for He was sorely weakened and the hurt was beyond even His mending and, some said, He saw portents of His ultimate defeat through Estrith's treachery. Yet, such was the justice of His cause, that where His tears fell, the blasted land was sown with His wisdom, to be harvested in the times to come so that He might rise again . . .'

Thus went one of the many tales of the creation of the Thlosgaral – a bleak and blasted scar of jagged and broken rockland cut deep into the land to the east of Arash-Felloren, between The Wyndering and the Wilde Ports. It ran north to south, and was the sole source of the crystals that were so important to the city and the Lowe Towns around it.

Many other tales existed about its origins. It had been made by

28

one of the Great Lord's Appointed, who had launched his given Power from his very hands to destroy Estrith's mighty army. It had been caused by one of Estrith's terrible lieutenants, in an attempt to tear apart the land itself and plunge it and the Lord's army into the ocean. It was the funeral pyre for the Lord Himself after He had been so treacherously betrayed and slain in the ninth hour of the Last Battle.

Not that all such tales referred back to the time of the Final War. Some said that long before people had come to the land, in times beyond any remembering, a star, blazing and thundering, had fallen from the heavens to tear open the great rocky cleft. Still others said that it came from perturbations in the bowels of the world itself. And one strange telling declared that the Thlosgaral was a flaw which stemmed from the very beginning of the world, from the First Heat in which all things were formed, and that in it were to be found the keys to the Forbidden Ways that spanned between the worlds.

The scholars and learned men of Arash-Felloren speculated and argued along less esoteric lines, seeking more logical explanations. But while much was learned about the place, none could determine how it had come about. Still less could they determine how the crystals had been formed, or even account for their many strange properties.

Whatever its origin however, the Thlosgaral was there, and it was an anomaly. An eerie and dangerous place, permanently hot and utterly different from the lands that bordered it. Strangest of all, it was given to moving, like a slow and stately ocean, though to rhythms and tides that no one could ever measure.

'Ever restless, His spirit seeks to break forth . . .'

Barran had come to the Thlosgaral quite inadvertently. At the time he was a mercenary and had been heading north following rumours of a great war pending there. Finding himself on the wrong side of the Thlosgaral he decided to cross it rather than retreat and move around it. But, like many before him, he misjudged the nature of the rocky desert and was taken unawares by one of its sudden, stinging dust storms. His horse had panicked and, while normally he might have regained control, a loose shoe brought it down, unseating him and knocking him unconscious. When he came round it was to find his horse bolted – with most of his possessions – pain suffusing his entire body, and three ill-favoured individuals looking at him suspiciously.

His immediate fear was of robbery, but a discreet check on his purse and hidden weapons reassured him. One of the three men came forward, offering him a battered canteen. After a momentary hesitation, Barran took it. The water had a slightly metallic taste, but he drank it eagerly and thanked the man. He could see now that though the men were dirty and unkempt, they did not have that air about them that would identify them as robbers. They were probably labourers of some kind, he decided.

Levering himself into a sitting position he made to stand up, only to discover, as all the pains in his body suddenly focused in one place, that his ankle had been injured in the fall. The three men watched impassively as he slid back to the ground.

Some cautious probing and manipulating told him that there were probably no bones broken, but it was going to be almost impossible for him to walk on that foot for some time. He cursed his horse, the desert, and fate generally but managed to keep his face impassive. Injured, and with his horse gone, he had little alternative now but to ask for help from these strangers – and a string of oaths might well be misunderstood.

'I can't walk,' he said. 'Can you help me to the nearest village?'

The three men looked at one another and held a brief, soft conversation.

'Nearest town's too far to reach today even for a good walker,' one of them said. 'And we can't be wasting time going there anyway. Least of all carrying you. You should've been more careful. We'll take you to our camp and tend you if you'll give us two months' of your labour.'

Barran gaped. He had had many bargains put to him in his time, but none quite as odd as this. Questions flooded into his mind. He picked one of them. 'What do you do?'

There was a hint of surprise in the three surly faces. 'Come from far away, have you?' the first speaker declared flatly. Barran nodded.

'Crystal miners,' the man said, answering the question without further comment.

Barran was no wiser. He reminded himself of his position. Lost and hurt and with little money and no food, this was no time for questions which might try the patience of his possible saviours. 'I'll work my way if there's work I can do,' he said.

'There's work.'

Despite the circumstances however, it was against Barran's nature not to bargain.

'But two months . . .'

There followed a brief bartering, at the end of which it was agreed that he would work for them for four weeks from the time when he could walk again.

As he hobbled along, his arms around the shoulders of two of the men, he congratulated himself. He had no intention of keeping any bargain, but he would have shelter and food until he was well enough to escape. And, apart from telling him that the leader of the group was called Aigren, the exchange had taught him something important – these people were fools. Later he learned that he had been very lucky not to be found by some of the wiser miners who worked the Thlosgaral – men who would have done as he would in their position – taken lost travellers as slaves.

His opinion of the men was reinforced when he reached what they referred to as their camp. It was a large, ramshackle wooden hut, leaning, so Barran thought, against a steep rockface. In front of it, three women were working with tall, double-handled pestles, and four children seemed to be playing in the dust that pervaded everything. All looked up as the men arrived but there was no greeting or display of affection, and Barran was given only a cursory glance as his presence was explained.

Whatever crystal mining was, there was a great deal of work involved and little or no money to be made at it, Barran decided, taking in the poverty of the scene and the weary appearance of even the children. Still, that was not his problem. He would adopt his normal practice when amongst strangers, of seeming stupid

31

and remaining silent while he listened and watched and learned.

Aigren picked up a long-handled hammer and pointed to a pile of rocks by the hut.

'Break those,' he said, thrusting the hammer into Barran's hand.

Barran looked at it and then at the rocks. His immediate reaction to the order and the surly manner in which it had been voiced was to use the hammer on his new employer – he'd killed men for less. But a twinge from his foot reminded him that he had few choices at the moment and, supporting himself on the hammer, he hobbled over to the pile. 'How small do you want them?' he asked, barely keeping the sarcasm out of his voice.

'The women'll show you,' came the reply, as the three miners disappeared into the hut. Barran stood for a moment leaning on the hammer and staring at the closed door.

'Work if you want to eat.' The voice was followed by a rhythmic pounding.

He started and turned round. The women were working with their pestles again, beating out a slow, insistent tattoo. It was one of them who had spoken. He caught her eye and nodded towards the rocks. 'Just break them?' he asked.

'Just break them.'

Not being able to stand, wielding the hammer proved to be no easy task, but eventually he managed to make an impromptu seat amongst the rocks from which he could work to some effect. Part of him rebelled at being obliged to do such menial and seemingly pointless work, but as he worked, he began to remember digging trenches and excavating under foundations in conditions that were far worse than this. At least no one was trying to kill him here. And, when need arose, he was good at this kind of undemanding, physical work – he just had to find his pace. The memory recalled, he gradually relaxed and was soon working with an easy rhythm, his hammer-blows counter-pointing the dull pounding of the women's pestles.

Still, it was hot. An airless, clinging heat soon brought sweat to his brow, griming the dust there into an unpleasant grittiness. He was tempted to complain about it, but the sight of the women working on, silently and steadily, prevented him.

After a while, the reason for what he was doing became apparent. The women were grinding the rock fragments that he made into a coarse powder. From time to time one of the deep mortars that they were using would be tilted and rolled along its bottom edge to be emptied where the children were playing in the dust . . . except that they were not playing. Like their parents they were working, nimble fingers spreading out the dust and young eyes searching through it intently.

After some time, one of them cried out and there was a brief halt to the relentless beat of the pestles as the women broke off and went to examine some find. At the second such call, Barran swung himself upright on his hammer and hobbled across to see what was happening. At first he could see nothing, then the child twisted his hand and a bright flash between his thumb and forefinger revealed a tiny crystal. The women nodded approvingly and one of them, wetting her fingertip, dabbed it up and took it carefully over to a small pot. Seeing Barran following her, she motioned him back to his work defensively. He gave an apologetic shrug and did as he was bidden, affecting an indifference he did not feel. The sudden brightness of the crystal had cut through more than the dusty air; it seemed to have cut right through him also. Almost in spite of himself, he was intrigued.

'That's what you're after is it?' he said, as he settled himself back on to his rough seat. 'They're very small for jewellery. Are they worth the trouble?'

'Jewellery?' The woman paused and half-turned towards him, then she turned back and delicately dropped the tiny find into the pot. Her face was puzzled as she stood up. 'Crystals are crystals. They're all precious.'

Barran resorted to honesty. 'I've never heard of such things before. What are they used for? Who wants them?'

The woman was filling a bucket with the rock fragments he had broken, throwing back on to the pile those that were too large. She looked at him with open suspicion. 'Everyone's heard of crystals,' she said stonily. Barran met her gaze. Under the grime and weariness was a strong face. He decided not to argue the point. He'd find out all he needed in due course if he was patient. 'I've come from far

33

away,' he said softly, but in a tone that ended the exchange.

The work continued as before, Barran breaking the oddly brittle rocks, the women working their pestles, and the children sifting through the dust. Barran willed his foot to heal quickly. He might be good at this kind of work but he had no desire to be doing it for longer than necessary.

There was only one more crystal found during the remainder of the day. Barran remained where he was, continuing his pretended indifference to what was happening. But this time, the women's inspection resulted in an excitement that had not attended the previous ones. Barran craned forward discreetly to catch the ensuing conversation but heard only, 'Ellyn, it's a tint – I'm sure it is.'

Ellyn was the woman who had spoken to him: Aigren's wife, he presumed. He did not hear her reply, but her manner was doubtful. She held up the crystal and moved it from side to side, peering at it thoughtfully for some time before she shook her head. There was an appeal from the first woman, of which Barran caught '. . . a rainbow vein hereabouts . . . always said so.' Then, apparently by way of compromise, the crystal was placed in a different pot to the two previous finds.

The brief snatches intrigued Barran further. What in the name of sanity was a tint? And what was a rainbow vein? That they were matters of some significance was confirmed almost immediately, for despite Ellyn's caution about the latest crystal, the mood of the women changed perceptibly. Even the rhythm of their pounding seemed to be lighter, and from time to time they spoke to one another. Once, Ellyn gave a tight, thin smile and looked up at the sky. For an instant, Barran, who had been desperately trying to hear what was being said, saw her as the younger, more hopeful, woman she had once been. The sight disturbed him.

Shortly afterwards, as the light faded, the men reappeared. In so far as he had thought about them, Barran had presumed that they had been idling the day away in the hut while he and the women did the work, but each was carrying a panier of rocks on his back. These they proceeded to tip on Barran's heap, making it

34

considerably larger than it had been at the beginning. He watched them blankly.

Then the pattern of work shifted. Barran was told to continue with his rock breaking but the women and children vanished into the hut, taking the mortars and pestles and the two small pots with them. Subsequently, several more paniers of rocks were brought out but eventually Aigren came to the door and motioned Barran inside.

The door was closed behind him immediately – and well bolted too, Barran noted, as a dull thud made him turn. A heavy crossbeam had been dropped into stout brackets behind the door. What would these impoverished people need such protection for? He set the question aside, with all the others.

It took a moment for his eyes to adjust to the comparative darkness, the process not being helped by a sense of disorientation. For, what he had taken to be a large lean-to hut built against a rockface was actually only an entrance hall to a cave. Furthermore, he realized, the cave was man-made. He had done enough sapping in his time to recognize the toolmarks. Despite himself, he was impressed.

'You cut this yourselves?' The question came out before he had time to consider it.

'Some,' Aigren replied, tersely. He showed no sign of enlarging on this comment and Barran remained silent. Just how foolish these people were he had yet to decide, and until he did so, it was important that he gave away as little as possible about himself.

He looked around. The light was coming from a few oil lamps perched on ledges cut into the rock, and the air was remarkably fresh for a cave. There was even a hint of a breeze, but there was a warmth in it that was not pleasant. The wooden entrance hall was apparently used primarily as a store-place for tools. It was more substantial than it appeared from the outside, though the roof and walls were canted and twisted as though a massive hand had tried to push the whole structure over. Surely it hadn't been built like that, Barran thought. And yet these solid rocks couldn't move, could they? More and more questions. He pointed to a bundle of hammer handles leaning against the wall. 'Could I use one of those

35

for a stick?' he asked. 'This hammer's a bit awkward for walking with.'

Aigren nodded.

Barran tested a few before picking one that would serve him both as a support and a well-balanced weapon should need arise. As he hobbled back into the cave, he saw that the women were preparing food while the men sat sullenly at one end of a long wooden table. Tentatively, he joined them, watching carefully for any sign of offence being taken. Now he should learn something. There was nothing like food after a hard day's work to loosen tongues, and they must surely want to learn about him – who he was, where he was from, how he had come there and so on. They were obviously not a garrulous group, but once the conversation started he was sure that their taciturnity would fade away and that he would be able to nudge events along to learn more about them and their strange trade.

He was to be disappointed however. The food was simple and filling, if gritty, but it was eaten in almost complete silence – a silence which deepened on two occasions when a distant creaking sound drifted into the cave. Everyone except Barran abruptly stopped eating. Aigren and the other men craned forward as if to hear some faint message in the noise, and the women and children watched them anxiously. Then the sound was gone and they were eating again, but the atmosphere was tense and Barran sensed that any attempt at conversation would be unwelcome.

And, quite suddenly, he was asleep. A great deal had happened to him that day – he had been unhorsed, knocked unconscious and injured, lost both horse and possessions and finally transformed from mercenary soldier into oafish labourer, working in a mine such as he had never even heard of, in an unfamiliar and bizarre land. What amounted to combat readiness had kept him alert so far, but as soon as that relaxed – and the bolted door and the food was sufficient to do this – his body sought to fulfil its own needs. He had a broken impression of being dragged from the table and laid down somewhere but, despite the pain of his injured foot, he remembered nothing until Aigren's voice intruded on him.

'Dawn, Barran.'

His eyes opened and though he was stiff and sore, he was immediately wide awake in anticipation of the violence that had so often accompanied awakenings in strange places for him. But all was quiet. He blinked to clear his vision. Aigren was walking away from him through the lamplit gloom. Around him, others were stirring. He saw that their beds, like his, were little more than rough blankets laid on the ground in a wide recess cut into the cave wall. He had slept in worse places, but the knowledge offered little consolation as the pains caused by his unyielding bed and his injured foot really began to make themselves felt. His hand landed on the hammer handle that he had chosen as staff and weapon and he levered himself up on it. As he did so, his attention was caught by a patch of deeper darkness further along the cave. He peered into it and saw others. Tunnel entrances, he decided. That must be where the men worked. Doubtless they had it in mind for him to work along with them eventually, and the opportunities for flight from underground would be considerably less than those he would have breaking rocks outside. He tested his injured foot gently. It was a little easier. Normally he healed quickly – as much a learned inner discipline as a fortunate natural attribute – and sitting while he worked the previous day had obviously helped. However, it would perhaps be in his best interests to exaggerate his incapacity.

Aigren was lifting the crossbeam that secured the side door. Barran hobbled awkwardly over to him.

'Is there any water? I'd like to wash.'

Aigren looked at him. For the first time, Barran sensed violence in the man – smouldering and distant, but there nonetheless. Be careful, he reminded himself, tightening his grip on his staff. You know nothing of these people and you're in no position to defend yourself properly here.

Aigren nodded towards a barrel standing by the side of the door. 'Water's for drinking,' he said. 'Some for washing in a couple of days maybe. Unless you want to walk to the river.'

Despite reading the answer in Aigren's face, Barran asked, 'Where is it?'

Aigren flicked his head. 'Half a day east.' There was a hint of a sneer. 'If you know the way.' Then bitterness. 'And if it hasn't moved.'

The comment meant nothing to Barran.

'Here.' It was Ellyn. She was offering him a canteen and a basket of bread. 'This will get you through the day.'

'See he earns that,' Aigren said to her harshly as he pushed open the door. Warmth, dust and a reddish morning light rolled into the cave. Ellyn gave Barran an enigmatic look as she walked past him.

The day passed much as the previous one until about noon when three men walked into the camp.

Chapter 5

Barran's interest quickened as soon as the strangers appeared. Their arrival was apparently unexpected but they were obviously known to the women, who suddenly became subservient and ingratiating. One of them ran, almost girlishly, to the hut, 'To get the men.'

Barran eyed the men surreptitiously while he continued his work. One was carrying a small case and was conspicuously better dressed than the others. He was also slightly ill at ease.

A client and two bodyguards, Barran decided. The latter were quite unmistakable. One of them was a tall hulking individual who rolled from side to side when he walked and whose arms arced away from his sides. He stood close to his charge, face set. The other was of more average build and had settled himself against a rock, apparently uninterested in the proceedings. The dangerous one, Barran concluded, as he watched the man looking indifferently about the camp. The first would be some moronic ale-house bruiser whose physical presence was intended to deter would-be attackers. Barran thought it unlikely that he would be able to use the sword that hung from his belt. The second, however, would be the one who anticipated and thought. He would go to some lengths to avoid trouble but would move in quickly with deadly force if real need arose. *He* would be able to use a sword – and the knives he would have secreted about him. Barran was grateful for the fact that he was sitting at a menial task and covered in dust. Just as he had read the man, so he knew that he himself would be the object of an intense inspection. He must do nothing to give away his own calling.

He turned his attention to the bodyguards' client.

The man was an incongruous sight against the bleak rocky

39

surroundings. He was anxiously – and fruitlessly – brushing dust from an ornately embroidered shirt and periodically mopping his flushed face. Barran knew two things about him already: he was important and he was a fool – or most probably so. The women's actions marked his importance and the two bodyguards gave some measure of his folly – men bought for protection could always be bought by others. And the man did not even carry a knife!

But who was he?

Aigren and the other two miners emerged from the hut. They were carrying a table and two chairs which they set down in front of the stranger. Awkwardly, Aigren swept a kerchief over one of the chairs and motioned him to sit. When he had done so, the man nodded, and Aigren sat opposite him. The other miners stood a respectful distance away.

The women having stopped working, Barran did the same. He leaned forward, rested his chin on the hammer and prepared to watch. The stranger glanced at him and there was a brief conversation which Barran deduced involved an explanation by Aigren of who this new worker was. The man looked at the smaller bodyguard who made a slight hand movement. Seemingly this indicated approval and the man turned back to Aigren again.

Not really expecting serious trouble, are you then? Barran thought. This must be a regular meeting – a routine affair. Had it been otherwise, a conscientious bodyguard would have been holding a knife at his throat while such a judgement was made. Much would be given away here if he had the wit to see it.

Aigren gestured to Ellyn, who, almost like a serving girl, brought the two pots containing the crystals to the table. A merchant, Barran decided. This would be interesting.

The man delicately lifted the lid of one pot, inserted a finger and stirred it around gently as he studied the contents. He seemed satisfied. Ellyn said something to him and pushed the other pot forward expectantly. This received a more thorough examination, with individual crystals being taken out and inspected closely. At one stage he opened his case and took out a large eye-glass to facilitate this. In the end, however, he shook his head slowly, and with an apologetic shrug towards Ellyn, carefully tipped the contents of the second pot into the first. Though she gave little outward sign, Barran could feel her disappointment. One of the other women actually gave a subdued cry.

Then, bargaining proper began. Aigren pulled out a bag from his tunic and slowly emptied the contents on to the table. Despite his control, Barran could not restrain a start as the crystals caught the dusty sunlight and transmuted it into a disproportionate brightness. The glint that he had seen between the child's fingers the previous day was multiplied manyfold. It seemed to reach out and pinion him, and something stirred deep within him. As did hard-learned warning signals. When he finally managed to pull his eyes from the crystals and back to the two men, he realized that he was holding his breath and craning forward with his hands clenched tightly about the top of the hammer handle. He cast a quick glance at the bodyguard by the rocks to reassure himself that his momentary lapse had gone unnoticed. Lucky, he reproached himself with some relief. But that had been a shock. He had no name for what he had just felt, but it was a long time since anything had moved him so. He had to force himself to keep his gaze away from the crystals.

Fortunately the bargaining was now under way. The merchant's high-pitched and whining voice weaving around Aigren's slow grumble gave Barran something to concentrate on. He had not been impressed by the ability of the miners to drive a bargain at their first meeting, and he had a strong suspicion that something similar was going to happen here. And, for some reason, even though it was not he who had sweated beneath the Thlosgaral to wrest these crystals free, he now felt a powerful resentment that they might be parted with at too low a price.

But so it proved to be. He had acquired some knowledge of the local currency on his way through the Wilde Ports and though he could not hear what was happening, he could see that the coins the merchant was stacking on the table were the wrong colour for the value that *he* had just placed on the crystals.

What kind of a dolt was Aigren? Couldn't he see the clothes this man was wearing – and the kind of men he was employing to accompany him? Items worth only what was being put on the table

41

did not need to be protected by one bodyguard, still less two!

And there was something else about the merchant. Something wrong about this meeting other than Aigren's incompetence. Barran could not help himself but lean forward intently as he reached out to snatch this elusive impression.

And it was there. Clear for anyone to see who had any vision worth speaking of! The man was *desperate* for the crystals – it was in his every gesture, in every inflection of his voice. He would have paid ten times what he finally conceded with a little moue of reluctance. Barran glanced round at the two other miners and the sullen faces of their wives and children, but they were oblivious to the reality of what was happening. Sheep for shearing. For an instant he actually considered intervening, but the notion quickly transformed itself into a heightened determination to find out more about this place, about the crystals and what made them so precious. And too, about the merchants and who they in their turn sold the crystals to. He must do this even if it meant delaying his escape. Somehow, there was a great deal of money to be made here.

Yet, even as this resolve formed, a sense of foreboding suddenly swept over him – a nameless fear which awakened his every battle instinct. But unlike the previous shock, this one he recognized as an old friend, awful though it was. More than once in the past it had saved him – made him turn to find an attacker at his back, made him seek out an ambush ahead. He ignored it at his peril. But what possible danger could there be here? The miners had offered him none – and they needed him for work. Besides, injury or no, they were so slow that he could probably deal with all three of them at once if he had to. The mines themselves were dangerous, of course, and he had no great love of confined spaces, but he had no intention of going underground. And the bodyguards would do nothing unless their charge was attacked. Then, as suddenly as the fear had come to him, came the answer. The hint of something unnatural about the slowness of the miners and their women, the anxiety of the merchant. It is this place that makes them like this. *Something about the Thlosgaral drains the life out of people.*

It was a vivid realization. Even though no reasoning came with it, Barran knew that this conclusion was true. He must not linger here or he too would degenerate into one of these dull-witted creatures. It added an urgency to the resolution he had just made.

Yet how was he going to learn *anything* from these people? Such conversation as he had heard so far had been confined to simple instructions and requests – and even these had been few in number. Perhaps tonight, with a bargain struck, there might be a small celebration of some kind that he could use to ease his way into their confidence? He dismissed the conjectures – they were beginning to cloud his mind. He wasn't going to fall asleep so easily tonight and, at the very least, he could ask outright what the crystals were used for and who bought them. Showing himself stupider than his employers might perhaps make them more talkative.

Aigren and the merchant were concluding their business, the merchant having produced a balance from his case and some kind of a measuring device. Aigren's face was immobile, but his posture was full of self-satisfaction. Barran wanted to strangle him.

After the merchant and his escort had left, there was a brief debate amongst the miners and their women, and then the men disappeared into the hut and the women returned to their pestles.

Barran found it difficult to concentrate. The light from the crystals seemed to have lodged within him so that when he closed his eyes they were there again, making all about them seem distant and gloomy – no longer real. He wanted to handle them, hold them up and scatter their light about him, peer into their hearts. He wanted to . . .

He wanted.

Wanted.

And mingling with this desire, two other contradictory needs pulled at him: the need for knowledge about the crystals, and the strange realization that the Thlosgaral was in some way a dangerous place to linger in. It did not occur to him that all thoughts of simply escaping this place, of his lost horse and possessions, of employment in the war in the north, were gone. As the Thlosgaral itself did every day, Barran had subtly changed.

However, the relentless rhythm of the group soon reasserted itself and Barran could not have said how much time had passed before he looked up and saw five men approaching the camp. Just as he had made an immediate assessment of the merchant and his bodyguards, so now he made one of these new arrivals, though this time it was easier. Their dress and demeanour were unmistakable: they were scoundrels of some kind. Barran noted however, that though they all wore swords, they were carrying staffs obviously fashioned from the hammer handles such as the one he had chosen for support. Robbers then, but perhaps not casual murderers, he concluded. He stopped hammering and discreetly reached for his own staff leaning on the rocks by his side.

In the few seconds which it took Barran to reach this conclusion, the new arrivals were seen, first by the children, and then the women. The children jumped up and ran to their mothers who ushered them to the back of the hut. Barran could see that the women were alarmed but not terrified. That was good.

A further look at the newcomers told him that they were little more than street ruffians. Nasty and brutal, but no match for a professional soldier. Still, he had no desire to defend himself against five opponents in his present condition.

'Stay where you are!' The command froze the children, but the speaker still chose to emphasize it by purposefully smacking his staff into the palm of his hand.

'There's no need to frighten the children, Fiarn,' Ellyn said, a hint of anger creeping through her sullen manner.

'It's as well they don't disturb your menfolk at their work, isn't it, Ellyn?' the man replied. He walked unhurriedly towards the woman. The others followed. 'You know how . . . concerned . . . they become when they have to pay the Landgeld.'

The woman bared her teeth as if to say something, but thought better of it. Instead she lowered her head to avoid looking at him. 'We've nothing for you. It's been bad lately – poor quality crystals and few of them at that.'

Fiarn nodded, full of mocking concern. 'Normally there's nothing I like better than listening to your tales, Ellyn. You've such an entertaining imagination. Not quite as slow as most around here – yet. But it's been a tiring day – there've been so many buyers about recently that, as you see, I'm actually having to do some of the collecting myself.' He took hold of her chin and forced her head round towards Barran. Barran made no response but remained sitting, carefully maintaining an expression of indifference. 'And things can't be too bad if you've taken on a worker, can they?'

The woman jerked her head free. 'He's just a traveller – got an injured leg – he's bound to us for a month, that's all. We'll be lucky if he digs enough to cover his food.'

Fiarn's expression became one of impatience and he pushed her to one side. 'Enough,' he said. 'Just get the money and don't waste any more of my time.' He walked towards Barran. The woman stared after him for a moment, then turned to go into the hut. 'And remember, don't go shouting for your men. You know what happened last time.' Fiarn raised his staff warningly.

As he drew nearer, Barran took his hand from his staff but made no effort to stand. If need arose he could do the man greater damage, more quickly, from this position than standing face to face. Fiarn was taller and heavier than he was, though he doubted he was as strong. And he could see a hint of that slowness about him that pervaded the miners. Everything about him confirmed street fighter rather than soldier, but Barran still needed to know a great deal more about what was happening here before interfering. He would have to hold his tongue and await events. Act slow and stupid.

He allowed himself to look confused as he met the man's gaze.

'What's your name, traveller?' Fiarn asked, towering over him.

'Barran, sir.'

'What are you doing in the Thlosgaral, Barran?'

'Came here by chance, sir. Thought it might be a short-cut. I'm not from round here. I was looking for work. I'm a farm labourer by trade, but these good people helped me when I lost my horse.' He became earnest. 'You haven't seen a horse wandering about loose, have you, sir? He's a—'

Fiarn raised a hand to silence him and then stared into his wilfully vacant eyes for a moment in amused disbelief. 'It's either sold or eaten by now . . . *farmer*,' he said, scornfully emphasizing the last word. Ellyn came out of the hut. She had a small pouch in her hand. Fiarn glanced from Barran to the purse and back again, then abandoned his interrogation and, shaking his head, turned

45

back to Ellyn. 'Have we seen a horse! Not often you come across someone even stupider than a miner,' he announced, for everyone's benefit. His men laughed. Snatching the pouch from the waiting woman, he took a handful of coins from it and dropped the rest on the ground.

'Just have it ready for me in future,'' he said grimly, holding a fist in front of her face. 'I know how much you get and I've had enough of these games.' Suddenly he was angry. 'You people have no gratitude for anything. You owe for the equipment, the right to dig here, and for protection from the robbers who haunt this place. Robbers who wouldn't hesitate to slit your throats while you slept – children and all. Don't forget it. Do you understand? Explain it to your husband very slowly when he gets back. He doesn't seem to have grasped his position fully yet and I don't want him coming round causing problems again. He was lucky not to have been more badly hurt than he was.'

They were gone.

Ellyn crouched down and picked up the money then silently returned to her work. Barran watched the three women for a while before he started working again. So many thoughts filled his head that he felt as though he was cutting through dense undergrowth in search of a clear path that lay nearby.

Slowly it emerged. These people had a valuable resource which they bargained away more foolishly than children. Then they allowed themselves to be robbed in silence. There *was* money to be made here. All that was needed was a little more information so that a plan could be formed. Then a little determination – a characteristic Barran had in great measure. That, and other less commendable traits.

For as long as he could remember, he had earned his living by fighting for other people. Through the years, all manner of lords and dukes and petty princes had employed him and his kind when their greed, intransigence, or just plain folly, had transformed a dispute of words into a dispute of swords. Without fail they had all claimed to be injured parties fighting for natural justice against treacherous enemies, though Barran could scarcely recall a time when he might have been inclined to believe such protestations.

Fighting first for one side and then the other as his commander of the moment negotiated better terms was a common occurrence.

One thing Barran did remember from the earliest days was that, on the whole, he was brighter than most of his companions and, fortunately for his continued well-being, bright enough to keep such knowledge to himself. And two things he soon learned. One was that while fighting and pillaging might satisfy certain needs within him, the money and power that he craved was to be found not by those who fought but by those who commanded their services. The other was that – like the merchant – those who had to buy the swords of others for their protection invariably became hostage to them. He had resolved long ago to profit from the first and avoid the hazards of the second.

Thus, he had worked diligently at the art of soldiering. He had a particular aptitude for the darker side of that art, for he could be vicious and cruel, delighting in hurting others, sometimes even where no gain was apparent – and the adulation and acclaim that that had brought him soon taught him the fundamentals of true leadership.

Eventually he came to have his own band of mercenaries and for a while it prospered. But despite his clear-eyed schemes and his savage bravery, slowly but inexorably the wild vagaries of combat took away trusted friends and battle-hardened allies alike, and left him approaching the middle of his life with no more wealth than he had once set out with, but many more scars, both inward and outward, and an increasingly desperate view of what lay ahead.

Yet it was all he knew and he could but follow the call to arms wherever he heard it.

And it was following such a call that had brought him to the Thlosgaral. Rumour declared that it was the Great Lord returned to mete out vengeance to those who had once dispossessed and banished Him, but Barran gave such nonsense no heed. It was more practical considerations that had lured him north – a reliable contact who had paid a portion of cash in advance, the promise of a good, well-written contract, offering many benefits not least amongst which was equitable shares of all profits from the campaign.

The events of the last two days however, had dispatched such remaining enthusiasm as he had for joining another army. The merchant had shown him the presence of great wealth in the vicinity; Fiarn had shown him opportunity. And here he was, a wolf amongst the sheep. With each blow of his hammer he saw a sunlit path to power and riches opening before him.

He stopped hammering and began to sketch out his new future. He must wait a little and build up his strength, learning what he could about the crystals, the merchants, and Fiarn and this whole frightful place. Then he would probably have to deal with Fiarn. Unless the man had others more powerful behind him, that shouldn't present too much of a problem. Only a fool would have approached a stranger and stood in front of him as he had – so vulnerable. He must have become so used to bullying women and weary men that he had lost whatever fighting edge he had once had. And there was that hint of the miner's slowness about him. Barran pursed his lips and nodded to himself, but even as he reached this conclusion, old habits cautioned him sharply – casually underestimating people thus could prove fatal.

'Work, Barran, if you want food.'

He started, jerked suddenly back to the present. It was Ellyn. He grunted and began breaking the rocks again. The admonition was timely – assume Fiarn is sharp and dangerous, he thought sternly. Assume he has allies. But don't linger. This is no place to be for any length of time. Again he felt afraid. The emotion inspired him.

'The man frightened me,' he shouted across to the women.

There was a slight faltering in the rhythm of the beating pestles. 'He frightens everyone,' Ellyn replied. She did not seem inclined to continue, but Barran noticed her jawline tighten. This woman was not yet completely crushed. Probably because of the children, he thought. One day, her anger might spill out.

'Where I come from, a debt is a debt. A lawful thing. Something to be given and repaid without reproach by either side. Why did he come with so many men and threaten you like that?'

Ellyn's pestle came down with unusual force, disrupting the rhythm. 'You must come from a long way away, Barran. Debts to the likes of Fiarn are never paid off. He and his kind own this place.'

'Own it? How can someone like that own a place like this? Is he a Lord or a Duke?'

All the women turned to him, pausing in mid-stroke. Managing an expression of naïveté, he looked at them briefly, without stopping his own work.

'There's no Lord, no Duke, dispensing justice and maintaining order around here, man. Not even in Arash-Felloren. Fiarn's just a bandit.' Ellyn almost spat out the words. 'One of a score or more such living off the backs of the mining families. The only respite we get from them is when they fight amongst themselves for the right to persecute us.'

Barran shook his head in feigned bewilderment. 'You should stand against him. There *must* be law somewhere hereabouts.'

Ellyn's shoulders slumped, her anger crushed like the rocks under her pestle. Barran cursed himself. Somehow he had stopped her talking. He took a chance.

'*Why* don't you stand against him?' he demanded.

Ellyn's temper flared briefly. 'Because others have done it, and been killed and maimed for their pains. Get on with your work and be quiet.'

Barran was content to accept the rebuke. In that short exchange he had learned a great deal about life in the Thlosgaral. And even more about his future. And it was good. Merchants desperate for the crystals, bands of men terrorizing the miners and fighting amongst themselves . . . It all held out great promise.

As if in confirmation, there was a cry from one of the children and the three women abandoned their work to examine the latest find.

Later, the men appeared. They had had a bad day. A rockfall had buried much of the work of the previous days and one of them had received an ugly gash to his arm. As a consequence they looked set for several days' hard work before they could expect to mine any further crystals. Ellyn read her husband's face as soon as he emerged from the hut, and Barran in turn read hers. She had become increasingly nervous as time passed and now he could see her

49

struggling not to flinch away even though she was holding her husband's gaze as she told him what had happened. For her pains she received a back-handed blow across the face that knocked her to the ground. It was followed by a furious tirade. The children scuttled hurriedly away from the fire and into the shadows. Not an uncommon scene then, Barran thought, but he watched impassively as Ellyn struggled to her feet, in the shade of her glowering, fist-clenched husband. Almost reluctantly her hand came to her bruised face.

Suddenly, and to his considerable surprise, Barran found himself attracted to her. Too long without a woman, he thought, as he looked at her, dishevelled and degraded. But it was not that – not that alone, anyway. There was something beneath the grime and despair. That strong face, and that momentary flash in her eyes as she had struck the ground – a flash that spoke of a knife between the ribs of her sleeping husband one night. He added a caveat – *if this place doesn't eat the heart and brains out of her first.* Then he looked at the husband. Jaw jutting in wordless anger, the man seemed about to strike her again, but though she backed away she did not cower. And there was that flash again. Dangerous, thought Barran, though he doubted that the man saw it.

'I couldn't do anything else, could I?' Ellyn shouted. 'He'd have started on me or the children, you know that.'

The man turned from side to side, like a trapped animal. Barran braced himself. Uncharacteristically he felt that he would intervene if the man renewed his attack on the woman, even though doing so might bring the rage of all of them down upon him. But no attack came. Instead the man let out an almost animal cry. Ellyn reached out to touch his arm but he dashed her hand aside. The two stood silent and motionless for what seemed to be a very long time, then the man said, 'Enough.'

His voice was suddenly very soft and controlled. At its touch, every part of Barran became alert. The man had passed beyond a certain point. He was going to do something wildly dangerous. Watching him intently, Barran could feel his own hands shaking and his breath coming faster. He paid no heed. They were familiar and appropriate responses and he was too experienced a fighter to

50

be afraid of being afraid. His body was preparing itself and he knew he could trust it. If the man turned against him, he would be ready – and his injured leg would not impede him.

Ellyn, though schooled in different sensitivities, also felt the change. 'What are you going to do?' she said, bending forward urgently and trying to catch her husband's eye. He did not reply and she repeated the question even more anxiously, this time seizing his arm.

'Get our money back from Fiarn,' he replied simply, brushing her aside roughly and picking up a long hammer.

Ellyn did not respond immediately but gazed at him vacantly as though unable to grasp what he had said. He was almost out of sight by the time she recovered. Then she was running after him, shouting, 'No! He'll kill you this time.'

When she reached him she seized hold of him and was dragged over the rocks for several paces before he stopped. Her shrill pleading ended abruptly as Aigren struck her again. She lay still. Aigren walked away without a backward glance.

It was only a little later, as the women were bathing Ellyn's bruised face and trying to console her, that Fiarn and his companions returned to the camp. They were carrying Aigren. As they dropped him on to the ground, Barran did not need to look at him to know that he was dead. Ellyn made to move to him but Fiarn grabbed her roughly.

'Didn't I tell you to keep him away?' he snarled. She was wide-eyed with fear. 'He was always trouble.' He kicked the body and swore. 'I've let you get away with too much. And what have I had in return? Endless ingratitude from Aigren and the lowest yield of any of my mines.' He was shouting now. 'I've had enough of you. I'm doubling the Landgeld on this place. You can—'

'No! You can't!' Ellyn snatched herself free and struck him a stinging blow across the face.

Don't do it, Barran thought, reading the woman's temper as Fiarn recovered from the shock and, his face contorted, lifted an arm back to strike her. White and shaking, Ellyn let out a piercing shriek and leapt at him, hands tearing at his face, feet lashing out wildly. Fiarn crashed to the ground, Ellyn flailing on top of him. It took Fiarn's companions some time to drag them both upright and, even then, three of them were having difficulty in restraining the demented woman. Fiarn's face was alight with rage. He stepped back and pulled out a knife.

'No! Put the knife away. We need to talk.' Barran's powerful voice cut through the din.

The camp was suddenly silent and all turned towards him — even the miners and their wives who until now had simply been watching events, completely bewildered. Barran remained seated, his staff resting casually across his knees.

Fiarn's expression became one of disbelief. 'Talk?' he mouthed.

'Talk,' Barran confirmed purposefully.

Fiarn gestured to his companions and made a circling motion with the knife. 'Fetch that oaf here. We'll see how well he talks with his tongue cut out.'

As the men walked towards him, Barran took in a deep breath and let it out slowly, at the same time forcing himself to relax. He tested his grip on the staff. This was going to be very dangerous. He would have preferred a great deal more information before making a move against Fiarn but, if Ellyn was killed, this group would disintegrate and . . .

And there was something about this woman . . .

Damn! Why was he doing this?

Two men were in front of him. All choices were gone now.

He let them reach down and take hold of his arms but resisted as they tried to drag him to his feet. Then, carefully favouring his uninjured foot, he stood up suddenly and drove his straight staff upwards. Propelled by legs, arms, and many years of harsh experience, the ends of the staff caught each man under the chin with appalling force, lifting both of them off the ground. The two of them were still collapsing as Barran slid his hands together and swung the staff round to bring it down with a crushing blow on the head of a third.

Urged by panic rather than consideration, Fiarn's fourth companion lunged out and grabbed the staff hastily. He was a big man and seeing his inadvertent success he grinned triumphantly at Barran. There was still a vestige of a grin on his face when Barran let go of the staff, drew a knife, stabbed him under the ribcage and, almost gently, prised the staff from his dying grasp.

In the span of scarcely half a dozen heartbeats, Fiarn's power in the Thlosgaral had been destroyed. All he could see, however, was Barran's awful focused intent as he moved towards him, his limping gait serving only to make him more frightening.

The blow that knocked the knife from Fiarn's trembling hand was scarcely necessary. He reached out to grab the end of the staff in the vague hope of defending himself, but it vanished upwards. As his eyes followed it, a blow behind his knees swept his legs into the air and sent him crashing down on to the rocky ground.

Through the clamour of his frantic breathing and his pounding heart, Fiarn became aware of a foot on his chest, the end of the staff pressing on his throat, and a voice saying, 'We need to talk.'

Within three years, Barran, with Fiarn as his lieutenant, held sway over more than a third of the mines that worked the Thlosgaral. Unlike his rivals however, Barran had extended his enterprise to include nearly all of the crystal merchants. His power grew relentlessly.

Chapter 6

'Come on, move yourself. It's nearly dawn.'

Dvolci's deep voice rumbled cavernously through the slumbering darkness where Atlon was floating. It provoked a response that Atlon felt was lucidity itself, but it was a distant and unintelligible grunt that actually drifted into the gloomy Wyndering room. There was an exasperated sigh, then a significantly more purposeful, 'Move yourself!' accompanied by a poke at the form under the blankets.

Atlon repeated the grunt more slowly and waved a vaguely defensive arm towards his tormentor, but otherwise did not stir. The poke was contemplated again but abandoned in favour of a vigorous shaking. Atlon swore into his pillow then plunged his head underneath it.

Dvolci chuckled darkly, 'Lie there, if you wish then. But you've made better choices. "Mattress was given a good beating only last week".' It was an alarmingly accurate imitation of Ghreel's voice. 'A beating, no less. There's house pride for you. I wonder what a bed bug with a headache thinks about people sharing its home.'

Atlon, abruptly awake, emerged from under the pillow and rolled over sourly, scratching himself. 'It's not even dawn yet,' he grumbled. A nerve-jangling grinding sound filled the room, making him clamp his hands over his ears.

'Must you do that?'

'It's my breakfast,' came the injured reply. 'Do you want some?'

Atlon forced himself to focus on his companion in the dim light. Narrow taunting eyes met his bleary gaze. Dvolci was sitting on his haunches and leaning forward intently. His sinuous body ended in a pointed head which was tilted ingenuously to one side. A taloned paw was offering Atlon a heavily scored piece of rock.

Atlon scowled. 'Get off my chest, I'm awake now.'

Dvolci slithered gracefully to the floor. He began chewing the rock again, revealing white and alarming teeth. Atlon grimaced at he noise and swung out of the bed.

'You'd think with all your learning, especially with your knowledge of the *Power* . . .' Dvolci hung mockery about the word '. . . you'd be able to wake up in a more civilized manner – greet the world with a little cheerfulness, perhaps.' He stopped chewing and looked up at the ceiling thoughtfully. 'It's almost as if you reverted to something more primitive when you went to sleep. Of course, you're not alone in that. It seems to be a very common human trait. Mind you, I've always thought that . . .'

'. . . humans are not a particularly well-evolved species yet.' Atlon finished the sentence as he slouched over to the stone sink and began pumping the handle. 'Unlike the felcis, they have no teeth worth speaking of, rather inadequate hands, and a quite pathetic digestive system, as I remember.'

Dvolci nodded sagely. 'Yes, indeed. One wonders at times how you've all managed to get this far considering such disadvantages.' He crunched the remains of the rock nosily. 'Still, don't fret, you're quite endearing on the whole. And your imperfections can sometimes add to your charm.'

'At least we don't irritate people by being brisk and hearty when we wake.' Atlon plunged his face into the cold water to end the conversation.

Dvolci delicately picked his teeth while Atlon washed and dressed.

'Where shall we go first?' he asked eventually. Atlon thought for a moment and then shook his head. 'I'm no wiser about that than when we started,' he said. 'We'll just have to keep asking and following the trade route back to its source – if it has only one source.' He frowned. 'I must admit, I'm surprised we've never heard of this city on our travels . . . what was it – Arash-Felloren? Does the name mean anything to you?'

'There's something vaguely familiar about it. It's got an old sound – very old – but I can't place it.' The felci gave a dismissive shrug. 'It's probably only a small town when all's said and done. You know how parochial people are – everyone thinks that *their* village is the centre of the whole world.'

Atlon looked doubtful. 'This is a big inn to serve a small town.'

'Well, we might learn something over breakfast. There are quite a few other people staying here.'

Atlon's expression changed to one of surprise. 'How do you know that?'

'I looked, of course,' Dvolci replied. 'While you were comatose in your pit I had a good prowl around the place.' His voice rose. 'And don't look at me like that. One of us has to stay alert. You know how treacherous your kind can be. This could be a den of thieves and murderers for all we know.'

Atlon buckled on his sword. 'I can look after myself quite well, thank you.'

Dvolci snorted. 'Half a day with the Queen's elite troops doesn't make you a warrior, you know,' he said. 'Especially when all you did was raid an empty fortress.'

'It could have been very dangerous.' Atlon protested defensively. 'And it was more than half a day. I spent a lot of time with them – as you know. They were quite impressed by me.'

Dvolci gave a scornful whistle. 'You mean they remembered you vividly – it's not the same thing.'

Atlon straightened up. 'Impressed. Their word, not mine. They said I was a very quick learner.'

Dvolci moved to the door. 'Why don't you try learning to wake up in the morning then.'

Breakfast at The Wyndering was both constant and variable. Constant in that Ghreel and the fare he served each week were always the same, variable in that those present on any two consecutive days were rarely the same.

Not that the latter was anything to do with the former, for Ghreel, oddly enough, was a remarkably competent cook. It was simply the location of the inn, which stood at a busy crossroads. All the traffic between the Wilde Ports and Arash-Felloren passed by it, as did such traffic as moved through the region north and south.

Thus, though he had imagined himself to be a solitary guest the previous evening, Atlon now found himself in a room with a score or so others, all busily eating at four long tables. Some were grouped together, others sat alone, but that they were all travellers was apparent from their dress and general demeanour. Beyond that however, Atlon could not deduce anything about their various trades and professions. Nevertheless he was relieved to note that they appeared to be an improvement on the group that had been decorating the place on his arrival. Two boys and, occasionally, Ghreel, were moving amongst them, serving food.

Atlon sat down at the end of one of the tables. Dvolci jumped up beside him. The man sitting opposite started slightly but Ghreel, who was lumbering by, gave an almost feminine cry. 'What the hell's that?'

The general hubbub dropped and all eyes turned towards him. He answered his own question. 'It's a rat!'

Embarrassed, but managing a smile as he met Ghreel's gaze, Atlon forced himself to be pleasant. 'It's a he, and he's a felci. He travels with me. He's my companion.'

'Not here he's not. He – it – isn't staying in my inn.'

Atlon looked around the room. There were at least three dogs lying under the tables. 'The dogs stay,' he said.

But Ghreel was not going to bandy words with this know-all teacher from far away. Momentarily forgetting Atlon's easy way of paying, he leaned forward menacingly. 'Get it out of here, or I'll throw it out.'

'You don't know anything about felcis, do you?' Atlon said. He motioned to a passing boy for food in the hope that morning routine might divert his irate host. Then he laid a hand on Dvolci's sleek neck. 'It's not a good idea to touch him. Felcis are a highly intelligent species and they don't like being mishandled. They're deep rock-dwellers, and—'

'I know a rat when I see one.'

There was a flicker of impatience in Atlon's eyes but he kept his tone conciliatory. 'Then when you look a little more carefully, you'll see that he isn't one, won't you? Look at him. He's nothing like a rat. He—'

Ghreel however, was not listening. He put his fingers to his mouth and whistled. One of the dogs pricked up its ears, then scrabbled to its feet and sauntered over to him. It was a large, muscular animal with torn ears and scars on its face bearing witness to its history as a fighter. Atlon gave Dvolci an inquiring look. The felci gave a slight nod and Atlon edged resignedly away from him.

Ghreel seized the dog by the chain around its neck and turned it towards Dvolci.

'See it off!'

Immediately, the dog set up a great clamour, barking furiously, its paws scrabbling on the rough floor as it pulled against Ghreel's grip in an attempt to reach its prey. The big man staggered as he struggled to restrain it. Atlon looked anxious but Dvolci seemed unconcerned by the uproar, sitting on his haunches and peering curiously about the room.

'Get it out of here or I'll let him go,' Ghreel shouted to Atlon above the din.

Atlon was about to reply when Dvolci gave a low whistle and turned towards the dog. As if seeing it for the first time he began to stare at it intently, tilting his head first one way, then the other. The dog redoubled its outcry at the challenge. Dvolci continued staring for a little while then dropped gently on to all fours and, crouching low, began to crawl slowly along the bench.

'Quietly, if you can,' Atlon hissed between clenched teeth as the felci crawled over his knees.

Dvolci made no response, but stopped briefly about two paces from the dog. Then, without warning, he leapt forward. There was a collective gasp from all those who could see him, and more than a few jerked their feet off the ground in a very unmanly anticipation of a wild flight by the felci. But it was suddenly quiet. In between frantic barks, the dog had found itself nose to nose with the felci and, for some reason, had lost interest in its loudly announced intention. Though all that could be heard was the felci's whistling, now very soft, the dog's ears flattened against its head, its tail curled tightly and protectively between its legs, and it dropped to the floor with a whimper. So sudden was this collapse that Ghreel almost overbalanced.

It took the innkeeper a moment to grasp what had happened, then he swore at the dog and yanked violently on its chain. But to no avail – the dog remained motionless, its head turned away from Dvolci. Eventually Ghreel drew back his foot to kick it.

'No!' Atlon cried. 'Leave it. I told you you didn't know anything about felcis. It's lucky your dog had a bit more sense. It could have been cut open from nose to tail by now.' Suddenly he was on his feet, very angry. 'And what the hell were you playing at anyway? Do you always set the dogs on to anything you happen not to have seen before? Is that the way travellers are treated at The Wyndering?' He waved an arm across the watching room.

Dvolci, leaving the scene of his triumph, gently bumped into the irate Atlon as he trotted back along the bench. 'Quietly,' he said, softly and with heavy irony.

'Get me my breakfast,' Atlon demanded to conclude his tirade, then he sat down. 'And be quick about it. I've paid enough for it.'

Ghreel was in no mood to argue. The unceremonious rout of his best dog, and the intensity of Atlon's sudden, and righteous outburst had left him feeling exposed and foolish. He affected an indifference to what was said about him beyond the limits of The Wyndering, but he knew that he had just made a mistake, not least in underestimating Atlon and that stupid animal. He was known for dealing 'firmly' with troublesome customers, but news of his subjecting one of his guests to such unjustified violence could spread like a grass fire and do his business great harm. He let go of the dog, which scurried quickly to the far end of the room then he aimed an angry blow at one of the passing boys. Apparently used to such treatment, the boy ducked and continued on his business, barely missing a step.

The various travellers returned to their meals but now the atmosphere was alive with chatter as, in the wake of the tension, they became as familiar with each other as old friends, telling the tale of what they had just seen to one another over and over. There was a great deal of laughter and knowing head-nodding, and eyes turned repeatedly to examine Dvolci and Atlon.

'Heading for the fighting pits, are you?'

The question had to be repeated before Atlon realized it had been addressed to him. It came from the man sitting opposite. Atlon apologized awkwardly then, as the words impinged on him, 'Fighting pits? What are they?'

The man gave him an uncertain, half-amused, half-suspicious look. 'The fighting pits,' he echoed, almost as if he had been asked where the sky was. 'Everyone's heard of them.'

Atlon shook his head. 'Not me, I'm afraid. I come from far away.'

The man nodded. 'I suspected as much when you were so polite to Ghreel. You staying here long?'

'I'm not sure. I'm travelling south for . . . some friends, but I'll need to find work locally to pay my way.'

The man gave him another look then seemed to reach a decision. He rested his arms on the table and leaned forward confidentially. 'It's perhaps as well you bumped into me, then,' he said. 'You have to be careful around here, you know. There are plenty of people who're only too willing to take advantage of a stranger such as yourself.' He leaned further forward and lowered his voice. 'But I think I can help you.' He looked at Dvolci and touched the side of his nose with his forefinger. 'I know my fighting animals, and that . . . is a fighting animal. He's not big, I'll grant you, but he's got it inside, you see. Heart. Guts. That quality only other animals can see.'

'Other animals, and you.'

Atlon, struggling to understand what the man was talking about, started slightly. It was his voice, but he had not spoken. Dvolci looked up at him innocently.

'Exactly,' the man replied, not realizing who had spoken and apparently not noting the sarcasm. 'Experience, you see. Saw it as soon as your . . . what is it? . . . Felci . . . looked at that dog. I saw what Ghreel didn't – the muscles under that fur, those claws.' There was unfeigned admiration in his voice. 'And the way it moved. It's intelligent too – look at how it's watching everything. You've got a fortune waiting for you in that animal, trust me.'

Still bewildered and a little fearful that Dvolci might intercede on his behalf again, Atlon said, 'I'm sorry if I seem foolish, but I

61

still don't understand what you're talking about.'

The man waved the remark aside airily. 'Strange you've never heard of the fighting pits,' he said. 'But there's nothing much to understand.' He tapped his head. 'Doesn't tax the brain. Animals fight in the pit, and people bet on them.'

Atlon's breakfast appeared in front of him but he scarcely noticed it. He was having difficulty in believing what he had just heard. 'You mean, people wager money on one animal killing another?' he asked uncomfortably.

The man shook his head. 'Oh no, there's not always a killing.' He smirked and returned to his meal. 'Lot of money goes into training a good fighter. Can't afford to risk losing them too easily, can you? No, people just bet on which will win.' He tapped the table as he spoke. 'People'll bet a fortune on a good fight.'

A sharp flick from Dvolci's tail and a soft whistle told Atlon to restrain his incipient indignation and to listen and learn. In deference to the felci's command, he managed not to speak, but his hands were shaking as he began to eat.

'I wouldn't have thought the authorities would allow something like that,' he said, after a while.

The man laughed outright, in genuine amusement, spraying food. 'Authorities! What authorities? No one has authority over Arash-Felloren. Quite a few think they do – the Prefect, the Council, the *noble* families and the like.' He gave the word noble a scornful emphasis. 'And a lot more would like to – the trading houses, the Weartans, the Kyrosdyn, the Guilds – all looking after themselves. But it's everyone for himself, really. Always has been, always will be. Arash-Felloren's too big for one man to control – even one man and an army.' He became avuncular and set aside this digression. 'I can see it's *very* fortunate you've met me. You must've come from far away indeed, by the sound of it. Don't you worry. No one could stop the pit fights even if they wanted to.' He rubbed his thumb and first two fingers together knowingly. 'There's far too much money to be made at it.'

Atlon chewed his food energetically to hide his increasing agitation. He tried to deflect the conversation. 'Who are the Kyrosdyn?' he asked.

62

The man's face twisted into an expression of distaste. 'Crystal-workers,' he replied. 'Why?'

'Crystals I know a little about,' Atlon said brightly, surprised at his good fortune in encountering this information, and more than a little relieved to have found something that would take him away from the fighting pits. 'Perhaps there would be work for me with them.'

The man cast an anxious glance at Dvolci then leaned forward again, urgent now. 'Listen to me. Don't you have anything to do with them. I've heard tell that working with crystals can do strange things to a man, and looking at the Kyrosdyn, I can believe it. They're a weird bunch. Humourless, scheming devils. Meddling with things they ought to leave alone.'

'What do you mean?'

'Oh, they have a finger in every part of the political squabbling that goes on. Eternally playing one side off against the other for whatever suits them, though no one seems to see it except us ordinary folk.'

'Why would they do that?'

The man looked surprised. 'I don't know – power, influence, control over the city like I said . . . who knows? They call themselves artists and craftsmen but they're no better than all the others really. Worse, in fact. Rumour has it there's a vast hoard of tints under the Vaskyros – they certainly employ enough guards to protect the place. But they're always looking to make more money. They're involved in all sorts of things that have nothing to do with the crystal trade, but always secretly – behind the scenes. If you ask me, they wouldn't be happy even if they *did* manage to take over the entire city. They'd want all the Lowe Towns, probably, even the Thlosgaral and the Wilde Ports.' His voice dropped to a whisper. 'And there's other things, too. They have . . . powers.'

He seemed to regret this last remark almost immediately and glanced quickly from side to side, as if even the mention of the Kyrosdyn had brought a malign influence into The Wyndering.

'Find out more,' Dvolci's whistled instruction was urgent.

'What do you mean, powers?' Atlon asked bluntly.

The man gave him a startled look.

'It's not important,' Atlon added hastily. 'I was just curious. I've seen all sorts of strange things in my travels, and heard some odd tales, but they all usually come down to trickery and craft in the end. Are you all right? I didn't mean to alarm you.'

The man bridled slightly. 'You didn't alarm me,' he said, a touch too loudly. 'But it's not something that's talked about a lot. The Kyrosdyn certainly don't like it. They always deny everything, play the innocent, the injured party. But everyone knows they meddle in things they shouldn't. They're queer things, crystals.'

The man fell silent. Though anxious to pursue the topic, Atlon sensed that nothing was to be gained by pressing him. Reluctantly he drew the man back to his original topic.

'I understand,' he said. 'Hypocrites. You can find *them* anywhere. The kind that wouldn't be seen at your fighting pits, but who'd have someone there making money for them.' He winked significantly.

The man nodded a confirmation but still seemed to be unsettled by the talk about the Kyrosdyn. The general hubbub of the room came into the awkward silence between them. Atlon was loath to lose this first tenuous contact with the crystal trade. 'Tell me more about these pits,' he said, setting aside his distaste and affecting enthusiasm. 'What kind of animals fight there? Not felcis, surely.'

'No,' the man replied, looking relieved. 'Never seen anything like him before.' His confidence began to seep back. 'Mainly it's like on like – cocks, dogs, cats, horses – fads come and go. But there're no rules – it's whatever the owners agree. In fact, a good mixed fight usually attracts a lot of attention.'

'And thus money,' Atlon added.

'Exactly,' the man replied, fully himself again. He pointed at Dvolci. 'You see, an animal like that – not big, not fierce-looking and, if I'm any judge after seeing him with that dog, not keen on fighting more than he has to – can do well for his owner. You'd be able to take him from pit to pit and make a lot of money before his reputation got widely known.'

Atlon could not think how to continue the conversation. The man misunderstood his silence. When he spoke again, his tone was almost reverential. 'Of course, if you're interested in real fighting – and *real* betting – you have to go to one of the Loose Pits.'

Atlon looked at him blankly.

'There's everything there,' the man went on, taking Atlon's continued silence as a question. 'All the animals that no one will challenge in the ordinary pits.' His voice fell. 'And some things the like of which you'd be hard-pressed to dream about. Terrible things. Things that might have been wolves or boars or worse once, but certainly aren't now.'

Atlon did not need Dvolci's softly whistled urging. 'What do you mean?' he asked.

Once again, the man looked about him. When he spoke, it was in a whisper. 'You need to see them to understand. Some say that the Kyrosdyn have actually *made* these things, but I've heard it said that they're bred from creatures which have been found in the lower depths.' He pointed a curled finger downwards. 'You know – in the caves.' He almost mouthed the words. 'Lower even than the old tunnels.'

Atlon leaned back. Suddenly he felt very cold. He had countless questions that he wanted to ask, but knew that this man could not answer them even if he had been willing to. 'This city sounds very interesting,' he managed to say. 'Lots of opportunities for an enterprising man.' He laid his hand on Dvolci.

'With the right kind of guide,' the man suggested.

'Indeed.' Atlon pursed his lips and looked thoughtful. 'As I said, I'm on a journey for some friends – travelling south. But it's not urgent, while my need for work is.'

The man smiled broadly. 'Work's the refuge of a desperate man.' He flicked a thumb at Dvolci. 'My name's not Irgon Rinter if good money isn't to be made by putting that in the pits.'

Atlon shook his head and pushed his plate to one side. 'I'd need to think about that. I've been a long time alone and he's been good company. I'm very fond of him. I couldn't throw him into a pit full of those creatures you were talking about.'

The man held up his hands in denial. 'There's no question of that,' he said reassuringly. 'To make money in the ordinary pits you try to remain unknown. But to get into the Loose Pits it's just the opposite. You have to make yourself well known – fight your way up – get a reputation. There's no money to be made betting on what happens when you just throw a cat to the wolves, is there? And fighter though he might be, he wouldn't stand a chance against some of the things in the Loose Pits.'

He looked at Atlon narrowly for a moment, then held out his hand. 'Your name, stranger?'

Atlon took the hand and introduced both himself and Dvolci.

Rinter reached across as if to stroke the felci, then catching Dvolci's eye, changed his mind. 'Odd kind of a name,' he said, with a nervous laugh. 'But then he's an odd kind of a creature, isn't he?'

'Odd kind of a creature!'

Atlon winced as Dvolci ground his teeth violently and repeated the phrase yet again.

'You told me to find out about him,' Atlon protested. 'And he's pointed us to the crystal trade. He could be useful.'

'Yes, yes, yes. I know,' Dvolci replied irritably. He ground his teeth again and returned to his diatribe. 'What kind of a creature is it that makes other animals fight just for the spectacle? A human, that's what. I should've torn his blathering head off.'

Atlon knew from experience that there was little point in attempting to stem Dvolci's onslaught on the character of Rinter and, consequently, humanity in general, but he could not resist a jibe. 'I thought you didn't approve of fighting.'

The felci glowered at him, then raised a paw to strike an arbitrary blow at the end of the bed. 'Don't damage the furniture,' Atlon cried hastily. 'We're hardly in favour with Ghreel as it is and I've no desire to be thrown out of here until we've got some more money from somewhere.'

Dvolci blew a violent raspberry then, for no apparent reason, ran round the room five times, recklessly bounding over anything that got in his way.

'Have you finished?' Atlon asked unnecessarily when he finally came to a halt.

Dvolci shook his head violently, sat on his haunches and began to scratch himself. 'Sorry,' he said, after a moment. He looked straight at Atlon. 'I don't think you've any idea what a difficult species you are to live with.' His voice was calm and assured now.

Atlon did not argue the point. 'Bad taste in your mouth again?' he asked gently.

'My own fault. I shouldn't get so angry. Especially about humans. And it's not as if I didn't know what you're like at your worst, is it?'

'It's not as if both of us didn't know,' Atlon added.

Dvolci jumped up on to the stone sink and began working the handle energetically. When the water started to flow he took several large mouthfuls, gargled noisily and then spat them out. He shook his head again, sending a fine spray of water in all directions.

'We go with him, though?' Atlon asked.

'Oh yes,' Dvolci replied without hesitation. 'If the reality of his life matches his gossip, we should learn some interesting things, moving in his circles.'

Atlon voiced his reservations. 'Not such a small town, after all, by the sound of it. And alarming as well.'

'You afraid?'

'Nervous,' Atlon conceded, pulling a wry face. 'There are times when I'd much rather be back at the Caves, studying in peace and quiet.'

'But . . . ?' Dvolci caught the doubt.

Atlon blew out a long breath and picked up his pack. 'But the only way to get back to that is to go forwards, isn't it?'

Dvolci gave a mocking whistle. '*Very* philosophical. You must write *that* one down.' Then he was serious again. 'We must find out all we can about these Kyrosdyn. Some of the things Rinter was saying about them were very alarming. Powers, for pity's sake. If that means what I think it means . . . if these people are using crystals to meddle with—'

'Yes, I know.' Atlon cut across Dvolci's concern. 'But if they are, they are. And they'll have been doing it for a long time. I'm sure *we'll* have no trouble in finding *that* out. We'll have to wait and see.'

'And caves beneath the city – and strange creatures?'

Atlon wiped his hand across his mouth nervously. 'I don't even want to think about what that might mean.'

'We'll have to find out.' Dvolci's tone held no enthusiasm at the prospect.

'I know, I know,' Atlon acknowledged grimly. He fluttered his hands as if to dispel an image in the air in front of him. 'In the meantime we've more pressing problems – like finding a source of income around here.' He slung his pack on to his back.

A trail of fine dust eddied about his feet as he opened the door. Stepping on to the long balcony, he looked up at the hazy sky and the low bright sun just breaking through the dust that hung permanently over the Thlosgaral. There was an unhealthy, almost feverish quality about it. The promise of a heat that would drain rather than sustain.

'Yes,' he said, answering Dvolci's earlier question. 'I am afraid.'

Chapter 7

Though not normally concerned by dirt about his person. Pinnatte nevertheless tried to remove the stain from the back of his hand. His first instinct was to lift it to his mouth, as an injured animal might, but something stopped him. At least he could see the mark where it was. If he sucked it into his body, who knew what it might spread through his system. Perhaps that was what the Kyrosdyn had intended – perhaps the mark contained some subtle poison. Pinnatte felt more pleased than unnerved by this conclusion. It confirmed his own assessment of himself – he knew how to survive on the streets; he was not one to be so easily trapped.

He was less pleased a few minutes later when a vigorous washing in the cold water of the fountain failed to make any impression on the stain. A chill slowly formed in the pit of his stomach. What had that freak done to him? He felt sick at the random chance of it all. Like most of the Guild of Thieves, he was meticulous in avoiding stealing not just crystals, but *anything* from the Kyrosdyn. Though an elaborate system of statutes announced otherwise, punishments in Arash-Felloren were usually dependent on the whim of the injured party. Weartans, typically, could be bribed, unless there were several of them, in which case a beating was more likely. The private guards who looked after noble houses were more immediately inclined to violence, but, incongruously, often hesitated to create a disturbance that might distress their masters. Those employed by the traders, by contrast, would often call on their master to join in, which they invariably did, and with relish. But no one *really* knew what the Kyrosdyn did. There were only vague and frightening rumours – mysterious disappearances and people returned who were silent and haunted – 'never the same again'.

Pinnatte had been luckier than average in his career. He had had many narrow escapes but had only been caught twice. On the first occasion he had managed to escape by paying a substantial bribe to a Weartan officer, while on the second he had had to serve a spell as a bound worker in one of the lesser noble houses. But as he stood looking into the bubbling water of the fountain he felt as though all the punishments he should have had were now about to be brought down upon him.

Hardly noticing what he was doing, he turned and began making his way through the crowded square. Again like a wounded animal, his instincts were now leading him to where he felt safest – Lassner's Den.

It's only a mark, he kept saying to himself, over and over, but there was no comfort in the thought. A darkness had come into his life that would not be so casually dismissed. He could see nothing beyond it.

Not that he was without resource. In a more practical attempt to push the concern from his mind, and in direct contradiction of his earlier vow, he had managed to steal two purses before he turned into the familiar twisted street with its uneven, cart-rutted surface and disordered tiers of neglect and abandoned dwellings on either side.

Lassner was in his usual position; apparently asleep, with his hands curled over the top of his stick and his chin resting on them. The dingy room, off an equally dingy entrance hall, had a welcoming air that Pinnatte had never noticed before. He threw the two unopened purses on the table in front of the old man. 'Clean cuts,' he said, as Lassner's eyes snapped open and looked at him sharply. The simple statement, meaning that the owners were unaware of their purses being taken, was more than a casual remark. A chase attracted attention. Faces otherwise lost in the crowd might be recognized, and perhaps remembered at a future time. A Den Master might decide that a particular area was to be avoided for the time being. Failure to report a chase was liable to bring down a punishment on the offender's head – sometimes severe, particularly if the chase had been brought anywhere near the Den.

Lassner half-closed his eyes to acknowledge the message then looked at the purses shrewdly before emptying them on to the table. After carefully rooting through all the pockets to ensure that nothing had been missed, he threw them to an old woman sitting in the corner, with a few rapid instructions about how they were to be altered. There was a brief, ill-tempered exchange at the end of which the woman turned her back on him and, muttering to herself, bent over her work. It was a regular ritual: Lassner issued the instructions, she ignored them and went her own way and, within a couple of days, the purses, as new, but quite unrecognizable, would be for sale on a stall somewhere. Lassner could sell the bark from a dead dog, his friends proclaimed.

Bony fingers flicked quickly through the coins and personal items on the table, assessing and ordering them. Personal items, like the purses themselves would be altered and resold, if possible, for the 'funding of the Den', though no one ever questioned the fate of the money from such sales. Coins would be returned to the thief, with a premium being paid to the Den Master. When he had finished, Lassner drew a pile of coins and a ring towards himself and looked up at Pinnatte.

'Agreed?'

'Agreed.'

Pinnatte did not actually agree. Lassner had been taking too much by way of premium lately, but nothing was to be gained by arguing the point. He swept up the balance of his day's work and turned to leave.

'What's the matter, lad? They *were* clean cuts, weren't they?'

The questions made Pinnatte start. For a moment he considered making an off-hand reply, but experience had taught him that it was pointless trying to keep anything from the old man once he had chosen to ask about it. Thus the tale which earlier he had hoped to tell bravely and with great style to win himself free lodge for a day or so, stumbled out almost incoherently.

Lassner's attention was rapt nevertheless, and a few sharp questions ordered the events as nimbly as his finger had ordered the contents of the purses. 'Bad mistake,' he declared when Pinnatte had finished. 'Very bad.'

'There was nothing to show who he was.' Pinnatte anxiously

71

repeated what he had already said. 'No staff, no robes, nothing. Just another plum for picking.'

Lassner frowned, but nodded. The excuse was accepted. Pinnatte did not normally make mistakes, least of all anything as serious as this. He reached out. 'Give me your hand.'

Pinnatte thrust out his right hand stiffly, half-fearing some form of punishment. But Lassner merely took it and examined the mark.

'A typical Kyrosdyn trick,' he pronounced disparagingly, releasing the hand. 'Something to make you fuss and fret – chew your nails over. And it's working, isn't it? Look at you. You're here, but your mind's skittering about the city like a cat with a tin on its tail.'

'He used Kyroscreft on me,' Pinnatte insisted. 'He just pointed at me and I couldn't move my legs. And he was surrounded by . . . something.' He rubbed the back of his hand. 'What if he's done something else like that to me?'

A flicker of impatience crossed Lassner's face and he let out a loud breath. 'You've got the makings of a good thief, young Pinnatte. That's why you're here and why I don't take much premium off you for the learning you're getting. You could go far – get a Den of your own one day, perhaps. But you've still a lot to learn; there's more to real thieving than just cutting purses.' He became unexpectedly confidential. 'Some of the best thieves in the city are heading trading houses or serving on the Council. The only difference between them and us is that we've got a sense of honour.' He waved his digression aside then tapped his head. 'Making people think they've seen something that they haven't, or seen nothing when they've seen something, is as important to you as learning how to use a sharp knife and a soft touch when you're taking purses.'

'There was no trickery,' Pinnatte protested. 'I felt what he did to me. I couldn't move my legs.'

Lassner shrugged. 'I'm sure you couldn't,' he conceded, 'as you thought. Kyrosdyn aren't people to trifle with, for sure everyone knows that. But from what I've heard, they can't do anything that I haven't known many a good thief capable of.' He became almost earnest. 'When you're frightened, your mind plays tricks, betrays you. They play on that. And play well. They're treacherous and clever.'

Pinnatte shook his head and made to speak.

'Listen to me, lad.' Lassner's tone made Pinnatte stiffen. The older man had an ugly temper at times, and though he no longer had the skills that had once made him one of the Guild of Thieves' finest, he was still highly respected, and someone to be reckoned with. 'What you need above all else in this business is to see things as they are. Not as you think they are, or as you think they ought to be, but *as they are*. Use your eyes, use your wits, look into the heart of what's happening. Let everyone else be confused, chasing shadows . . . *but not you*. You need to be the one who sees what's really happening.'

Pinnatte nodded earnestly. Tempered with relief that no punishment was coming, it was a mixture of respect and fear that was holding him there now that he had told his story. Though he was listening to the old man, he had no idea what he was talking about. How could you not see something the way it was? he thought scornfully. All he wanted to do was get to his room and set about his hand with hot water and a stiff brush. Lassner looked at him for a moment, then his eyes narrowed shrewdly. 'Get some hot water and give that hand a good scrub,' he said.

Despite himself, Pinnatte gaped and momentarily stopped rubbing his hand. The old man chuckled darkly and waved him out of the room. 'You see how easy it is, lad, when you use your head and your wits. See things as they are.'

The demonstration made a vivid impression on Pinnatte, but his dominant concern soon returned. Within a few minutes he had collected a pan of hot water from the grumbling and dangerous boiler at the back of the building, and made his way up the rickety stairs to his own room on the first floor. There he began vigorously scrubbing his hand, grimly determined to remove the Kyrosdyn's mark, no matter what Lassner chose to say about it. Within a few minutes the back of his hand was red raw. But the mark was unchanged. As he stared at it, the memory of the sudden loss of the use of his legs, and the Kyrosdyn's eerie presence, returned with dreadful clarity. His hand was trembling as the brush slipped from

73

it and clattered on to the floor. For a moment, fear threatened to overwhelm him completely. Unclear, but intense visions rushed in upon him, telling him of a future where somehow he would be irrevocably bound to the service of the Kyrosdyn. A crystal glittered in front of him.

'I'll have your worthless soul. Bind it in here. Listen to its futile struggling. Trapped. For ever.' The voice, the manner, everything, chilled him.

'When you're frightened, your mind plays tricks, betrays you. See things as they are.'

Lassner's words entered his swirling confusion. He latched on to them. Lassner, at least, he knew. Insofar as anyone could be trusted, Lassner could – whatever else he did to his charges, he didn't lie to them. A trick, he'd said. Something to make him fuss and fret . . .

'And it's working, isn't it?'

But he hadn't been able to move his legs. And the stain wouldn't go . . .

A howling cry built up inside him.

For an instant there was only darkness – closing all about him.

Then, years of assessing consequences made themselves felt. If he gave in now, succumbed to the darkness and the howling inside him, what would follow? He might be one of Lassner's favourites at the moment, but that would soon change if he became a trembling clown who sat shivering in his room all day.

Another future unfolded in front of him, displacing that of the Kyrosdyn's bondage. One in which he had neither Den nor Den Master. In which he was without friends and companions, sliding relentlessly down through the complex social order of Arash-Felloren, down to begging and scavenging around the decaying slums that pocked the city, down to scuttling about the tunnels and sewers, capable of preying only on his own kind, down to some dismal, unsung death.

The cry found a different voice, soft and strangled and full as much of anger as fear.

'It's a mark on the back of my hand,' he whispered desperately through clenched teeth. Nothing more than some fancy dye like

74

the old woman downstairs used to colour purses. You could scrub that until the skin peeled and it wouldn't come off. That's all it was. That, and a mess of sinister-sounding threats. How could he be put in a crystal, for pity's sake? It made no sense. A grown man caged in a thing like that. It was ridiculous! How could he not have laughed outright when the words were spoken? Lassner was right, they were tricks, that's all – tricks. Still, now he really knew why the Kyrosdyn weren't to be trifled with. They were good at playing tricks – very good. Even Lassner had made him think for a moment that he could read minds. Who could say what could be done by someone who practised that kind of a deception day in, day out, just as he did cutting purses?

He was breathing heavily, forcing air in and out of his lungs as he did whenever he was about to tackle anything particularly difficult.

'It's a mark on my hand,' he said again. 'Nothing more. Like the old woman's dye, it'll wear off in time.'

He walked over to the window and looked at the mark closely in the dust-filled sunlight. He was still shaking from his ordeal but, seen with his new vision, the mark looked quite innocuous. He blew out a relieved breath. It was fortunate he hadn't made a bigger fool of himself in front of Lassner.

As he twisted and turned his hand, he fancied that the mark had a slightly green hue to it.

He flopped down on the crude mattress that served for a bed. He felt drained. It had been a bizarre and terrifying day. He needed to think, to rest.

He looked at the faint lines and patches of colour that were the surviving remnants of a painting that had once decorated the cracked and stained ceiling. A painting done presumably when the house had been part of a more salubrious area, though it had had many tenants since then. The shapes and patterns were reassuring in their familiarity. He was fortunate indeed just to have a roof over his head, let alone to be part of a Den, especially Lassner's Den. But even as the thought came to him, so did another, provoked, perhaps, by the vision he had just had of the dismal, degraded future that might lie in front of him. He must never again allow anything to happen that might bring him to the head of that road, yet while he was out in the streets, snatching such things as he could, the risk would always be there.

'Some of the best thieves in the city are heading trading houses or serving on the Council.'

Lassner's words told Pinnatte nothing that he did not already know. Indeed, such ideas were an envious commonplace amongst all the city's thieves. But Pinnatte saw them now as he had never seen them before.

It was not enough to be a stealer of purses.

True, he was good at it, and it would always make him a living. But what kind of a living? The cracked ceiling suddenly looked tawdry and squalid, exuding nothing but countless years of neglect. The question came again. What kind of a living? He sat up.

This was not enough.

He had been scared out of his wits today – for what? For a lousy room in a lousy house and a few coins to jingle in his pockets. The memory of the Kyrosdyn's purse returned, bringing a new message this time. He could not have afforded such a purse with the proceeds of an entire year's thieving. And if he *had* stolen the purse, what would he have sold it for? A mere fraction of its true worth. There would have been shaken heads and in-drawn breaths from even his most reliable buyers – 'Difficult to sell quality stuff like this.' But someone, somewhere, would sell it for something like its real price, and walk away with *his* money.

'See things as they are.'

Pinnatte nodded to himself. Lassner's advice was sound. He would do just that. And though it was not a conscious decision, he started with Lassner himself. Questions began to form such as had never occurred to him before. They were disturbing, but Pinnatte could do nothing to stop them. Who was this old man that so dominated his life, sitting in his dingy room all day and living little better than his Den charges? His Den Master was not only a respected man amongst the city's thieves, he was, reputedly, a wealthy one. But surely no one would live like that if they had the wealth to live otherwise? And could even Lassner afford such a thing as that Kyrosdyn's purse? Suddenly Pinnatte had no doubts about the answer. It was No. And with that realization, starker contrasts burst in upon him. This was only the man's *purse*! His miserable purse, a trivial thing, a minor item of property. Whatever its value, it was the least indication of the man's true wealth. If he had a purse like that, what would be the worth of the rings on his fingers, or the clothes on his back? What possessions would he have back at the Vaskyros? What did it cost him to employ a bodyguard to follow him round all day? Was it likely that such a man would now be lying on an ancient, crushed mattress, staring up at a cracked and grimed ceiling?

Pinnatte ran his hand across his forehead. He was sweating with excitement. Whatever else had happened today, a new pathway had been opened for him. He looked at the mark on the back of his hand. It held no terrors now. It had been a stupid, petty gesture by a man discomfited by a mere thief. But it had unbound that thief. Turned him into someone entirely different.

Pinnatte lay back. Only minutes before he had been tired, but now he was wide awake. Now he must think. It was one thing to concoct grandiose ideas, but quite another to do something about them. For one thing, he was bound to Lassner for another year. Not by any written document, but by his word – the code which every thief in Arash-Felloren honoured. Well, nearly every thief. Those who were rich and powerful enough – or dangerous enough – to go their own way did so, accountable to no one, but that was not a choice available to Pinnatte. To break his word to Lassner would be to bring repercussions on his head which would leave him without any allies, and more concerned with saving his life than enriching it! Thus, Lassner must not learn of this new-found ambition. Care must be taken to see that he got no wind of it. He might not be able to read minds, but he read people well enough. Any hint of disloyalty or untrustworthiness and Pinnatte's other future could yet come to pass.

A slight twinge of guilt intruded into Pinnatte's exhilaration. Was he right to do this? Lassner was the nearest thing he had to a father. The old man had taken him in some five years ago when he had been changing from one of the city's homeless waifs into a wild and unstable young man, destined to end his days on someone's knife or under a hail of Weartan staffs in an alleyway somewhere. Lassner had given him a home, of sorts, and had also taught him many things, not least a modicum of discipline. Now he had taught him something else, albeit unintentionally.

The moment passed. His obligation to Lassner was based on necessity, not affection. And some of Lassner's teaching had been brutal. The old man could use his stick for more than leaning on and Pinnatte had received many beatings in his early days until he had learned that Den Master really meant Master. And now, contrary to his constant protestations, the money he took by way of premiums was excessive. Pinnatte did something he had never done before other than to evaluate his day's takings – he did a calculation. There were at least forty in this den; few of them earned as much as he did, but most of them would earn at least half as much . . .

He scowled with effort. Arithmetic was not his strongest suit but it was good enough to show him that Lassner would be making a great deal of money out of his charges – a great deal of money for which he did very little. In fact, he did nothing, Pinnatte decided, except sit in that damned room like a scavenging crow.

And what did Lassner do with all this money? Pinnatte was suddenly angry. Unlike the majority of his Den-Mates, he had a shrewd idea where much of Lassner's money went – it disappeared into the pockets of the men who ran the gambling rings at the fighting pits.

Pinnatte had only been to the pits a few times but, on one occasion, quite by chance, he had seen Lassner there. He had not recognized him until, at the height of the excitement, a hood had slipped to reveal the old man at the very edge of the pit, wild-eyed and frenzied like the rest of the spectators. Pinnatte was about to shout across to him when the fight came to a sudden and, apparently, unexpected end. The change of expression on Lassner's face struck Pinnatte like a blow, seeming, as it did, to mingle in an obscene harmony with the final pitiful whimper from the pit. He felt the acrid stench of the place filling his entire being, and his greeting died before it formed. Whatever had happened, it was bad, and Lassner would no more want to be seen thus by one of his charges than be seen naked in the street. Pinnatte backed discreetly into the crowd, resolving to act with the utmost surprise if he chanced to bump into his Den Master before he had a chance to get away. Some imp, however, held him there. He had rarely seen Lassner outside the Den and was curious about what the old man was up to, particularly in view of his violent reaction at the end of the fight. Thus, against his better judgement, but keeping carefully out of sight, he had watched him for much of the evening. It proved to be an unsettling revelation as he saw Lassner part with substantial sums of money in predominantly unsuccessful wagers. When he finally left, Pinnatte had made a further resolution to say nothing to anyone about this insight. At the time, it had been out of a mixture of loyalty and fear for, though he had been uncomfortable about what he was seeing, he still presumed that Lassner would only act in the best interests of the Den – and who was he to question his Den Master about such a matter? Over time however, his assessment of Lassner's altruism had gradually changed, and though his suspicions about the gambling were strengthened into certainty by his growing experience of the man, and such contacts as he had at the pits, he still remained silent. Nothing was to be gained by exposing Lassner's folly to the others, and a great deal was to be lost.

Now however, the matter, having simmered over the years, seemed to have been brought to a boiling conclusion by today's shaking events. He would not be Lassner's creature any longer. He would work now to break away and to earn himself the kind of money that would meet the needs of his new aspirations.

He rubbed the mark on his hand.

Chapter 8

Dreaming about breaking away from Lassner was one thing; doing it, quite another. Pinnatte was an experienced and skilful thief and he knew more 'useful' people in his trade than Lassner would have guessed. Further, over the years he had done an unusual thing for a thief: he had accumulated some money. It was carefully hidden in discreet niches about the city, and while it was not a great deal, it would at least buy him board and lodge for a week or so, if need arose. He had managed to achieve this by not declaring all his 'earnings' to Lassner – a matter requiring very careful judgement and a stern control over his natural greed, for the Den Master had an uncanny knack of knowing when he was being given purses that had already been lightened, and he was brutal to anyone he caught. One of Pinnatte's earliest memories after he had joined the Den was of Lassner's stick hissing violently through the air and of an offender trying vainly to escape, his cries mingling with Lassner's curses.

'Not for your greed, you vermin. For your stupidity in thinking that *I* was stupid!'

The recollection reminded Pinnatte again that striking out on his own was not only a daunting prospect, but probably hazardous. Yet it did not radically diminish his new-found resolution. He would just have to continue being careful.

Why the day's events should have brought the idea of freedom to him, he could not have said, but he knew now that he would not be able to turn away from it. All that was to be decided was the manner in which his parting from Lassner was to be achieved. Vague notions came and went, leaving nothing in their wake that would direct him to the next act in his quiet rebellion. Gradually his enthusiasm turned into frustration until, in the end, he was pacing the floor, fists clenched.

There had to be a way!

There had to be a place for him somewhere other than this dismal Den.

He stopped. He was at the window, staring out at the street and the familiar decaying buildings opposite. On an impulse, he turned and ran out of the room and up the several flights of stairs that led to the Den's deserted attic. From here, a little nimble footwork carried him through a dormer window, up the roof and on to the ridge. He paused to catch his breath, then, leaning against a chimney stack, gazed around.

He had first come to this place some years ago thanks to a scornful challenge by one of the other Den-Mates. His meeting of it had enhanced his status within the group dramatically but, more important to him, both then and since, was the knowledge that here was a place to which he could retreat and be alone. The bright blue sky and the cool breeze of that successful day had been like a benison, and some part of it was always with him when he came here. Even now, when the sky, strained by the relentless heat of the long summer, looked grainy with effort, he still felt a lightening inside him as he looked along the hump-backed ridge and out across the familiar roofscape.

As far as he could see, in every direction, there were buildings. Walls and rooftops rose and dipped in a chaotic landscape, their jagged contours adding to those of the innumerable and long-forgotten hills upon which the city had grown. In the distance he could make out the Vaskyros, spiky against the dusty sky. It was thought to be the highest building in the city but Arash-Felloren was so hilly that no one building could dominate it and, from so far away, it looked small and insignificant. The scaffolding that encased it — solid, elaborate and confusing at close quarters — became only a cobwebbed raggedness. Pinnatte had never known the Vaskyros to be free of the paraphernalia of masons and builders and their allied trades. Time after time, walls, towers, spires, high-spanning arches had been started, abandoned, restarted, changed, demolished, but never to any discernible plan. Few bothered to ask any more why the Kyrosdyn were always altering their building.

'Women can't ever make up their minds.'

He recalled the sarcastic explanation and the sneering face as if the words had been spoken within the hour, although it must have been years ago and he could not now remember even the name of the speaker. Nor could he remember the name of the older man who had rebuked him, though he remembered a strangeness in his gaze. 'Hold your tongue, boy. A man who rises to become Ailad of the Kyrosdyn is to be respected. A woman who does it is to be feared. It bodes no good for any of us.' The sneering face had chosen not to pursue the matter.

Work on the Vaskyros had indeed begun shortly after Imorren had become Ailad. That much Pinnatte had learned from Lassner, though he had learned precious little since. As far as he could determine, that had been some time before he was born and, insofar as he ever thought about it, he shared the common view that the endless changes to the building were the folly of people with too much money and too little work to occupy themselves with. Not that, until today, the Vaskyros had ever occupied his thoughts very much. Still less did Imorren. She was an even more distant figure than the Prefect, although admittedly, together with other female notables, she featured occasionally in his wilder flights of fancy, when some adventitious act of courage on his part would lead him on to wealth, power and, above all, sensual gratification. For all her years, Imorren was said to be a 'striking' woman. Pinnatte had never seen her at close quarters and was not quite sure what that meant, so he usually assumed the best.

He rubbed his hand. Imorren was in his thoughts now, but not as an idle dream. What kind of woman could she be, to control the Kyrosdyn as she did? He let the question float away. It brought back to him the memory of his encounter with the Kyrosdyn and the fear that hung about it. The fear was less now, diminished by confession, revelation and physical effort, but it was still there. Yet too, the thought of Imorren brought an unexpected encouragement. This woman had risen through an organization dominated by men and, somehow, for whatever reason, she imposed her will not only upon them but on their very fortress. *It would be how she wished it to be, regardless of any obstacle or opposition.* The realization was visceral and sudden. Pinnatte found he was holding his breath. She would allow *nothing* to stand in her way.

He must be the same.

Steadying himself against the chimney-stack he turned around slowly to look at the full panorama of the city. Buildings, large and small, ornate and simple, faded gradually into a complex patchwork and thence into a mottled uniformity: all detail, all individuality gone. But still the buildings would be there – and the city went on and on. He knew that he would see the same sight from the roof of any other building he chose to climb.

And just as his sensing of the ambition of Imorren had shaken him, so now the vastness of Arash-Felloren forced itself on him for the first time.

He was the merest mote! He was nothing.

How big was the city? Did it ever end?

'No man has ever walked across it. So far does it reach, so densely woven its ways, that any who have tried to span it have never returned.'

'A lifetime is not long enough to walk a different street each hour.'

'Sunset and sunrise are ever-present in the city.'

Ale-house legends uttered with the unimpeachable conviction of unnumbered but sincere and variously poetical drunkards rose up to answer his question. They were a nonsense, of course. A city couldn't go on for ever . . . could it?

How would he know? He, who had never travelled more than half a day from the Den! He had heard of the Thlosgaral to the east, where the crystals came from – and of the Wilde Ports beyond, though he had no idea what they were – but in every other direction . . .?

And there were other tales, more foolish still – yet they were tales that even drunkards whispered. There were more tunnels and caves beneath the city than streets and buildings above it. There were more *people* beneath the city than above it. And there were other things beneath the city, in the caves . . . ancient and terrifying things. And buildings that just vanished, to be replaced by different buildings and strange people speaking unintelligible tongues, or that reappeared elsewhere in the city, the inhabitants seemingly unaware of any change. It was even said that there were places where a single thoughtless stride would carry a man into the past or the future.

Pinnatte shook his head to break free of the city's unexpected grip. He was only partially successful. The immensity of Arash-Felloren was not so lightly set aside. But his perspective had changed. Still he was as nothing in such a city, but what did that mean for him? It meant that there were countless places where he had never been, countless places where he could find another home, countless people who did not know him, countless opportunities. All he had to do was look for them, and then reach out and take them.

Slowly his mind spiralled back to some semblance of calmness. Now he must think. He sat down on the ridge and leaned back against the chimney-stack. His problem was starkly simple – he needed money. A great deal of it. The solution was less clear – where was it to be found, and how might he go about acquiring it? He was good at what he did, of course, very good. But that knowledge merely heightened the need for him to look to other than purse-cutting to serve the needs of his new ambition. He was one of the best in Lassner's Den, but even if he paid no premium, the money he made would not be sufficient for him to live much better than he did at present. And it was a risky business. Many a purse contained little or nothing, while all held danger. And how much better could he become at this craft? He could not take many more purses each day than he already did, and twice the number would not bring him anywhere near the realm where he might sport a purse such as the Kyrosdyn had casually taunted him with.

And too, seeping into all these thoughts was the presence of Lassner. Another realization came to Pinnatte as he sat gazing at the dimming western sky. He still had a great deal to learn from the old man. He smiled to himself. Wasn't it Lassner after all who had taught him to smile and make a friend rather than an enemy?

'Won't stop you robbing him in the end, will it? But there's no need to be unpleasant about it.' Pinnatte's smile turned into a chuckle and he felt an unexpected surge of affection for his mentor.

Thoughts of Lassner brought his mind back to where much of his premium was spent, thanks to the good offices of his Den Master: the fighting pits.

When Pinnatte had gone there originally, it was to see what opportunities the crowds offered for easy pickings. He had learned two things very quickly. One was that there was a great deal of money to be found there; the other was that he was unlikely to be able to make off with any of it. He relied on his ability to move quickly through crowds to save him when things went amiss, but that would be out of the question around the pits where the crowd was so packed that it was sometimes impossible to move at all. Adding to this assessment of his chances was the fact that the typical pit crowd was not one he would wish to antagonize. This too, was immediately apparent. The air stank of bloodlust and savagery, and it needed little sensitivity to see that there was more cruelty and viciousness around the pit than in it. Subsequently he had had a dream in which he was seized in the act of taking a purse and hurled bodily into the pits to be torn apart while his eager-eyed captors slowly passed money to and fro, waging on the nearness and the manner of his end and discussing in leisurely terms the techniques of the raging animals. The dream had recurred several times after his first visit and each time he had lurched out of sleep, bolt upright, gasping and covered in sweat. It came less frequently after he forced himself to go to the pits again, hands firmly tucked in his belt and knife tightly sheathed, and it had stopped altogether after he had learned about Lassner's gambling.

Also deterring him from trying to pursue his trade at the pits was the fact that many of those present were from the darker fringes of Arash-Felloren's criminal fraternity: those who earned their money by bludgeoning people in the street, or even in their homes; those who kidnapped and extorted; those who even preyed on their own kind and who killed at the behest of others. He, and most of the Guild, affected to despise such as these for their brutality and lack of skill or finesse, but the scorn was always carefully hidden. Fates worse than being thrown into a fighting pit were waiting for those who needlessly provoked such individuals.

Yet the pits were the only place that Pinnatte knew of where substantial sums of money were conspicuously available . . . True, there were banking and credit houses, and there were the larger shops and market stalls, but it was beyond him to attempt to rob any of those. They invariably had their own guards who would watch the likes of him constantly from the instant he appeared. He looked down at his clothes to confirm this. Perhaps he could smarten himself up a little? He imagined himself preened and elegant. 'Some of the best thieves in the city are heading trading houses or serving on the Council.' But Lassner's words only reminded him where he stood in the city's social and criminal hierarchy. He hadn't the faintest idea how such people did their thieving; he was lacking far more than decent clothes. With a twinge of regret, he let the peacock image fade.

Yet, incongruous though it seemed, he knew that he should be working to acquire that knowledge; he should be thinking about how he could take money from these people. Just because it was difficult did not mean that it could not be done, even by him. He placed the notion carefully to one side, quietly resolving to think about it from time to time.

He could always resort to burglary, of course, but that held even less charm than cutting purses. True, he was a good climber, but he liked to have several avenues of escape available at all times and the prospect of encountering an enraged householder while clambering through a window high above the street gave him vertigo.

Inexorably his thoughts gravitated back to the pits. Was there anything more for him there than anywhere else? Purse-taking was out of the question and he had no money for placing wagers – not that that would have earned him much in view of what happened to Lassner's money, and he, presumably, knew something about the business. Besides, it had not taken Pinnatte very long to realize that the people who made money out of wagers were those who set the odds – the men who ran the pits – and they were very jealous of anyone attempting to usurp their rights. But even as he reviewed his prospects at the pits he realized that they offered opportunities not found elsewhere in the city: they brought together people from the highest to the lowest. They were places of levelling.

'We're all blood-lusting brothers under the skin,' Pinnatte had once heard someone say, with a grim, knowing laugh, when all eyes had been temporarily drawn away from the conflict to look at a group of smartly dressed young women whose frenzied shrieking was overtopping that of the blood-soaked animals.

His stomach rumbled. Despite the day's happenings, bodily needs were making themselves felt. He was pleased now that he had managed to bring enough money back to ensure he would be fed for a day or so. Clambering to his feet he took a final look around the city. The western sky was reddening with the setting sun while a dull, brooding redness on the eastern horizon marked the Thlosgaral. There *would* be a place for him somewhere, he resolved.

Then, almost childishly, he slid perilously down the roof on to the top of the dormer, leaned over and, seizing the edge of the window, swung slowly out over the street, taking his weight on his arms until his feet gently touched the sill. As he usually did, he paused for a moment and peered straight down defiantly into the tapering perspective of the building to the crooked pavement below. Then he was inside again, the attic of the Den closing about him familiarly, at once sheltering and oppressive.

A little later, he was eating and listening to the noisy chatter of his Den-Mates and Lassner's regular harangue about the failings of modern Guild members in comparison with their predecessors. He found that he had to struggle to prevent old routines from brushing his new ambitions aside and, from time to time, he glanced down at the mark on his hand. The sight of it brought only a hint of fear now. It was as if the Kyrosdyn had written a subtle sign for him that would keep him reminded of this violent day, and of Imorren and her relentless will, for ever.

After he had eaten, he set off for the nearest of the fighting pits. He strode out as if the simple act of walking would carry him to his new future. Hitherto, his visits to the pits, perhaps everything he had ever done, had been without any clear purpose. But no longer. Now he was going to watch and learn as never before.

Now he would look continually for anything that would lead him to that place that was his.

As he marched through the ill-lit streets, a figure, drifting from shadow to shadow, moved silently after him.

Chapter 9

The road from The Wyndering to the city was a well-trodden one, and Atlon and Rinter were soon part of a steady stream of travellers. There were as many travelling away from the city as towards it.

Atlon looked about him constantly, taking in such as he could of the busy scene. He would have questioned Rinter about many of their fellow travellers, but his new found guide sat his horse with a preoccupied air that did not invite interrogation. Their silent progress puzzled Atlon somewhat. Rinter had, after all, shown an enthusiastic interest in Dvolci, conceding even that he had never seen a felci before, yet now he asked nothing about him. Nor did he ask about Atlon's homeland or the nature of his journey. In similar circumstances, Atlon was sure that he would not have been so restrained.

Rinter's silence, in fact, had two causes. Firstly, he had little interest in where Atlon had come from. In common with most of the citizens of Arash-Felloren, he knew that while a world existed beyond the city, it was an inadequate and inferior place, and held nothing that could not be found in excess in the city itself. Secondly, in answer to Atlon's unspoken question, he was indeed thinking very hard about Dvolci, though solely with a view to luring Atlon into placing the felci in the pits. He had been quite truthful when he claimed to be a good judge of fighting animals, and Dvolci's demonstration with Ghreel's dog had impressed him greatly. Furthermore, an unusual creature like that should prove to be a considerable attraction. Not many chances such as this came a man's way, and he mustn't let it slip away. He had been less truthful about his contacts and organizing ability.

Atlon unsettled him. It didn't help that the man kept the damned animal as a pet, of all things, but there was more to it than that. The horse he rode, for example, was splendid – well muscled, well proportioned and with a look in its eye that Rinter could scarcely meet. It occurred to him that it might have been some kind of a war-horse – a cavalry mount, perhaps? But how would someone like Atlon come by such an animal? He didn't look like a soldier, and he certainly didn't behave like one. Then, for a moment, Rinter found himself teetering on the edge of panic. Was *he* the one who was being lured here? Was Atlon's seeming naivety merely a device to instil confidence? He had a brief vision of some mercenary, once sure and alert, lying dead in the mountains, treacherously murdered while he slept. He cleared his throat and cast a side-long glance at his companion. Nothing Atlon had said or done had given any indication that he was anything other than what he claimed to be – a teacher looking for funds to continue his journey. But that meant nothing. Rinter knew enough violent characters to be aware that smiles and affability were not always what they seemed. What was he getting himself into, meddling with this stranger? Should he just slip into the crowd and leave him while he could?

But to lose the chance of getting that felci in the pits . . .

Easing his horse back a little, he studied Atlon carefully. Senses heightened by his instinct for self-preservation, he noticed almost immediately that Atlon sat his horse as though he were part of it, so much so that the horse was responding to signals that Rinter could not even see. Neither Atlon nor the horse were disturbed by the increasing clamour of the traffic as they drew nearer to the city. No, Rinter decided with some relief, this was no stolen animal. Wherever Atlon had come from, he had been riding all his life and he had been with that horse for a long time. His initial assessment of the man had been correct. He may or may not be a teacher, but he was harmless. The image of the murdered mercenary faded and Rinter urged his horse forward again.

Thus far, Dvolci had remained on Atlon's shoulder, also looking about himself curiously, although occasionally he would disappear into Atlon's back-pack and reappear, chewing.

'If it wasn't for all these hills, this would be like one of the roads to the Great Mart,' he said softly into Atlon's ear.

The reference to his homeland gave Atlon a momentary spasm of homesickness. He looked around. 'Not really,' he said, a little more harshly than he had intended. 'The horses are a poor lot on the whole, ill-tended and ill-controlled. And there's little or no semblance of line discipline on the part of riders round here.' He shot an angry glance at a large, heavily laden cart as it swayed past him very closely, obliging his horse to step sideways. 'This road's in an appalling state, too.' He slapped his hand on his sleeve, sending a cloud of dust billowing into the sunlight. 'Why in the world it's not paved, with this amount of traffic using it, I can't imagine. I suppose people round here must like choking on dust in the summer and sinking in mud in the winter.'

'What?'

Rinter's voice made Atlon start. Dvolci chuckled and jumped down from the horse. As he ran off, a dog on a nearby wagon barked furiously after him, provoking a stream of abuse from its owner.

'I'm sorry,' Atlon said. 'With travelling so much alone, I'm afraid I'm in the habit of talking to myself.'

But Rinter was not interested. The sight of Dvolci's brown sinuous body scurrying into nearby rocks shattered the vision of a lucrative future that he had already invested in the animal.

'It's running away,' he cried out in alarm, standing in his stirrups and pointing frantically. His horse protested, making him drop heavily back into the saddle.

Atlon smiled. 'He'll be back when he's had a good look round,' he said reassuringly. 'It's just that he's not too keen on crowds.'

Rinter massaged his behind. 'He's not going to like the city, then,' he said, affecting a heartiness he did not feel.

Atlon laughed. 'He'll be all right. He mightn't like crowds, but he's been in busier places than this, and he's extremely curious.'

'You seem very easy about it.'

'Felcis are intelligent and resourceful – Dvolci more than most. And he knows I need him more than he needs me.'

You've been *far* too long on your own, Rinter thought, though

93

he managed to keep it from his face.

Atlon turned his attention to the people around him again. Despite his slightly irritable response, Dvolci's remark had been accurate: apart from clothes and accents, the crowd in essence was little different from that which could be seen any day travelling to and from the great market in his homeland. With the exception that is, of the number of wagons and riders that were being escorted by groups of armed men. It took no soldier's eye to see that these men were not formal escorts for the purposes of decoration or for declaiming their master's status, but men ready and used to action, albeit only street-fighting in many cases. He asked Rinter about them.

Rinter seemed surprised. 'No disrespect, but you must come from a *very* sheltered place,' he said. 'They're just for protection, that's all. None of the bigger merchants will risk sending goods across the Thlosgaral without one.'

'There are a great many robbers there, then?'

Rinter gave a strange laugh and shook his head as he replied. 'Yes and no.' He looked around then nodded discreetly towards a rider being escorted by four men on foot. 'Those men, for instance, belong to Barran. They're there to protect that merchant, as I said.' He lowered his voice conspiratorially and gave Atlon a knowing wink. 'But the person who controls most of the robbers in the Thlosgaral is Barran himself.'

Atlon frowned. 'I don't understand.'

Rinter's expression became that of a man faced with the need to climb a large hill. The last remnants of his concern about Atlon as a secret assassin faded utterly. 'The merchant has a choice. He can try to cross alone, in which case he risks being robbed. Or he can employ some of Barran's men and be substantially guaranteed a safe passage.'

'Against . . . Barran's robbers,' Atlon said slowly, his frown deepening. Rinter nodded then waited for Atlon to grasp what he was being told. In a moment there would doubtless be an indignant outburst from this naïve newcomer.

It did not come, however. Instead, Atlon grimaced and blew out a long breath. 'There's much wrong with this city of yours, I fear,' he said quietly, as though to himself.

Rinter felt suddenly indignant. Who was this man, this teacher, to criticize his city – the finest city in the world? He was about to give voice to his outrage when he remembered why he was here. The prospect of the felci as a source of income intervened to soften his response, though his tone was still heavily sarcastic when he spoke. 'You have no robbers in your land, I suppose. That's why you wear a sword.'

Atlon paused before he replied. 'My remark was out of place,' he said quietly. 'I apologize. Yes, sadly we *do* have robbers – and worse than yours by far. Just as there's darkness in each of us, so it emerges as darkness in any community.' His eyes became distant. 'No matter from how far or how near you look, there's always darkness and light mingled. Always.' He laid a hand on the hilt of his sword. 'And you're correct, we do go armed – a duty and a tradition. Each of us must be prepared to defend his neighbour as well as himself, mustn't he?' He slapped the hilt and smiled. 'Be prepared to bring a little light into matters if necessary.' He made a mock sword thrust with his hand.

Rinter returned the smile involuntarily, even though he was not sure he understood what Atlon was talking about. Suddenly, and uncharacteristically, he wanted to know more about this newcomer. What kind of land was it he came from? What had brought him so far from home? Where did he get that horse from, and where had he learned to ride like that? And, not least, what did 'and worse by far' mean?

His curiosity did not last long however, as his dominant concern returned in full force. They were drawing ever nearer to the city and he had still not thought of a strategy that would put Dvolci in the pits – *if* the damned animal hadn't got itself lost! He could improvise as circumstances allowed, if necessary, but he preferred not to do that. Things could go wrong even when you had a plan, but without one . . .

He would have to force the issue.

'How much money have you got?' he asked bluntly. The words were no sooner uttered than he was wishing them back, but Atlon did not appear to be offended.

'Enough for a few days at The Wyndering,' he replied.

Rinter decided not to overreach himself by asking how many were a few, but in the absence of any better inspiration, pressed on with his direct approach. He nodded significantly. 'You really should give some serious thought to putting the felci into the pits.' Despite himself, he glanced anxiously around to see if Dvolci was anywhere in sight. 'Even with a few minor fights, you'll make at least enough money to give yourself a month at The Wyndering.' This was not true, but he embellished it anyway. 'And have some left to carry you on your journey.'

Atlon used this abrupt return to Rinter's main concern to reiterate his own. 'I'll have a look at them,' he conceded, anxious not to alienate his guide with too resolute a refusal. 'But I think I'd rather be looking for a more conventional way of earning something. There must be schools, places of learning, surely? Or families that want tutors?'

Rinter was beginning to feel helpless. He lied. 'You'll have to be in one of the Learned Guilds to get that kind of work, and you can only join those if you've been educated in the city.'

Atlon frowned. 'I've never heard of anything like that before,' he said.

'You've never been to anywhere like Arash-Felloren before.'

As though falling back on a poor alternative, Atlon moved to his real interest. 'Well, I've worked with crystals in the past – I'm quite good at it actually. Surely I wouldn't need to be in a Guild to get a job in a crystal workshop, would I?'

Caught unawares by Atlon's casualness, Rinter had shaken his head before he realized it. He resorted quickly to dark warnings. 'You'll not get paid much. The Kyrosdyn didn't get rich by paying well. And they're hard masters.' His concern became genuine. 'In any case, you don't want to be near people like that. They're very odd – dangerous even.'

Atlon refused to be cast down. 'I'm sure you're exaggerating,' he said cheerily. 'All the crystals-workers I've known in the past have been welcoming once they see your interest is sincere. They tend to be preoccupied, I'll admit, but it's a delicate job and needs a lot of concentration.' Seeing from Rinter's gloomy expression

96

that the warnings were about to be renewed, he offered a compromise. 'Let's have a look at your fighting pits, then you can show me where the crystal-dealers trade and I'll find out for myself.' He looked at Rinter earnestly. 'I'll pay you what I can for your time, of course. You've been very patient and helpful.'

Rinter made a vague, half-accepting, half-rejecting shrug, accompanied by a grunt. This man kept catching him off-guard.

Atlon put his fingers to his mouth and whistled. After a moment, a brown shape appeared as if from nowhere, and nimbly threaded its way through the wheels and hooves grinding the dusty highway. Atlon casually swung low out of his saddle, held out a hand, then swung back equally effortlessly as the felci clambered up his arm and on to his shoulders. There was a small burst of spontaneous applause and cheering from a group of men in a cart moving in the opposite direction, but Atlon did not even realize that it was for him. Rinter too, found that he could do no other than applaud the action.

'You ride very well,' he said. 'Been doing it all your life, I'd say. Are you sure you're a teacher and not a cavalryman?'

Atlon, uncertain what to do with a compliment, stammered, 'Everyone rides in my country. It's a . . . tradition.' Adding weakly, 'We like horses.'

Equally uncertain what to do now he had *given* a compliment, Rinter coughed awkwardly and turned his attention back to his problem. He felt much more relaxed now that Dvolci had returned. It seemed that the thing was well-trained, after all – that would doubtless be useful. And the way it had moved through those wagons and horses! It hadn't faltered once. The road might as well have been empty. Every time he looked at the animal he felt its potential as a pit fighter more and more. But, he realized resignedly, he was going to have to direct events as they happened. Any more attempts to persuade Atlon and he might just turn away and pursue his own search for employment.

The two men rode on in silence.

Atlon had not known what to expect of Arash-Felloren but, there being many hills on the journey, he had hoped that at one turn in the road he might find himself on a high vantage overlooking the city. That would have enabled him to compare it with the hyperbole that marked such descriptions as Rinter had offered him, and hence give him a measure of the worth of the man's words. But Arash-Felloren was built on, and surrounded by hills, and this, coupled with its sprawling size, ensured that no place existed anywhere, save the clouds, from which it could be viewed as a whole.

Thus it took Atlon a little time to realize that he had actually entered the city. They had passed through two small villages on the way and, on reaching another untidy cluster of buildings lining the road, Atlon had assumed that this was a third. After a few minutes however, it dawned on him that the traffic about them was becoming more confused and that they were encountering many more side roads than previously. Glancing along some of them, he saw houses and other buildings in far greater numbers than might be expected in a village.

'We're here?' he asked tentatively.

Rinter pursed his lips. 'Sort of,' he replied dismissively. 'This is just the outskirts really. There's nothing much to see around here except houses.'

'Nothing to see! The man's blind,' Dvolci whistled softly into Atlon's ear. 'Look at the buildings. They're fascinating. All manner of styles. No two of them the same.'

Atlon nodded. 'But the people, Dvolci. Look at them. There must be . . . one in ten of them who seems to be in need of some kind.'

Rinter's angry voice intruded. He was cursing an old woman who was trying to make her way across the road. She was struggling under the weight of a large bundle clutched in her arms and she staggered as Rinter's horse reared slightly.

'Be careful!' Atlon shouted, angry in his turn. He jumped down from his horse and ran across to the old woman.

'Are you all right?' he asked, taking her arm. She did not reply, but just looked at him with a mixture of alarm and bewilderment. 'Can I help you with that?' he tried again, indicating the bundle, but the only response she gave was to wrap her arms more tightly about her burden and edge away from him. Then, without a word, she turned and scurried away.

Rinter was shaking his head as Atlon remounted. 'You're wasting your time trying to help half-wits like that,' he said. 'The city's full of them.'

A combination of the old woman's unexpected response and fear of losing his only guide to the city kept Atlon silent, but it was an effort and his horse stamped its foot and shook its head, sensing his inner tension. He leaned forward and spoke to it softly.

Rinter had watched the incident with concern. Keeping a good fighting animal as a pet he could just about understand, but stopping in the middle of the road to tend to some old fool who hadn't the wit to look where she was walking, was beyond him. What kind of a man was this? From his general manner and conversation, he didn't seem to be weak in the head, but something must be wrong with him. In some ways he behaved like a foolish child, yet he must be in his thirties and there was a hint of care lines on his face which belonged to a much older man, so he had had troubles in his time. And too, he could not have travelled this far without being able to fend for himself effectively.

Unnervingly, the image of Atlon as a deceiving killer slipped once again into his mind. Vividly. His hands tightened involuntarily about the reins. Atlon might not be simple, but that did not mean that he wasn't crazy. Rinter had heard of people whose minds were incompletely formed and who belonged to a long gone and darker age. People who could mimic normality to perfection until the opportunity came to slip from behind the mask and reveal their true selves – to their victims. His mouth went dry. How would you recognize such a person? He watched Atlon talking to his horse, as if some clue might lie in his demeanour. As he did so his eye fell on Atlon's sword. It was well crafted and had a used and practical look about it. Probably cuts firewood with it, he forced himself to think, but the thought did not convince and the idea that Atlon might be a murderer refused to fade as it had before. Rinter reached a crisis. Perhaps he should walk away from this man now, forget about him, his strange animal and his even stranger ideas. But the felci had made too deep an impression on him when it had

99

intimidated Ghreel's dog into retreat, and the lure of success at the fighting pits after years of dealing with mediocre animals was irresistible. He rationalized. Atlon had done nothing untoward to warrant such a judgement, and after all, he *was* a foreigner – he was bound to be peculiar. In any event, he reassured himself, there was no reason why he should ever find himself alone with the man. He cheered up. It helped in reaching this conclusion that he was in the middle of a crowded street.

Curses from other riders halted by Atlon's abrupt stop brought both Rinter and Atlon back to the moment. Atlon raised a hand in apology but Rinter returned the verbal assault in kind and they set off again. Rinter adopted a fatherly manner. 'If you don't mind my saying so, Atlon, you'll have to learn to be a bit more . . . forthright, dealing with people around here. The strong shall inherit the world, as they say. If you don't stand up for yourself, people here will take you for a fool, and will take everything else you have as well.'

'Yes,' Atlon said enigmatically, leaving Rinter with nothing else to say.

As they rode on, the character of the buildings changed in that they became generally taller, though the plethora of different styles was still bewildering. Great piles of ornately carved masonry jostled with austere straight lines and seductive, arching curves. And crooked ramshackle buildings, obviously of great age, squinted out from between them all defiantly. All the older buildings and many of the new bore signs of movement. Street traders too, began to abound: some with fixed stalls, some with outrageously decorated carts, and others who carried their stock in their hands and accosted passers-by. All were shouting and none could be heard. Rinter, in common with most other riders, Atlon noticed, was fairly free with his foot in dismissing any who came too near.

'It's a vigorous place at least,' Atlon said to Dvolci.

'So's a weed patch,' Dvolci muttered back. 'This place isn't vigorous, it's running wild.'

Rinter turned to Atlon with a look of pride. 'I'll wager you've never seen anything like this before,' he said.

'That's true,' Atlon replied. 'My country's much flatter. It's an

100

odd feeling, walking either up or down at every turn. And our buildings are not quite so . . . varied, nor so crowded together. We also usually build down rather than up, so the buildings are not so high, but often quite deep.'

Rinter pondered this revelation, then thrust his city forward again.

'Deep!' he exclaimed, prodding a finger downwards. 'This whole city's underlain by tunnels. Level after level. Some you could get two carts side by side down, they say. And so many that no one's ever managed to draw a map of them.' He laughed. 'Mind you, no one's ever managed to draw a map of the streets yet, there's always so many people building and changing things.' The finger prodded again, with even greater pride. 'And under the tunnels are the caves.'

Atlon inclined his head to acknowledge this laudation then said, 'Tell me about the caves. I'd be interested to see them. And Dvolci's a cave animal. He likes to spend time underground whenever he can. Too much sky for too long upsets him.'

Rinter's joviality faltered. 'Nobody goes down there unless they have to. There's people and things down there that you don't want to meet, believe me.' He laughed again, but the sound was forced. 'There's queer enough things live in the tunnels, let alone the caves.'

'*Nobody* goes into them?' Atlon repeated. 'I thought you said the Kyrosdyn found animals down there for the Loose Pits.'

'Nobody *normal*,' Rinter emphasized. 'A few cracked miners, maybe – outcasts, fugitives from the Guild of Thieves and the like. As for the Kyrosdyn, no one really knows how they come by their animals, but they're capable of anything – that's why you don't want to be working for them.' He waved the uncomfortable thoughts aside. 'I wouldn't worry about what fights in the Loose Pits. The felci might be tough but he's not tough enough for there. You take my advice, I know this business; with the right kind of handling there's a lot of money to be made from the ordinary pits. You'll be staying at better than The Wyndering before we've finished.'

'I'd like to see the Loose Pits though. They sound interesting.'

Rinter turned away casually to hide the smile he felt he could not contain. Coming round to the idea, are you? he thought. Things were starting to move his way. 'It might be possible,' he said. 'But they don't happen as often as the ordinary pits and they're expensive to get into.' He was pleased he had managed to drag in a reference to Atlon's need for money. 'Still, I'll make some inquiries.'

Atlon gave a nod of thanks. 'Have we much further to go?' he asked.

Rinter shook his head then pointed. 'This way.'

The street he led them into was only marginally less busy than the road they had just left, and Atlon had to ride in file behind him. They had not gone far when their surroundings changed radically. The buildings they had passed through hitherto had been unfamiliar to Atlon and widely varied, but they were nevertheless evidence of some prosperity. Now he was riding through all manner of sheds and makeshift buildings which sprawled, seemingly at random, over the undulating terrain, transforming the path he was following from a simple thoroughfare into part of a maze of ill-defined alleyways. He looked back to see at what point this change had occurred, but all he could see were shacks and hovels. It was as though the city had never been.

The squalor of the place was almost palpable and the atmosphere was not improved by such people as he could see. All of them looked surly and unwelcoming and they were everywhere – leaning out of windows, sitting on steps, asleep on the ground, standing in groups or just wandering about with varying degrees of purposelessness. Worse, Atlon felt that every one of them was turning and examining him with cold, judging stares.

The noises filling the place were as inseparable as the tangled alleys. Everyone seemed to be talking at once, as though they were all involved in a desperate debate. Everyone talking, no one listening, he thought. Not good. This conclusion was confirmed as from time to time he heard outbursts of violent cursing and shouting. Even such laughter as he heard was jarring and unpleasant.

Weaving through the clamour were unidentifiable bangings and clatterings as of tradesmen working, though Atlon could see little sign of anyone doing anything useful. And there was livestock, he realized, though this he noticed because of his horse's gait as it delicately stepped between the hens that were wandering about, seemingly indifferent to the passers-by. Other sounds, and scents – and there were many scents hanging in the still, warm air, most of them unpleasant – told him that there were also pigs and even cows nearby, but these he could not see. Several times he caught sight of incongruous splashes of green – a bent and twisted tree growing in a tiny, improbable space between two buildings and straining towards the light, a small garden full of weary-looking herbs and vegetables, grass-choked gutters, and creepers clambering over broken and stained walls.

And it was unpleasantly hot. Atlon made to loosen the collar of his tunic but it was already undone.

Even more disturbing than the heat, the noise, and the general demeanour of the citizens was the feeling that he was riding through people's homes as his horse, following Rinter, picked its way through lines of washing and other patently domestic paraphernalia that littered the place. He felt it most acutely when, ducking to avoid jutting eaves he several times found himself staring in through open windows.

'Not much different inside than outside,' Dvolci said to him softly, echoing his thoughts.

'Spare me one of your lectures on the failings of humanity,' Atlon said. 'I'm having trouble enough with this myself.' Dvolci did not reply.

Rinter, by contrast, seemed to be very much at home – a gesture here, a nod there, the occasional reply to a shouted greeting – and all with the air of a busy man dealing with people who, for the most part, were his inferiors. Atlon, filling with questions at every stride his horse took, found it difficult to stay silent. Just as he had not been able to gain an overall impression of the city as they approached it, so now he hesitated to extrapolate from what he was seeing. Nevertheless, when the winding pathway became wide enough he pulled alongside his guide and asked, quite unable to keep the incredulity from his voice: 'Is the whole city like this, away from the main streets?'

Rinter turned to him, puzzled. 'Like what?'

'Like this,' Atlon replied, with a small but encompassing hand movement. He searched for words that he hoped would not cause offence. 'Disorganized, crowded. It's . . . it's no place for anyone to live.'

Rinter's expression showed no enlightenment. He looked about him, following Atlon's gesture, then shrugged. 'Everywhere's different, if that's what you mean,' he said. 'There's other places like this, of course – Spills, they call them, I don't know why. Some are better, some are worse – much worse. They get cleaned out from time to time.' He leaned forward and spoke confidentially. 'You have to understand. These people here – they wouldn't know how to live any other way. It's what they're used to. It's all most of them are fit for.'

Atlon frowned at the response and seemed inclined to pursue the subject, but another turn in the path had brought them to a place where the shacks and huts were replaced by blackened façades and scorched timbers. Some areas had been completely levelled. A faint smell of burning hung about the place, catching at the throat and adding a subtle menace to the scene which the sound of a few unseen children playing nearby deepened rather than alleviated. It took Atlon a moment to realize that what he was looking at were the remains of dwellings similar to those he had just ridden through. Rinter reined his horse to a halt. He looked worried.

'What's happened here?' Atlon asked, affecting not to notice his concern.

'I've no idea,' Rinter said softly. 'It wasn't like this a week or so ago. I'd have come another way if I'd known. It might've been a dispute between families. That happens from time to time.'

'And the people who lived here?'

Rinter shrugged.

Atlon's eyes narrowed angrily, but before he could speak, Rinter was urging his horse forward. 'Come on,' he shouted back. 'We'll take a chance. It's not far now. It's not worth going all the way back.'

Atlon was not reassured by his tone, but he had little choice other than to follow. For a few minutes they cantered through the

104

bleak, dead landscape, Rinter obviously ill-at-ease travelling on a horse at speed, Atlon alert.

As they rounded a bend, a figure stepped out in front of them sword in hand.

Chapter 10

Rinter reined his horse to a clattering halt, nearly tumbling from his saddle in the process. Atlon, by contrast, while remaining slightly to the rear of Rinter, moved quietly to one side, positioning himself to the left of the man standing in the centre of the pathway. It was an innocuous movement, intended to provoke no response, but it was also one that placed him where the man would need to take a backhand stroke if he wished to attack, thus allowing the horse enough time to retreat or to lash out with its forelegs and end the matter. It had been trained thus, but so had its countless sires and dams through the ages, and the movement to protect both itself and its rider was almost instinctive. As was Atlon's complete trust in it. It was the way of his people. He knew that the horse was in a place of its choosing and that it would wait until he instructed it or until the man offered a real threat.

Dvolci's head emerged discreetly from Atlon's pack but he did not speak. Atlon reached up and gently touched the sleek head, though whether to reassure the felci or himself, he could not have said. Dvolci retreated.

As Rinter struggled to quieten his horse and regain his seat, Atlon took in the swordsman's appearance. His manner was authoritative and confident and he was wearing a uniform of some kind: dark brown, almost black trousers and a tunic of the same colour with insignia on the arms and shoulders. It was clean and well-tended, a marked contrast to the dress of the people Atlon had been seeing since they entered the Spills, or, for that matter, to both he and Rinter. His initial alarm eased. Despite Rinter's claims that no civic authority existed in Arash-Felloren, this could only be a representative of such a body.

'What are you doing here?' the man demanded of Rinter.

Rinter stammered and attempted an ingratiating smile. 'Just passing through, Weartan,' he said, rather too heartily and with a hint of a stammer.

The man waved an arm across the charred remains of the buildings all about them. 'Are you blind or something? Can't you see this area's being renewed?'

Rinter's stammer worsened. 'I . . . I . . . saw no marker, Weartan, or we'd have turned back. Just rode straight into it. I thought it was perhaps a feud . . . a private clearance.'

The Weartan raised his eyebrows in weary disbelief. 'Name?' he intoned with heavy patience.

'Irgon Rinter.'

'Where are you going?'

'We were going to the pits – the Jyolan pits.' He pointed vaguely, then indicated Atlon. 'We've come down from The Wyndering – this was the shortest way.'

The gesture drew the Weartan's attention to Atlon.

'He's a stranger here, a traveller,' Rinter volunteered. 'He—'

The Weartan waved him silent and began a close scrutiny of Atlon. Atlon met his gaze calmly.

'That's a fine horse you're riding,' the man concluded. 'Where did you steal it from?'

The question startled Atlon and he was not able completely to keep an edge from his voice as he replied. 'The horse is mine, sir. Has been since it was a foal. It's not an exceptional animal where I come from. My people take a pride in their horses.'

The Weartan looked unconvinced.

'It's got an eye I don't care for.'

'He's nervous,' Atlon said. 'The smell of smoke's disturbing him.' Then, apologetically, 'And I'm afraid your sword's frightening him.'

Atlon had taken control of his voice and his quiet manner caused the Weartan to hesitate and glance down at his sword. For a moment it seemed that he might sheathe it, but in the end he simply lowered it to hang by his side. His voice was less harsh when he spoke again. 'I can tell from your accent that you're not city bred. What're you doing here?'

'I'm looking for work to pay my way so that I can carry on my journey south.' Atlon gave a disarming shrug. 'I'm afraid I didn't know how expensive everything was here. I've nothing left. I met this gentleman at The Wyndering and he kindly offered to help me find something.'

The Weartan's expression announced that he considered Rinter's altruism to be extremely improbable. 'Well, all he's found you so far is trouble.' He studied Atlon thoughtfully for a moment, then flicked a thumb over his shoulder. 'On your way. Don't come back here, and if you see anything like this, keep out of it or you might find yourself losing your horse and the coat off your back if you've no money to pay a fine.'

Atlon bowed. 'Thank you, sir. I'll do as you say,' he said. 'But I've no idea where I am, or even how to get back to the city. And if Rinter has offended, perhaps I can speak for him. He wouldn't be here but for me.'

The Weartan looked at him as Rinter had done on several occasions: as though he were a rare and improbable animal. Then he thrust his sword into its sheath and pointed along the path, impatient again. 'Go that way, slowly. This ... gentleman ... and I have matters to discuss about his offence. He shouldn't be too long.' He glanced at Rinter significantly. 'If he's sensible.'

Atlon gave his guide an inquiring look, but Rinter urgently motioned him to do as he was told.

'I didn't realize you could be such a sycophant,' Dvolci said softly, when they were some way from the two men.

'Diplomat is the word you're looking for,' Atlon replied, looking back anxiously over his shoulder. 'What are they doing?'

'Just talking, by the look of it.'

Then the path carried them around a bend and down a slope, and Rinter and the Weartan vanished from view behind the charred landscape. Atlon reined in his horse and waited.

'See if there's anyone else about,' he said. 'This place has given us too many surprises already.'

Dvolci clambered out of the pack and disappeared into the remains of a nearby house. Uncomfortably, Atlon half-drew his sword, pondered it for a moment, then dropped it back into its scabbard and took hold of a heavy staff that hung from his saddle. Hefting it familiarly, he swung an arcing blow first to one side and then the other. This was what he would use if necessary, he thought. Not as casually deadly as a sword, and at least he could use it properly.

Dvolci returned. 'He's coming,' he said as he dropped back into Atlon's pack. 'And there's no one else about. That Weartan seems to be leaving as well.'

Rinter came trotting around the bend. Despite his obvious discomfort at having to ride at even modest speed, he looked relieved.

'Luck's with us today, Atlon,' he said, wiping a soiled kerchief over his flushed face. 'Let's get out of here before it changes.'

'Who was that?' Atlon asked as they moved off. 'And what were we doing wrong?'

'That was one of our blessed Prefect's guards. One of the virtuous souls charged with the task of keeping order in the city.' There was considerable irony in Rinter's voice. 'Fortunately for us, he was on his own, and he was one of the more honest ones.' Rinter's brow furrowed as a thought occurred to him. 'Or perhaps that was just because he was on his own.' He shrugged the possibility aside. 'Anyway, it doesn't matter. It's enough that he was content with only a small payment.'

'Payment? What for?'

Rinter's expression became weary again. 'It must be very difficult, being a teacher,' he said. 'Explaining the obvious all the time.'

Atlon's eyes narrowed. The squalor of the Spills, the sudden transition to this ravaged area and, finally, despite the calmness he had affected, the encounter with the Weartan had all conspired to shake him badly, and his willingness to be treated as a foolish relative from the country was deserting him rapidly.

'It is,' he agreed, though there was a menace in his tone that made Rinter glance at him nervously. 'But you do it anyway. It's the safest in the long run. You never know who you might be instructing.' He urged his horse to move a little faster and, reaching across, took the reins of Rinter's horse. It was a swift and expert movement. 'We'll be quicker if you let me do the riding. You just hang on and tell me which way to go. You can explain the obvious to me while we ride.'

Naked fear appeared on Rinter's face as his horse quickened, first to a canter and then to a modest gallop. It was no cavalry pace, but it was faster than Rinter had ever travelled and, after an initial fumbled failure, he made no further attempt to stop Atlon's assumption of command, concentrating instead on following his advice, and hanging on. Nor did he make any attempt to 'explain the obvious' to his companion – partly because his sarcasm now seemed inappropriate, but mainly because he was holding his breath. A stern demand from Atlon made him release it sufficiently to gasp out a direction whenever a fork appeared in the road, in time to ensure that the pace of the charge did not falter. Rinter closed his eyes as well as held his breath as the two horses galloped around a corner.

The path wound and undulated through the blackened wreckage, and where the two riders passed, the horses' hooves stirred up a cloud of black ash which lingered behind them in the heavy air. At one point they encountered two Weartans, but though Atlon deftly steered the horses past them, his appearance was so sudden and his progress so relentless that they leapt to one side instinctively. When they recovered, coughing in the dust, the riders had vanished from view.

Then, as abruptly as they had entered the destroyed area, they were out of it and riding through squalor and disorder different only in its details from the one they had passed through previously. Atlon reined back the horses to a walk, returned Rinter's reins to him, and motioned him to lead on. 'You *did* want to get away quickly, didn't you?' he said pleasantly. 'I thought it was the least I could do after you'd been so helpful bringing me here.'

Rinter was patting his chest with one hand and gesticulating vaguely with the other. It was some time before he could speak coherently. His opinion of Atlon had undergone a drastic change during the brief chase. Whatever else this stranger might be able to do, he could ride like no one he had ever seen before. And when

111

he was riding he was a very different person from the one who had just politely returned his reins to him.

'There won't be a problem with those two officers, will there?' Atlon was asking. 'I don't want to break any of your laws, but I presumed you didn't want to speak to them.'

Rinter shook his head. Seeing the two Weartans brushed casually aside was the one part of the ride that he could recall with relish. 'No, no. You did right. We were lucky with the first one; we mightn't have been with those two.'

'You must explain to me about these people. They wore the same uniforms and the one who stopped us was obviously used to people accepting his authority. Who are they? And why were all those houses – those shacks – burned? And what did he mean, the area's being *renewed*?'

Rinter raised a hand to stem the questions; when he spoke it was with the embarrassed air of someone explaining about a crazed relative kept in the attic. 'They're Weartans, the Prefect's Guards. They—'

'Prefect?'

Rinter frowned, though only because he was trying to order his thoughts. 'The Prefect is head of the city, or at least is supposed to be.'

'Like a king, or a Ffyrst?'

Rinter was still struggling. 'I don't know what a Ffyrst is, but the Prefect's not really like a king. He's appointed by the Council.'

'And the people appoint the Council,' Atlon offered.

Rinter looked as blank as he had at the mention of a Ffyrst. 'No, of course not. The Prefect appoints the Council.'

This time it was Atlon who frowned. 'But . . .'

Rinter wanted to be free of the subject. He was recovering from his enforced gallop and was anxious to get back to the business of luring Dvolci into the pits. 'It's very complicated,' he said. 'Everyone has fingers in everything – the Noble Houses, the Trading Combines, the Congress of Artisans, mercenary groups, the Kyrosdyn.' At the last moment he managed to mumble the word Kyrosdyn, loath to risk turning Atlon's thoughts back in that direction. 'Even the Guild of Thieves has a say, one way or another,' he added heartily. 'Then there's the Weartans and the hordes of clerks and scribes and jumped up little jacks-in-office running round, making their own rules up. They're always there, no matter who the Prefect is or who's on the Council.'

Atlon was screwing his eyes up as if that might clarify matters for him. 'It *is* complicated, as you say. And, with all due respect, it doesn't seem to be a very good way of looking after a place like this.' He looked around at the makeshift shacks and the surly people they were passing, but Rinter did not notice.

'It's the way it's always been,' he said. 'Different groups all jostling for power and influence.' He sneered. 'And for what?' He turned to Atlon and looked at him squarely. 'This place is just too big, too full of too many opinionated people, to be *ruled* by anyone. You might as well say you rule a river because you stand in it and fill a bucket. These people do more harm than good, meddling with things that'll work themselves out anyway. Everyone's only looking to survive, that's all. I don't know why they can't leave things alone.'

There was a passion in his voice that took Atlon by surprise. And Rinter had not finished. His fist beat the air. 'Too big. They say that in the old days, when the Great Lord built the city, His enemies lost an entire army trying to occupy it – literally lost it – just disappeared without trace. It's that big. And these fools think they can take charge of it as though it were a market stall.' He spat. 'You want to keep clear of people like that. You stick with me. Simple folks like you and me have got to look after each other. There's always a living to be made here if you're sharp enough.'

Atlon however, was still having difficulty with the seeming lack of civic order that Rinter was describing. 'But there must be laws, surely? And courts of some kind where people can settle disputes or where criminals can be examined.'

'Oh, there's laws enough to choke every street twice over. And courts and tribunals and assizes and boards and benches and all manner of grey-hearted "servants of the city" looking to separate you from your money. That's if you get that far, if all your money's not gone in buying off the Weartans. Personally, I'd rather take my chance against the Guild of Thieves. At least they're honest robbers.'

Atlon decided to leave the subject. It was more than possible that Rinter's view of the matter was jaundiced for some reason, but it would contain an element of truth for sure. He renewed his earlier resolve to be watchful and to be careful about whom he trusted.

As they talked, they had left the Spills and were now making their way along a paved street, bounded by high brick and stone buildings. Atlon was glad to feel something of permanence about him after the aura of transience and decay which had pervaded the ramshackle constructions of the Spills.

He was pleased also, to be amongst people of a less overtly surly demeanour, for the street was quite busy. He looked back, but once again, the city's curved and sloping streets had removed the Spills from view. It was as if they and the burned buildings and the Weartans had never existed.

Like a dream.

The thought was fleeting but vivid and peculiarly unnerving, and Atlon hastily turned back to the solid reassurance of his present surroundings.

The upper floors of the buildings were distinguished by barred and shuttered windows, though many of these were thrown open, as if greeting the bright sunlight. At street level, many of the frontages were brightly decorated and there were all manner of shops, interspersed amongst what Atlon took to be warehouses and other commercial premises. Looking round, Atlon identified a dozen trades almost immediately, and noted many more that meant nothing to him. And there were the inevitable stalls and peddlars hawking their goods.

Dvolci was at his ear again, whispering softly. 'I think your little run through the Spills has improved our guide's attitude,' he said. 'But his account of how this place is governed was disconcerting, to say the least. It verges on anarchy. You really must be very careful.'

'I realize that,' Atlon replied, a little testily.

'No, you don't,' Dvolci countered coldly. 'Your people – in fact, all the people you know – live free but within a framework of order of some kind. These people seem to be unfettered – running wild. And you're too immature a species to cope with it, especially crowded together like this. This place is as dangerous as a battle front, even if there *aren't* people fooling around with crystals and the Power.'

Exposing the follies of humanity was one of Dvolci's many amusements and he frequently delighted in proving his point by rousing his antagonists to fist-clenching fury. Now however, his voice was level and calm: the voice of someone bearing the ancient wisdom of his kind. It was a timely reminder and Atlon nodded in acknowledgement.

'I understand,' he said.

'Here we are.' Rinter's voice ended the soft exchange. He dismounted.

They had stopped outside a tall, solid-looking building which, insofar as Atlon was able to judge, seemed to be much older than its immediate neighbours. Flanked by two narrow alleyways, it stood alone. Carved figures, weathered and featureless, stood guarding the corners of the roof, lichen stains running down the walls from their feet. And where most of the other buildings had plain bars sealing the upper windows, this one had elaborately worked metal frames, some portraying strange and sinister-looking animals, others gaunt and malevolent faces. By contrast, it was a face of remarkable beauty that decorated the massive keystone of a circular arch which spanned the entrance. Unlike the rest of the building it appeared to have been untouched by time, and the rough-hewn stones of the arch rose up to it as if in homage.

Dvolci nudged Atlon and pointed to it discreetly. Atlon drew in a sharp breath and circled his hand over his heart. Then he coloured and drew his hand down his tunic awkwardly as though to wipe the gesture away.

'It's all right,' Dvolci said. 'More than a few of your learned elders would have done the same under the circumstances. It's a frightening piece of work.'

'I've never seen . . .' He looked at the face again.

'No. Leave it. It's only a piece of stone – a skilled piece of carving. There'll be more potent manifestations of Him about this place to be dealt with, if I'm not mistaken. Let it go!'

Dvolci had to repeat his last instruction to make Atlon tear his gaze from the face. With an effort he forced himself to look at the gate sealing the entrance. This was a heavy timber, two-leaved contrivance, obviously newer than the rest of the building. In crude lettering across the top, it bore the legend *The Jyolan Pits – The Oldest Fighting Animals Arena in the World* while the rest of it was covered with notices in varying states of decay, and garish, ill-drawn pictures of blood-stained animals fighting one another.

'Delightful workmanship,' Dvolci said acidly.

By now, Rinter was in earnest conversation with someone through a grille in a wicket-door. Atlon dismounted and walked to the gate. Though he made a deliberate effort not to look at it, he felt as though the face on the keystone was watching him intently. He studied the many notices littering the gate. They meant little to him. Times, prices, special appearances of named animals, cancellations, were displayed indiscriminately, along with a wide variety of extravagant claims about the 'unbridled ferocity' of the 'specially selected' animals, and more than a few sentimental eulogies for recently deceased 'fighters'. On a small and very old notice, partly hidden behind another, Atlon found the fighting rules. They were very simple, while on a much larger notice, the wagering rules were displayed. Atlon studied them intently for a little while – they were in an extremely fine print – but was obliged to give up after only a few lines.

'I think they mean, give us all your money and go away,' Dvolci summarized. 'Or else.'

Rinter was with them again. He was agitated. 'There's a problem, I'm afraid. I'd hoped you'd be able to get in right away and see what happens, but there's a special fight tonight and they're closed until then.' He fidgeted and looked up and down the street anxiously. 'And I've got other matters to attend to before tonight.'

Atlon hid his relief. 'We – I'll – look around the city until then,' he said, his tone conciliatory. 'Find somewhere where I can water the horse. Find my way about.'

Rinter fidgeted a little more while he debated this proposition then reluctantly accepted it. 'Go that way,' he said, pointing. 'Otherwise you might end up in the Spills again. Keep to the main

116

streets, don't go wandering off down any alleyways.' He nodded towards the mouth of the alley by the side of the Jyolan building. 'And remember where this place is so that you can find your way back.'

Atlon smiled. 'You sound like my mother,' he said.

Rinter grinned weakly, made a tentative start at a couple of sentences, then shrugged. 'You've no timepiece, I suppose?' he said. Atlon shook his head. 'About sunset, back here, then,' Rinter said, looking at him earnestly.

'Sunset,' Atlon confirmed.

As he prepared to mount, Rinter snapped his fingers. 'Walk your horse,' he said knowingly. 'You'll be less conspicuous. And don't leave it with anyone. In fact, don't leave it at all. And keep where it's busy. And . . .' The words faded, leaving Rinter tapping his foot nervously. He had been about to tell Atlon to avoid any of the crystal marts, but decided at the last moment that it was probably wiser *not* to remind him about them, now that he had got him at least as far as the door of the pits.

But he was not happy at seeing his future prospects wandering off unguarded into the city, and he stood staring after them even when they disappeared from view.

He would have been even less happy had he been privy to their conversation.

'A fortunate parting of the ways,' Atlon said. 'I think he would have been more than a little persistent about your fighting if that place had been open. Now let's see if we can find someone who deals in crystals.'

Chapter 11

Imorren could scarcely contain her fury. It was many years since she had known emotions, of any kind, so strong that she had had to struggle to master them, and the knowledge that such traits still lurked within her unsettled her profoundly, adding to her anger.

The room in which she sat, upright and still, was a coldly glittering place of polished white stone and elaborate crystal constructs. It was the Hall of Endings and Beginnings – the Chamber of the Ways – and it lay deep within the Vaskyros. Nine domes formed the ceiling, borne on carved walls and slender, many-sided columns that seemed at once to reach up in fearful praise and to hang like moonlit icicles. Rare, tinted crystals swept out intricate, abstract patterns over the entire Hall: patterns within patterns, endlessly, smaller and smaller, drawing the eye into unknowable depths. Full of subtle complexity they tumbled from the domes, down walls and columns, to spill across the floor like frozen tributaries to a silent ocean – an ocean which lapped, motionless at the feet of crystal towers whose surfaces and edges drew light from an unseen source to cut and shape yet more patterns. Jagged and bewildering symmetries formed in every direction.

To a mean-spirited man, it was merely a place that would demonstrate extravagant wealth, while a craftsman would fall silent in the presence of such ancient skills practised at their finest. But to Imorren, the Hall of Ways was, above all, the essence of her purpose: the place that all her will was focused upon and which in its turn, she believed, focused upon her such of His will as could reach into this realm. Eventually it would form the gleaming heart of the Way that would bring Him forth.

'Learn all that is to be learned of these things,' she had been told. 'And make that which is without flaw.' And thus she had striven to build. Yet the Hall was not perfect – nor ever could be, she knew. All was flawed in this mismade world, and would inevitably be so until He came again. But the paradox did not disturb her. '*Your* perfection will make good all blemish,' He had said. 'Trust in me.'

And she had. And been raised above all others as He had promised.

And now, rage had come upon her. Not the rage with which she had sworn vengeance on His enemies – pure and absolute, and which sustained her constantly – but a rage larded with pettiness and bitter gall, a manifestation of that grossness in her character that she had worked so relentlessly to excise. A manifestation of her humanity. Would she never be free from its cloying presence?

She sat for a long time in the stillness of the Hall before revelation suffused her: her anger was not a petty spasm but a timely reminder – perhaps a touch of His will reaching across the voids? Just as she struggled incessantly to grasp the deep mysteries of the Power and the crystals that would enable her to perfect this enclave and shape the Vaskyros about it, so she must ever struggle to master and understand the flaws inherent in mankind that she might use them to manipulate those whom she needed, while remaining unmarred by them herself.

Slowly she turned to look into a mirror mounted on the arm of her chair. There were few mirrors in the Vaskyros. Mirrors were dangerous, especially in the unseen but ever-present and resonant flickering of crystals. Capturing reality and folding it back upon itself, they could be random doorways to the worlds beyond. And that which was random was beyond control, and thus anathema.

Yet too, they were needed. Paradox again. For only through mirrors could those ways be made that stretched without end and were filled with the rushing of light to and from those places an infinity away which were ever beyond the reach of light.

She turned the mirror until her face was framed in it centrally. It was a beautiful face, showing nothing of her true nature and bearing none of the signs of the years that it should have. It was necessary that she be thus, she reasoned, only vaguely aware of another human

120

frailty fluttering nearby – vanity. Black hair framed the slender, grey-eyed face, against the reflected pattern of the Chamber's inexorable symmetry.

The glowering expression that had been there when she first entered the Chamber was gone and, as she stared at herself, a slight tautness about her jaw gradually faded. She righted the mirror, so that it faced its partner on the other arm of the chair, then spoke.

'Enter, Rostan.'

Her voice was calm and measured and she spoke as though to someone immediately in front of her, but the Chamber carried it through to the cause of her anger, standing outside at the centre of a circular entrance hall. Rostan was a tall, lean individual, dressed immaculately in the formal robes of his order and bearing his staff of office. Had he been dressed thus when he was abroad in the city, Pinnatte would not even have considered trying to steal his purse. Indeed, he would probably have crossed the road to avoid him.

Though he had been standing straight and immobile, as befitted his position, his leader's voice drew him even straighter. The only other betrayal of his inner turmoil was a tightening of his grip about the staff, and a hesitant attempt by his other hand to check the perfect fall of his robes.

The two doors to the Chamber opened silently as he approached, and a crystal-etched pathway pointed him directly to the chair upon which Imorren sat. As he passed through the doorway he lowered his head, after the manner of a novice. It was an involuntary response rather than a wilful attempt to placate the Ailad. He knew well enough that Imorren was not one to be diverted from her concerns by a trivial show of respect. Fear it was that bent Rostan's head, and a fear that grew with each footstep he took. At the end of the path, he knelt.

The coldness of the Hall was no pleasant contrast to the heat of the relentless summer searing the city. It was not a thing of temperature, it was of the spirit and the mind and, for Rostan, it chilled both now.

There was a long silence.

'Look at me, Rostan.'

The softness of the voice served only to chill him further.

'Look at me!'

Twice bidden! Rostan cursed himself and forced his eyes upwards. Such moisture as still softened his throat dried up as he tried to meet Imorren's searching gaze and failed.

'Ailad,' he managed to say.

There was another long pause.

'Kyroscreft, Rostan. Kyroscreft. How long is it since that word was last called out in the streets?'

Rostan swallowed. He was about to say simply, 'Many years,' but caught himself in time. 'It had been many years, Ailad.'

'Had, indeed, until?'

The look of regret on Rostan's face was not feigned.

'Until today, Ailad.'

'Until today, Rostan. When you, the Highest of the Order, saw fit to pursue a petty thief through the streets like an aproned merchant after a stolen cheese.' Despite herself, Imorren's rage spat itself out. 'Then you compounded your folly, first by using the Power to restrain him, and then by allowing him to escape.'

Aware that more was to follow, Rostan remained silent, fixing his eyes somewhere vaguely on Imorren's face. Not for the first time he found it impossible even to imagine the time when they had been lovers – the time before she had become Ailad.

'Is it not enough that we have continually to divert our energies from our true purpose by binding ourselves with alliances to other powers in this place?' The gesture that accompanied this was slow and sweeping, yet it seemed to rend the air, so still had Imorren been. Reflected images of it moved silently about the Chamber like accusing fingers. 'Is it not enough that we must waste our energies in feuding with yet others? Are we so secure in our position here that you should so cavalierly risk releasing the wild ignorance of the mob against us?'

'I . . .'

Imorren's eyes flashed, cleaving Rostan's tongue to the roof of his mouth. He could not have said whether it was the force of her presence or whether she had subtly used the Power against him by way of a demonstration.

'Granted, there have been times when it suited our ends to allow such civic strife – when diversions were needed to draw attention from other matters. But rarely. Usually, anything we have gained from such incidents has been fortuitous. And in all cases, sacrifices have had to be made.'

She fixed his gaze with hers.

'However, you do not need me to tell you of this. There must have been a reason for your conduct. For you to risk such a thing when we are so far along our way; when we are stronger in the city than we have ever been; when so few could reasonably expect to assail our influence.'

She fell silent and looked at him expectantly.

Rostan had been clinging to the hope that an admission of error might be sufficient to assuage Imorren's anger, once he discovered that she had learned of his escapade. But by the same token, her learning of it meant that others had learned of it – and Imorren would put the discipline of the Order above all other things. Worse, far worse, he would have to tell her what he had done to Pinnatte. She obviously did not know about that.

Or did she?

What *did* she know?

She was impossible to read. And so sensitive! Even searching her face for clues might bring a rebuke down on him.

As would delay.

He would have to tell her everything, and as truthfully as possible. However dangerous that might be, anything else would be far more so.

He made no attempt to keep the fear from his voice or his manner. He would not have succeeded, and the attempt would have angered her further. He lowered his eyes.

'I erred, Ailad. I conducted myself in a manner that was not fitting. I have no excuse.'

He tried not to cringe as he waited through the silence that followed. A small part of him told him to prepare to use the Power to defend himself, but he chased it from his mind, for fear that the slightest hint of defiance might show itself in his manner. Had he looked up he would have seen a flicker of uncertainty in Imorren's eyes. She had not anticipated either so immediate or so abject a confession. Following in the wake of the uncertainty came clear suspicion. This was worse than she had thought.

For Rostan, the silence continued unbearably.

'I did not ask for an excuse, Highest. Excuses are for novices and acolytes and lesser initiates – for those who have paid too high a price for a tint, or ill-cut a stone. You are above excuse.' Her voice fell. 'I asked you for your reason.'

The word *reason* hissed out, echoing about the Hall, from column to column, from crystal tower to crystal tower, magnifying, debating – judging. As the sounds, transformed, returned to him, it was as though the frozen ocean at his feet was suddenly thawed and about to engulf him. Rostan managed not to gibber, but the words he spoke were unknown to him until he spoke them.

'I have no reason, Ailad. When the purse was snatched . . .' He looked up and met her gaze again. 'I felt such . . . fearful confusion. They were primary crystals and of a water and a size that's found scarcely once in fifty years. Just to be near them was to feel the future opening up before us. And even as I felt them slip away from me, I felt also not only *your* anger and reproach, but that of the whole Brotherhood at my betrayal of their trust. The tireless working of those who had gathered the price of the stones, the work – our work – our *holy* work, set back perhaps for years. For a moment, I was indeed reduced to the state of a clumsy novice.'

Even in his terror, Rostan had sufficient control to avoid mentioning the fact that it had been Imorren who suggested they transport the crystals in this casual manner rather than in a heavily-escorted coach. 'One purse in a crowd. Where best to hide a book but in a library?' she had said. She had even allowed herself a hint of a smile as she had echoed the thieves' dictum: 'No one will steal a Kyrosdyn's purse. But a coach and escort could bring larger predators on to the streets.'

Rostan snatched at the implication of this memory.

'Then it occurred to me that a deeper matter might be afoot than the random snatching of a purse. Had the thief perhaps been sent by Barran himself? With all due respect to the man, he is a consummate opportunist and quite ruthless, and more than capable of stealing back something he had just sold to us.' Rostan began to warm to his tale. 'And he has skilled cutters in his pay. Unthinkable though it might be to us, the crystals could be . . .' He hesitated. To cut such stones would indeed be unthinkable; even the idea of it disturbed him. He forced himself to continue. 'The crystals could be cut to make many smaller ones, which in their turn could be sold to us.'

'I am aware of Barran's character,' Imorren said. 'But he has a keen grasp of reality. Don't compound your folly by maligning a man who has always traded honestly with us.'

'It was a fleeting impression, Ailad, joined almost immediately by others which pointed to Barran's rivals as being the culprits.' He had his excuse! He could barely keep the relief from his voice. He might yet survive this encounter. Until . . .

What did she know?

He went on hastily, loath to think ahead. 'It was this that made me pursue him, even when the purse had been recovered. I wanted to question him, to bring him here so that the truth could be discovered. Knowledge of whoever had laid the plot could be nothing other than valuable, either as a lever against Barran or as a token to buy his future loyalty.'

There was another silence. As was her way, when she spoke, Imorren offered nothing that he could support himself with.

'But you did none of these things. The thief escaped you, humiliating the Brotherhood in the process – and you know what that might cost us. And we know nothing of his motives. Was he just a fool in the wrong place at the wrong time, or was he indeed a tool of weightier foes?' She leaned forward slightly, and Rostan heard again the murmuring of the seas at his feet as she said, 'And you used the Power like a carnival fraudster, causing the word Kyroscreft to be loosed amid the herd.'

Rostan affected an expression of deep and puzzled concern as he bowed his head. Another inspiration was coming to him. 'Strange circumstances seemed both to protect the man and to lead me to him, Ailad. Though he held the crystals for only a moment, their potency seemed to cling to him. It was such that I could feel their presence almost tangibly – hanging in the air. Run though he might, it would avail him nothing, I knew. He was joined to me –

to us.' Imorren's eyes narrowed slightly and she turned her head slightly to one side. Rostan, eyes lowered, did not notice the movement. 'And, indeed, I found him at the fountain in the square as easily as if I had agreed to meet him there.' He paused uncertainly. 'Yet too, he was able to oppose me. He resisted both voice and gesture.' He moved his hand as he had in front of Pinnatte's face. 'And the crowd were drawn to him in some way.' He shook his head then gave a guilty shrug. 'When he threw off my guard, Gariak – and you know how powerful he is . . .' Imorren made no acknowledgement. 'When this . . . skinny bundle of rags tossed him aside so casually, I'll swear I felt the Power being used.' He looked up and held out a hand to forestall a protest. 'It makes no sense, I know, but I felt *something*. And when he suddenly made to dash into the crowd, I reached out and held him before I realized fully what I was doing.'

He bowed his head again. He had almost convinced himself of the truth of the tale he was weaving. A conspirator both by instinct and training, he had naturally followed the safest path, lying only slightly, and making the rest of the story logically consistent.

But still the real enormity of what he had done had to be told.

'And still he escaped.'

Imorren's voice returned him to the present. He clung to it, pathetically grateful.

'He must have been protected by someone. How else could he have taken back control of his voice and swayed the crowd?'

'Do not question me, Rostan. You forget yourself.'

The cold rebuke made Rostan stiffen. He may have spun a plausible tale but even a hint of euphoria was premature. 'Forgive me, Ailad,' he said quickly.

Imorren looked down at him. He was lying, of course. Rostan had always had a spiteful disposition. Almost certainly it was this that had made him pursue the would-be thief. But he had had the wit to accept full responsibility and to make no mention of her contribution to the affair. And his tale had revealed some strange aspects to the incident. That the thief had tried to snatch the purse offered no puzzle. It was obviously a random event. Rostan, for some unfathomable reason, had worn no sign of his office, and the quality of his clothes would have marked him out as a rich man. Nor had there been any conspiracy. The thief, by throwing the purse back, had obviously been horrified when he realized what he had done. And Barran had a peculiar honesty – he set store by his word. In any event, he was too clear-sighted to risk stealing and re-selling the crystals. They might be worth a fortune, but Barran's relationship with the Brotherhood was worth far more. And no one else could have known what was happening. Yet it was strange that a mere street thief could resist Rostan's power. It was possible, that in his spleen, Rostan's control had been poor, but even so . . .

She set the thoughts aside. They could be pursued at leisure. Nothing had come of the Kyroscreft cry and Rostan's tale had confirmed the information which she had already received. But as he had been speaking, she had gradually become aware that something more serious had happened – something that she had not learned about and which he had not yet found the courage to confess to her.

She spoke slowly and softly. 'Do you deserve my forgiveness, Highest?'

Rostan felt the words searching into him.

She knew!

She knew!

It took all of his control to prevent himself from gasping for breath, but he could do nothing about the sweat that appeared on his brow.

How could she . . .?

It didn't matter. He must speak immediately. Delay now would surely damn him. As, probably, would confession. Yet it was all that was left to him.

'I spoke as I did because I am adrift amid confusion and uncertainty, Ailad.' He made no attempt to stop the tremor in his voice. 'I do not know why I did what I did, save that I followed an inner calling. If I have erred, then I make no plea other than that, and will accept the wisdom of your judgement.'

The tautness in Imorren's jaw that she had carefully relaxed before Rostan's entry, returned. As did a look in her eyes that would have frozen the words in his mouth had he seen it.

'There was a strangeness about the man, Ailad. Indeed, as I said, there was a strangeness about the whole affair. Trusted with such an errand, what could have made me act so recklessly? Why had the power of the crystals clung to him so? Why had he been drawn to me, and I to him? Why would I use the Power as I did? And how could he have opposed it?' His voice became almost a whisper. 'I knew the folly of what I was doing, even as I did it, but I could not stop myself. But, at the end, as I looked into his eyes – his defiant, mocking eyes – there was a certainty. Everything that had happened seemed suddenly to become part of a whole, a guiding. There had been a purpose to it. I *knew*. I was but a tool. I must play the part given me.'

In His name, what had this dolt done? All of Imorren's considerable will was scarcely sufficient to prevent this roaring thought from being voiced. When, after a long pause, she spoke, it was with painful deliberation as she struggled to refrain from committing some atrocity against the man for his lingering telling. Whatever he had done, he was the strongest of the many props that sustained her, and to destroy him would be to injure herself and thus the Brotherhood. She managed to remain outwardly calm.

'And now the certainty has become doubt?' She commended herself on managing a hint of motherliness.

'I Anointed him.'

As Rostan heard the dreaded words coming from his mouth, it seemed to him that all movement in the Hall ceased. His pounding heart and every part of his body were no more. Dusts motes ceased their wavering journeys. The endless silent song of the crystals was stilled. Even the light passing through the air no longer moved for fear of what was to follow.

And Imorren too, for a timeless moment, seemed to have absorbed the cold heart of the Hall and become a pallid ice statue.

Then the movement returned, frenzied and panic-stricken, washing away from her in terror. Rostan, however, remained motionless, filled with the ancient knowledge of prey, that flight will but bring the predator down.

Imorren sat slowly back in her tall chair. With an unseeing gaze, she looked at her hands then rested them on the polished arms of the chair. Once again she was part of the many symmetries of the Hall.

Rostan, forcing himself to keep his eyes open, saw only the flickering remnants of this movement that the Hall's myriad reflecting surfaces carried back to him through the shining floor. It was as though a cloud were gathering over him, or the shadow of a fearsome bird. He waited for Imorren to turn the Power against him.

As she surely must. And nothing he could do would protect him from it. Imorren's skill with the Power was of a kind that he could not even aspire to.

But Imorren remained motionless. It was as if she were being held immobile by the remorseless patterning of the Hall.

And indeed, she did not move because she could not move, for Rostan's revelation had unleased two opposing aspects of her character and the conflict between them demanded her every resource.

Only minutes before, she had found herself in the grip of an anger she had long thought conquered, but that was as nothing compared to the emotions possessing her now. It was as though that anger had been the work of skirmishers from a far greater army lurking in ambush for her. Had Rostan drawn a knife and lunged at her, he could not have delivered her such a blow, so great was the shock of this assault.

Not since she had heard the terrible news of His dispatch from this world had she known such ferment. As the enormity of Rostan's words impinged upon her, a black hatred surged up within her which, had it been given free rein, would have destroyed every last remnant of Rostan, and probably much of the Vaskyros, perhaps even herself. Out of the unknown darkness it had come, from a direction she did not even know existed, full-armed and terrible.

But even as it welled up, so had her appalled dismay that so much uncontrolled human savagery should still exist within her.

129

For a moment, it seemed that all she had achieved would be swept into nothingness, like smoke in the wind. But years of brutal self-discipline had provided her with other unknown resources, and before the destruction was unleashed she found that a colder, crueller rage had arisen to stay the onslaught.

To and fro the two forces swayed, a grim dynamic equilibrium: Imorren, greatest of all the Ailads of the Kyrosdyn, and Disciple of the One True Light against the primitive frenzy of her own corrupted human origins. For a time that could not be measured, there was only turmoil and confusion, but slowly, she became aware of a conscious thought hovering above the field, like a single silver star in a golden sky, bright and clear.

This is a testing!

He reaches across the unknown Ways, to test me yet!

As He must ever.

For there can be no perfection here until He returns, and even the soundest of vassals might be found wanting in the splendour of that time.

The screaming hatred faltered, and other thoughts rallied to her.

The Anointing was to be the culmination of her work here. The act that would open the Ways to His return. Yet too, it was a deed fraught with unknown perils, set as it was, at the very limits of the Brotherhood's knowledge. There was sufficient understanding to know that the consequences of failure could be terrible, and great doubts existed. When should it be? In what manner should it be done? And, not least: by whom and to whom? There was a presumption that one of the Kyrosdyn would be the Chosen, perhaps Imorren herself, but it was no more than that – a presumption. All calculations, all reasoning, failed before any of these conclusions could be made with certainty, dissipating themselves into regions of wild nonsense and seemingly confirming irrefutably that the only certainty was uncertainty. There was *no* understanding of the consequences of success, save that the Ways would in some manner be opened.

Yet Rostan had done this thing. Casually, in a market square brawl with a street thief! An individual who had fled, to hide in this vast city. He had applied the unguent which only he and she dared carry, and impressed it with the Power.

Hatred flared again, feeding on the fear she could scent rising from the form crouched at her feet. Brutally, she forced her mind to pursue its course.

Rostan was many things, but he was *not* a fool. He was the Highest of the Order and deservedly so, with skills, knowledge and ruthless ambition far above anyone else in the Brotherhood, save herself. It defied all his training, indeed all logic, that he should have done this thing in a fit of petulance.

But he had done it!

And he had lied about the reasons why he had done it. She could smell that too. She had not attained her present position without developing an unerring sense for prevaricators and liars. Perhaps he *had* done the deed as an act of spleen. The idea did not invoke the response it would have done scarcely a dozen heartbeats earlier; the clamouring fury was abating as her mind gradually took control of the events. The only question to be asked was: What had caused such a complete loss of control in him?

Testing.

The word came to her again. She pondered it. It would be presumptuous to assume that He would test her alone, but . . .

What was the word Rostan had used?

Guiding!

Could it be that He had reached out from His distant, scattered fastnesses, to show us the way over the final abyss at the edge of which all our resources had foundered and where we had so long trembled?

She closed her eyes. It was as though she was once again at His feet, learning of the world that was to be when His enemies had been destroyed and He was once more free of the cold northern land in which He had been bound.

Another of Rostan's words returned – certainty.

Yes. She felt it too. His hand was there. It was so.

It was so!

She opened her eyes and breathed in the splendour of the Hall which she had created. She was herself again. Very calm. There

131

were only the merest rumblings of anger at the very edges of her mind. It had indeed been a testing. A grim trial, but she had been found whole.

She looked down at Rostan. Though he did not appear to be moving, she could feel his entire body quivering.

Like the heart of a crystal, she thought. The idea amused her.

Yet Rostan had been chosen to do the Anointing. What she would have perceived as a weakness, He in His wisdom had seen as the tool to begin the making of the Way. She was humbled. No calculation, no logic, no instinct, could have led her to such a conclusion.

Fleetingly the thought came to her, 'Am I too being used?' but she dashed it away. It was heretical. Her faith, above all, must be total.

'Leave me, Rostan. I must ponder this.'

There was a brief pause while Rostan disbelievingly took in the words. Then relief overrode the questions bursting in upon him, and, with such dignity as he could muster, he rose, bowed and retreated silently from the Hall. It was an unsteady leaving, his legs were shaking so violently.

As the doors closed silently behind him, so the Hall became intact again. Imorren looked about her, moving her head slowly from side to side, taking in its rich and intricate perfection. Echoing the many patterns, details within details were beginning to unfold in her mind – consequence upon consequence. Rostan must not know of the honour that had been bestowed upon him, of course; he had always had a tendency to vanity and the thought would fire his ambition, perhaps even cause him to turn his eyes once again to her position. And that would mean his death, which would not be in the interests of the Brotherhood. He was too valuable an asset to be lightly cast aside. And too, who could say what further use He might find for him in due course? Rostan must know that he had erred but that, with redoubled effort, the damage could perhaps be repaired. That would be fitting.

The thief would have to be found, but that should present no problem. As time passed and the effects of the Anointing grew, even the dullest of novices would be able to find him.

But these were mere details. She looked at her hands as she had when Rostan had told her the fateful news. A cold smile lit her face. She could feel it all around her. The world was different now. As was she. Just as when she had heard the news of His defeat, and sworn her terrible oath of vengeance, so it was now. She had been renewed, re-forged, shown the way forward.

His time was near.

Chapter 12

'This place is incredible,' Atlon said. 'I've never seen so many people, and so many trades being plied in one place. And so many different buildings! I'm beginning to think that Rinter was telling the truth after all.'

'What about?' Dvolci grunted acidly.

'About the size of the place. I thought he was just telling us a local's yarn. Every street you look down, there are others branching off – more shops and stalls, more people . . .'

'. . . More noise, more stink, more dust.' Dvolci chattered his teeth irritably. 'This place is rapidly becoming the stuff of my worst nightmares.'

'Ah, confirms your darkest fears about what mankind can sink to when it's so inclined, eh?' Atlon said mockingly.

'I don't need any confirmation of that, I've seen you in battle.' Dvolci's tone was unexpectedly grim. Atlon reached up and touched the felci's head.

'Come on,' he said gently. 'It's a bewildering place, for sure, but at least it's full of energy and bustle. The people here are getting on with their lives. Not like those we saw in the Spills.'

'Oh yes. Plenty of energy and bustle, but to what end? And how many of these people do you see smiling?'

Atlon had no answer to the first point and, looking around, could only concede the second. As usual however, when Dvolci was in this vein, Atlon found himself provoked to speak in defence of his own kind.

'They're probably all very busy,' he said, knowing it was a mistake even as he spoke.

'To what end?' Dvolci rasped again. 'Getting rid of appalling areas like the Spills, perhaps? Renewing them, whatever *that* meant. Riding down potty old women?' He snorted. 'You know what they're doing well enough, don't you? They're busy wasting this minute in their haste to get to the next, that's all. Every one of them. You can smell it. You people can be staggeringly unaware of where you are, at times.'

Despite himself, Atlon raised his voice. 'Even at home, people don't go around grinning at everybody else all the time.'

'No, but they know what matters. They stop and talk with friends, pass the time of day. You don't see pushing and elbowing like this even on market days.'

Atlon gave up. There *was* a testy, impatient quality about the bustle around them, and his own training and temperament gave him as clear an insight into its true nature as Dvolci's.

'People have their different ways,' he persisted. 'And the heat *is* a bit wearing.'

Dvolci did not pursue his victory. He was silent for a little while, apparently lost in thought.

Then: 'Do you remember those . . . rat things – the ones we met in the tunnels?' he asked eventually.

Atlon looked at him blankly.

'You can't have forgotten. A great black sea of them – bright red eyes. We all had to dive for cover.' Then he tutted to himself. 'I'm sorry. You weren't there, were you? I forgot. Anyway, I'm sure you've heard the tale.'

'Many times, now you mention it.' Atlon just managed to keep an edge from his voice. It had been a nasty incident for those involved, one of many in a dark time – a time whose shadow still lingered with sufficient menace to draw him out on this journey. 'What's your point?'

'I keep seeing them when I look at these crowds. Rats, trampling over one another, trying to escape from that creature chasing them.'

Atlon frowned. This was not a re-opening of their well-rehearsed spat. Dvolci rarely referred to those times. Now he had a serious point to make. 'You're being unusually severe,' Atlon said. 'There's no panic here, still less any ancient predator. We're new here. It's confusing. We're just not used to these people's ways.'

Dvolci looked around again. 'Just speaking as I feel,' he said thoughtfully. 'The image persists and I can't ignore it. There's something about this place that's very unsettling – something more than the crowds and the general confusion. I don't know what it is, but I'll not find it by staying quiet, you know that.'

Atlon nodded. He too, had been sensing something disturbing about the place, something other than the general clamour. It had grown as they had neared the city. And Dvolci's intuition was sharper than his by far. It would be foolish not to pay heed to him.

They walked on, a gentle eddy in the torrent.

'On the topic of fruitless activity, we seem to be doing little better ourselves,' Atlon said, as they reached the top of another hill to find the street opening out into a wide square. 'We've passed all manner of shops and stalls and traders – I've never seen so much relentless buying and selling – but nothing that seems to have anything to do with the crystal trade.' He grimaced. 'And the day's slipping by. I'll have to find some kind of employment if we're going to stay here. I don't think our host Ghreel is over-burdened with charity for impoverished travellers.'

Dvolci jumped from Atlon's shoulder on to the horse and, standing upright, scanned the square intently.

'Nothing here, either,' he declared, returning to Atlon's shoulders.

Atlon blew out a worried breath and then cast an anxious glance at his horse. That was another problem. He must tend the animal before he bothered about himself. Perhaps if he could see one of the Weartans he might be able to seek advice, though from Rinter's comments, and his own limited contact with them he did not relish the prospect.

As he gazed around the square he could see many more streets joining it.

'We'll have to look at each one before we decide where to go next,' he said wearily. Atlon was finding it increasingly difficult to keep his concerns for the immediate future at bay. In the mountains, in the countryside, he could fend for himself without too much difficulty, but here, surrounded by stone and brick and thousands of his own kind, the natural resources of the terrain seemed to be peculiarly limited. And, standing behind these worries were those about the purpose of his journey. That would have to be addressed, and soon.

'Come on, then.' Dvolci's command set the horse walking.

'Don't do that!' Atlon said crossly, hastily taking hold of the bridle. The horse was supposed to respond only to his voice – and neither he nor his companions at home had ever managed to work out why their horses would obey Dvolci. But then, there were many things that felcis could do which puzzled finer minds than Atlon's.

'Well, you were dawdling.'

The brief exchange dispelled Atlon's mood. His innate optimism came to the fore, albeit not very convincingly. He'd find something eventually. He should worry less about himself and more about his horse and Dvolci. The felci was not averse to travelling on his shoulder, or on the horse, but he much preferred to wander free. Today's journeying would be taxing him sorely though he made no complaint.

They were about halfway along one side of the square when a familiar noise penetrated the hubbub and drew Atlon's attention like a beacon. Following it came an equally familiar smell. It did not take him long to find the source of both. On the far side of the square was a blacksmith's forge. It was a large and prosperous-looking establishment situated incongruously between a shop selling elegant clothes and one selling all manner of what appeared to be medicinal items. Over the wide entrance was a wooden sign bearing in bold letters the legend HEIRN – BLACKSMITH and displaying inaccurate but brightly painted pictures of harnesses, horseshoes and various other iron implements. The real counterparts of these hung under the sign and could be seen along the walls of the interior. As could the glow of a furnace and the shadow of a large figure working at an anvil. Atlon began making his way across the busy square. As he drew nearer he saw a large water trough and a long wooden bench in front of the forge.

He was about to lead his horse to the trough when he remembered he was in a strange place. 'May I water my horse?' he shouted to the hammering blacksmith.

The man looked at him narrowly for a moment, then struck a few

138

more blows and plunged the hot iron shoe into a bucket of water.

'From out of town, are you?' he said, through the hissing steam.

'Yes. Just arrived today.'

There was a pause as the man withdrew the steaming shoe, examined it, then hung it with others on a nail. He was almost a head taller than Atlon, with short-cropped black hair. He was also powerfully built, but his manner exuded no menace as he emerged from the forge, wiping his hands on a dirty rag. A white grin split his grimed face as he stopped in front of Atlon and looked down at him. 'Thought so,' he said, pushing the rag into his belt. 'It's a public trough, young man. Even the Prefect gets some things right from time to time. Like listening to people, for instance. Water your horse with pleasure. And yourself too, if you want – though I wouldn't recommend the trough water.' He produced a flask from a clutter of equipment hanging on the wall and held it out. Atlon smiled and pointed to one hanging from his saddle. 'Thank you,' he said. 'You're very kind, but I've sufficient for the day.'

The blacksmith nodded, took a long drink from the flask himself, then poured water into his cupped palm and splashed it over his face and neck. The ablution merely rearranged the dirt on his face, but he looked cooler. He pointed hesitantly at Dvolci, sitting on Atlon's shoulder. 'Does your . . . pet . . . rat want a drink?'

Atlon felt Dvolci stiffen. He reached up and touched him nervously.

'It's all right,' Dvolci's whisper was heavy with restraint. 'If he thinks you're a young man, his eyesight's probably not too good. Lift me down, I want to get a closer look. This one's interesting.'

Atlon did as he was told. 'He's not a rat, he's a felci,' he said to the blacksmith. 'And he's not a pet, he's a friend. Someone who's travelling the same way. He's also very curious – can he stretch his legs around the forge? It's not very comfortable for him sitting on my shoulders or the horse all day and it's too dangerous for him on the ground.'

Dvolci stood up and, resting his forefeet on the blacksmith's knee, stared up at him. The blacksmith smiled and reached down to stroke him. Unexpectedly, the felci did not avoid the huge hand.

The blacksmith could be trusted then?

'I can see he's no rat now. My apologies. I've never seen a . . . felci . . . before. In fact, I've not even heard the name.'

'That's not surprising,' Atlon said. 'They're mountain creatures, and they don't bother too much with people.'

The blacksmith nodded. 'As wise as he's fine-looking, eh?' Then, a little concerned: 'He won't frighten the horses, will he?'

'No,' Atlon replied, indicating his own horse.

Dvolci dropped on to all fours and sauntered off into the forge. The blacksmith watched him for a moment, then splashed his face again.

'Poor weather for this kind of work,' Atlon said, putting his horse to the trough.

'It is indeed,' the man replied. 'Never known a summer like it. Day after day, no clouds, no rain. It feels as if it's been like this for ever and will go on like this for ever.' He chuckled. 'Still, I suppose with the first cold wind and rain, it'll all be forgotten. Winter's kiss and all. Shrivels most things.' He turned casually to look at Atlon's horse. Almost immediately his interest quickened. 'May I?' he asked, eyes widening.

Atlon nodded.

The blacksmith was silent as he ran his hands expertly over the horse, but he could not disguise his enthusiasm. The horse's quiet response confirmed Dvolci's assessment to Atlon.

'How much do you want for it?'

The blacksmith's manner was so blunt and open, that Atlon could not help laughing. 'He's not for sale, I'm afraid.' He looked at the smith squarely. 'Would *you* sell a horse like that if you had one?'

The unexpected question made the smith start. 'I could do,' he replied hesitantly, after a brief reflection.

'Yes, but you wouldn't, would you? You couldn't part with it. And I doubt you've any *need* for such an animal, so you wouldn't buy it in the first place, even if it was for sale.'

The blacksmith's brow furrowed as he considered this reasoning. 'Are you sure you're from out of town?' he asked.

Atlon laughed again and ignored the question. 'Tell me, does everyone in this city buy and sell all the time?'

The blacksmith ignored the question in its turn. 'Where are you from?'

'The north.'

The blacksmith's expression darkened and the furrows deepened. 'Heard there's been a war up there.' Atlon said nothing and the blacksmith did not pursue the matter. 'Never been much beyond the city myself, though I've heard tell of a land to the north that's full of fine horses and riders. A place where the people ride before they can walk and spend more time in the saddle than on their feet.' He was examining the harness now, with the same attentiveness he had shown to the horse.

'We like horses,' Atlon said.

'I can see that.' The smith moved to the horse's feet. He lifted one and let out a low whistle. Then he stood up and cast an equally assessing eye over Atlon. 'This is better tack than I've ever seen, and I'd consider myself a master of my trade indeed if I could make shoes half as good as these.' He straightened up and pointed to the sign above. 'I'm Heirn. Not much of a signwriter, as you can see, but the best blacksmith in the whole of Arash-Felloren. Until the man who shod your horse arrives, that is.'

Atlon gave a slight bow. 'It was a woman, actually,' he said. 'And she's well content to stay where she is.'

'A woman!' Heirn laughed loudly and shook his head. 'Then I'd be doubly lost if she set up here. I'd probably have to marry her to stay in business.' He thrust out a hand. Atlon watched nervously as his own hand disappeared into it, but the big man's grip was very gentle.

'My name's Atlon,' he said. He waved vaguely into the forge. 'And my friend's name is Dvolci.'

'Welcome to the centre of the world, Atlon,' Heirn announced, raising an ironic eyebrow. He motioned Atlon to the bench and sat down next to him. His long legs sprawled out, so that passers-by had to move around him. Taking another drink from his flask he leaned back against the wall. No sooner had he settled himself than Dvolci appeared from the forge and, quietly clambering on to his lap, curled up. The blacksmith began to stroke him.

141

He looked from Atlon to the horse and back again and seemed to come to a decision.

'Your first day here, you say?'

Atlon nodded.

Heirn pursed his lips. 'You'll have to forgive my speaking to you like this. I wouldn't normally, to a stranger. Not my affair. But I can see from your manner and your horse . . . and your . . . friend that you're an honest kind of a man, so there's things you'll need to know about this place.'

Atlon was finding it increasingly difficult to maintain any sense of caution about this bluff figure.

'I'm sure there is,' he said, meeting Heirn's inquiring gaze. 'It's bewildering, to say the least. I'd appreciate any advice you can offer.'

Having gained permission, Heirn now seemed uncertain about where to start. After taking another small drink and clearing his throat, he said, 'Answering your question, most people do buy and sell here, myself included. It's the way of things. Anything's to be had in this city if you know where to look. And everything's for sale if you know the price.' He leaned towards Atlon, confidentially. 'But there's more than a few people who just take. Some with fast words, others with . . .' He stopped stroking Dvolci and punched his fist into his palm, very gently, as if reluctant to disturb the apparently sleeping felci. 'Watch your horse and your goods carefully – very carefully. And your back. And trust . . .' He hesitated. 'Trust no one.' He pointed significantly at the staff hanging from Atlon's saddle. 'Don't be afraid to use that if you have to. A man needs to be able to fend for himself here.'

Atlon gave an acknowledging nod. 'I'll heed what you say, but you seem rather harsh in your judgement of your fellows.'

'That's also the way of things here, I'm afraid. There's plenty of good things and fine people in this city, but more than enough bad ones to mar the whole, and there's no point saying otherwise. As I said, I wouldn't normally talk to a stranger like this, but there's something about you, and I've a feeling I wouldn't sleep easy tonight if I'd let you go on your way innocent of what could happen to you here.'

142

Almost in spite of himself, Atlon was moved by the man's genuine concern. 'I'm truly grateful to you,' he said. 'Perhaps I might ask more advice of you?'

The blacksmith motioned him to continue.

'I'm staying at a place called The Wyndering.' A thought suddenly jolted him, bringing his hand to his head. 'And I've no idea how to get back to it, now I think about it.' He waved the problem aside. 'But that wasn't what I wanted to ask you.'

The blacksmith chuckled. 'It's no great problem, young man. Any road east is likely to take you back to The Wyndering sooner or later, but ask what you want to ask, and then I'll tell you the easiest way.'

Atlon thought for a moment, but finding no subtle approach, voiced his problem directly. 'I need work. I've got things to do in the city that'll take me some time, and I've only got enough money to keep me at The Wyndering for a few days.'

Heirn glanced at the horse again as if considering making another offer for it, then rejected the idea. 'What can you do?' he asked.

'I'm a teacher by profession, but I can work crystals and that's the business I came here to learn about. We've been wandering the city all day in search of a crystal merchant or a workshop of some kind, but without success. Can you tell me where I can find one?'

Heirn wrinkled his nose unhappily. 'Not a good business to be involved in, crystals.' He looked at Atlon earnestly. 'I wouldn't have taken you for one of those poor souls drawn here in hope of finding the rainbow vein, or looking to find the streets strewn with crystals. You've not heard such tales, have you? Because if you have, I suggest you turn about and head for home right away.'

Atlon shook his head. 'I've no idea what the rainbow vein is, and I've got all the real wealth I need. I just need money so that I can buy food and lodging for my horse and myself. And as I have to learn about the crystal business, and have some skill in working them, a job in a workshop or with a merchant would probably serve both ends.'

The blacksmith's expression did not ease and he folded his arms and let out a noisy sigh. 'Why crystals, of all things?' he asked. 'There's miners, diseased and broken, all over the Thlosgaral, trying

143

to wrench the damned things from the ground. There's Barran gradually taking control over the whole trade, and who knows what else, by murder and extortion. And then there's the Kyrosdyn.' He shook his head. 'They're stranger than ever since Imorren became Ailad. I wouldn't even hazard a guess at what they're up to, other than that it's for no one's good except their own.' He became stern. 'Arash-Felloren's always been a wild place, but it's much worse now than it was when I was young. And I'd say most of its problems these last ten, twenty years, stem, in one way or another, from crystals. None of my business, of course, but I wouldn't recommend anyone I called a friend to have anything to do with them, be it digging, buying, selling, working – anything.'

Atlon was weighing consequences. He had had few qualms about raising the matter of work with the blacksmith but the purpose of his journey was a different matter. But, as he had reminded himself barely minutes earlier, it would have to be addressed, and preferably sooner rather than later. Both his horse and Dvolci had signalled their trust in this man and neither gave that lightly. His own instinct was to do the same. Still, he should be cautious. He had strange things to relate, and Heirn was nothing if not down to earth. It was difficult to judge how he would respond. He met Heirn's gaze.

'I appreciate what you're saying, and your frankness. I know only too well that crystals can present problems, but I don't really have any choice. I'm tasked by others with discovering about the crystal trade in the city, and I must do it.'

'Why?' The question was abrupt. Like any resident, Heirn might criticize his city, but the threat of prying outsiders struck deeper chords.

'The tale's not fully mine to tell,' Atlon replied. 'But there's no ill intent involved, for what you feel my word is worth. It's just that as crystals have caused difficulties here, so they've caused them elsewhere. Far further away than I suspect you'd imagine.' Heirn was watching him intently. He continued, softly and slowly. 'Also, in the hands of certain people, crystals can be used for far more than making mere ornaments.'

Heirn's expression announced that he was being told something he already knew. He nodded and flicked a thumb back into the forge, almost relieved. 'I use them to make my iron stronger, or harder, or easier to work – whatever's needed.' The thumb moved on to the shops on either side. 'Don't use them myself but some swear by their medicinal qualities, and crystal needles – good ones – are better than anything I can make.'

Atlon held up a hand that was both restraining and reassuring. 'Yes, I know that crystals have many valuable uses, perhaps more than we know, but they can also be used . . .' He hesitated. Was he going too far? Could this man really be trusted?

More than anyone he had met so far for sure, he decided finally. A colder thought came: should he prove . . . difficult . . . Heirn could always be made to forget! Atlon suppressed a shiver as he set the thought aside. That would be a last extremity. It was up to him to see that such a conclusion was unnecessary. He pressed on. 'They can also be used as weapons. Not just for hardening the tips of spears and the edges of swords and knives, but as a means of harnessing and directing forces – natural forces – to unnatural ends. Awful ends.'

Heirn's expression became suspicious. 'Let me show you something.' Atlon stood up and began searching through one of his saddlebags. After a brief struggle he pulled out a small flat box and opened it as he sat down again by the blacksmith. Inside, each in its own shaped recess, lay two rows of crystals. Heirn stared at them uncomprehendingly for a moment, then he drew in a sharp breath. Very quickly but with a deliberate affectation of casualness, he reached across Atlon and closed the box.

'They *were* tinted crystals, weren't they?' he said incredulously under his breath. He was still maintaining an air of massive unconcern, but his eyes were flicking up and down the street frantically.

'Most of them, yes.'

'Including a green one?'

'Yes.'

'In the name of sanity, man, keep them out of sight! Have you no idea how much that green alone is worth, let alone all the others?'

'A great deal, it would seem, judging by your response.'

145

Heirn closed his eyes as if searching for guidance. 'A great deal indeed. I don't know what they're worth where you come from, and I'm no expert in these things, but I suspect you're casually carrying around with you crystals worth more in this place than I've earned in ten good years. I'd say that not only have you no need to seek work, you've no need either to fret about your food and lodging for a very long time.' He laid a powerful hand on Atlon's arm. 'I pride myself on being an honest man but there's wealth in that box that would tempt *anyone*. You're really going to have to learn about this city. There are people here who wouldn't hesitate to cut your throat for a fraction of what you're carrying in that box.'

Atlon slid the box gently from under Heirn's hand and slipped it into his pocket. 'They're worth a great deal where I come from also,' he said, 'but in a different way, I think. I—'

Heirn, increasingly agitated, interrupted him. 'Let's get back inside. Too many eyes and ears out here. And for pity's sake, keep your hand on that box. There's pickpockets about as well as cut-throats.' Uncertainly, he shook Dvolci gently to wake him, then lowered him to the ground before standing up and striding back into the comparative gloom of the forge. 'Bring your horse,' he called over his shoulder. 'There's stalls back here.' Atlon hesitated for a moment then tapped his horse and moved after the smith, keeping his hand in his pocket. The horse followed him.

At the back of the forge, Heirn opened a door and beckoned Atlon. Atlon whispered something to his horse, which positioned itself so that it could see both the door and the entrance to the forge.

The door opened on to a small room. There were no windows, but Heirn was turning up an oil lamp which lit the place adequately. A small table stood at the centre, surrounded by old, well-worn chairs. A few bedraggled papers were scattered about the table, some covered in figures, others with sketches. There was also a plate with the remnants of a loaf on it.

Heirn indicated a chair and pulled one up for himself. He ran an arm across his brow.

'Did I really see what I think I saw?' he asked, studying Atlon

146

anxiously. 'Or was it just the brightness out there after being so long at my anvil?'

Atlon took the box from his pocket, laid it on the table and opened it. Heirn leaned forward to examine the crystals, then sat back and put his hands to his temples. He was wide-eyed when he looked at Atlon. 'Who are you? What can you want here – looking for work with these in your pack? Have you no idea what they're worth?' He leaned forward again and reached out as if to touch the green crystal, but his fingers curled as they drew near. 'They're dangerous, aren't they?' he asked nervously.

Atlon made to close the box then changed his mind. 'They can be,' he said. 'They can have a very . . . peculiar effect on people. But only if you handle them for a long time or are surrounded by a great many or . . . do other things with them.' He picked up the green crystal and held it out to the smith. 'Look at it. Hold it. No harm will come to you. Especially with me here.' His mouth twitched as if that might draw the words back. He hurried on. 'Perhaps here, in this city, this stone could indeed bring you coffers full of coins, but I think, like me, you know what true wealth is. You know that, beyond a certain point, those coins would be merely dross. Worse, perhaps, they'd become a burden, binding you to a life you didn't want. Imprisoning you. Have you constantly looking up and down the street in fear, as you just were.'

Heirn nodded, but Atlon was not sure that he was even listening as his shaking hand took the crystal. He held it up between his thumb and forefinger and peered at the hissing lamp through it. A green hue suffused his face, making him look sinister and dangerous.

'See it as it is,' Atlon said softly. 'A beautiful thing come down to us through spans of time we can't even measure. Full of echoes of the forces that shaped the world. Bound there in the endless complexity of its structure.'

Heirn was breathing heavily and his hand was still shaking as he placed the crystal back in the box. His fingers hovered over the box uncertainly for a moment as if receiving warmth. Then he ran his arm across his brow again. He looked distressed. 'There've been times in my life – dark times – when I'd have laid you out

147

and left you in an alley for the least of these.'

Atlon stayed silent.

Heirn slowly closed the box and pushed it away from him. Many emotions were playing across his face, not the least of which was fear.

'Tell me the truth of all this, stranger,' he said coldly.

Atlon looked at him uncertainly, then at Dvolci.

The felci jumped on to his knee and placed his forefeet on the table. He studied Heirn for a moment then turned to Atlon.

'Tell him,' he said.

Chapter 13

Heirn started violently and jumped up with a cry, knocking his chair over. The plate slithered to the edge of the table then tumbled off and broke noisily as it struck the floor.

'Tricks!' Heirn shouted angrily. 'Damn you. I should've known.' He levelled a fist at Atlon. 'Out! Now! Do you think I'm a child? This is Arash-Felloren. You don't trade here without meeting every conceivable piece of charlatan trickery sooner or later.'

Atlon looked up at him in considerable alarm. The smith's menacing figure filled the entire room.

'He thinks you're throwing your voice,' Dvolci hissed urgently.

Heirn made to move around the table to implement his command by force. Dvolci scrambled on to the table, stood on his hind legs, and let out a series of high-pitched whistles. Heirn hesitated and stared down at him.

'Sit down, Heirn,' Dvolci said quietly. 'I didn't speak earlier because since we left home, this is invariably the reaction we get when I do. I apologize if I startled you.' A hint of irritation crept into his voice. 'Though why you humans should consider yourselves the exclusive users of this particular language defies me. It's not as if it's a particularly good one. Horses don't get upset when I talk to them in *their* language.' He sighed. 'Still, that's the way it seems to be, so I've learned to hold my peace. Now *please* sit down, I'm getting a crick in my neck.'

Heirn glanced warily from Dvolci to Atlon several times.

'Please,' Dvolci repeated.

Slowly, and watching Dvolci intently, Heirn picked up his chair and sat down.

'Thank you,' Dvolci said, dropping back on to all fours.

There was an uncomfortable silence. Dvolci pushed the box towards Heirn and flicked it open. Heirn looked at the crystals sourly.

'It's not a new trick, you know,' he said. Atlon frowned, puzzled. 'They're fakes, aren't they? Imitations. You had me believing you for a minute. Let me guess. You were going to tell me they were part of your father's collection and that you'd part with them for a hundredth of their value because you were in desperate need of money?'

Atlon looked down for a moment, unable to meet the accusation in Heirn's eye. 'No,' he said. 'I understand how you feel, and I'm sorry I've handled this in such a way as to make you think that. It's just that I . . . we . . . are on our own in a city the like of which neither of us has ever seen before, and I'm gradually realizing that the task I've been given is perhaps beyond me.' He leaned forward. 'The crystals are genuine. They're not my father's but, in a manner of speaking, they do belong to my family. They're not for sale at *any* price, and anyone who tried to steal them would soon find that he'd made a serious mistake. Crystals have the potential for doing harm beyond anything you can imagine, and I have to find out where they're coming from. I want nothing from you except a little help to find work so that I can get money for food and lodging. But if I've offended you . . .'

Heirn tapped the box uncertainly.

'Do as I said – tell him,' Dvolci said sternly. 'I trust him, and so does the horse. He's as honest as we're going to find, and everything's led us to this city. From what we've heard, this must be the source. Insofar as we expected anything, we didn't expect a place like this, and we can do nothing without someone to help us.'

Heirn was watching Dvolci closely. He crouched low, bringing his head level with the felci's. 'You really talk, don't you?'

Dvolci stared back at him. Atlon cleared his throat warningly. 'Yes,' Dvolci said. 'I do talk. And I scratch and shake myself and pick my teeth.' He did each of these in turn, the last involving revealing his ferocious teeth and prying delicately between two of them with an equally ferocious-looking claw. 'I also eat . . .' He

150

looked around then jumped off the table and picked up a piece of the broken plate. 'Rocks, preferably, but this will do. May I?'

Without waiting for a reply he put the fragment in his mouth and began chewing it noisily and with great relish.

Heirn winced and sat back in his chair. He was beginning to look helpless.

'Are you all right?' Atlon asked. Heirn nodded, very slowly. 'I think so,' he said. 'Though I wouldn't be surprised if I woke up in a moment.'

Atlon picked up the box and put it in his pocket. 'I appreciate your caution, but let's go back outside into the sunlight. I doubt anyone will be interested in two men talking on a bench, and I think you'll feel much easier out there.'

'You're probably right,' Heirn said unhappily. Then, host again, 'But mind you keep your hand on that box.'

'It's perfectly safe,' Atlon assured him.

On their way back through the forge, Heirn paused and spent a few minutes tending his furnace, anxious to have normality about him again. Before he returned to the bench he went to a basin in the corner and washed his face thoroughly. As he sat down, he offered Atlon his flask again. Atlon took it and thanked him.

'I'm sorry about startling you like that. But I've told you no lies. I *am* a teacher, I *do* have to find out about the crystal trade, and I *do* need work.' He looked round at the busy square. 'And we can walk away from you right now, if that's what you want.'

Heirn followed his gaze. 'You said that crystals are doing harm even in your country?'

'No,' Atlon replied. 'I said they caused difficulties. There've been . . . incidents. We want to act now before they start doing harm.'

'What kind of incidents, and who are "we"?'

Atlon looked up at the grainy blue sky. 'I belong to a group of scholars, an Order founded a long time ago and given the task of gathering knowledge against the day when an ancient enemy might return to this world.'

Heirn's eyes were narrowing. Dvolci, lying on the bench beside him, and resting his chin on the blacksmith's lap, said, 'Listen to him, Heirn. This is no child's tale.' Though his voice was soft, there was a quality in it that commanded the smith's attention. 'You yourself mentioned rumours of war in the north. Well, there was a war. Fought and finished several years ago, now. At least, we hope it's finished. It happened because Atlon's people, and others, let things become legend and tradition that should have been kept alive and real. And then the "legend" returned and many are dead and maimed now as a consequence. Because of that neglect, people are travelling far and wide, learning about the world that lies beyond their own realms, some searching for those who pledged alliance to the old enemy and led His army, others searching for signs of the corrosion that He might have secretly spread before He was discovered.'

Heirn shuffled uncomfortably. 'Be patient,' Dvolci said. 'I live in the mountains, well away from people, if possible, and Atlon lives – or used to live – in a lush flat land where the towns and cities are full of low buildings and wide, wide streets, and where the people take a pride in caring for one another. So this tale's no more bewildering for you than this city is for us.'

'I'm doing my best,' Heirn said, 'but it's not easy. A large part of me is saying, see these two off and get on with your work.'

Atlon looked back into the forge. 'You say you use crystals to change the qualities of your iron?'

Heirn was thankful to be back on safer ground. 'Not crystals like those in your box, or even such as a woman might have in a necklace or a ring,' he said. 'Just the very small ones – they're like dust, almost. There are different mixtures. And you have to use them sparingly.'

'Because they're expensive?'

'No, not really, though they're not cheap, but if you use the wrong quantity – too much or too little – the iron will be spoiled.'

'Why?'

Heirn's mouth dropped open as he made to continue his explanation and could not. After a moment, he shrugged. 'It's just the way it is,' he said. 'Like the heating and the cooling, it has to be done a certain way, or it doesn't work. The iron'll be too brittle or too soft.'

Atlon jabbed again. 'Why?'

Heirn's reply was full of frustration. 'I don't know!' he exclaimed. Then he stammered, 'I . . . I just know these things. I learned them from my father and he from his before. And I've learned from others, and experimented . . .'

'You wouldn't say it was magic, then. Or trickery.'

Heirn became indignant. 'No, of course not. It's . . . it's . . .'

'The way it is,' Atlon said.

Heirn let out a noisy breath. 'Yes,' he said, with finality. 'What is it you want me to say? What kind of a question is it you're asking?'

'One I knew you couldn't answer. It could have been any one of thousands. Why does a flower open in the morning and close at night? Why do the clouds change shape? Why rain, why snow, why wind?'

'And why am I sitting here?' Heirn made to stand up. Atlon laid a hand on his arm.

'Please, bear with me,' he said. 'I need to make you understand. You know that many things are so, but not why, and it doesn't trouble you. You've seen them all so many times that you take them for granted. But, imagine, if you didn't know how to harden your iron, and if someone came along and added a little more than a pinch of crystal dust in the melting and then produced an edge that was hard and keen, what would you think?'

Heirn was still debating stepping back into the gloom of the forge, but a combination of his natural courtesy and Atlon's earnestness held him there. 'I've no idea,' he said after a moment. Then, reluctantly, 'I'd probably think it was a trick.'

'Just like my crystals, or a talking felci, or this,' Atlon said. 'Look at that horseshoe.' He pointed casually back into the forge. As Heirn turned, the horseshoe slid to the end of the long nail it was hung over, and clattered to the floor.

'No!' Dvolci hissed furiously.

'No choice,' Atlon retorted sharply. 'He has to understand.'

Heirn's head jerked from side to side as he intercepted this exchange and at the same time tried to keep watching the fallen shoe.

'I did that,' Atlon said, before he could speak. 'It's a skill as commonplace to me as tempering iron is to you. I know the how, but only a little of the why, save that it touches deep into the power that's in all things. The power that can be harnessed and magnified with crystals and directed to great ill by anyone so inclined.'

Heirn was clenching his teeth, both curiosity and a growing alarm conspiring to stop him from walking away from these strange visitors. He was almost snarling when he spoke.

'The flowers open every day. My edges are always true if I've done my work properly. Do it again.'

Two more horseshoes slid off the nail. Dvolci's hair stood on end and he was baring his teeth. 'Enough!' he shouted.

Some of the passers-by, sensing a quarrel, turned to look at the trio. Dvolci clambered recklessly over Heirn's knees and brought his face close to Atlon's. Though he did not raise his voice again, his anger was unmistakable.

'If there are people abusing the power around here, and there's every indication that there are, they'll probably be deranged, and certainly dangerous. Acting like this, you might as well have had our names called out for everyone to hear.'

Atlon flinched away from the felci's outburst, then, scarcely less angry, snapped back: 'I'm aware of that. But time and our money are slipping away from us and we need help. Half a day's talking wouldn't have convinced him a tenth as much as moving those shoes.' Unable to hold Dvolci's glare, he became defensive. 'Besides, no one's noticed anything. And who's going to pick up a fleeting ripple in a crowd like this? I was going to show him a simple focus using a crystal, but that might have been less effective and even noisier.'

Dvolci's manner softened slightly. 'It was still reckless!'

'All right! But—'

'But nothing.'

Heirn stood up, tumbling Dvolci to the ground and effectively ending the dispute. He picked up the horseshoes and carefully examined the nail from which they had fallen, then he looked at Atlon.

'I'm not doing it again,' Atlon said, anticipating the request.

'Dvolci's right, it *was* risky – and it could draw attention to us. But it was the only way I could think of, to get you used to the idea that some of us possess skills that you'd consider impossible. Then perhaps it might be easier for you to understand the nature of the enemy we fought and how dangerous His followers might still be.'

Heirn was absently sliding the horseshoes back and forth along the nail. Delicately he lifted one of them over the large round head as if testing its weight.

'Why would you want me to know about this enemy of yours? And whose attention are you frightened of?'

The residue of Atlon and Dvolci's argument vanished and they looked at one another uneasily.

'Because He wasn't just *our* enemy,' Atlon said, stepping back into the forge. 'He's an enemy to every living thing. Had He defeated us – and He nearly did – you'd have known about Him by now. Your city would have been razed or enslaved. And you'd have been either in chains or making them.'

Heirn seemed inclined to disagree but did not speak.

'And the people we're afraid of?' Atlon patted the pocket containing the box. 'Anyone who has knowledge of the Power and who uses these. Probably your Kyrosdyn, from what we've heard. They do have strange powers, don't they?'

'So it's said,' Heirn replied tersely. 'But supposing I accept this tale of yours – and it's a wild one, you'll admit – what's the difference between you and them with your power and your crystals?' He tapped the horseshoes, making them jangle.

Atlon stood silent for a long time, silhouetted against the bright clamour of the square beyond.

'We use the Power very rarely,' he said eventually, his voice low. 'It offers always the easy path, and the end of that is invariably corruption and degradation. As for crystals, they magnify this manyfold; we use them even more rarely, and then only with great caution and after much deliberation.' He paused. 'But perhaps you're right and there's very little between myself and the Kyrosdyn if the truth be known.' He turned and looked out at the square. 'Born in this city, I might well have become one of them.'

Heirn stared at him intently. 'That doesn't answer my question though.'

'I can't,' Atlon said, shaking his head. 'You know the Kyrosdyn better than I do, and we're just two bizarre strangers performing party tricks and talking wild tales, as you say.'

Heirn stopped fiddling with the horseshoes and shoved his hands deep into the pockets of his apron. 'I hope I'm not going to regret this, but I've spent most of my working life trusting my judgement about people, and I've been luckier than many I know. For all your foolish tales and tricks, you still don't strike me as either mad or bad, and as you've not tried to get money out of me so far, I see no harm in listening to you at least.' He indicated the bench again. As he walked past Atlon, he said confidentially, as though someone might be eavesdropping, 'Besides, I'd no more trust a Kyrosdyn than I'd use the anvil for a boat.'

'Smith!'

The harsh voice made both Heirn and Atlon start. Standing in the entrance was a robed and hooded figure. Dvolci drew in a hissing breath and quietly retreated behind a stack of rusty iron chains lying on the floor.

Heirn shot a glance at the figure, then, turning back to Atlon, reached up and began pointing to the rows of horseshoes hanging from the wall. 'I'm sure you'll find one that'll suit your horse's problem, sir,' he said briskly. 'Feel free to examine any of them, while I attend to this gentleman.'

As he approached the new arrival, he took the rag from his belt and wiped his hands on it as he had when he greeted Atlon. He positioned himself squarely in front of the man, obliging him to step back slightly, out into the street, and obscuring his view of the interior of the forge.

'Yes, sir. What can I do for you?' he said, folding his arms and standing very straight so that the newcomer had to look up at him.

The figure was not intimidated, however. 'Has anything unusual just happened around here?' The voice was that of someone used to commanding obedience.

Heirn craned forward slightly, peering into the hood. Atlon, watching from the corner of his eye as he pretended to be examining

156

the horseshoes, noted that the figure seemed to lose some of its assurance.

'Unusual, sir? What did you have in mind?'

There was clear impatience in the reply. 'Unusual, man! Unusual! Out of the ordinary. Something that doesn't normally happen, something you couldn't explain.'

Heirn became bluff. 'Well, sir, I've only to sit on my bench there and watch the square for a half a day and something unusual's likely to happen. I'm sure if I sat there long enough I'd see as much of the world as any seasoned traveller – and not get saddle-sore into the bargain.' He laughed loudly at his own joke but the figure only stiffened. 'Then there's you coming, sir. That's unusual. Don't get many Kyrosdyn Brothers stopping by, you not generally being horse-riders. And as for things I can't explain, they're legion. Why do flowers open in the morning, why wind, why rain, why snow?'

The Kyrosdyn stepped past him angrily and strode up to Atlon.

'And you – have *you* seen anything strange in the last few minutes?' His manner was no different from that he had adopted with Heirn.

Atlon's jaw tightened, but he continued looking at the horseshoes as he spoke. 'You are a member of an Order of learning, aren't you? A thinker, a searcher after knowledge and the great truths of the world?'

'Yes.' The reply sounded forced, prised out by the unexpected question rather than given willingly.

Atlon nodded, but still kept on examining the horseshoes. 'Then the only unusual thing I've seen recently is a member of a so-called learned Order addressing a respected craftsman and a complete stranger with an inexcusable lack of civility. Good day to you.' He tapped one of the horseshoes and leaned forward around the Kyrosdyn to look at Heirn. 'Blacksmith, when you've finished with this gentleman, I think I may have found what I need.'

Heirn's eyes widened and his mouth dropped open. Not because of Atlon's abrupt dismissal of the Kyrosdyn, but because he was suddenly surrounded by a deep silence, and everything about him seemed to have been transformed into an unnatural but carefully

157

arranged tableau: Atlon, smiling pleasantly, holding out the horseshoe to him, the Kyrosdyn, rigid and staring at where Atlon had been, and he himself, unable to move. He was sure that, had he been able to turn around, he would have found that the square behind him was no longer there. And the atmosphere in the forge was like that before a thunderstorm, with the motionless Kyrosdyn at its quivering heart.

Then, just as suddenly, it was gone, and the clamour of the square was washing over him like a surge of relief. Without speaking, the Kyrosdyn spun round and strode out of the forge, obliging Heirn to step quickly to one side to avoid him.

Dvolci emerged hurriedly from behind the chains and ran across to Atlon. 'Make sure he's gone,' he shouted urgently to Heirn, then to Atlon, 'Are you all right?'

Atlon was breathing heavily and rubbing his hands together. He nodded. 'I think so, yes,' he said shakily. 'Did you feel it? I'm sorry about the trick with the horseshoes. I didn't think for one minute that there'd be anyone who—'

'It's all right, it's all right,' Dvolci said, at once anxious and reassuring. 'Neither did I really. And did I feel it? How could I not?'

Heirn interrupted them. 'He's gone. Stormed across the square straight as if I'd thrown him. People had to jump out of his way.' He looked at Atlon. 'What the devil happened?'

Atlon swayed and reached out to steady himself against the wall. 'Help him, man,' Dvolci cried angrily. 'Get him out into the open air.'

Heirn draped a massive arm about Atlon's shoulders and led him gently from the forge. He repeated his question as he sat him on the bench, and crouched down in front of him, though this time his voice was full of concern. 'What the devil happened? You look awful.'

Atlon closed his eyes and let out a long, slow breath. Colour gradually returned to his cheeks. He opened his eyes and scanned the square without moving his head. 'He's gone,' he said to Dvolci. 'And I can't feel anyone else about.' He drew a shaking hand across his forehead and looked at Heirn.

'My little demonstration with the horseshoes was a mistake, I'm afraid,' he said. 'I put you in danger. I'm sorry. I never thought . . .' His voice faded away and he shook his head.

'There was no reason why you should,' Dvolci said. He gave a violent shudder.

'Are *you* all right?' Atlon asked.

Dvolci was dismissive. 'Of course I am,' he said. 'It was just the thought of what all this means.'

Heirn interrupted with strained patience. 'Will you please tell me what—'

'Did you know the man?' Atlon asked him.

'No. They all dress more or less the same, and they usually keep their hoods well forward. And they have their own smiths for such work as they need. I did the odd thing for them when I was young, but they're bad clients – argue your price down to next to nothing, then argue about your workmanship, then you have to wring your money out of them, drop by drop.' He grimaced angrily as old memories returned.

'Well, answering your previous question, if that man's typical of the Kyrosdyn, then it's them I'm afraid of. And much more so now than before.' Atlon put his hand to his head. 'I can hardly believe it.'

Heirn was about to speak again but Dvolci answered his question. 'He nearly attacked Atlon with the Power,' he said. 'Right here, out in the open, with no regard for human flesh or the consequences. I've never seen such grotesque, such frightening, indiscipline.'

'I don't know what you're talking about,' Heirn said.

'Yes, you do,' Dvolci said. 'I saw the hairs on your neck standing on end even from where I was.'

Heirn gritted his teeth and looked up and down the square uncomfortably before replying. He had to force the words out. 'I just shivered, that's all. You know – a goose walked over my grave.'

'In this heat?' Dvolci was derisive. 'You were scared stiff. And rightly so, too.' There was such force in his last remark that it stopped Heirn's protest. 'Think yourself lucky you were on the edges of it. And we can all thank those who taught Atlon that sometimes it's better to receive than to give. I shudder to think what would have happened if you'd retaliated.'

Atlon tried to stand up then changed his mind. 'There was nothing to retaliate against, fortunately,' he said. 'Otherwise I probably would have done. But he didn't actually do anything. That was just a little fist-clenching. He wasn't *that* indisciplined.'

Dvolci snorted. 'Don't be ridiculous,' he blasted. 'He reached for the Power as if it were no more than scratching his backside. He must use it all the time, it's appalling.' One foreleg came up nervously. 'Did you respond at all – even a little? Do you think he realized you had the skill too?' His teeth chattered anxiously. 'And what if they're all that powerful?'

'No, I didn't respond, but more by good luck than anything else,' Atlon replied. 'And no, I don't think he suspected anything. He wouldn't have left so easily, if he had. As for them all being like that, then all we can do is return home with the news.' He slapped his knees with unconvincing heartiness. 'But we'll have to find out more about these people and what they're doing. We can't go back crying the alarm on the strength of one chance encounter, can we?'

'We mightn't survive another,' Dvolci said darkly. 'He was using a crystal, you know.'

'I know,' Atlon confirmed. 'Though I can't think how.'

Dvolci was angry again. 'Don't be so obtuse. You *know* how.'

Atlon shook his head. 'It can't be.'

'Can't be? Of course it can! You said it yourself before: the easy path – corruption and degradation – and crystals magnifying the way manyfold. Someone who uses the power so casually is totally under its sway – totally! He's probably addicted beyond recovery. Tumbling headlong into hell. And it's hard to imagine he's alone.'

Atlon turned to Heirn. 'What do the Kyrosdyn look like?'

The smith shrugged. 'I've not really seen all that many. As I told you, they usually keep themselves hooded. But such as I have seen look pale . . . unhealthy.'

'Gaunt?'

160

Heirn nodded. 'Too much working indoors in ill-lit workshops, I suppose.'

'But they're . . . vigorous, for all that?'

Heirn nodded again. 'Yes,' he said. 'Though I'd use the word tense rather than vigorous – stiff, jerky and sudden in their movements. And they've always been arrogant and unpleasant.'

For a moment, Atlon looked much older. He shook his head slowly as if reluctant to accept his own conclusion. 'I'm afraid you're right,' he said to Dvolci.

Heirn sat down heavily beside Atlon. 'I'd value an explanation,' he said. 'One I can understand. I've no idea what you're both talking about, and, pleasure though it was to see one of them dismissed like a stray dog, even *I* felt something strange happen.'

Atlon was matter-of-fact. 'The Power I used to dislodge those horseshoes, he was prepared to use against me. Except that what he was threatening to use was many times stronger. It was akin to your smashing me with your hammer for the same offence.'

'But he didn't actually do anything?' Heirn looked at him anxiously, searching for reassurance.

'No,' Atlon replied. He looked unhappily at Dvolci. 'Had he done, I'd probably have defended myself instinctively. I don't think I could have done otherwise. And who knows what the consequences of that would have been . . .' He paused and studied the smith for a moment. 'But he raised the hammer, Heirn. Would you have done so in those circumstances? I doubt you'd have raised anything other than your eyebrows. What he did was not the act of a truly sane person. If the others are the same, then they're much more than just another group of people scrabbling for power and wealth within the city. They're profoundly dangerous. They're liable to bring this place down in ruins.'

Heirn grimaced. 'I can't accept this,' he said with a broad wave of his hand. 'No disrespect, Atlon, but you're beginning to talk nonsense. You've no idea what this place is like. How big it is. How many conflicting groups there are. The Kyrosdyn are an odd lot, for sure, and undeniably not people to trifle with. But the city's full of determined and organized groups. Always has been. The Kyrosdyn are one of the oldest – they're supposed to go back to

161

the very beginnings. Why would they want to harm the place? And *how* could they? If they started to muster mercenaries, news would be all over the place in days – hours, even – and that would unite almost everyone against them, not least the mob. It's happened before with other groups.'

The trio sat in silence for a long time, each absorbed in his own thoughts. Eventually, Atlon looked up at the sun, now quite low in the sky. 'It's getting late,' he said, standing. He held out his hand to Heirn. 'Thank you for your help and your kindness to two strangers,' he said. 'I apologize for the problems we've caused you. I won't ask you to accept what I just told you, though it *is* true. The Power unleashed is something far beyond anything you've ever known and you'd think me truly mad if I tried to explain it to you, so I won't. If I could ask you to direct us back to The Wyndering, preferably avoiding any of the Spills, we'll be on our way and trouble you no further.'

Heirn too, stood up, and took the offered hand. He looked down at Atlon sternly. 'The trick with the horseshoes, I thought could probably be just that – a trick. But Kyrosdyn don't come to my forge, and that one was here like a dog after a rat. That's a puzzle. Then your manner, your horse, the tack, the shoes, and not least the crystals, all mark you out as being someone unusual. Another puzzle. And the business with the Kyrosdyn. As I said, even *I* felt something. Yet another. You've given me so many questions that I'm unlikely to sleep tonight as it is.' He leaned forward, looming over Atlon. 'But this city's my home, and the home of many good people, for all it leaves a lot to be desired, and if the Kyrosdyn are a danger, I'd like to know more about it.'

Atlon glanced up at the sun again. 'So would I,' he said. 'But I've still got the problems I arrived with, and one day less in which to solve them. I need work to pay for food and lodging. Until I get that, there's precious little I can do about the Kyrosdyn or anything.'

Heirn nodded thoughtfully. 'It occurs to me that, you coming from such a horseloving land, you might have some rudimentary skills in say, leatherwork, shoeing, and the like.' He gestured back into the forge. 'I've usually got a few horses back there that need tending for a day or so. I could perhaps offer you food and board in return for a little help. And while we worked, you could talk.'

Atlon looked at Dvolci uncertainly. Heirn, the inveterate bargainer, pressed his offer before the felci could contribute his thoughts.

'I don't think you want to work in a crystal workshop any more, do you?' he said significantly. 'Or get too close to *any* of the Kyrosdyn. At least for the moment.'

Atlon's expression conceded the point.

'Then you're hired?' Heirn asked encouragingly.

Relief lit Atlon's face. 'Yes,' he said, smiling broadly. 'You're very kind.'

'I'm very curious,' Heirn admitted bluntly. He looked up and down the square knowingly. 'And as we're not likely to get any customers at this time of day, I'll shut up and we'll go along to my place. It's not far. We can have something to eat, then perhaps . . . talk a while, eh?'

After he had damped down the furnace, it took Heirn only a few minutes to swing a series of heavy shutters into place. They were robust and ingeniously designed to provide no leverage points for would-be thieves, but they were scarred with various impacts nevertheless.

'Who'd want to steal what's in here?' Heirn said as he saw Atlon examining them. 'But they try. Always they try. It's a pity they don't put the same effort into plying an honest trade.'

As they moved away from the forge Dvolci clambered on to Atlon's shoulder and whispered urgently in his ear. 'He's come back.'

Atlon nodded. 'Yes, I know.' He spoke to Heirn. 'The Kyrosdyn's back.'

Heirn looked around, startled. 'I can't see him.'

'He's here even so. How far is it to where these people live?' he asked.

'The Vaskyros? Quite a way – why?'

'Could he have been there and come back since he left the forge?'

'No. Not even if he'd been riding.'

Atlon's face became grim. 'We'll have to deal with him.' He looked around anxiously at the busy street. 'Is there any secluded way we can use to get to your home?'

Chapter 14

Pinnatte felt good. Very good. In fact, he could not remember when he had last felt so good. It was as though his every heartbeat reinvigorated him as he strode through the gloomy streets towards the Jyolan Pits. Among the many fantasies that he toyed with on the way was one that had him seeking out the Kyrosdyn who had left the mark on his hand, and thanking him for setting him on the path to finding a new future for himself. It made him glow and he rubbed the back of his hand delightedly.

As he neared the Pits he made a conscious effort to calm down. Strutting conspicuously through the darkened side streets and alleys was not only out of character, it was foolish. Once or twice he actually fancied that he was being followed, though when he spun sharply on his heel he caught no sudden tell-tale shift in the shadows behind him. However, drawing attention to himself in the Pits would be particularly unwise. He was known to be one of Lassner's Den-Mates, and if he were to act the way he felt, the eye of every Pitguard in the place would be drawn to him inexorably. The very least that would happen then would be Lassner hearing of his excited behaviour and presuming, naturally, that he had been less than honest about his takings for the day. The worst that could happen would see him trying to convince the Pitguards that he hadn't suddenly had a 'stroke of particularly good fortune' which he might like to 'share' with his old friends. No, this night was for watching, not being watched. He must be his old, insignificant self.

Apart from his own safety, this was the correct way to behave in any event. He had no clear idea of what he intended to do, or to whom he might wish to ally himself, but he knew that it would have to be done discreetly – *very* discreetly. He had seen enough in his time to know that the people who were *really* successful – the likes of Barran, for example – were not flashy and raucous, but modest in their public appearances, and silent and secret in their business dealings.

Barran . . .

The name had slipped into his mind unexpectedly. He mulled it over. To be part of Barran's ever-growing empire was an improbably high aspiration, but then, today was proving to be an improbable day. And if he was looking to improve his lot, there was really not much point in following the star of just another Den-Master, someone precious little better than Lassner.

Why not Barran? he decided extravagantly. There was no harm in dreaming, though even in his elated state he knew there was little chance of finding a way into such a man's service – not least because he had no idea where to start.

He came to the top of a rise and joined the street that led to the Jyolan Pits. To his surprise, it was much busier than usual, with almost everyone walking or riding in the same direction. And while there were some familiar faces to be seen, the majority were not the typical night people that were usually to be found here. He joined the stream.

Intrigued, he was taking a considerable interest in the crowd as he rounded the final corner before the Jyolan – part professional, part curiosity. As he looked ahead however, he stopped with a violent intake of breath, and all thoughts of the crowd were gone. In front of him, chilling and awful, was a malevolent, winking face. It filled the entire street. His knees started to buckle and his mouth dried as he saw that the surging crowd, now no more than a black flood, was disappearing into its gaping, blazing maw. For an instant, heart pounding, he was about to turn and flee back into the darkness, to the safety of his Den. But even as the intention formed, the image changed. He gave a nervous, self-deprecating laugh. It was only the Pits. Normally, all that could be seen of the place at night was such as the inadequate street-lighting revealed, and whatever light spilled out of the entrance door. Tonight however, the place was illuminated. The high-arched entrance was ablaze and lights on the roof played on the carved figures there, making them seem to move like restless guards around a flickering campfire. Lights too, hung all about the front of the building, and some had been placed behind the windows to the upper floors, to glint through the ornate metal frames like so many squinting eyes. Pinnatte let out a noisy breath and shook his head to dispel the residue of the image that had greeted him.

Everyone around him was heading towards Jyolan, to join an already large crowd gathered there – a much larger crowd than was usual, he noted as he drew nearer. And much more excited. *And* richer, he realized very quickly, as he reached the outer edge of it. He could see liveried manservants, maidservants, grooms, formal guards and more than a few individuals whose sharp-eyed attention to their surroundings marked them out unequivocally as bodyguards to the very quietly rich. Coaches bearing the insignias of noble houses and rich traders were arriving and leaving, or just standing in the street, their horses skittish in the noisy crowd. There could have been real pickings for him here had he so chosen, but though he could feel his instinct for theft stirring, he kept it sternly under control. Apart from his new-found ambition, purse-cutting at the Pits was profoundly foolish even under ordinary circumstances, with so few avenues of escape and so many Pitguards about. Apart from the fact that most of them knew him, they guarded their exclusive right to separate the spectators from their money most jealously. To be caught stealing by them meant a beating – no smaller matter in itself – but with the place alive with mercenary bodyguards, always alert for an opportunity to justify their wages to their employers, he could end up with a hand over his mouth and a silent knife under his ribs for his pains. No one would even know he was dead until the crowd moved away and he tumbled to the floor. And then there was the crowd itself. He'd heard tales of would-be thieves who'd been literally torn apart by a fighting-pit crowd.

He shook off the thoughts and, thrusting his hands deep into his pockets, as if to emphasize that he was keeping them out of trouble, he settled into the crowd's shuffling progress. Whatever was happening was perhaps fortunate. At least he could look happy and excited and no one would remark on it especially. But, what was going on? The Jyolan Pits were the oldest in Arash-Felloren and, reputedly, had once been the finest, but now they were rather down-at-heel and definitely not the kind of establishment that attracted this class of clientèle.

A man, similar in build to himself, was jostled into him by a passing horse. Pinnatte caught and steadied him.

'I'm sorry,' the man said after he had finished cursing the rider.

Pinnatte gave an uncharacteristically gracious nod. Then the man was stretching up and looking from side to side as if searching for someone. His modest height however, proved to be too much of a problem in the growing crowd.

'Something special on tonight?' Pinnatte asked.

The man nodded absently, still trying to look around. 'Yes, more's the pity,' he said. 'It's a Loose Pit.' He made one more quick inspection of the crowd then gave up. Turning to Pinnatte, he spoke as if they had known one another for years, as is the way with strangers thrust together in crowds. 'I ask you, how often do the Jyolan have a Loose Pit? Once in a green-cheese moon, that's how often? – Never. And they have to have one tonight of all nights.'

A Loose Pit! Pinnatte thought. He hadn't expected that. But it accounted for the size and quality of the crowd.

'You haven't seen a man wandering about looking lost, have you?' The man was speaking again. He held a hand above his head. 'So high. Long riding coat and a big hat.' He leaned forward. 'Fine horse. And probably got a rat on his shoulder.'

Pinnatte's eyes widened. 'A rat?'

'Well, a sort of rat.'

Pinnatte shook his head and smirked uncertainly. 'No,' he said.

'You're sure?'

'I'm certain. I've only just arrived, but I'd have noticed someone with a big hat and a rat on his shoulder.' Pinnatte's smirk became a laugh. 'You were waiting for him?'

The man nodded and grimaced. 'He's new in town, he's probably got lost.' He swore. 'I shouldn't have let him wander off. Years I've been training animals for the Pits – not in a big way, you understand, but I know my business – and that rat-thing would have made me a fortune. And the owner, of course,' he added hastily.

'You should've seen the way it backed down Ghreel's dog at The Wyndering.' He swore again.

Pinnatte had no great interest in some failed Pit-animal trainer, but the crowd was holding them together and he seemed affable enough. Besides, it dawned on him, failed or not, this individual would know more about the men who ran the Pit than he did. He could be useful.

'He might be anywhere in this lot,' he said. 'Perhaps you'll see him inside.'

The man looked unhappy. The crowd continued to edge forward. Pinnatte offered consolation. 'Besides, I don't think a rat would've stood much chance in a Loose Pit, would it?'

'Oh no,' the man said. 'It wouldn't even have got in, of course – an unknown fighter and all. But its owner was beginning to show a real interest. I was sure that if I could've got him in here and talked to him – shown him the way of things – he'd have been really enthusiastic. He needed the money, and that's always a help.'

The crowd tightened around them. He held out his hand. 'Irgon Rinter,' he announced. 'You haven't got any animals you'd like trained up, have you?'

Pinnatte introduced himself, untypically using his real name. 'No,' he replied. 'Not unless you count the bed bugs in my lodgings – they're bloodthirsty enough for here.'

Rinter cackled. 'Maybe we should run a miniature fighting pit. Fleas, maggots, spiders and the like.'

'I don't think two fleas battling to the death would pull a crowd like this,' Pinnatte said off-handedly. He was not too keen on joining in Rinter's humour. 'What's fighting, do you know?' He slapped his pocket. 'More to the point, what's it going to cost to get in?'

'A lot,' Rinter said. 'They'll have opened up the top terraces for this crowd and I'll wager they'll be charging the normal Pitside prices just for *them*.' He leaned forward and tapped the side of his nose. 'As for what's fighting,' he said, in a conspiratorial undertone, 'according to my friends inside,' he nodded towards the building, 'it's something *very* special.' He looked around as though someone in the heaving crowd might be eavesdropping, then mouthed rather than spoke his revelation. 'Something the Kyrosdyn have found.'

He pointed downwards significantly. 'From the caves.'

Pinnatte was genuinely impressed though he managed not to show it. He rubbed the mark on his hand unthinkingly.

'Why here?' he asked, for want of anything better to say.

Rinter maintained his conspiratorial air. 'I don't know. It's unexpected – only heard about it myself this afternoon. But I've heard it said that Barran's been taking an interest in the Pits. Probably looking for new businesses now he's in control of so much of the crystal trade.'

But Pinnatte was not listening. The words Kyrosdyn and Barran had collided in his mind and were echoing there, taking on a life of their own. They began to circle round and round like high-flying birds of prey, their very presence slowly paralysing him. Then all meaning was gone from them and, sounding over and over, they became a cacophonous babble – a chaotic choir of innumerable voices crying out in a harsh and alien language.

And something was pressing down on him.

He could not breathe! It was though an iron ring was tightening around him. He should go no further. He should get away from here!

'Are you all right?'

Rinter's voice filtered weakly through the clamour. Pinnatte seized it and clung to it desperately, and to the grip that was shaking his arm. The choir wavered and the ring tightened. He must get away.

'Are you all right?'

Somehow, Pinnatte forced his head back. He *had* to look up – to find air to breathe above this choking press – to see if anything was indeed circling high above in the darkness, preparing to swoop down on him.

For he *would* be able to see it, he knew.

But instead, his eyes met those of the face carved on the keystone of the arch that spanned the entrance to the Pits. They seemed to reach out and embrace him. At their touch, he felt the sense of oppression lifting from him, or rather, being lifted from him by some unknown agency and replaced by one of elation. And the grip about his chest was gone too.

'Are you . . .'

Rinter began his question for the third time. He continued shaking Pinnatte's arm.

'Yes, thank you,' Pinnatte said, putting his hand over Rinter's reassuringly to still it. 'Just felt a bit dizzy for a moment. The crush, I expect.'

But his mind was racing, and he could not stop staring at the face. How could he have come here so many times and never noticed anything so beautiful? This was a word he could not remember having ever used before, but it did not disturb him. It must be the lights, of course, he thought, but that had a false, inadequate ring to it as an explanation. It was something more than that, for as he edged forward, the face seemed to be following him, telling him not to be afraid, telling him that all would be well, that great things lay ahead of him, that he was protected. His body was permeated with the knowledge. It was unlike anything he had ever known.

Then a sudden eddying shuffle ran through the crowd and he was carried under the arch. For a moment, it was as though he had been plunged into darkness, even though the lights inside the building were brighter than those outside. Part of him cried out in pain at the separation, but then the image of the face was with him again, distant now, but still sustaining him. And it remained there even though normality began to close about him again as the crowd slowly moved across the stone-floored entrance hall of the Pits.

'Probably the heat, as well.' It took Pinnatte a moment to realize that Rinter was diagnosing the dizziness he had claimed.

He nodded and smiled broadly. 'Well, it's gone now, and I'm in the mood for watching a good fight.'

The sound of angry voices rose up ahead of them. Rinter stepped up on to the broad foot of an iron stanchion to locate the source of the commotion. 'Looks like we'll see one before we get inside,' he said. 'Someone's objecting to the price.' He jumped down quickly and there was a ragged movement through the crowd as a figure, dripping blood through the fingers of his hand clasped over his mouth and nose, elbowed his way against the flow. Abuse and laughter followed him.

Pinnatte joined in. What an idiot! Fancy arguing with the

171

Pitguards, especially in front of a crowd like this. Even so, he discreetly thumbed through the coins in his pocket. If Rinter's previous estimate was correct, this was going to be an expensive evening and he'd no desire to go struggling back through the crowd, bloodied or not. He had plenty, he decided, after a second count, though he felt a brief twinge of unease about spending so much money. Still, he'd earned it today, and it would be folly indeed to walk away from an event like this, not only because of what it was – the *first* Loose Pit at the Jyolan, and with a Kyrosdyn animal as well – something from the caves – this would be a boasting point for years – but because of what he might learn and whom he might yet meet in such a crowd. Admittedly, all he had encountered so far was one unsuccessful Pit animal trainer, but he had made no effort to do that, and it was still a step into the world he wanted to explore. If, as Rinter had intimated, Barran was going to start taking over the city's Pits as he had taken over much of the crystal trade, then the Jyolan would be a good place for him to begin. Old, respected, and long past its best, it occupied a building the constant complaint about which, by those who went there regularly, was that it could be used far more effectively than its present owners allowed.

'Had a good day, young Pinnatte?'

He jumped. He had been so absorbed in his thoughts that he had not realized he was so close to the inner gate. The greeting came from one of the Pitguards.

'Could have been better,' he replied. It was his normal response. It was the normal response for most of the citizens of Arash-Felloren to such a question. He noted that the Pitguard was wearing not only a livery, but a new, albeit ill-fitting one, and that some of the others standing by the gate were unknown to him. He considered an ironic remark about the livery but decided against it; he did not know the man all that well, and he was looking both particularly proud and keen-eyed. Further, Pinnatte suspected, from the glances being exchanged, that the apparently friendly greeting had only been to identify him to the other Pitguards.

'How much is it tonight?' he asked.

The Pitguard wearily indicated a large notice dominating the inner gate. Having prepared himself, Pinnatte managed to keep his mouth from dropping open, but he still felt a wrench as he parted with the money. Then he was through.

'Thought we'd never get here.' Rinter was by his side again. He looked around. 'Well, well, look at this. It's not only the top terraces that have been opened.'

In front of them, the crowd was being shepherded with varying degrees of politeness by more strange Pitguards through a row of arched entrances. Rinter was drawing Pinnatte's attention to two arches at the end of the row. These were normally dark and completely blocked by piles of rubbish. Now they were brightly lit and the rubbish had either been removed, or pushed aside.

'That way,' a nearby Pitguard called out before Rinter could say anything else. The man was pointing towards one of the newly-opened arches with a heavy baton which he hefted in a manner markedly at odds with his polite demeanour.

The building that housed the Jyolan Pits was very old, and no one now knew what it had originally been used for. Nor could a use be readily deduced from its construction, save that it must have been for some kind of public assembly. Externally, apart from being unusually ornate and patently much older, the building was not vastly different from most of its neighbours in that it was, in essence, a large rectangular block. Internally however, all was curved, sinuous and confusing. An oval arena with a central circular platform, raised and fenced, lay at its heart. It was surrounded by steeply stacked terraces on the lower steps of which the spectators usually stood. Around these in turn, were several levels of cloistered balconies, each of which, disconcertingly, protruded further than the one below, forming an arching line which drew the eye upwards until the outer walls finally swept up to form a domed ceiling. The balconies were normally empty and the rows of arches and their broad separating columns which formed the balustrades, hovered around and over the assembly like dark, sightless eyes, giving the place not only a gloomy atmosphere, but, at times, a sinister one. More sinister yet was a circle of sharp-pointed hornlike spikes which unfurled from the ceiling. Each one bent downwards as if bowing in obeisance to a solitary barb which hung from the crown

173

of the dome. Its curving sides swept down from a broad base to an almost needle thinness, at the end of which was what appeared to be a clear crystal about the size of a child's fist. In the light now seeping from the balconies, this occasionally flashed bright, like a solitary silver star.

Stranger than this central hall however, was the access to it, which consisted of a complex tangle of interweaving and inter-linked passageways. Like the streets of the city itself, these twisted and turned, dipped and rose, to no discernible logic. Some were wide and spacious, while others were narrow, with low, claustrophobic ceilings, though none maintained the same shape for any great length. And for each of these passages, there were innumerable other conduits threading unknowable pathways through the ancient stonework. These ranged in size from some that a stooping man might pass along, if he were so inclined, to others scarcely large enough to accommodate a probing forefinger. Whatever the passageways were for, it was questionable that even the widest were intended for people as all of them had uneven, curved floors, sometimes almost semi-circular, which broke the strides of walkers and constantly forced them into the centre, away from the walls.

One of the wilder tales that the smaller passageways spawned was that they moved. Ways that were seen one day were gone the next, and new ways appeared where none had been before. It was even said that, in the past, people, alone in the building, had heard voices and had wandered off and never been seen again. Certainly, sounds echoed strangely along all of the ways and even when all else was silent, a soft moaning filled the place. Sometimes it was like a wind from a distant and bleak land, while at others it had a living, chilling quality to it.

It was along one of the narrower passages that Pinnatte and Rinter found themselves walking, part of a long file of would-be spectators. Pitguards, or crudely-written signs directed them at the many junctions. As at the entrance, there was an aura of hasty organization about everything. All around was the ringing clatter of feet on the stone floor and the echoing sounds of many people speaking too loudly. Excitement was the predominant mood, generated by the unexpected staging of a Loose Pit, the opening of the balconies, and the appearance of new, liveried Pitguards. But too, some part of the clamour was perhaps for reassurance in the long twisting passageway, with its low, oppressive ceiling and the uneasy light from intermittently placed oil lamps adding an escort of milling shadows to the moving line.

Rinter and Pinnatte were not immune to the general mood, but they moved along in silence, bonded enough by the new experience to stay together, but not enough to share any gleeful anticipation. Eventually, after a sudden steep incline, they were walking up a curved stone stairway. It opened out on to a cloistered passageway that formed one of the higher balconies. Though it was wide, the outer wall curved noticeably inwards and was paralleled by the inner face of the parapet wall, giving the scene that greeted the two men an odd, canted appearance as they stared from left to right, uncertain which way to go. They had little time for deliberation however, as the press behind carried them forward.

There were many people already there but there was still plenty of space along the parapet wall for the incoming crowd and Pinnatte and Rinter did not walk too far before choosing a place to stand. Peering out over the arena, Rinter looked immediately downwards, searching curiously along the lower balconies opposite. Pinnatte however, found himself looking upwards, towards the ring of curved spikes that crowned the dome. For a giddying moment he felt that he was looking not up, but down on the scene and that the spikes were like the petals of a great flower that had opened to release a central, solitary bloom that now seemed to be sweeping up towards him. Though not afraid of heights, he tightened his grip on the edge of the parapet involuntarily, as if he might tumble into the dome. He smiled uneasily as he realized what he was doing and the unsettling sensation passed as his gaze moved from the dome along the tapering stem to the solitary crystal. He moved his head slightly as if that might improve his view and, catching a light from somewhere, the crystal flashed brilliantly. The light seemed to Pinnatte to pass into him, unhindered by his body, and fill him utterly, shining to the heart of what and who he was. It embodied all that was perfect and pure, and he was once again outside the building, staring up at the face carved into the keystone of the entrance arch, though this time, it was alive and radiant, and the entire crowd behind him was staring also, in reverence and awe.

'I never realized how big this place was.'

Rinter's voice, grating and sounding unnaturally harsh, cut brutally into the deep silence of Pinnatte's vision. Flooding in its wake came the babble of the gathering audience. Pinnatte grimaced and his hands were halfway to his ears before he remembered where he was. Rinter, however, was too engrossed in the scene below to notice the reaction. Pinnatte took a deep breath to calm himself and looked again at the crystal. It glittered as brightly as before in the comparative gloom, but its strange, penetrating presence was gone. Unexpectedly, he was possessed by a terrible rage that Rinter's mewling should have torn this wonder from him, and his mind was suddenly filled with a vision of the animal trainer flailing and screaming as he hurled him from the balcony into the arena below – a fitting sacrifice. But, just as suddenly, the mood was gone, leaving Pinnatte oddly empty and a little puzzled that such a violent image should cause him so little concern. He had been subjected to violence many times, and was not afraid to use it himself when he had no alternative, but it was always a regrettable necessity and certainly it was not his way to take vengeful delight in it. And yet the reason he had not attacked Rinter was not because of any moral scruple, but because the light from the crystal stayed his hand. It seemed to be reassuring him, telling him to remain calm: it was not lost, it was merely elsewhere; it had existed always, and would return to him. And it told him other things as well, just as had the carved face. It told him again of a future quite different to the one he would have thought was his but days ago. He took another deep breath. Just a reaction to all that's happened today, he thought. So many changes. It wasn't a very convincing explanation, but he'd think about it later. He forced himself to pick up the threads of Rinter's continuing remarks.

'There must be three times as many people here as normal, and there's space for as many again – look.' Rinter was almost having to shout to make himself heard above the clamour coming from every angle.

Pinnatte followed Rinter's pointing hand down across the lower balconies and the terraces around the arena. The man's estimate was probably right, he decided. There were far more there than he had ever seen before, and though the balconies were lined with people, they were far from crowded.

'Where've they all come from?' he asked. '*I* didn't know there was going to be a Loose Pit here tonight and I live quite near.'

Rinter turned to him questioningly. 'Never been to one before, eh?'

Pinnatte shook his head.

Rinter became avuncular. 'Loose Pit people are different from ordinary Pit watchers, Pinnatte. Richer, as you can see. More knowledgeable and discerning by far. Connoisseurs, you might say. And very well connected.' He gave a knowing nod with the last remark, then leaned close. 'For instance, when I was here earlier with my . . . colleague . . .' He frowned at the sudden memory of Atlon and Dvolci, and cast a quick glance across the hall as if he might suddenly see them. It did not halt the momentum of his new tale, however. 'When I was here earlier, they were closed because there was going to be something special tonight. But it wasn't this. Not a Loose Pit. There was no hint of it. They'd have told me right away – me being known here. Don't ask me why, but this has come about within the last few hours. But those people . . .' Without looking away from Pinnatte, he pointed over the parapet, towards the crowd on the terraces below '. . .Are connected. News of a Loose Pit gets to them quicker than if it was being taken by a galloper. I've seen it happen before. They come from all over.'

Pinnatte inclined his head and pursed his lips by way of acceptance of this information. After allowing for a little licence by the teller, the suddenness of it all seemed quite plausible. The entrances to the passageways they had come along had only been roughly cleared of rubbish and the lighting and signs they had met all bore the hallmarks of hasty preparation.

Then he wondered whether Lassner was amongst the crowd – whether his Den Master was one of the chosen many who supported these very special events. The thought brought a flicker of bitterness. If Lassner was there, it would doubtless be his,

Pinnatte's, money that the old fool was wasting with his inept wagering. And, presumably, wagers too would be much higher than normal tonight. Almost as though he had accidentally picked up a hot coal, he let the thought go quickly – it was an unnecessary burden. All he needed to think about Lassner now was how to get away from him without causing problems that were likely to pursue him into his new future. *Now* he was going to enjoy the experience of the first Loose Pit at the Jyolan, and *his* own first Loose Pit.

Enjoy.

This too puzzled him a little. Though he came to the Jyolan fairly frequently, he would not have described himself as a great follower of the sport. In fact, there were times when he found it unpleasant and distasteful, not least the behaviour of the crowd. It touched something in him that he rebelled against. He went there as much for something to do as for any other reason – usually it was not an expensive evening. Tonight, however, continuing the mood that had started to possess him as he had sat on the roof of Lassner's Den, he was actually beginning to feel excited. Perhaps it was the general mood, or just the strangeness of everything that was happening here. Perhaps it was the prospect of the yarns he would have to tell over the next few months. Then again, he thought more cynically, perhaps just parting with the extra money had induced in him the idea that what he was about to see must be worth paying a lot for.

Whatever it was, he was glad to be there.

'Any sign of your friend?' he asked.

Rinter's mouth twisted irritably. 'No. I doubt he's in here even if he's found the place. He didn't have much money and he still needed quite a bit of persuading. I might go back to The Wyndering tomorrow to see if he's still there. That rat thing was most impressive. I wouldn't like to lose it.' He shrugged regretfully. 'But I'm afraid he might be another lost opportunity now. I should never have let him wander off on his own. He was very . . .' He looked at Pinnatte while he searched for a word. 'Innocent,' he decided.

Pinnatte replied with an arch look that made Rinter chuckle craftily. He gave Pinnatte a friendly punch on the arm. 'Well, better

I show him the ways of the city than some unscrupulous individual who wouldn't have his best interests at heart.'

'Of course,' Pinnatte concurred with mock solemnity.

The two men laughed as they turned their attention back to the arena.

It was the first time that Pinnatte had really looked at the scene below since they arrived and he was immediately struck by the remarkable view of the arena. It was not as good a view as Pitside, of course, but it was much better than he had imagined it would be when the Pitguards had directed them up here. Rinter was not as impressed. 'I hope they're big, whatever's fighting tonight,' he said. 'It's going to be difficult to see any niceties from up here.' He leaned back from the wall and looked up and down the balcony. 'Have you seen any blues?'

'No,' Pinnatte replied. 'But there's plenty Pitside.' He pointed. 'And they're signalling up here. There must be some further round.'

The blues were the 'officials' who controlled the wagering at the Pits. Wagering between individuals was expressly forbidden, and though it was common, it was risky. Anyone caught doing it would routinely lose any money and valuables they had on them, by way of fines, and could well be given a beating to emphasize the point. Ostensibly the blues were independent of one another, officially appointed by the Prefect, but everyone knew that they were chosen for their peculiar mathematical skills and, like the Pitguards, were employed by the people who organized the Fights. They were called blues because of the bright blue neckerchiefs that they wore, bearing the insignia of the Prefect in silver thread at one corner. Although it was a characteristic of them that they were loud in proclaiming their honour and honesty, it was a commonplace that they worked together to ensure that the odds remained decidedly in their, and thus their employers', favour. Nevertheless, such judgements were invariably forgotten in the heat of a Fight and the blues were never short of customers. They communicated with one another above the din and confusion of the Pits by means of frantic elaborate hand signals involving great manual dexterity and many violent slashing and throat-cutting gestures. Several of them were standing around the Pit, signalling to others on the terraces and up to the balconies.

Rinter studied them for a while then pursed his lips and shook his head. 'Not for me tonight, I think,' he said. 'Minimum bet's too high.'

Despite himself, Pinnatte was impressed. 'You understand all that arm-waving?' he asked with a mimicking gesture.

'Enough,' Rinter replied. 'I've picked it up over the years.'

Before Pinnatte could pursue this intriguing discovery, a trumpet sounded. Four repeated notes echoed around the crowded hall and the audience fell silent.

Chapter 15

Another trumpet joined the first. Then another. The sounds cascaded over one another, filling the hall. Traditionally, fighting pits always opened with a fanfare of some kind. More often than not it would be a teeth-clenching affair of split notes and dissonances, though occasionally it could be martial and stirring. Pinnatte liked that – he responded to music, and a good fanfare thrilled him. So much so, that when he heard one he would walk back to the Den, whistling a tuneless and inadequate descant to its echoing memory softly under his breath.

But this was such as he had never heard before. It was not merely confidently and accurately played, it had a driving, rhythmic power that seemed to pick him up and shake him. At its climax, he felt as though he was being transported to another place, far above and beyond this shoddy hall with its degradation and its stench of bloodlust and greed. He was wide-eyed and gaping in amazement when eventually the sound faded, and he felt as if every hair on his body was standing on end. How could such magic exist in a place like this?

Then a biting pain shot through his right hand and, for a moment, suffused him horribly. It was as though his body was rebelling against his elation at the music and it brought him crashing back to normality. Somehow he managed to reduce an anguished cry to a sharply indrawn breath, but he could do no other than seize his hand and hold it tight against himself. The pain began to fade almost immediately.

'What's the matter?' Rinter asked.

'Nothing,' Pinnatte answered, grimacing. 'I hurt my hand earlier and just caught it on something.' Rinter nodded with casual sympathy and returned to watching the arena below. Unexpectedly, Pinnatte found that he was relieved at the other man's lack of concern. He did not want to show the stain on his hand to anyone: it was his, and his alone. Fleetingly it seemed to him that the pain and the music were associated in some way – as if the pain were indeed a punishment because the music had taken him somewhere he should not be. He did not dwell on the notion, for it made no sense.

Then the pain was gone completely. Slowly he released his hand, fearful about what he might see when he looked down. He edged back a little from Rinter and, manoeuvring himself into the light from a nearby lamp, nervously examined the back of his hand. To his relief he saw that nothing had changed. There was no sign of inflammation or swelling, still less anything that might have caused a violent and sudden reaction. Indeed, the stain seemed to be a little fainter. Very tentatively, he prodded it with his finger. It did not hurt. He prodded harder. Still there was no pain. Whatever had caused it, there was not even the slightest tenderness now.

A raucous cheering came up from the crowd, dissipating his lingering concern about his hand. Like the fanfare, the roar grew in intensity and, also like the fanfare, it seemed first to pass through him and then to carry him away. This time however, he was not so much lifted out of himself as possessed by the wild-eyed and ravening excitement that was filling the hall. For the first time, the characteristic stink of the arena reached him. It had a peculiarly vivid intensity, almost as though for an instant he had been given the heightened senses of an animal. It mingled with the smell and roar of the crowd, exciting him still further. He heard, or rather felt himself joining in the noise even before he was again looking over the parapet to see what it was for.

The cause lay in the floor of the high platform at the centre of the arena, where three curved and overlapping sections were slowly drawing back to reveal a growing circular opening. Pinnatte stiffened as the oval arena became a great eye, with the dark circle that formed its pupil widening as if at the joy of seeing him. As it stared up at him, his own eyes widened in response.

Then a faint bloody thread was worming in the depths of the darkness. Only slowly did he realize that he was watching someone emerge through the opening. The image of the eye lingered however, until the man stepped on to the platform.

He was a familiar figure, to be found in all the fighting pits, though Pinnatte was not used to seeing him from such an angle. He wore a bright red, broad-brimmed hat, and a long coat of the same colour decorated with an elaborate gold tracery. In his right hand he held a slender silver staff, half as tall again as himself. This was the Master of the Pit, ostensibly the supreme authority over all matters that occurred in the arena. His decisions were not to be disputed, however arbitrary they might seem, however enraged the crowd. He it was who signalled the beginning and the ending of each fight and who determined the winner when any doubt existed. He also enforced discipline in the arena, the merest touch of his staff causing animals to release even the most tenacious of grips and leap back in pain. More than once, Pinnatte had seen a similar fate meted out to irate owners who had so much forgotten themselves in the heat of the moment as to approach the central platform and argue with the Master.

Following this tall and dignified figure came two men dressed in tight black tunics and trousers. They too carried staffs though they were shorter than the Master's. These were the Judges of the Pit, though why, no one knew, for their opinions were neither sought by the Master nor offered to him. Their duties consisted of regaling the crowd with the breeding and fighting pedigrees of the various animals, with goading those that were reluctant to fight, and with dispatching any that were badly hurt.

Other figures entered the arena next through doors in the side of the central platform. They entered quietly and without ceremony. Carrying heavy staffs and long knives, they were known as the Clerks of the Pit. It was their task to implement any instructions from the Master and to help the Judges with the dispatching of animals – sometimes a difficult and dangerous duty – and to clean up the arena after each fight. Normally they were a motley, ragged group of individuals, but tonight even they wore liveries – pale brown in colour, not dissimilar to that of the arena floor. They were greeted with mock cheers and whistles which most of them managed to ignore.

The Master extended his arms with his palms upwards and turned round to encompass the entire crowd. The cheering became genuine and very loud, fading only as one of the Judges stepped forward to speak. Rinter and Pinnatte craned forward in anticipation of having difficulty in hearing a solitary voice from so far away. So did everyone else. It proved to be unnecessary however. When the man spoke, some quality in the construction of the hall carried his voice in such a way that it was as though he were standing only a few paces away from everyone there. A murmur of surprise rumbled through the hall, but he spoke through it. He had an ironic lilt to his voice.

'Welcome to you all, my friends. Welcome to the Jyolan Fighting Pits . . .'

'He's a new one,' Rinter said. 'And the Master, too.' Pinnatte nodded.

'Welcome to the *new and future* Jyolan Fighting Pits.' There was a cheer from parts of the crowd. 'Tonight is not what it was going to be. Even this morning, this night was not foreseen. But changes have come about and tonight's contests will show you things that will remain with you not only when you leave, but for the rest of your lives . . .'

'That won't be long at this rate. Get on with it,' someone shouted.

There was some laughter, and the Judge turned and levelled an open hand in the direction of the heckler. 'And we may decide to finish the evening by throwing some extra fresh meat to our magnificent winners.' This was greeted with a raucous cheer from those standing near the man and, satisfied, the Judge returned to his speech. 'Those of you who come here regularly, may doubtless be surprised at what you've found tonight.' He indicated the opened balconies.

'And at the prices,' came a cry. There were some angry voices raised in agreement with this.

The Judge gave an airy wave. 'Quality, ladies and gentlemen. Quality. If you want to see rabbits, rats and bad-tempered dogs nibbling at one another, there are plenty of other places to go to.' He became dismissive. 'Some, I've no doubt, would probably *pay*

184

you to go in and watch. But for what we have tonight, a grand re-opening, as it were, what you've paid is the merest trifle. You'll not regret the modest amounts we've asked from you – not ever. For you are the fortunate, the privileged few whom fate has chosen to be present at the very beginning of a future which will see the Jyolan Pits restored to a splendour and fame that will exceed even its past greatness, the few who'll be talking about tonight's events to their great-grandchildren.'

Despite the unusual nature of the Judge's preamble, sections of the crowd were becoming restless. The man faltered. Slowly, the Master of the Pits raised his staff vertically and brought the end down on to the platform with a crack which, like the Judge's voice, carried round the entire hall. Very few of the crowd did not start at the impact and the hubbub faded rapidly.

The Judge cast a hasty look over his shoulder at the Master who gave him a sharp nod to continue. He cleared his throat. 'My friends, we are providing you with this spectacle tonight, because the Jyolan – always one of the finest pits – now has patrons who rank amongst the city's wealthiest and most powerful.' He bent forward and put a finger to his lips. 'Patrons who, as is the way with people of discernment and delicate sensibility, prefer to give their support, discreetly and silently.'

'It's Barran, I'll wager,' Rinter nodded significantly to Pinnatte. He spoke softly, as if his voice might travel around the hall like the Judge's. 'I told you there'd been talk of it. And it'd take someone like him to see the potential in a place like this.' He rubbed his hands gleefully.

The mention of Barran brought Pinnatte fully back to his reason for being there that night. 'Have you ever met him?' he asked.

'Who?'

'Barran. Have you ever met him?'

Rinter paused for a moment then took on a proprietorial air. 'Well, with his business interests, he likes to keep himself to himself and there's not many get close to him, but I have met him – and spoken to him – and, of course, I know Fiarn from the old days. You've heard of Fiarn?'

Pinnatte looked at Rinter with considerably renewed interest.

185

He had accepted that this newly-found acquaintance might be a pit animal trainer – plenty of people claimed to be that just because they had a fierce dog which they occasionally entered in minor pits – but it seemed highly improbable that he would know people such as Barran or even Fiarn, not least because he was standing here in the cheapest part of the hall. Still, for some reason he had taken a liking to the man and he was loath to jeopardize their casual friendship by taxing him too closely on such matters. Nevertheless, first things first, he had a future to find for himself.

'Yes, I've heard of Fiarn,' he replied. 'Used to look after miners in the Thlosgaral, didn't he? Until he started working for Barran.'

The Judge below was beginning to describe the animals that would be fighting in the first contest. As was usual, the speech was full of flamboyant hyperbole and, also as usual, most of the crowd was scarcely listening.

Rinter chuckled knowingly. 'Oh yes, that's one way of putting it. Fiarn used to look after the miners all right.' He turned round and leaned back on the parapet wall. 'In fact, I worked for him for a while – looking after the miners.' His face darkened and took on an expression almost of regret after this boast. 'But it wasn't for me. Not my kind of work. Fiarn's a hard man – brutal when he wants to be. And I couldn't help but feel sorry for the miners – or their families, anyway. It's difficult to feel sorry for the miners themselves – they're a dismal, driven lot at the best of times.' His expression became reflective. 'People go into a world of their own after they've worked in the mines for a while. You can see it when you look into their eyes – they're not there really, though I wouldn't like to know where they are. And the Thlosgaral's a creepy place – downright frightening at times. You know it moves, don't you?' Pinnatte nodded vaguely. The Thlosgaral was not something that came up often in normal conversation, but he had heard tales about its constantly changing terrain. Rinter cast a glance back into the arena – the Judge was still talking. 'But yes, Fiarn "looked after the miners" until Barran made him a better offer.'

'What was that?'

Rinter chuckled again, then laughed openly. 'A typical Barran offer – work for me or die. Mind you, it was more than he offered the rest of Fiarn's gang.' Pinnatte raised an inquiring eyebrow. Rinter looked at him squarely, as if making a judgement, then he leaned forward and spoke softly. 'It almost makes you think there's someone keeping an eye on you, the way things work out, doesn't it?' His voice fell lower still. 'I'd left Fiarn only days before he and the others picked a fight with Barran and ended up . . .' He drew his finger across his throat. Abruptly, the humour went from his manner and real fear came into his eyes. He turned quickly back to the arena.

This time, Pinnatte was genuinely impressed. Whatever Rinter might be, there was no denying the sincerity of his last reaction. This man had actually met Fiarn, Barran's most trusted and feared lieutenant. He edged closer to him. 'You think Barran would've done the same to you?' he asked, almost whispering.

Rinter's cheeks puffed out and he searched the arena below as if anxious to be firmly back in the present again. 'No doubt about it,' he said. 'If I'd been there then, I wouldn't be here now. I can take care of myself better than most would think, to look at me, but being able to fight wouldn't have made much difference from what I've heard since. Fiarn's men thought they were fighters – and they were, after a fashion, but Barran's a real fighter – a mercenary who's fought in battles far away from here, and he took them just like *that*!' He snapped his fingers. 'Four men in as many heartbeats.'

The story excited Pinnatte. He could hardly help himself. 'Do you know Fiarn now?'

Rinter hesitated, torn between telling the truth and bolstering himself with a fanciful tale. The latter would have been his normal response, but this young man was oddly engaging. He had the look of a thief – probably a Den-Mate – but he seemed intelligent, and there was something about him . . .

Untypically, he opted for the truth. 'Not really,' he said. 'We parted friendly enough. He knew I wasn't much use for his kind of work – he only gave me the job because I was out of luck at the time and we'd known one another as kids. But we went our separate ways. I've seen him a few times since – had the odd drink and talk about old times – but I'd hardly claim to be a bosom friend.'

A roar from the crowd drew both men back to the arena. The Judge had finished his rambling introduction and, with his companion, was retreating to stand at the edge of the central platform. Two doors had opened in the outer walls of the arena, on opposite sides. As Pinnatte and Rinter began to watch again, the first contestants and their owners emerged from the doors. The two dogs were dark grey, squat-headed and bandy-legged, and both were straining at their leashes. The Master of the Pit looked down at each in turn then made a motion to one to move towards the other. This would determine the direction of movement of the first part of the bout. It was a long-established tradition which ensured that all sections of the Pitside crowd would be able to see some of the action at close hand.

'Can you take me to meet him?' Pinnatte could hardly believe the words he was speaking. What was he thinking about, making such a request of so casual an acquaintance? And what could he possibly say to a man like Fiarn, even if he did meet him? And say something he would have to, for to trifle with such a man . . .

He took a sharp hold of his thoughts as they careened recklessly into innumerable futures.

Rinter's head jolted round, but somehow Pinnatte managed not to flinch away from his shocked expression. Right or wrong, the words were out.

'Can you take me to meet him?' he asked again in the hope that attack would be his best defence.

Rinter did not speak for a moment, then he said both hoarsely and urgently, 'I . . . Watch the fight!'

Keeping his eyes fixed on him, Pinnatte nodded an acknowledgement, though with a slightly apologetic expression that indicated postponement of the question rather than abandonment. He leaned forward enthusiastically over the parapet wall. Rinter had not actually refused! Pinnatte had no idea what had prompted him to speak as he had, but he could sense that an important seed had been sown, and that it should be left to germinate for a while. And in what more favourable surroundings than these? Even allowing for the Judge's exaggeration, this was probably going to be an exciting evening, and Rinter would almost certainly be even more forthcoming at the end of it than now. Pinnatte felt very relaxed.

The two dogs were brought together, or rather kept apart, for they were both still leashed, and their owners were keeping them sufficiently far away from one another to ensure that no serious damage could be done too soon. Each time one of them charged it was yanked back before it could make contact with the other. This was a wilfully provocative procedure which was used to raise both the animals' fighting fury and the crowd's anticipation to an even higher pitch. Slowly the snarling protagonists were dragged around the arena, followed at a watching distance by the Clerks and, around the platform, by the Master with the two Judges, one on each side of him, all bending forward and studying the proceedings intently.

Rinter, apparently recovered from the shock of Pinnatte's abrupt question, was soon totally absorbed in the fight. He pulled a seeing glass from his pocket and peered through it. 'I thought I'd seen them before when they first came out,' he said. 'They're from the same litter. They're brothers. This should be a very interesting night indeed if they're starting with these two. They'd normally be brought on near the end. They really hate one another.' He cackled. 'I always say if you want a truly vicious fight, keep it in the family.' He handed the glass to Pinnatte, who placed it uncertainly to his eyes. Though he had observed others using seeing glasses before, he had never actually used one himself, and at first he could see nothing other than a disconcerting rainbow shimmer. He drew his head back, blinking.

'Move it backwards and forwards,' Rinter said, taking his hand and demonstrating. 'And turn this.'

Pinnatte did as he was told. Then, abruptly, he was looking at the two dogs as though he were standing at the Pitside. He gasped and jerked back from the vision, more than a little disorientated.

Rinter seized his arm. 'Careful!' he cried. 'That's a good glass. I don't think dropping it from this height would do it much good – not to mention whoever it landed on.' He seemed suddenly to be in remarkably good humour. He motioned Pinnatte to continue his watching.

Cautiously, his tongue protruding slightly, Pinnatte brought the glass to his face again, then he rested his elbows on the parapet to steady himself. The sight was incredible. On reflection he decided that even at Pitside it was unlikely he would have such a good view. For a moment, his old self reemerged. If he could steal some of these, he'd make a fortune selling them to the crowds that would be flooding here. He set the idea aside for future consideration and turned the glass from the dogs to the Pitside crowd. It did not take him long to appreciate the wealth that was gathered there – expensive clothes, lavish jewellery, bulging purses and, of course, bodyguards, both liveried and otherwise. He had to remind himself strongly of the consequences of succumbing to the temptations that immediately began tugging at him. It did not help that the first wagers were being taken and he could actually see large quantities of money changing hands as the blues scurried about in a frenzy of activity. Some of it was even the notarized linen money that was becoming popular amongst the city's wealthy.

He followed one individual for a little while then it became too much for him and he reluctantly handed the glass back to Rinter who replaced it in his pocket. Looking now at the crowd as a whole, Pinnatte could see that all the terraces were alive with dots of blue moving to and fro frantically gesticulating to one another. And so too was the balcony he was standing on, he realized, as he became aware of activity going on behind him. Apart from a reluctance to indulge in it from what he knew of Lassner's experience, wagering was in any event a mystery to Pinnatte and he had always had a little awe for these strange people who worked out and constantly changed odds and whose spoken language was only marginally less difficult to understand than their elaborate hand signalling.

Rinter was tapping his purse uncertainly.

'No,' Pinnatte said, with a determined shake of his head. 'Go with your first judgement. It's too expensive tonight. Why spoil a good evening by paying even more than you already have? I don't think the blues will miss your contribution tonight.'

'You're right,' Rinter said stoically, giving his purse a final slap and abandoning it. He seemed relieved that someone had made the decision for him.

When the dogs had made two circuits of the arena, they were pulled apart and the activity of the blues stopped almost completely. Then, at a signal from the Master, they began another circuit. This time, however, they were allowed longer leashes and it was not long before blood had been drawn from both of them, although great efforts were made by the owners to ensure that they did not actually come to grips. Despite this, one would occasionally succeed in seizing the other and then one of the Clerks would dash forward and insert something into the offender's mouth to prise it open. This was far from popular with the crowd, who loudly abused the owner for his carelessness – and his intelligence, appearance, parentage, and general manliness. Such incidents were always followed by another flurry in the wagering, as calculations were made about the effect the incident had had on each dog, and whether the Master would have deemed it to be an offence against the honoured rules of the sport should the ending prove to be inconclusive and his decision be required.

The greater part of the fight was occupied thus, with the dogs being separated after each circuit. This was supposed to be for the Master to examine them and determine their fitness to continue, but in fact it was for the owners, who could choose to withdraw their animals if the fight was not proceeding as they wished – this often being determined by any wagers they had placed.

Then the Master gave the signal that the dogs were now prepared for the final stage of the fight. By an odd coincidence this decision was almost invariably reached at the same time as most of the betting had stopped, and when the crowd had reached a level of excitement from which it could only fall away.

The two dogs were released. Foaming and blood-spattered, they crashed into one another.

Rinter was laughing. 'Those two must have given their mother a rare belly-ache when she was carrying them. Look at them. They're almost human the way they go at one another.'

Pinnatte barely noted the remark, however; he was completely engrossed in the fate of the struggling animals as they began rolling around the dusty arena in a confusion of flailing legs and clashing jaws. The Clerks stepped in to goad them on whenever they stopped and just stood panting and staring at one another. Though he could no longer distinguish one from the other, Pinnatte suddenly wanted one of them to win, and to win outright, tearing the throat out of the other and leaving it to gasp its last to the roar of the crowd. It was not all that common a conclusion, happening, when it did, usually to animals that were nearing the end of their usefulness. Nevertheless, he wanted it. He was sweating. Though he had often been to the pits before, he had never had so powerful, so visceral a response. It seemed to possess him utterly. And yet a part of him was still and silent – watching – watching him coldly from some strange eyrie, far away, in another place. He could feel himself as part of the crowd, his body shaking to its will as he screamed at the betrayed animals. He could hear his voice as part of the awful howling chorus, and at the same time he could see his own tiny figure, distant and preposterous, bouncing up and down on the crowded balcony. One shimmering mote against thousands.

Abruptly, it was over, the Master deftly using his staff to separate the two animals and declaring one of them the winner. It was a nicely timed moment, provoking an equal mixture of abuse and cheers from the crowd. Pinnatte was venting the former and, for a moment, as he slid giddily back down to normality, he wanted one of the owners to dispute the decision and receive the Master's staff for his temerity. But all was orderly and mundane: the owners reined in their dogs, by now exhausted as well as injured, and left the arena quietly; the Clerks began cleaning up the mess that had been made; the Master and the Judges conferred on some matter, and the crowd settled back into a state of noisy expectancy. Spasmodic cheering accompanied the movement of the blues through the crowd as wagers were settled. Rinter had taken out his seeing glass and was watching them with interest. 'Smiling as ever, when they've got their backs to the crowd,' he said sourly. 'It's a good thing you reminded me not to bet, or I'd have been the cause of some of that now if I had.' He pocketed the glass. 'I gather you enjoyed yourself,' he said with a laugh. 'Mind you, I got quite involved, too. That Master certainly knows his job. Couldn't have finished that fight better myself. I wonder where they got him from?'

Pinnatte certainly could not affect a cool indifference to the conflict as the memory of his behaviour returned. He was both elated and disgusted. Unconsciously he rubbed the back of his hand. The whole experience had been something the like of which he had never known before. Would it happen again in the next fight? he wondered. Did he want it to? He had no clear answer. 'It was exciting,' he conceded awkwardly, leaning over the parapet as if fearful of what Rinter might read in his face.

The scene below was unchanged. The blues had settled back into comparative stillness, and were hovering at strategic positions, ready for the next frenzied burst of effort. The Clerks had finished tidying the arena, and the Judges were standing as if waiting for an instruction from somewhere. It was the usual, too-long pause between fights. The Master was turning round slowly, looking at the crowd, and the general hubbub ebbed and flowed.

Playing with us, Pinnatte realized. The thought burst into his mind with extraordinary vividness. It was as if he should have known it all his life. That was the Master's job – not simply the controlling and adjudicating of the fights, but the sensing of the will of the crowd and, by his control of the rhythms of the fights, the manipulating of it.

To what end?

To the profit of those who employed him, of course – those who owned the Pits.

It was obvious. Why had he never seen it before? Why had he not noticed this subtle, vital underplay in the great game of wringing money out of people?

Briefly he felt the distant detachment he had experienced at the heart of the fight. It didn't matter that he hadn't noticed it before. He noticed it now, and it intrigued him. He had been right to search out a new future for himself, and he had been right to come here as the first step – finding himself at the first Loose Pit at the Jyolan! And meeting Rinter, who knew Fiarn! As Rinter himself had said, it was almost as if someone were looking after him – manipulating his destiny the way the Master was manipulating the crowd. And more would happen tonight, he knew.

He could feel it.

He rubbed the back of his hand.

Below, a hooded figure at the Pitside turned and looked up at him.

Chapter 16

Barran dropped down heavily into a chair and, leaning back, looked at the elaborate array of angled and irregular-shaped mirrors lining the wall in front of him. By each one was a decorated circular grille. He had been there for some time, but still he could barely believe what he was seeing. It was the culmination of an incredible day.

Even without this room, the whole of the Jyolan building was amazing! How could the Kyrosdyn have owned it for so long and done so little with it? When he had been merely a casual Pitside spectator he had seen the potential of the place, with its remarkable arena and enormous, largely unused audience space. Later, as his interest had grown, he had done careful calculations to assess its real worth. But, as today had passed, these calculations had been set at naught and his estimate of the value of the place had grown considerably. And the discovery of this room had set even his new evaluation at naught.

The Kyrosdyn's neglect of the Jyolan puzzled him, but their failure to use this room defied him utterly. It needed no sophisticated thinker to see its value in the scheming world of Arash-Felloren's incessant power struggles, yet the lock had been rusted almost solid and, when it was finally freed, the door had opened into a room that was thick with dust. No one had been in it for years.

He leaned back again and smiled broadly. It was a sight few had ever seen. So much had come to fruition so quickly. Even now he found it difficult to grasp all that had happened in one day. It was as though a boulder blocking a choked river had just been torn free and he was being swept along on an uncontrollable torrent that would carry him from high and spartan mountains plains down into lush and fertile valleys.

For months he had been quietly pushing at the owners of the Jyolan – or those he thought to be owners – and there had been no response. Nothing but evasiveness and indifference. It was a perfect reflection of the way the place was run, but it made no sense. As a business it was obviously bumping along, barely making a profit, and slowly, but quite perceptibly, deteriorating in every way. He had offered them all manner of different deals, from various forms of silent partnership to outright purchase. He would put money into the place, get a decent Master, some better animals, smarten the place up. He had threatened and cajoled, gently and reasonably persuaded – but all to no avail. He had been on the verge of resorting to direct violence when, during one of their routine meetings to discuss the crystal trade, Rostan had made a casual remark about the one-sided negotiations. It was unusual, because Rostan did not make casual remarks – especially when discussing business. Barran, as was his way, had confined news of his interest in the Jyolan to only his immediate officers, so Rostan's comment had been to tell him that the Kyrosdyn were involved and were interested in his proposals. This having been declared, albeit covertly, Barran knew that the negotiations should continue.

He was both impressed and concerned by Rostan's timing – the Highest must have been watching developments keenly, but was he, Barran, becoming so predictable? It was a salutary reminder that although he had a long and relatively stable relationship with the Kyrosdyn, he should never take them for granted. He did not remotely understand what drove them but he knew that their power was far greater than they allowed generally to be known, and their commitment to their own self-interest was total. All were pawns in Arash-Felloren.

The peculiar reticence of the Jyolan's apparent owners now made sense. The Kyrosdyn were obsessive in all things, rarely doing anything openly or directly. Barran knew then that his pursuit of Jyolan would go the way of all his negotiations with them – it would be convoluted and slow. He had learned to deal with that through the years, and he immediately abandoned his intention for more direct action. Nothing would be gained from it, and much could be lost. The Kyrosdyn would deal with him, either directly or indirectly, when they were ready and not before. All he had to do was persist with his approaches and ensure that he assessed their financial need accurately when they finally succumbed – and, for all he did not understand their motivation, he was good at that now, his normally taciturn exterior disguising an obsessive deviousness of his own.

Why they should be interested in having him involved with the Jyolan was a question that he knew was not worth pursuing. Perhaps they wanted to keep close to him because of his increasing control over the mining and distribution of the crystals. Perhaps it was for some completely different reason. Still, it did not matter – it was sufficient that both parties now knew where they stood. All that would be needed now was patience and watchfulness.

He had thus been more than surprised at the startling suddenness of the Kyrosdyn's actions today. It was unprecedented and, even now, he wondered what vital signals he had missed in all the confusion.

There had been the summons to attend on Imorren. That was a fairly rare event in itself, but being marked 'urgent' made it unique. There was, of course, no indication of what she wanted to discuss, but he had gone to the Vaskyros immediately and without questioning the messenger. He had met Imorren several times in the past. In the early days she had tried to oppose him as he had begun taking control of the distribution of the crystals, but she had been too late. By then, having carefully studied the demand for the strange rocks, he had quietly dealt with almost all the disparate groups who dominated the miners, and replaced them with his own men. He had allowed a few to remain and operate, on the grounds that should he gain absolute control, his various enemies would almost certainly unite against him. As it was, there were sufficient crystals being traded outside his control to keep them all divided.

Since his first meeting with Imorren, when he had shown her the benefits of stability in the crystal trade, he had had no serious problem with the Kyrosdyn; each had an interest in ensuring the well-being of the other, and though never overtly stated, this was clearly understood. Nevertheless, Imorren disturbed him. Over the years, he had seen no change in her physically – no subtle hardening lines in the face, no filling out of her form. And she had always looked far younger than the age that her known history in the city indicated. But more than that, he had always found her unsettling to be with. For a long time he wondered why he felt no attraction to her. She was undeniably beautiful but, whenever he was with her, a coldness rose up inside him to forbid all thoughts of desire. Was it something in those searching grey eyes? Or that fine, too-symmetrical face? Or that serpentine quality in her movement? He had never found the reason, and he had long given up searching for it. Perhaps it was no more than his natural instinct for survival. To be in any way emotionally attached to Imorren would have soon seen him under her sway, and turned from a near equal into a mere vassal. He would not have won the wealth and power he had today. Indeed, he could have been dead.

Still, it was curious. And insofar as he could pretend to understand her – the most impenetrable of the Kyrosdyn – he sensed too that she was as puzzled as he by this strange distance between them.

Meeting her today however, he knew that he had the advantage in whatever bargain was to be struck – and there *was* a bargain to be struck or she would not have contacted him in such a manner. As she entered the room, he could feel her agitation, even though her appearance was as calm as ever. He stood up and paused deliberately, looking squarely at her.

'You asked to see me, Ailad.'

'You wish to acquire the Jyolan?'

Sitting staring at the mirrors, Barran congratulated himself again that he had managed to avoid any reaction to this brusque question. Such directness he had never known from any Kyrosdyn, not even from the novices whom he occasionally met in his day-to-day dealings with them.

Having taken this first assault without responding, he had been tempted to make an evasive reply to see how much further Imorren's directness might go. But a wiser part of him reminded him who and what she was, and that if she was being so blunt, she was telling him that she had a genuinely urgent need and if he did not fulfil it, and fulfil it now, someone would be found who would. He knew well enough that his worth to the Kyrosdyn was a matter of balance. If, for example, they considered anarchy in the crystal trade to be to their advantage, they would not hesitate to have him assassinated. Thus he must accept her message and reciprocate.

'Yes,' he said simply.

There was no hesitation in what followed.

'It is yours for . . .' She quoted a price that was almost exactly what he had hoped to pay in the end. Again he wondered how predictable he was becoming. 'But . . .'

The word pinioned the elation that was starting to well up in him.

'You must open it tonight – fully, and with a Loose Pit. We shall provide you with suitable animals for the closing contest.'

Looking back, he felt a twinge of regret for his slight faltering at this point. He should have just bowed and left. As it was, he fumbled into details: 'I shall need the full co-operation of the present staff,' and it was she who bowed and left, answering the request with a curt nod – and was that a hint of irritation, or triumph? Details were for other, lesser fry to deal with.

He had lost that part of the confrontation certainly, but he had no serious regrets. It had been a well-laid ambush and he had handled himself quite well, all things considered. Years of secrecy and deviousness on the part of the Kyrosdyn had made him ignore the possibility that one day they would resort to directness. He shook his head and smiled to himself again. There was always something to be learned – or, more correctly – to be re-learned. Whatever Imorren had gained from their bargain, he may or may not discover in due course; it was of no great concern. All that mattered now was that *he* had the Jyolan, and for the price that he wanted.

Not that the sealing of the bargain had been easy. Imorren's demand for a Loose Pit in a matter of hours had been a taxing one, and Barran's current euphoria was tempered by physical fatigue as a consequence. Tentative plans, made in anticipation of the ultimate acquisition of the Jyolan were dragged out, ruthlessly pruned, and implemented with unprecedented vigour, Barran himself at his finest, coaxing and menacing alternately, as each problem required.

The least of these had been announcing that a Loose Pit was to be held. As Rinter had told Pinnatte, news somehow seemed to travel amongst the followers of the Loose Pits faster than it could be carried by a good horseman, and so it had proved. More problematic had been the gathering of decent animals. Here, the senior Kyrosdyn Brother who had appeared from nowhere to give him a bunch of keys and, 'to be of service, friend Barran', had proved to be invaluable. His actions had confirmed finally to Barran the truth of the long-established rumour about the Kyrosdyn's considerable interest in the fighting animals themselves. He was also heartened by the man's arrival because it clearly indicated Imorren's desire for his success in the venture. However, the thought of the Ailad's directness after so many years of intricate deviousness, buzzed about him all day like an unseen and irritating insect, though he dared not take the time to pause and think about it.

The most difficult problems had arisen from the neglected condition of the building and the revelation of its confusing and complex layout. Even now, Barran was not entirely certain that everyone had returned from the crowds that he sent in to move years of accumulated rubbish, and to hang lamps and mark the ways to the various balconies. And, despite Imorren's tacit agreement about co-operation, the existing staff had been precious little use. Sluggish and dilatory by dint of years of practice, they did not fully grasp Barran's sense of urgency until he sent two of them sprawling. Even then they added little but confusion, seeming to know almost nothing about the building other than what lay on the ground floor and basement where the animals were held before fighting.

Only one was of any real value – a frail, wizened individual who remembered 'the place, like it used to be. Long before *they* came, with their frosty ways.' He it was who guided Barran's men through the maze of passages to the different balconies, though, to his initial alarm but subsequent delight, they had to carry him much of the way.

When they returned him from this tour of the building he refused the handsome sum that Barran offered him with an airy wave. There was a sparkle in his eye that Barran hoped would be in his when he reached that age.

'Put it away. Put it away,' the old man said excitedly. 'I should be paying *you*. Waited years for this. Seen the place going down – tragic.' He cast a significant glance at the back of the Kyrosdyn, talking to someone nearby, and, laying a confidential hand on Barran's arm, beckoned him to bend down. 'There's other places here that *you* need to know about,' he whispered, giving a massive wink and touching a finger to his lips. 'One, very special.'

'Show me,' Barran said quietly.

The old man had led him along more twisting, winding tunnels, showing him lines of small rooms that, to Barran, could have been private quarters, and a series of larger rooms which might once have been dormitories.

'What are these?' he asked, as they came to one of them.

The old man shrugged. 'I've seen them used as store rooms, junk rooms, meeting halls, quarters for special guests, all sorts of things, but what they were originally, I've no idea.' The admission of ignorance seemed to offend him and his manner became defensive. ''Course, no one knows what this place was built *for* – or even *when*.' He lowered his voice. 'But it's a queer place, you know. There's some say these tunnels actually move.' He put his hand into one of the circular openings in the wall. 'Especially these small ones.' He removed his hand and wiped it on his trousers. 'Can't say I believe it myself, but I've seen and heard more than a few things here over the years that didn't make any sense, so . . .' He left the sentence unfinished and looked up at the arching ceiling. 'And I've always had the feeling that the place is bigger inside than outside.'

'It's just confusing,' Barran said, becoming a little impatient at what he took to be the old man's ramblings. 'I don't think there's a straight line in the place. It's difficult to keep your sense of direction.'

But the old man was not listening. He was wandering off along the hall, motioning Barran to follow. As they neared the door at the far end, the Kyrosdyn came through it. He gave a display to indicate that he had been looking for Barran for some time and, ignoring the old man, walked fussily up to him and took his arm to direct him back the way he had come. 'I think you should look at the large cats that have just arrived. I'm not sure . . .' He staggered slightly as Barran did not respond to the pressure on his arm.

'In a moment,' Barran said, catching a plea in the old man's face.

'But—'

'In a moment,' Barran said sharply, with a look that forbade any further debate.

There was a brief flash of anger in the Kyrosdyn's eyes, but he turned away quickly and gave a sulky shrug.

Then they had come to the room he was now sitting in. As they neared it, the Kyrosdyn became increasingly agitated. 'I'll look at the animals shortly,' Barran told him, though more by way of a goad than a reassurance, sensing that this was not the cause of the man's concern.

At the door the Kyrosdyn had stepped forward and, taking the keys from Barran, had selected one and inserted it in the lock. His manner was one of strained helpfulness and, to Barran, seemed to be covering something approaching desperation. This continued as he made a half-hearted attempt at turning the key before he yanked it out, announcing, 'It won't move. It's probably broken, or rusted.' He turned to walk away, adding off-handedly, 'Besides, this room was never used.'

Intrigued by the man's anxiety, Barran laid a gently restraining hand on his shoulder. 'I'll have someone work on the lock. It won't take a moment. Some of my men are very good at that kind of thing.' He became hearty. 'Failing that, we'll break in.'

Though the Kyrosdyn said nothing further, Barran could feel his nervousness. He took some delight in it. He traded with these people, but he had never liked them. They were a cold, twitchy lot, and to see one struggling to conceal ordinary human emotions appealed to him.

'They never liked this place,' the old man whispered to him as his men were working on the door. 'It scares them. Don't know what it is, but when they first came here, they took one look at it, then sealed it, and never came near it again.' Barran nodded.

When the door finally creaked open, the old man grabbed a lamp from one of the men and with a command, 'You lot wait here,' stepped inside, drawing Barran after him. At first, the room seemed no different from many others he had been shown, though along one wall was a decorated timber panel. Before he could speak, the old man took hold of the edge of the panel and heaved on it. Barran watched for a moment, then helped him. The panel slid reluctantly to one side.

The old man stepped back and held the lamp high. For a moment, the wall looked like the many-faceted eye of a huge insect as the edges of row upon row of dusty mirrors – or what appeared to be mirrors – sparkled in the lamplight. The Kyrosdyn, who had followed them, hissed audibly and stepped back quickly into the doorway. Placing the door between himself and the mirrors, he lifted a hand to the collar of his robe and pressed, almost as though he were testing his pulse.

Then, looking constantly over his shoulder at the door, the old man was softly explaining something to Barran. There was a grille by each mirror. The old man clicked his fingers and demanded, 'Keys, keys!' of his increasingly wide-eyed companion. Barran hurriedly retrieved them from the Kyrosdyn and watched in continuing amazement as the old man showed him how the grilles worked. He moved very close to Barran. 'I might be old, but I'm not stupid. I know what a man like you can do with a place like this.' He became almost inaudible as he directed a scornful finger towards the figure hovering behind the door. 'Me, you and them. We're the only ones who know about this place. They won't say anything. Look at him – I told you, the place scares them witless. *I* won't say anything – I'm just glad the Jyolan's in good hands again . . .'

'I won't be saying anything either,' Barran said, anticipating the advice he was about to be given. His mind was reeling with the impact of what he had just seen and heard. Opportunities upon

203

opportunities were unfurling one within another in a great confusion. But the background to this ferment was simple and clear – *this room must be his and his alone.* 'And I won't forget who showed it to me.'

The remark was wilfully ambiguous, for even as he was speaking he was considering having the old man and those who had opened the door killed. The thought was a natural one for him, but he did not consider it for long. Killing the men would cause far more problems than it solved, and who could say what else this old man knew about the Jyolan? He placed a defending arm about the frail shoulders and drew him close. 'I'm in your debt,' he said. 'What do you want?'

As he had refused money earlier, so the old man gave a dismissive wave. 'I told you, I'm just happy to see the place waking up again. And now you've got it, you'll really look after the Jyolan, won't you?'

Barran looked at him doubtfully. 'You want nothing?'

'Well, a good place, Pitside, regular, would be nice,' the old man conceded.

'It's done.'

The old man beamed.

'And come to me if you find you want anything else.'

The pressures of organizing the Loose Pit had obliged Barran to leave the room after this declaration, though he had found it far from easy. It was not until much later that he had been able to return and reflect on what he had been shown.

He looked at the array in front of him, tapping his lips with the key that the old man had given him. Leaning forward, he inserted the key into a hole in one of the grilles, and turned it. It was very stiff, but eventually it moved and voices began to float into the room. They were echoing and strange, but they were clear enough. He listened for a moment, then closed the grille, and his normally immobile face was briefly split by a smile which was full of both childlike wonder and cunning anticipation.

On each of the mirrors could be seen not a reflection of himself, but some part of the Jyolan Pits. And from the grilles could be heard the sounds from that same place. He sat back and took in the scene as though he were an emperor viewing his domain from a mountain top. Some of the mirrors were still and dark, others were alive with activity. But from here he knew that he would be able to watch and listen to almost everything that happened in the Jyolan in complete secrecy. He could ensure that the Master and the Judges were doing as they had been instructed, note the trends in the wagering, see who was there with whom, who was there with someone they shouldn't be with, *and what they were talking about* – all the fragments of information that would be so important to him in his expanding business. His early career as a mercenary had taught him the importance of good intelligence not only in fighting, but in making deals, and he had put that knowledge to considerable effect since coming to the city.

He had heard that there were supposed to be devices in some of the older buildings which enabled scenes to be viewed and overheard from a distance and in complete secrecy. Arash-Felloren, however, was full of such nonsensical tales, and he rarely gave any of them credence. The people here were greatly given to exaggeration about the wonders of their precious city and, in his experience, it gave them at times a gullibility remarkably at odds with their normally sharp and shrewd nature. It was no great surprise to him that they would find it easier to accept that some of the major political changes which had swept the city through its long history were due to these fantastical mirror and echo ways rather than the patient treachery and convoluted cunning of their own kind. But here were those self-same devices, just as the gossips and tale-tellers had always declared.

Briefly he wondered how many other of the city's wild tales might prove to be true – precious few, he trusted, since some of them were extremely alarming. Though the thought was almost immediately swept aside by the many other matters vying for his attention, it twisted a tiny cold knot of fear deep in the pit of his stomach before it left. There were so many strange things in this city! Even this chilling acknowledgement could not survive long in the heat of Barran's elation, however. Not now that this incredible room was all *his*!

But he must clean the place up. The mirrors were covered with a film of dust. He reached out and made to wipe one of them with his sleeve. To his horror it quivered then moved, and the view it was reflecting blurred and vanished. He snatched his hand away fearfully and, for an instant, saw his new future crumble in the wake of his careless destruction of this incredible acquisition. But the mirror slowly sighed back to its original position. He let out the painful breath he had been holding and pressed his hands together to stop them shaking. Then, very carefully, he took the surprisingly thick edge of the mirror between his thumb and forefinger and supported it while gently cleaning it with a kerchief. It misted as his breath touched it and the image faltered slightly, revealing a faint reflection of his anxious face, but it steadied almost as soon as he released it.

He made a note that one day he would have to find out how these things worked. He was never comfortable with things whose workings he did not understand, particularly if he was relying on them for anything important. Once he had been given charge of an elaborate siege engine and, full of youthful pride and believing the claims of the inventor, had made wild claims about its value in a forthcoming assault. 'What'll you do when the string breaks?' an old sapper had sneered to general amusement at the height of one such peroration. Stung, he had sneered back, and in the subsequent mêlée had killed the sapper. Subsequently, the machine proved to be not only useless, but dangerous to its operators, and the mocking comment had returned to bite deep into him. Like a barbed arrow, it had stayed with him ever since. He rarely relied on anyone absolutely. Even now he always carried several knives and, though he had had little cause to carry a bow for many years, he still had two spare bow strings secreted in different pockets.

Yet, unusually, he could think of no one to whom he might turn with such a problem, save perhaps the old man, though he suspected that he knew only that the Ways were there and what they did. Indeed, he suspected that the strange irregular mirrors and their grilles were perhaps beyond anything that the craftsmen of today's city could even aspire to. His doubts broadened into certainty. There would be no one. He could not even think of anyone who could construct the building, with its innumerable twisting tunnels and passages and alarming balconies. And if there were someone who understood the mirrors, there was the problem of secrecy . . . Whoever learned of this device would have valuable information – too valuable. Grim amusement bubbled up within him. That was probably the very reason why no one knew how to make such devices now!

He set the problem aside with all the others that the day had brought. It was not important at the moment. He could clean the mirrors himself, and it was encouraging that, even though they had probably not been used for many years, they seemed to work perfectly.

He relaxed and once again admired his new dominion. Several of the mirrors showed the arena from different angles. After a little searching, and more careful cleaning, he found the old man, incongruous amid the conspicuous wealth that stood around him, but smiling happily. Barran chuckled as he saw an attractive young woman engaging him in conversation. Probably thinks he's a rich eccentric, he thought. He had a suspicion that the old man was not as frail as he made out and that he was going to get more than a good Pitside place for his efforts. Barran reached out to open the grille by the mirror, then changed his mind.

He turned to the other mirrors showing the Pitside. Even though he knew that he was both too excited and too tired to make rational plans, he could not stop himself from speculating and scheming as he looked at the wealth and power that was gathered around *his* arena. He let the ideas come and go for a while, though he deliberately avoided dwelling on any of them. Then, reluctantly, he drew the timber panel over the mirrors and left the room, carefully locking the door and placing the key in a safe pocket.

As he walked along the dimly lit passages his physical fatigue began to take its toll and his thoughts reverted to more immediate concerns. Not least was the matter of why the Kyrosdyn had suddenly decided to sell. Why had they not used the place to its full? Surely they must know what they had given him! They must want him to become even richer and more powerful than he already was. But why?

207

He stopped and straightened up, and made an attempt to dismiss these unanswerable questions once and for all. Just get through this day successfully – go and check the animals in the basement – go and check the takings. As he paused, the sound of cheering from the arena floated along the passageway. As it passed, it left a lingering echo like a low moan. It was like the sound that could sometimes be heard in the Thlosgaral, and the old memory made Barran shiver. He looked around at the many dark orifices pocking the walls and the ceiling and even the floor. They looked like so many eyes.

Could it be that someone, somewhere, was watching and listening to *him*?

Chapter 17

Pinnatte pointed. 'Who are they, down there? And why've they all got their hoods forward?'

Rinter followed Pinnatte's hand then peered through his seeing glass. 'I've no idea,' he said after a moment. 'They're rich, though. Look at their clothes – simple, but very expensive if I'm any judge. I doubt they even noticed tonight's Pitside prices. As for keeping their faces hidden . . .' He shrugged. 'Some of these rich folk are a bit odd, that's all. They don't like their friends knowing that they come to the Pits, especially the Loose Pits – mixing with the common herd and all that. It's not all that unusual. Why?'

'That one there – the woman in the centre – she looked straight at me, just then.'

Rinter laughed lecherously and nudged him with his elbow. 'Heard that some of these young ladies get worked up in more ways than one when they're watching a good fight, have you? Fancying your chances?'

Pinnatte was flustered. 'Why not?' he stammered, eventually managing to muster some indignation at the implied slur on his manliness in Rinter's tone. It passed Rinter by.

'Well, for two reasons,' the older man said. 'First, it's unlikely she was looking at you at this distance. She could just as well have been looking at me.' He laughed again. 'And second, how do you think you're going to find her in this crowd? Not to mention the fact that she might have her hood forward for a good reason.'

'What do you mean?'

'She could be ugly as sin – or three times your age.' Rinter's face became suddenly thoughtful. 'Mind you, that's no—'

A cheer from the crowd ended Rinter's exposition. One of the

Judges had stepped forward and raised his staff to announce the next fight.

'Give me your seeing glass,' Pinnatte said. Rinter handed it over with a leer. Pinnatte focused on the figure that had looked up at him. The robe she was wearing was indeed simple, but even he could tell that it was expensive. Though he could see nothing of the wearer, he felt drawn to her. It was no ugly old woman, he knew. As if acknowledging his observation, the woman inclined her head slightly. The movement cut through him, and she seemed to be so close that he wanted to reach out and touch her. The Judge's voice and the noise of the crowd faded to a distant, background rumbling.

Then she moved forward suddenly, slipping from his view, and Rinter was shaking his arm. 'Come on. Wake up. You don't want to miss this.'

'This' was the entry into the arena of a large dog and an equally large cat, black and muscular. Both had two leash-holders who were wearing thick gauntlets and leggings and who were already finding their task an ordeal as the two animals strained to reach one another. A third man accompanied each animal, carrying a staff with two prongs at one end and a loop at the other. These individuals pranced and strutted about the arena, swinging and waving their staffs in an elaborate and acrobatic drill as if it was they who were there to entertain the crowd. Their true function became apparent almost immediately however, as the cat suddenly twisted round and lashed out at one of the leashmen. A loop closed deftly about its neck and dragged it to one side before it could pursue its attack. There was some applause from the crowd.

Rinter was slapping his purse. 'The dog doesn't stand a chance,' he said, bouncing up and down. 'Look at that cat. It'll open it up with one blow as soon as they close.'

'What are the blues saying?' Pinnatte asked, pointing to the flurry of arm-waving breaking out on the terraces, the object of his desire having been forgotten for the moment.

'The same,' Rinter said after a brief study through his seeing glass. 'I should bet now before the odds drop.' He screwed his face up in indecision. Pinnatte was reminded of the times when he had discreetly watched Lassner debating about a wager. It had given him an insight into wagering which was subsequently confirmed by observation. No one beat the blues! He also felt a distaste, he realized. What was important here was the quality of the fighting, not this sordid scrabbling for money.

'Don't do it,' he said calmly. Rinter looked at him sharply, surprised by the authority in his voice. 'Don't do it,' Pinnatte repeated. Then he smiled. 'Enjoy the evening, remember? Save your money until you've found your man with the rat. The cat looks strong, but . . .' He ended the sentence with a shrug. Rinter, not altogether happily, took his advice.

For the first three or four circuits he seemed to be regretting it as the dog cowered away from the cat's angry, spitting attacks. But as the leashes were let out, the dog began to show an unexpected fleetness of foot and an ability to move in very quickly, wreak damage with a tearing bite, and retreat. It was not always quick enough though, and in the end, both animals being seriously hurt, the Master declared no winner. It was not a popular decision either with the crowd or the cat's owner, who strode forward, waving a clenched fist at the red figure. The Master looked at him coldly, but made no reply other than partly to lower his staff. The owner sobered abruptly and with an apologetic bow, retreated.

'Well, at least the blues seemed to appreciate that decision,' Pinnatte said.

Rinter nodded knowingly. 'Indeed,' he said. 'I'm glad we met. That's twice you've saved me money.'

Pinnatte gave a disclaiming shrug. He was beginning to feel strange. He had never had any great love for the Pits, but now he was finding himself utterly engrossed. In future – in his new future – he would come here much more, and find the money somehow to buy a place at the Pitside where he could watch events more closely. Even from high above the arena he could feel the animal ferocity of the conflicts as never before. He searched for a word.

Purity.

That was it.

There was a purity about the hatred that the animals expressed. A perfection. A totality of focus that, to Pinnatte, neither he nor

211

any other human could begin to possess. No doubts, no vagueness, no troublesome distractions of conscience or fear of hurt. He looked up at the solitary crystal seemingly floating in the thickening air like a distant, watching star – it was another glittering perfection.

This place must have been a temple once. A holy place. The thought flooded through him like a revelation and he could do nothing but stand motionless, scarcely daring to breathe for fear that the moment might just as quickly vanish.

As it was, the feeling faded gradually, but the memory of it remained with him for the rest of the evening as a parade of animals in various combinations were brought to the arena to fight one another. Sometimes they had to be goaded, sometimes they had to be restrained, but in every case, under the watchful tutelage of their caring owners and the Clerks, there was an inexorable climax, savage and rending, which left blood and sometimes entrails splattered across the dusty floor.

Pinnatte shouted and cheered with the rest of the crowd but, increasingly, only because he felt the need to keep hidden his true, inner responses – his growing empathy with the fighting animals. He seemed to feel each move they made, to taste as they did, scent the air as they did, feel his muscles and sinews quicken and dart as theirs did. And both the ecstasy of victory and the terror of defeat became one to him, as though they were merely different aspects of a common need which now he had the insight to understand. But even as he revelled in this vision, some part of him knew that the clarity which he now had was like that found in a dream and that, when all was over, he would have no words for it – just a lingering desire.

Several times as the evening passed, the hooded figure at the Pitside turned and looked up at him.

Then it was the last contest. The realization struck Pinnatte like a winding blow, dragging his soaring spirit back to his body leaning against the parapet wall. He wanted to cry out in pain. This should not stop. Such a thing should be without end. This was the true way. But he needed no animal instinct to know that amongst his own, he must be as they were, that to be too different was to risk finding himself in the centre of an arena even more

212

savage than that below. He looked round at Rinter and the other spectators lining the balcony like a cautious predator – pack leader, but fearful of the pack. Then, suddenly, a cold wave of profound bitterness and hatred swept through him. It seemed to come from beyond him and it was unlike anything he had ever known. He became the merest speck of dust borne along by forces which were as uncomprehending of him as he was of them. Yet too, there was humanity here – foaming rage and a blood-streaked lust for vengeance that reached back through times beyond his comprehension, to roots that vanished terrifyingly into the great heat of making.

Or was it re-making?

The vision faltered and, almost tragic in character, the faintest hint of bewilderment seeped into it before, abruptly, it was gone – torn away as though by a jealous hand. Pinnatte felt his own hand tightening about the edge of the wall to steady himself.

'You sure you're all right?'

Rinter's voice was garbled and distant. Somehow Pinnatte managed to smile and nod, though he did not trust himself to speak.

'You just looked a bit odd,' Rinter advised him paternally. 'It's probably too much excitement. You can get very involved at times – it's happened to me before now. And it's been quite a night.'

Pinnatte nodded again and forced out an uncertain, 'Yes.'

The very utterance of the word brought him fully back to the present. Maybe Rinter was right. Maybe he had just let the excitement of the night get the better of him. But he knew that was untrue. Something very strange had just happened. Something he would have to think about. But later. Now he must see what the culmination of this night was to be. He leaned forward.

The Judges were sharing the announcement this time, sometimes speaking together, sometimes alternately. It was a bizarre duet. Pinnatte watched the two men fixedly, patiently waiting for them to be gone. He heard the words, but paid them no heed.

This time, three dogs were to be pitted against one – 'a very special animal, brought to us by an honoured supporter of the Loose Pits who wishes to remain anonymous.'

'It's the Kyrosdyn,' Rinter hissed. 'I told you so. They've

brought something up from the caves. Now this will be a sight to see.'

Pinnatte did not respond. His gaze moved to the hooded figure below. She was leaning against the Pitside wall in the same posture that he was. Then, for a heart-stopping moment, she reached up and took hold of her hood. Pull it back, let me see your face, he willed desperately.

As if toying with him, the woman moved her hood back a little, then slowly brought it forward again. Pinnatte drove his fingernails into his palm. His mouth was dry and his breathing shallow.

Then his frustration seemed to fill the hall and the atmosphere became like that before the breaking of a violent thunderstorm. Pinnatte felt omniscient, as though any movement he made now might sweep aside the entire crowd.

Be silent, he thought viciously as he looked again at the Judges.

At the same time, the two men ended their peroration.

The Master raised his staff and brought it down heavily, twice. It did not make the sharp crack that it had made when he had done this earlier to silence the crowd, but more a sound like a muffled funeral drum. It echoed ominously about the hall.

As it faded, the doors opened in the side of the arena and three dogs emerged. They were larger than anything that had appeared in the arena that night, being perhaps half the height of a tall man. And their strength was demonstrated by the size of the two leashmen who restrained each one. At their appearance, the storm broke and a tumult of cheering and whistling filled the hall. In reply, the three dogs began a frantic barking, tugging at their leashes and rising up on their hind legs.

Pinnatte bared his teeth. *Bay as much as you like – you are doomed.* The thought filled him – possessed him – as though it were not his, and, for an instant he had the feeling of someone else looking out through his eyes. At the same time, a twisting spiral of fear wormed deep inside him.

He was in danger! Something was happening to him that he must fight, or he would be lost for ever.

Then both sensations were gone, and he was himself again.

Or was he?

214

He drew his hand across his mouth. It was damp – almost as though he had been slavering at the prospect of what was to come.

And what was to come? He could feel something stirring within him, a cruel, relentless will being drawn towards the focus of the waiting crowd. This time however, wrestling with his desire to stay, he felt also an unsettling urge to turn and flee from this awful place.

The hooded figure leaning against the Pitside wall moved her head from side to side as if distressed. Her companions turned to her, concerned, but she raised a hand to reassure them – or dismiss them.

Pinnatte did not notice the incident. His eyes were now fixed on one of the arena doors, and his ears were filled with the baying of the three dogs. He felt as though someone were tightening a band about his chest.

Slowly, the door began to swing open. It moved with agonizing slowness, and the tightness about Pinnatte's chest became unbearable as the door swung inward to its fullest extent, disappearing into a black void.

Then, it seemed to him that the blackness itself was moving – shifting, changing, drawing itself together and leaking out into the arena. For a moment, Pinnatte could not separate the images he was seeing from the sensations dancing in his mind. It was only a puzzled exclamation from Rinter that brought him back again to the balcony, with the gritty stone parapet wall under his hands. The dark shape became the form of another dog. It was quite large, but still smaller than the three animals frantically barking at it. So anxious were they to attack that they were threatening to drag their leash-holders into the fray. By contrast, the new arrival was being led quietly into the arena by a solitary figure.

Pinnatte turned to Rinter for the seeing glass, but his companion was peering through it intently, his brow furrowed.

'Well, it's ugly,' he declared flatly after a moment. He handed the glass to Pinnatte. His reaction seemed to be shared by most of the crowd and the creature was greeted with a mixture of jeering and incongruously polite applause. 'It doesn't seem very enthusiastic. One leashman, and it's not even pulling. It must think it's out for its evening walk.'

Pinnatte steadied his elbow on the parapet wall and focused the glass on the animal. As Rinter had said, it was indeed ugly. A pointed head, wolf-like except for a bulging forehead, jutted forward beneath hulking, muscular shoulders, and a curved back sloped down to rear legs that were shorter than the forelegs. Its eyes appeared to be closed and it had an uncomfortable, loping gait which, even to Pinnatte, did not bode well for its chances in avoiding its three opponents, still less in counter-attacking. Was this incredible night about to peter out in farce and anti-climax?

Yet there was something odd about this dog. Though it was making no effort to pull at its leash, either to attack or flee, its pointed head was moving slowly from side to side as if it were examining the crowd. It ignored the three dogs almost completely, although once it paused to stare at them briefly. As it did so, it twisted its head slightly to one side then lowered it horizontally, until it almost touched the floor.

Almost like an obeisance, Pinnatte thought. Yet it was not like any movement he had ever seen a dog do before. In fact, he decided, everything about the animal was unfamiliar. It seemed to have none of the characteristic movements of a dog.

Then: it *wasn't* a dog, he realized. It had the look of one, and perhaps its ancestors had been dogs, but that must have been a long time ago. This was . . .

What?

An abomination!

As the word came to him, Pinnatte felt again the urge to be away from this place, to set aside everything that had happened this night as a tawdry and shameful aberration. It could not stand against the force that held him there, however – the longing – the lust – to witness, to be part of, another scene of combat. He could feel the hunting fury of the three dogs, the straining to launch themselves at this solitary and silent intruder. Yet, oddly, he could feel nothing of the creature. The cruel will he had sensed before its entrance was gone. It was still, silent and seemingly docile.

'Out for its evening walk.' Rinter repeated his previous remark.

'What a flop! I'm having a wager on this one – it doesn't stand a chance. Look at the odds. They're tumbling with each step it makes.'

He made to move away, but Pinnatte, still holding the glass on the creature, took his arm. 'I don't know Barran, but it makes no sense that he'd end a night as splendid as this has been, with something that would send everyone away disappointed.'

Rinter pulled his arm free. 'Anyone can make a mistake. Maybe the Kyrosdyn are playing some game of their own. Leading him on for some reason.'

'Maybe,' Pinnatte agreed doubtfully, still peering through the glass. 'But there's something strange about this . . .'

He stopped. Full in his view, the creature was looking up at him. Its hooded eyes slowly opened and Pinnatte found himself staring into two yellow pits. And into recognition. It knew him!

Without taking its gaze from him, the creature did as it had before, canting its head to one side and lowering it almost to the floor. This time however, it bent its forelegs. This *was* an obeisance! Pinnatte could not tear his gaze free – did not want to tear it free. It was fitting that he should be acknowledged thus. All was well.

The creature opened its mouth and uttered a low, moaning howl. The sound had a strange poignancy and, as it rolled around the hall, Pinnatte was once again looking down the vertiginous span of long-gone times, through endless tortured and unintelligible memories that were not his. Then the creature was once more walking quietly by its leashman and the memories were gone. Pinnatte took a deep breath and finished his advice. 'Don't wager on this animal losing. It would be a mistake.'

Rinter fidgeted uncomfortably. 'I don't see how. Just look at it. I'd like to try to get the entrance price back, at least.'

'You won't. You'll lose,' Pinnatte said, returning the glass to him. 'Just watch.'

Before Rinter could pursue the matter, the Master signalled for the fight to begin and the first wave of wagering was ended.

At the outset it looked as if Rinter's judgement was going to be correct. As the leashmen brought the three straining dogs close, the creature made no response other than to continue looking about the hall. When they began to snap at it, it simply jumped away awkwardly, as if surprised. The crowd began to whistle and boo, and there was a frenzy of activity amongst the blues.

After two such circuits of the arena, the Master gave another signal and the leashes were extended, allowing the animals to come closer. Again however, the creature did not seem to know what was happening and made no effort to defend itself other than by trying to avoid the dogs' increasingly ferocious charges. Even then, it never once tightened its leash, although the men holding the dogs were having considerable difficulty in keeping their feet. Three or four times the creature was actually knocked over.

The crowd's anger grew. As too did Pinnatte's curiosity. Still he could feel nothing from the strange animal – not even fear. And he had felt a lot of that tonight.

Then, the Master gave the final signal. The dogs and the creature were separated by only twenty paces and the man holding the creature bent down, unhooked the leash and moved quietly to one side. One of the Clerks spoke to him, but he just shook his head politely and leaned against the wall, his arms folded. The Clerk shrugged his shoulders. The creature sat down and the catcalls from the crowd turned to a cruel laughter.

At the same time, the three dogs were released. As they shot forward towards the waiting creature, the leashmen, together with the Clerks, ran quickly from the arena.

Unexpectedly, the three dogs stopped their headlong dash as they reached the creature and began circling it, snarling ferociously, but seemingly uncertain.

'It's neither running nor fighting. They don't know what to do,' Pinnatte said, as much to himself as to Rinter. The crowd became strangely quiet, as if they too did not know how to respond to this behaviour. Nor too, it seemed, did the Master who, for the first time that evening, began to show signs of real activity, moving to the edge of the platform and leaning forward to study the encircling dogs and the silent creature. Even without the seeing glass, Pinnatte could read the uncertainty in his posture.

Eventually he reached out with his staff to touch the creature, but the creature's leashman signalled to him and he withdrew it.

Pinnatte turned from the arena to look once again at the hooded woman. She was leaning forward with her elbows on the Pitside wall. As he looked at her, she lifted one hand slightly and dropped it as though she too were discreetly signalling to someone.

The creature was on its feet with such suddenness that the entire crowd gasped. Though it scarcely seemed to move, it had hold of one dog's left foreleg. Pinnatte could see the yellow eyes blazing and, as though a smothering curtain had suddenly been torn away, he could feel the creature's awful presence. It filled him with both stark terror and soaring elation. So overwhelming was the sensation that he did not hear the sound of the dog's leg being crushed, or see the violent shake of the creature's head which tore the limb free and sent it arcing bloodily out of the arena and into the crowd.

'Ye Gods!' Rinter's voice mingled with the great roar that went up and the cry of the wounded dog so that Pinnatte felt rather than heard it. As the dog, yelping piteously, hopped away, the creature loped after it, making occasional charges at it, but stopping short so that the dog kept stumbling and having to struggle to its feet.

Pinnatte was enthralled. He could sense the fear of the one and the rapture of the other. For rapture it was. The creature was feeding off the dog's terror, he realized. And it was revelling in the crowd's wild-eyed goading. What kind of an animal was this?

The other dogs, silenced for a moment by the sudden attack, were keeping their distance and confining themselves to barking, as if that alone might frighten the creature away. But there was a high-pitched quality to the sound that robbed it of any menace.

More courage than sense, Pinnatte thought. You'd be better advised trying to escape.

Almost as though his thought had reached the dogs, one of them turned away from its fruitless pursuit and began jumping at the wall of the arena. The creature turned immediately and ran towards it. It lowered its head as it ran and its ungainly gait was suddenly gone. As had happened before, the entire crowd gasped at the speed of the creature. It covered the length of the arena and leapt up to catch the would-be fugitive in mid-air in little more than two heartbeats. As it landed, a single blow from its fore-foot tore open the side of the dog.

Seeing this, the third dog followed the example of its luckless companion, voided its bowels and, jumping on the creature's back, cleared the arena wall.

Uproar filled the hall: cheers and laughter from those members of the crowd who were well away from the frantic dog, cries of panic and terror from those who were not. But, for Pinnatte, rising above it all was the cry of the creature – a bellow of appalling fury at the escape of its prey. It possessed him so totally that, for a moment, he was completely at one with the creature, consumed by its ravening frustration.

Then, something within him reached out and dashed the creature's will aside; it was an angry dismissal.

The creature hesitated for a moment, then seized the injured dog by the neck and shook it so savagely that, despite its greater size, the dog was lifted clear of the ground and smashed into the wall. To Pinnatte, the act seemed casual, petulant even. Then the creature was walking over to the remaining survivor, now lying down and whimpering as it licked the bleeding stub. It stopped as it saw the creature approaching and flattened itself along the floor, its ears drawn back, its eyes wide. The creature seized it and dispatched it as contemptuously as it had the other, then it let out another roaring bellow of rage before dropping down at the feet of its leashman. The man had not moved throughout the entire proceedings. As it lay down, Pinnatte felt all contact with it ebb away. The curtain had returned. He folded his arms on the parapet wall and let his head slump forward on to them. He needed darkness for a moment.

But Rinter was digging him excitedly in the ribs. 'Don't go nodding off. There's another show going on down there.'

Reluctantly Pinnatte looked up. The Master and the Judges had gone, and the Clerks were removing the remains of the two dogs, but Rinter was directing his attention to the pandemonium on the terraces as the escaped dog dashed to and fro in search of escape. Despite the fact that two such animals had been easily dispatched by the creature, it was not something that anyone would face by choice. Further, it was demented with fear and attacking anything it came near with the appalling efficiency of a trained fighting dog. Bodies were being crushed and trampled underfoot as the crowd swayed this way and that, in belated response to the dog's frantic twisting and turning. And as much damage was being done by people wildly waving swords and knives about in vain attempts to protect themselves. The whole scene was being cheered on by the crowds watching from the safety of the balconies.

'Perhaps it was just as well we couldn't afford Pitside tonight, eh?' Rinter chuckled.

Pinnatte suddenly went cold. What had happened to the woman with the hood? Was she caught in that awful mêlée? Foolish fantasies of an heroic rescue flitted through his mind as he peered urgently over the balcony. But she was gone. As were her companions. He did not know whether to be relieved or disappointed. He slapped his hands down on the parapet.

'Come on, let's go.'

Rinter looked at him in exaggerated alarm. 'And run into that thing, taking chunks out of everything it comes near?' He motioned Pinnatte back to the wall. 'No, thank you. Let's watch the fun from up here. When someone's caught it or killed it, that'll be soon enough to go down.'

The fun, however, did not last a great deal longer, though the dog was neither caught nor killed. It simply disappeared.

Rinter and Pinnatte joined the slow-moving queue that was leaving the balcony. There was still a great deal of commotion rising from the terraces, but this was mainly injured and shocked people shouting for help, and of little interest to watch.

'Serves 'em right, rich bastards,' someone said behind Pinnatte. The remark was greeted with cries of approval.

The Jyolan's twisting passageways, gloomy in the poor lamplight, were crowded with swaying figures shuffling unsteadily over the curved and uneven floors. Though a ceaseless babble of voices echoed all around him, Pinnatte noticed that no one in his immediate vicinity appeared to be talking. It gave him a strange, detached feeling – one intensified by the sounds which emanated from the many openings in the walls and which seemed to be trying to speak to him – urgent, hissing whispers, dark, rumbling gloatings, distant high-pitched screechings which wavered fearfully – sometimes even a clear voice speaking an unfamiliar language, or two or three words that made no sense – once, even his name – but each slipped away from him as he strained forward to listen.

So absorbed was he that he started when a sudden rush of sound announced that he was near the entrance hall. Reaching it, he and Rinter found themselves confronted by uproar and confusion as a great crowd struggled to pass through a single narrow gate in the heavy iron railing that divided the entrance hall. The crush was being fed by streams of people from every archway, some blood-stained and wild-eyed. Here and there, Pitguards were struggling to establish order but, increasingly unable to move themselves, they were merely making things worse.

Fear clutched at Pinnatte as the press closed about him and he felt himself being lifted off the floor. It threatened rapidly to turn into panic as he was carried forward. Then he caught the eye of a young boy clinging to a woman who was struggling to keep him safe in the lee of a stone column. His shirt was torn and covered with blood. The boy looked straight at him, his eyes filling the world – full of bewilderment and fear. Something in Pinnatte lurched back to his own childhood when, albeit briefly, the world had been happy and safe. The memory mingled with sights he had seen tonight – and the emotions he had felt – and a wave of nausea and shame passed over him.

Through it, far away, he heard himself saying, 'We must do something.'

Then, desperately, he was pulling his arms free and reaching up to take the shoulders of two men in front of him. Trapped themselves, they could do nothing but curse as he began to scramble up them, painfully dragging himself free of the crowd. Then he was running across the top of the crowd, jumping from shoulder to shoulder, steadying himself occasionally against the stone ceiling or someone's head. Rinter, pinioned and fearful, watched open-mouthed as his new-found friend squeezed between the top of the railing and the ceiling and dropped down out of sight on the far side.

Pinnatte, born along by urgency rather than clear intent to this point, stared helplessly at the crowd in front of him, pressed against the railing. Hands were reaching out to him. Someone shouted, 'The bar, lad! The bar.'

Pinnatte dithered for a moment before he took in the words, then he saw the bar that was holding the main double gate shut. He swung on it. But it would not move – the pressure of the crowd was wedging it tight. He bent down, put his shoulder underneath it and thrust upwards, his legs straining.

Let them struggle and squirm, flawed worthless things that they are. Let them fall and grind one another into the dirt. It is the way it should be. It is the way it *will* be.

The thought rang in his mind, cold and malevolent and hideously clear.

It stunned him. His strength drained away.

Then another thought filled him – just as powerful. He must atone for what he had felt tonight.

And he was pushing again, his legs throbbing and the bar cutting into his shoulder.

For a timeless time, there was only pain. Pain that had been for ever and would be for ever. In his shoulder, in his legs – everywhere.

Then a rending screech cut through it and the bar swung upwards, out of its housing.

The gate burst open, hurling Pinnatte to one side. Only chance saved him from being crushed against the railing, so violently did the two halves swing back. As it was, he fell awkwardly, scuffing the back of his right hand on the rough floor and banging his head.

A dizzying blackness came and went many times. The din of the crowd came and went with it, roaring and echoing in his ears. He was vaguely aware of trying to stand and of his legs not obeying.

Then someone was dragging him to his feet.

'Did you see that?'

The voice was proprietorial. Rinter's face slowly came into focus. There was someone with him. Someone large.

'Saved us a lot of problems with that stunt, lad,' the figure said. 'What's your name?'

Pinnatte grimaced and put his hand to the back of his head.

'It's Pinnatte,' Rinter answered on his behalf. 'Friend of mine. Oddly enough, he was asking if he could meet you earlier, Fiarn.'

Rinter's face blurred again, then the blackness returned to swallow it completely.

Chapter 18

Heirn sat bolt upright, wide awake, his mouth gaping. He had been about to cry out in terror in the tangling depths of a dark and vivid nightmare.

Not since he had been a child had he known such a dream.

Yet, on the instant of waking, it fled. And, with each pounding heartbeat, its black tattered shadows flickered further away, beyond any hope of recall.

But still he felt compelled to remain motionless – some lingering fear telling him that they might mysteriously return if he moved too soon.

Gradually his breathing eased. He reproached himself for a fool as the familiar night sounds of his home enclosed him. There were faint hints of music coming from an inn in a nearby street, the occasional unidentifiable bump echoing through walls and floors from some other occupant of the building, and the usual intermittent clatter of night-time traffic – footsteps, voices, rumbling wheels. The sounds from outside were a little louder than usual because he had left the window wide open in an attempt to keep his room cool in the unusual and persistent heat that marked this summer. It had little effect. Even when there was a breeze silently searching the streets – which was not the case tonight – it was rarely sufficient to disperse the heat that had been assiduously stored by the brick and stone buildings during the day and which they released each night.

The dream had left him sweating and clammy. Rooting through the folded bedclothes at the bottom of the bed, he found a solitary thin sheet and, lying down, pulled it over himself. He made no effort to sleep. It would have been to no avail anyway; he was too wide awake now – indeed, it surprised him that he had slept at all after what he had seen and heard that night.

At Atlon's request, on leaving the forge Heirn had taken a detour which led them through deserted alleys and across open derelict sites. It was not a way he would have chosen, but it should have been safe enough at that time of day, and both Atlon and Dvolci seemed convinced that the Kyrosdyn who had accosted them at the forge was following.

They were walking quickly along a narrow cobbled road between two windowless buildings, Atlon leading his horse, and Dvolci trotting along beside them. 'I can't see anyone,' Heirn said, looking round yet again. His new companions' seemingly obsessive concern about the Kyrosdyn was beginning to disturb him.

'He's there nevertheless,' Atlon replied. He glanced significantly at Dvolci who ran off down the alley.

'So what?' Heirn asked impatiently. 'He's only one man. And low in the Order, I'd say – probably a young novice judging by his manner. If needs be I'll thicken his ear for him.' Atlon did not respond, causing Heirn to raise his voice. 'Why would he follow you? To rob you? They're a peculiar lot, but they aren't street thieves.'

An angry voice behind them forestalled any reply.

'Stay where you are!'

Atlon stiffened. 'Keep moving,' he said urgently, taking Heirn's arm and increasing his pace.

'I said, stay where you are!'

The voice had the same petulant arrogance as when its owner had addressed them in the forge and it was suddenly too much for Heirn. It was bad enough that he should be subjected to that kind of attitude in his own forge where possible customers might be allowed a little licence. But in the street – with friends!

He turned round angrily.

'No. Come on,' he heard Atlon say, but he pulled free from his grip and raised a hand, both to reassure him and to tell him to continue on his way. This was a matter between two locals. It wasn't something for outsiders.

The Kyrosdyn was striding purposefully towards them. Heirn held out his hand as if to slow his progress before he came too close.

'Who the hell do you think you're talking to like that?' he shouted.

Without breaking step, and even though he was still some distance away, the Kyrosdyn waved his arm as if to brush the irritating impediment aside.

Something struck Heirn, sending him crashing against the wall.

Even as he was staggering backwards, he took in the sight of Atlon turning, his face alive with anger and fear, his mouth forming the word, 'No!' At the same time, he saw the horse, seeming to mimic its owner, rearing and backing away, white-eyed, its hooves clattering noisily on the cobbles. Then he struck the wall, and for a few winded moments he was unaware of anything.

When he recovered, the Kyrosdyn had reached Atlon and was confronting him. Furious, and though he had no idea what had happened to him, Heirn made to lunge at the hooded figure. But he could not move. Something was holding him against the wall.

'Who are you?' he heard the Kyrosdyn demanding of Atlon, his voice muffled and distant. 'And who has taught you to dabble with the use of crystals?' He stepped forward menacingly.

Atlon reached out and held him at arm's length. He indicated Heirn. 'Let him go,' he said.

The Kyrosdyn looked down at the hand on his chest. 'You dare touch me – one of the Chosen?'

'Let him go,' Atlon repeated, his face suddenly grim.

The Kyrosdyn closed his eyes and his face became tense with concentration.

Atlon stepped away from him. In stark contrast to the Kyrosdyn, he seemed to be completely relaxed and calm. 'No,' he said, with a menacing softness that made Heirn stop struggling against his unseen bonds. 'You don't know what you're doing.'

Then the Kyrosdyn's eyes were wide and his hands were extended towards Atlon. It would have been an absurdly theatrical gesture, had it not been for the malice that his posture radiated. Heirn felt the force restraining him falter and shift, but not enough to allow him to move. Atlon leaned back a little and turned away with a pained expression as if a blustering wind had thrown dust in his face. As he did so, the Kyrosdyn staggered back several paces and collapsed on to his knees.

Then Heirn was free.

His immediate instinct was to seize the Kyrosdyn and beat an explanation out of him, but before he could move, Atlon seized his arm with an unexpectedly powerful grip and began dragging him along the alley.

'Quickly, run.' He slapped his horse, which set off ahead of them, then he let out a piercing whistle. Heirn tried to remonstrate, but Atlon's urgent tugging kept him off-balance.

They had gone barely twenty paces when a high-pitched shriek reached them. Resignation filled Atlon's face as he stopped and turned. The Kyrosdyn was clambering unsteadily to his feet. To Heirn it seemed that the man was shimmering, as though he were looking at him across a scorching landscape.

Atlon stopped and lowered his head. 'Go on, Heirn,' he said, his voice soft again. 'There's nothing you can do, and you could well get hurt.'

Heirn backed away from him hesitantly. Born and bred in Arash-Felloren and having prospered honestly, he was neither fool nor coward, but Atlon's initial desire to flee, and the now awful resolution in his quiet voice left him floundering. As he hesitated, he looked again at the swaying Kyrosdyn. There was a manic quality about the man which contrasted so starkly with Atlon's calmness that it gave him the truth of Atlon's words. He had no explanations but he knew that something terrible must surely flow between two such opposites. And there was nothing he could do.

Nevertheless, he would not leave.

Something brushed past his leg, making him jump violently. It was Dvolci.

'Do you want me to deal with him?' he asked Atlon, baring his teeth.

Atlon, without taking his eyes from the Kyrosdyn, shook his head. 'The state he's in, there's no saying what might happen if he tried to fight you off. Or who else might be drawn here. I'll try to calm him, but speak to the horse – he'll attack if I go down. Tell him to guard Heirn. And get them both away safely.'

Dvolci replied with a reluctant grunt and backed away. 'Stay by me,' he said forcefully to Heirn as he passed him. 'And if I say run – run! Don't argue!' He clambered up on to the horse and perched himself on its head. Though still obviously frightened, the horse not only made no attempt to dislodge him but quietened a little as he bent forward and whispered to it. It edged sideways a little, towards Heirn.

'What's happ—?'

'Shh!' Dvolci slapped down Heirn's pending question. Even as he did, Atlon was straightening up and holding out both hands to the Kyrosdyn, palms upwards, as if greeting a friend.

'Turn away from this,' he said, very gently. 'No harm's been done so far, and there are other, wiser ways for you to travel through your life.'

'He's wasting his time,' Dvolci said, as much to himself as to anyone else. 'The man's corrupted beyond redemption. Too little skill for the Power he's using, and even less judgement.' He hissed angrily.

The Kyrosdyn did not reply but reached out with both hands, as he had before. This time, Atlon did not move other than to open his arms wider. Heirn could see nothing passing between the two men, but where before the Kyrosdyn had staggered a few paces, this time he was lifted into the air and thrown back twice the distance. He landed heavily and lay still.

Atlon started towards him.

'Leave him,' Dvolci cried. 'Let's get away while we can.'

Atlon hesitated, looking from the fallen figure to his friends then back again.

'We can't leave him,' he said finally. 'He might be hurt.'

Dvolci muttered something viciously under his breath then ran after him. Curiosity overcoming his fear, Heirn followed them.

'Leave him,' Dvolci said again as they reached the fallen man. 'If he's dead, he's dead – and no loss. If he's alive, he's still lost.'

Atlon however, paid no heed, but knelt down and began examining the Kyrosdyn. He pulled the man's hood back and reached out to check his throat pulse. The Kyrosdyn's eyes opened and his hand seized Atlon's wrist.

Despite himself, Heirn stepped back, startled by the suddenness of the action and the expression on the young man's gaunt face.

'Thief,' the Kyrosdyn said hoarsely.

'No,' Atlon began. 'I was just . . .'

'Thief.'

Still holding Atlon, the Kyrosdyn brought his other hand to the elaborate kerchief about his neck and pressed it tightly. Atlon frowned uncertainly at this strange gesture. Then suddenly, he cried out in alarm and started back, struggling to break the grip on his wrist. But it was too strong. His free hand shot out in front of Kyrosdyn's face as if he was protecting himself from something. An image came to Heirn of himself making the same gesture in front of his overheated forge, though he could neither see, hear nor feel anything happening here.

'No! No!' Atlon was shouting repeatedly, as though he were trying to make himself heard over a roaring wind. 'No! You'll . . .'

His words faded as the Kyrosdyn tightened his grip about his own throat as if some greater effort was needed. Then, abruptly, the man's eyes were unnaturally wide and full of a terrible realization. Heirn turned away, unable to watch such pain. For a moment, the Kyrosdyn's back arched and his mouth gaped in a silent scream, then he went limp.

'. . . kill yourself,' Atlon finished, almost whispering, as the man's lifeless hand released his wrist. With a hasty gesture he drew the Kyrosdyn's hood forward then placed his ear in front of the open mouth. When he sat up he completed the task that had brought on the attack; he reached into the hood and checked the man's pulse.

'He's dead,' he announced finally. He bowed his head.

'What's happened?' Heirn demanded. 'What did you—'

'Find them!' Dvolci's urgency cut across the question and through Atlon's distress. 'Find the damned things quickly. I knew they were doing it. I could smell it in the air. I told you you were wasting your time. You could've been killed, then what? Anyone who uses the Power like that . . .'

'All right, I know!' Atlon blasted back at him furiously.

Dvolci retreated a step and shook his head vigorously, as though dispatching the budding quarrel before it grew into anything worse, then he began tugging at the Kyrosdyn's neckerchief. Heirn, fearing some atrocity on the corpse, reached down to take hold of him. But Atlon was already intervening. Carefully he unfastened a delicate clip that secured the neckerchief then gently removed it. As he turned it over he let out a resigned breath. Neatly worked into the pattern of the kerchief was a row of small green discs. Dvolci chattered his teeth as he bit back some comment. Heirn gasped. Though, on his own admission, he knew little about crystals, as with those that Atlon had shown, so now he recognized the brilliant green sheet that was glistening even in the gloomy alley.

'These must be ten times the value of those *you're* carrying,' he said breathlessly. 'Who is this man, carrying wealth like that so casually around his neck? I thought he was just a typical novice, but he must be a Higher Brother. What are we going to do?'

Atlon shook his head. 'For this one, nothing,' he said. 'He's beyond any help.' He stroked Dvolci's head, though for his own comfort, not the felci's. 'He paid the price of what he was doing. It was inevitable. I did my best to protect him from himself, but . . .' His voice tailed off.

'I don't understand. What's happened to him?' Heirn persisted.

Atlon looked down at the green crystals. 'Like me, he has – had – some skill in the use of the Power. Unlike me, whoever instructed him led him grievously astray, teaching him to use it – misuse it – through the crystals.' He folded the kerchief and put it in his pocket.

'What are you doing?' Heirn exclaimed, horrified. Then he immediately answered his own question. 'You can't do that. Robbing him. Isn't it enough that you—'

He stopped uncomfortably.

'Murdered him?' Atlon asked rhetorically, but without any rancour. 'I didn't murder him. I defended myself, then I tried to stop him from killing himself.' He stood up. 'If anything killed him, it was these.' He patted his pocket. 'I'll wager they were clear, or scarcely tinted a few moments ago. Now they're tainted

231

with all it was that animated this poor creature.'

Heirn's mind was whirling. 'I don't know what you're talking about,' he said agitatedly. 'The man was alive, now he's dead. And you're stealing from him – taking crystals worth an unimaginable amount. We have to tell someone about this – the Weartans, probably. And find out who those things belong to – his family – the Order – I don't know.'

Atlon looked down at the dead Kyrosdyn and, for a moment, his face distorted as though he were about to weep. His voice was unsteady when he spoke. 'You must do what you see fit, Heirn, but Dvolci and I can't stay. If this man's typical of the Kyrosdyn, then what they're doing is unbelievably dangerous – to themselves, to everyone around them, and not least to this city. I have to learn more about it. My people must be told. They're the only ones who can do anything. If the Kyrosdyn learn about me, they'll seek me out, just as he did, and sooner or later they'll find and attack me, just as he did. The consequences could be appalling.' He took the neckerchief from his pocket. 'As for these, to leave them here might be to sentence some passing innocent to death.' He took Heirn's arm. 'I know you've no reason to believe me, but I had no true hand in his killing. What happened to him he brought on himself.'

'I don't know,' Heirn said uncertainly, remembering the unseen force that had held him helpless against the wall. 'This city's the way it is because too many people walk away from things – refuse to accept responsibility for anything unless they see some gain in it for themselves. I—'

'We haven't time for this,' Dvolci said impatiently to Atlon. 'If this one felt you moving a horseshoe from the other side of the square, there's no saying who felt what's just happened.' He turned to Heirn and motioned him towards the body. 'Just look at him.' His voice was powerful and commanding. 'See what those precious crystals did to him. Ask yourself, how could Atlon possibly have done that?' Heirn stared at him uncertainly. 'Look at him! Lift his hood back. Look at his face, his hands.'

Frowning and reluctant, Heirn knelt down by the dead man and hesitantly lifted back his hood. The pale sunken face of an old man

232

stared up at him. He started back, then edged away from the body, looking from Dvolci to Atlon. 'I don't understand. I could've sworn he was a young man. The way he carried himself, spoke, everything about him. This man's withered almost . . . he must be incredibly old. Scarcely able to walk, I'd think, let alone strut about the way he was.'

'He was young,' Dvolci said bluntly. 'A foolish, misguided young man who used crystals to amplify whatever skill he had with the Power. In his ignorance he went beyond where he should have gone and ignorance is often a fatal condition. Doing what he did, he changed the nature of the crystals and they took back what they had given him – and more. That's why they're green now. He was like a child with an assassin's poisoned blade.'

Heirn was shaking his head. Atlon laid a hand on his shoulder. 'This is not the time or the place to explain this. Dvolci's right. He and I *must* leave immediately, there's no saying who'll have been drawn to this. I need your help now even more than before, but I understand your concerns. Do you want to stay, or will you help us?'

Heirn grimaced and looked from side to side, then up at the narrow strip of darkening blue sky above. The high buildings looked back impassively. 'Say something – one word – anything that'll help me. I'm lost in all this. Him – young, then old – crystals turning from clear into greens, you say – into a fortune – it's not possible. And as for stealing them, leaving a dead body lying here for the dogs and the vermin, it's . . .' He fell silent.

'There's nothing I can tell you, here, now,' Atlon said, taking the reins of his horse and turning it round.

'I can,' Dvolci said coldly. 'Look at these.' He opened the dead man's robe further. Livid circular scars marred his neck where the kerchief had been.

Heirn winced. 'Burns,' he exclaimed softly. 'Bad ones too.' He leaned forward. 'And new?'

'Portals to the soul I'd say if I was being poetic,' Dvolci said simply, gently closing the robe and covering the dead man's face. 'But choked and fouled drains would be a better description. The crystals did this to him. Quickly or slowly, they'll do it to anyone

233

in time. Especially these, in this state. That's why we can't leave them. Please help us. We came to this city because we were concerned about something in our own land – to learn, nothing more. Now it looks as though we might be back in a war we'd thought finished years ago.' He placed a paw on Heirn's arm. 'This is a fearful place for us both. I can understand your confusion and doubt – you don't know us and you *do* know the Kyrosdyn; we're outsiders, they're city people. It's your judgement, but we're more lost than you can possibly imagine. Help us, please. We'll tell you what we can, but help us get to somewhere safe.'

Heirn stood up. With a final look at the dead Kyrosdyn, he said, 'There'll be other bodies found tonight, I suppose. There always are – every night.' His face was pained. 'I never thought I'd be . . .' He stopped and straightened up. 'I'll take you home as I promised. But I *must* know what's happening.'

Heirn levered himself over on to his left side and gazed at the open window, a dim rectangle, yellow in the reflected street lights.

All three had been silent for the rest of the short journey to Heirn's home: Atlon and Dvolci as if they were listening for something, Heirn increasingly fretful about the wisdom of what he was doing. Scarcely had he shown them into his rooms and sat them down however, than Atlon's tale was pouring out.

'Sixteen years ago – I'd only just become a senior Brother in our Order – we discovered that an . . . old enemy . . . had returned to the land to the north of us.'

'Is this what you told me back at the forge?' Heirn interrupted starkly. 'I'm warning you, I'm in no mood for fireside tales.'

Atlon was unexpectedly grim and his face looked old in the early evening light that was percolating into the room. 'Yes, it is,' he said. 'And it's no child's tale, Heirn. It's a tale of a real war – one in which real battles were fought.' He tapped his finger to his temple savagely and gritted his teeth. 'Battles I can still see when I close my eyes at night. Bloody wounds, hacked limbs . . .'

Dvolci let out a low, soothing whistle.

Atlon fell silent. 'I'm sorry,' he said eventually. 'That's not your problem, is it? It's difficult to remember that while my countrymen and our allies were fighting and dying, the rest of the world was oblivious to what was happening. And still is. Or that, to them, the enemy we faced was nothing more than an old legend.'

'This . . . enemy . . . has a name?' Heirn asked impatiently.

It was Dvolci who replied. 'I think you'd call Him, Sammrael.'

Heirn frowned uncertainly then tried a scornful smile as if that might somehow dismiss all that had happened that day. 'Sammrael is the name of the man we call the Great Lord – the legendary founder of Arash-Felloren. But he *is* only a legend – a tale for children. And if he's anything, he's no ogre but a heroic figure – a noble man done down by petty and treacherous enemies.'

Atlon's gaze shrivelled his already waning smile.

'Listen carefully, this isn't going to be easy for you,' he said slowly. Heirn opened his mouth to speak then changed his mind. Atlon went on.

'No one knows who, *or what*, He truly is. It's believed that He was one of those who came from what we call the Great Heat at the beginning of all things.' Heirn's brow furrowed but he stayed silent. 'His sole intent seems always to have been to destroy the world that the others shaped. No one's ever fathomed why this should be, but His deeds testify to it, over and over – as do many of the names He's known by – the Great Corrupter, the Enemy of all Living Things. He's slipped into legend simply because the last time He was here was so long ago – far beyond most people's reckoning. Even we made the mistake of thinking He'd gone for ever, and we *knew* He'd been as real as you or I.'

Heirn protested, 'You can't ask me to believe . . .'

Atlon raised a hand to stop him. 'I'm not asking you to do anything except hear me out,' he said urgently. 'Who or what He is, how or why He came into being is, in any case, of no concern. But His reality *is*. That's a matter of unbroken, documented fact. I'm loath to burden you with this but we need your help. You can walk away from us at any time, but I'm asking you not to until you've at least heard what we've got to say. And when you feel yourself slipping into unreality – when you think you're listening to the ramblings of someone deranged – remember the horseshoes

235

I moved and how it drew that wretched man to us. And remember the force that knocked you against that wall and held you pinned there.'

Heirn, his jaw set, looked away from him, but did not reply.

'It could well be that He did found Arash-Felloren,' Atlon went on. 'He'd many citadels about the world and I've . . .' he paused and took a deep, nervous breath, '. . . I've seen His image once already.' He stiffened to suppress a shiver. 'And there's a feel about the whole place which is . . . disturbing.' He kept his gaze fixed on Heirn. 'The enemy we faced was this Great Lord of yours – be under no illusions. I felt the touch of His minions. When He last walked amongst us, corrupting and destroying, a Great Alliance of peoples eventually defeated His armies and, as they thought, destroyed Him, though we think now that He was only scattered, dispersed across many different worlds and times.' He waved his hand to set aside the distractions that were clamouring to be heard as justifications for his story. 'Whatever the truth of it, some focus, some Power in His old fastness, made Him whole again.' He could not keep the anger from his voice. 'And our Order – nearly as ancient as He Himself, and tasked with the duty of watching for His Second Coming and gathering knowledge to protect the world should it happen – saw nothing, felt nothing, heard nothing. Blind, under the rocks – inward-looking . . .'

'Enough!' Dvolci stopped him. 'That debate's finished.' Then, to Heirn: 'Suffice it that His return was discovered and He was defeated again, this time before He could spread too much of His corruption out into the world.'

'But?' Heirn said, picking up the inflection in Dvolci's voice.

Atlon answered him. 'But we don't know how long He'd been . . . whole. How many agents of His had gone out into the world, or how far. What harm they were still doing. And agents there'd be. That was always His way. Working silently and insidiously, like rot in the heart of an old tree, so that, one day, when the wind blows . . .' He brought his hands together in a soft clap.

Heirn cleared his throat nervously, as though half-fearing that he was being made the butt of some bizarre joke. 'I can't doubt that you've fought a war against someone,' he said. 'But you're asking a lot of me to accept that your enemy was some fictitious creature suddenly returned from the depths of time.' He looked at his hands. 'I've seen and heard some strange things, but I'm still a blacksmith – a practical man, dealing with practical matters. Men live and then they die – all of us. And they don't come back to life. How can a man do what you've described? It's not possible.'

'I've no answers for you, Heirn,' Atlon replied. 'He's not a man – perhaps not even a mortal creature as we understand it. I told you, we don't know what or why He is, but that's the case with many things. What we do know is that He's taken human form twice now and on both occasions brought untold horror into the world – horror that long outlived His apparent destruction. Horror that was eminently practical and of this world!' He leaned forward and spoke very quietly. 'We can only assume that, whatever's happened to Him, He will try to return yet again. And He'll succeed if we don't remain vigilant.'

There was a long silence. Heirn sat with his head bowed in thought. Atlon and Dvolci waited.

'I don't know what to make of any of this,' Heirn said eventually. 'I don't doubt your sincerity, but what you've told me just makes no sense. Yet . . .' He was pinned helpless against the wall again – then looking at the shrunken form of the young man made suddenly old. 'I can't just brush it all to one side as so much nonsense.' His distaste for this conclusion was written clearly across his face. He snatched at practicalities.

'These agents you mentioned. Do you think they might have come here, to Arash-Felloren?' he asked.

Atlon gave an unexpected shrug. 'When the war was over, many people were sent out into the world. Some to track down those who'd committed crimes in His name, others to seek out those who'd simply been led astray. Still others went out just to learn more of the world which we'd so long neglected.' He looked at Dvolci. 'As I told you back at the forge, we came looking for the source of the crystals that had been appearing in our land.'

Heirn nodded, though the conversation they had held, sitting in front of his forge, seemed now to have happened years ago.

'There'd been "incidents", I think you said.'

'Similar to what happened to the Kyrosdyn,' Atlon confirmed. 'Though nothing remotely as bad as that.' Almost mimicking Heirn's mannerism, he looked down at his hands. 'But, because of who my countrymen are descended from, most of us unknowingly have some aptitude for using the Power. And when that's done in certain ways and in the close proximity of certain crystals – alarming and dangerous things can happen.'

Heirn's hand went to his neck. 'Like those burns?'

'It can cause those kind of injuries, but they're only an incidental effect of what's really happening.'

'Which is?'

Atlon did not reply immediately. 'I don't know that I can begin to explain it to you, Heirn. It isn't easy to grasp, not least because it's far from being fully understood. Not even my teachers would pretend to understand it other than vaguely, and most of them have been studying it for longer than I've been riding. It's something that seems to lie near, perhaps even at the heart of everything we think of as being our world, our existence.' He looked around the room. 'What we call the Power is some attribute – some quality – that pervades all things; in a way, it connects all things. These chairs, that fire grate, those pictures, those flowers – ourselves even, are . . .' He sought inspiration on the ceiling. 'Different manifestations of it – different concentrations, for want of a better expression.'

Heirn looked at him blankly, and Atlon shrugged unhappily.

'It's the best I can do,' he said weakly. 'I did say it wouldn't be easy.' He pressed on. 'Put crudely, given the right circumstances, a crystal will draw the Power into itself, through the pulses, the meridians . . . in a way, storing it so that it can be used later. It's a hazardous thing to do, full of strange, unexpected dangers. It's appallingly addictive for one thing. We – my Order – use crystals like that only sparingly and not without great thought for the consequences. It seems however, that your Kyrosdyn use them quite recklessly.' His expression became distant and he shook his head in disbelief.

'In attacking me the way he did, that foolish young man went far beyond what I imagine he'd been taught to do. When I resisted him, he drew so savagely on the crystals at his neck that he actually changed their character.' He brightened a little as a comparison came to him. 'Like a piece of iron,' he said, holding up his clenched hands as though gripping a bar. He demonstrated as he spoke. 'If you bend it a little, it springs back. But if you bend it too much, it remains bent. It's changed in some way.' He lowered his hands, uncertain about his effort. The expression on his audience's face told him nothing.

Heirn looked at Dvolci. 'Portals to the soul? Choked and fouled drains?'

'Stab wounds would be as kind a phrase,' Dvolci replied sourly. 'The passage of too much too quickly in too small an area.'

'It was as if the crystals had suddenly become a great pit,' Atlon said, abandoning his iron-working analogy. 'Or a great whirlpool into which the energy that animated him, and everything nearby, was drawn irresistibly. Drawn and transformed.' He looked old again. 'I didn't even dare try to save him once it had started. It was all I could do to save myself and you.'

Heirn was silent for a moment, then he held out his hand. 'You're right,' he said flatly. 'It's not easy. Show me the Kyrosdyn's crystals.'

Atlon pulled out the neckerchief and handed it to him. Heirn unfolded it carefully and laid it on a small table. The green crystals were brilliant, even in the fading light. Tentatively he made to touch one, looking at Atlon as he did. Atlon reached out calmly and took his hand. 'It's possible you've some natural gift with the Power,' he said. 'People who work and shape materials often have.' He closed his eyes then, after a moment, nodded as if confirming something to himself. 'Crystals like these are something *you* should handle as little as possible. They won't do what they did to the Kyrosdyn because he had some conscious skill in using the Power and he wilfully misused it, but they'll do you no good in the long run.'

He picked up the neckerchief and examined the crystals closely. His face became angry. 'These have been cut and worked to get the greatest efficiency out of them. It's first-class workmanship and it shows a considerable knowledge of how they can be used.'

239

His anger changed into fear and then into a wrenching helplessness.

'This is awful,' he muttered to himself, putting the neckerchief down and leaning back into his chair.

Heirn ran a finger over one of the crystals. It tingled slightly – not unpleasantly – but he withdrew his hand quickly as the sensation ran up his arm. Looking at his finger, he saw that the tip was white, as though cold. He felt a peculiar urge to touch the crystal again.

Heirn rolled on to his back. The chimes of a distant clock drifted through the open window. Too early to get up, too late to get much worthwhile sleep. He'd be done for in the morning! But the strains of the day made his body give him the lie and, scarcely had the thought occurred to him than he was falling asleep. The last thing he recalled before he succumbed was Atlon briskly rolling up the neckerchief and returning it to his pocket. Then he had leaned forward and taken Heirn's hand. As he held it, the whiteness of the finger faded, and the urge to touch the crystal again passed.

Atlon's gaze had been searching. He asked no questions, but he seemed to know of Heirn's unexpected need. 'They are subtle beyond any knowing, Heirn. They bind and compel. You, who should be master, become slave. They are His things. And whatever the Kyrosdyn were once, they are His now, for sure.'

Chapter 19

Imorren's entourage scuttled uncomfortably behind her as she strode along the passage in the lower reaches of the Jyolan building. Senior members of the Kyrosdyn Order – mostly elderly Higher Brothers – they were used to her normally measured and careful progress and were having the greatest difficulty coping with her now rapid and determined step. There was certainly no question of maintaining the stately dignity that typified their escort duties about the Vaskyros. But then, many things had disturbed the Order's long-established proceedings that day – rumours about Rostan being involved in a street disturbance, even stronger rumours that he had committed some dreadful folly resulting in his solitary audience with the Ailad – not a special thing in itself, but it had been keenly noted that he was both immaculate and palpably nervous beforehand, and untypically flustered and edgy afterwards. Then suddenly, pandemonium erupted, or what passed for it in the stern, regimented life of the Kyrosdyn. The secret ownership of the Jyolan was to be transferred to Barran. Like insects disturbed by a plough, the Order's clerks and scribes had been sent scurrying between the Vaskyros and Barran's city headquarters bearing hastily drafted contracts and agreements to implement this. Barran was also to be discreetly helped to organize a Loose Pit *that same night* – this had prompted even more frantic scurrying. And the newly found creature, its existence known only to a few, was to be used. Rippling through the Order, news of this in particular carried silence in its wake as each of the naturally obsessive and conspirational Kyrosdyn paused to ponder the intentions of their subtle and enigmatic Ailad. The normal work of the Brotherhood came almost to a complete halt and the Vaskyros was alive with whispered questions. But the Ailad had sought no advice, and no overt questions would be dared. Her commands were not to be debated. Obedience was all – obedience and efficiency.

And her will had prevailed. What she had demanded had come to pass. And insofar as any of the Kyrosdyn could pretend to know her mood, it was known that she was pleased. Not that this lessened the Kyrosdyn's collective curiosity, but it did enable them to take solace from their faith in the rightness of the Order and its leader.

Thus it was too, that no hint of complaint or question arose from the escort bustling along after Imorren.

Accompanying, and discreetly supporting the less steady were several of the Vaskyros's unliveried bodyguards, while two carefully groomed Pitguards walked on either side of Imorren. They had been given the task of leading the Ailad along the complicated route, but it seemed from the outset that they were not needed. At each branch and junction – and there were many – Imorren continued in the correct direction without hesitating.

Thug turned businessman and aspiring diplomat, in common with most of Barran's senior aides, one of the Pitguards attempted a courtesy to break what was becoming an unnerving silence.

'You're familiar with the Jyolan, Ailad?'

There was no reply, but a tap on the shoulder and a shake of the head from a large bodyguard precluded any further attempt at conversation.

Finally they came to a wooden door. The same Pitguard, anxious now to atone for his apparent error, hurried forward and opened it fussily. Imorren stepped through, signalling the others to wait.

'Close the door,' she said, without turning.

It swung to with a dull thud.

Lamps were hung at random about the vaulted chamber where she now stood. They threw hazy shadows between rows of squat stone columns, but their light seemed to make little impression on the heavy darkness. As the sound of the door echoed and faded, there came the soft rustle of someone moving. Imorren turned towards it and a tall figure emerged from the shadows. He stopped in front of her then slowly went down on one knee and lowered his head. Imorren rested her hand on his shoulder.

'Keeper, you did well. Leave us for the moment.'

There was a hesitancy in the man's posture. 'Have no fears,' she said, almost maternally. 'What danger could *I* be in?' She motioned him to stand and indicated the door.

The man bowed and left the chamber.

When the sound of his leaving had died away, Imorren stood for a while in the silence, her head moving slowly from side to side as if she were testing the air for an elusive perfume. She pulled back the hood of her robe.

'Come,' she said. 'Don't be afraid.'

The silence descended again. Imorren waited, motionless, showing no signs of impatience. Indeed, she was smiling slightly.

'Do you think to hide from *me*?' she said, as to a child.

There was a sound, delicate, like grains of sand sweeping across a windy shore, and out of the shadows from which the Keeper had emerged came the creature that had ended the Jyolan's first Loose Pit.

Head lowered, it moved directly towards Imorren, stopping in front of her, as its Keeper had done, without command. She crouched down and took its ugly head between her hands.

'You too did well, blessed one,' she said. Yellow eyes met hers. She stoked the creature's head. 'How long is your line?' she said softly to herself, a hint of wonder in her voice. 'How long have your kin roamed the depths, keeping alive His memory, waiting for Him to come again?' Slowly it closed its eyes and opened them again, as if wilfully accepting her authority. She gripped the coarse hair of its neck and bared her teeth. 'Would that you'd returned but a few years earlier – been with His armies when the enemy came against Him. They'd have scattered like scalded ants before you. And you'd have seen the weakness in His erstwhile lieutenants, wouldn't you? Hollow vessels that they were. No ancient loyalties, old familiarities, would have blinded you to their inadequacy.' Her mouth curled into a vicious snarl – feral and cruel in the yellow light. The creature tried to pull its head from her hands as if afraid, but she held it firm.

The mask of her normal face returned. 'But these things are not

243

for our questioning. It was His will that I left Him, and who can say why you came so late? And the past is the past. His wisdom in these things is beyond our judgement – who can say what stratagem's afoot? For He is with us yet, is He not? This city is His place. Beneath the clutter and clamour of the creatures who infest it for the moment, His presence lies firm and whole, deep in its ancient foundations. He is strong here. And His will reaches out to us. How else could you have sought out your Keeper and come to us? How else could Rostan have been so used?'

She hugged the creature's head tightly. A low rumbling came from its throat and she laughed in response. It was a cold and desolate sound that darkened the vault where true laughter might have lightened it. Her voice fell to a whisper, and she spoke quickly, almost excitedly. 'And He will be with us again soon, blessed one. More and more my dreams are filled with the true form of the Vaskyros – stronger, clearer each time. Perhaps the Anointed will complete its shaping to open the Ways. Perhaps . . .' She stopped. Speculation was pointless. The Way of the Anointed was, by its very nature, unforeseeable.

But she could not remain silent. 'You saw him, didn't you? As did I. Glowing like a beacon of hope, high up in the darkness above the arena. And *I* feared that he might be lost.' She laughed again. 'He was drawn to us. He will bind himself to us more tightly than any bonds I could make.' She stopped again, struck by something. 'And perhaps more. I hadn't thought such a thing possible, but . . .' Agitated, she turned away from the creature and looked into the darkness. She was herself again when she looked back. Her voice became a whisper again as if the words she was about to speak might overwhelm her. 'Could he prove to be more than a guide?' She drew in a long, tense breath. 'Once, I'll swear, I felt His eyes upon me, His presence around me again.' She wrapped her arms about herself then stood up and began walking down one of the aisles, as if the thought would be too much, contained in a motionless frame. The creature moved silently by her side. 'I was right to seize the moment – to follow the wild rushing that Rostan had unleashed – to bring you out into this noisy world, so full of richness for you.' She stopped and began stroking the creature again. 'Soon, the

Anointed will be truly ready, then . . .'

She grimaced and put her hands to the sides of her face as though to crush her head. As, earlier, she had discovered the human frailty of anger within her, so now she felt elation. It was no less despised.

She blazed inwardly. There had been such learning this day! And re-learning! Learning that she was still flawed, that she must ever beware the clinging power of her humanity with its treacherous emotions lying always in wait to bring her low – contaminating her, marring her for His work. Learning again that she was but His servant and that His ways were not to be questioned or doubted – her faith must be absolute. Learning again that the power she had seized and accumulated in this city of powerful people, great though it was, was as nothing to what would be.

The elation faded, unnoticed amid her greater lusts.

The creature whimpered. 'We must be patient, blessed one. Our travails are nothing to His.' She knelt down by its side and draped an arm across its shoulder. 'But you *were* patient tonight, weren't you?' she said. 'You waited and waited, and played their foolish games. Then you were deprived of what was rightly yours. Your prey was snatched from you.' She became uneasy. The creature was no threat to her, she had more than enough Power to control it, but the Keeper had indicated concerns even though he had not voiced them. The creature was a unique instrument of His will, a memory of His crafting in the Great Age when His Power had spanned the world. It would be foolish of her to imagine that she fully understood it, and perhaps reckless of her to use the Power to control it. There was no telling what damage might be done. Then, slowly, strange, vivid images of the final encounter in the arena began to seep into her mind.

The creature was touching her in some way!

And she knew.

Though it showed no signs of distress, the antics of its three victims had served to rouse the creature without satisfying it. Its need suddenly filled her, leaving her at once exhilarated and starkly cold. It was not good that the creature was struggling against whatever forces were restraining it. As with people, the best control was had by fulfilling needs, not denying them.

She tightened her grip about the creature, holding it close. It did not resist.

As with the Anointed, she would have to have faith. Faith that His servants need not be bound by doors and chains for they could do no other than follow her as she followed Him.

'Go down beneath the city,' she whispered, picturing in her mind the labyrinthine tunnels that underlay the city. 'To the place above that you came from. Seek out a victim – sate your need. You must be whole. Return.'

The creature bent its forelegs and lowered its head as it had to Pinnatte in the arena. It made a strange mewling noise then drew its head back and let out a low, trembling howl. It was not loud but it was such as Imorren had never heard before and it struck right through her. In others, she knew, it would instil the deepest fear, but to her it was more a hymn of affirmation – this creature was indeed a harbinger of a new age. Nevertheless, her skin – all too human – crawled in response. The lamps seemed to flare at its touch and as the howl echoed around the vaults it was as if the whole chamber were breathing a long sigh of recognition and delight.

The creature walked away from her silently and vanished into the darkness.

Imorren rubbed her hands down her arms to quieten her rebellious flesh. Then the presence of the creature was gone. As with every other chamber in the Jyolan, many passages joined this cellar, passages that plunged far beyond the confines of the building itself.

It was an ancient building.

He was moving through the darkness, powerful confident limbs remembering their honing at the other end of the long darkness. Scents assailed him, old and familiar, rich and heady, feeding the need that drove him and drawing him on. And there were sounds too, distant and distorted, as though they were being carried on a buffeting wind.

Then he stopped and dropped low, listening, feeling. Ahead was prey. All around was prey. And no danger! An expectant shudder ran through him, culminating in a low, rumbling growl. He began to crawl forward.

What . . .?

He was here and not here – two things – two minds . . .

He did not belong!

The thought made no sense. Thoughts did not belong. He *was*. This was the way of things.

And the noises disturbed. And the lights, hovering, watching . . .

But he crawled on, sensing every movement in the air about him, every crack and flaw in the ground beneath him so that as he crawled, even he could not hear himself.

The scents that filled him drew him forward – and repelled. And the thoughts – no, the sensations – that flooded in their wake, were ecstatic, unspeakable.

Protest. 'No!'

Noises. And lights. They hurt.

'Did he say something?'

'He's been making all sorts of queer noises.'

Soon there would be prey near. A low growl to warn it, to make it flee – and then the chase, terror growing as it flew, etching a luring trail through the swirling air, on and on, screaming.

Good.

'Pinnatte!'

The sound crashed in on him, forming about him – giving him shape – tearing him free. The dark images fell away from him like a fouled cloak. And the dancing lights began to come together – hovering ovals.

Faces.

'Rinter?'

His own voice ran achingly through his head.

'You gave us a fright. Thought you'd been really hurt when that gate burst open. Are you all right?'

Pinnatte made to push himself upright but a hand stopped him. 'Lie still.' It was a woman's voice. He tried to turn to her, but his head protested painfully and the room began to sway.

'I said, lie still,' came the voice again, authoritative. The hand returned, immovable. 'I don't think you've had anything more than a nasty bump, but you're going to have a fine headache for a while.'

Moving more carefully, Pinnatte managed to turn to his physician. She was a middle-aged woman. Quite tall, he thought, though it was difficult to tell from where he was lying. She was certainly no frail thing, judging from the determination in the hand restraining him. Most striking however, was her face. She had been handsome once, he thought. Not beautiful – handsome. At the same time he realized there were more important things he should be considering, but the thought enticed him. Now, though there were lines of care etched into it, the dominant impression the face gave was one of strength – great strength – the kind that only a woman can possess and which comes when she has stood alone against all troubles and then pressed on into and through the darkness.

'Hello,' he said weakly.

She looked at him intently for a moment then, apparently satisfied, took hold of his hand and began examining it. 'Hello, yourself, young man,' she said while she was doing this. She frowned.

'It's only a graze,' came a man's voice from somewhere behind her. She made no response but motioned to someone to bring a lamp closer, then raised Pinnatte's hand close to her face.

'Nasty,' she said, very quietly. She shot a quick inquiring glance at Pinnatte as if expecting to see something she had missed. 'It looks almost like a crystal stain.'

A large, heavy individual eased her to one side and a battered face bent down to examine the hand curiously. 'You worked in the Thlosgaral, lad? In the mines?' he asked, returning the hand to the woman. His expression was a mixture of puzzlement and concern.

'No,' Pinnatte replied. 'Never been out of the city.'

The man shook his head. 'Couldn't be,' he said emphatically. 'Look at him. He's a bit skinny, but he looks fit enough. He's a Den-Mate or I'm a donkey – city through and through. Half a day's walk from here and he'd be lost. There's no way he'd learn to do that or even get the opportunity, for that matter.' He looked at the hand again. 'Besides, it looks almost green to me. No one but a lunatic would do *that*.'

The woman looked doubtful. 'Yes,' she began, 'but . . .' She shrugged. 'Couldn't be, as you say.' She stared at the hand pensively. 'Still, I'll put some drawing salve on it. It won't do any harm, and the cut needs cleaning anyway.' She lifted a loose cloth bag on to her lap and, after some fumbling, produced a small jar. 'Long time since I've needed this,' she said, wrestling briefly with the lid. Then a clean, pungent smell assailed Pinnatte and she was liberally pasting something on to the back of his hand.

A violent burning ran up his arm. With it, powerfully, came the knowledge that he must not allow this to happen!

He gave a loud yell and tried to snatch his hand back, but the woman was too strong and the action simply drew him upright. The pain in his arm was replaced by an even greater one in his head which suddenly felt as though it were about to burst. He slumped back, banging down on a cushion that was serving as a pillow and making the pain in his head even worse. He could do no other than lie still and moan until the pounding began to ease. As it did, he became aware of laughter around him. Very hesitantly he opened his eyes. Even his nurse was smiling a little.

'Some hero,' someone was saying. There was more laughter.

'The ointment will deaden it for a while and draw anything out that shouldn't be there,' the woman said. 'It's old-fashioned, but it's good.' She was bandaging his hand. The burning had stopped now and the hand felt cold. Still he had the feeling that this should not have been allowed, but it was much weaker now – and the tightening bandage was reassuring.

Cautiously he looked slowly around as far as he could, without actually moving his head. Apart from Rinter, the woman and the big man with the battered face, there were Pitguards milling about. He was lying in a room which, unusually for the Jyolan, had a plain, flat ceiling and four straight walls. It retained however, the Jyolan's long-neglected appearance, walls and ceiling being decorated with anonymous stains and peeling paint.

The Pitguards were coming and going at the far end of the room, attending to some kind of business with a man sat at a table. Almost all of them looked across towards the small group and one or two came over to look at Pinnatte curiously.

The events that had brought him here returned to Pinnatte as his vision continued to clear and the pain in his head settled into a comparatively tolerable throb. After a little while, he began to feel not only at ease, but very pleased with himself. He had no idea what had prompted him to clamber over the crowd, but it had turned him into an object of some admiration by men of whom he stood in awe. Even though his thoughts were occupied almost totally with his present circumstances, a small part of him was registering the fact that the esteem of these people could prove very useful in the future.

'You'd be best advised to rest for a while,' the woman said.

'I don't think I can do anything else,' Pinnatte replied. 'Is it all right if I stay here for a while?'

'Stay as long as you like, lad,' the big man said. 'Barran will see you get more than a bed for what you've done. A few minutes later opening that gate and there'd have been a lot of people killed for sure.' He shook his head. 'We'd have been up to our necks in Prefect's men, Weartans and lawyers for months, all looking for their share. Business would've gone to hell. As it is, it's only half a dozen or so got killed. We can soon pay them off.'

Pinnatte had little idea what the man was talking about and just looked at him blankly.

'This is Fiarn, Pinnatte.' It was Rinter. 'I told you about him earlier. We were talking to you when you passed out.'

Despite his general weakness and confusion, Pinnatte's thoughts soared. Meeting Fiarn was worth even more to him that the goodwill of a score of Pitguards. He lifted his bandaged hand to take Fiarn's. It was still cold and although he saw Fiarn's fist envelope it, he could feel nothing. It was as if it no longer belonged to him. He left it hovering for a moment when Fiarn released it then tried to move his fingers. Nothing happened.

'It's the ointment,' the woman said, sensing his concern. 'I told you, it deadens. You could chop a finger off and not feel it. Don't worry, it'll be back to normal in a few hours.'

Fiarn nodded knowingly. The woman thrust the jar and various bandages back into her bag and spoke to him. 'I've done all I can here. I'll get back to Barran downstairs and see what I can do there.'

Somewhat to Pinnatte's surprise, Fiarn's posture in front of the woman was politely deferential, as though she were in some way his superior. He even bowed slightly when she left. The impression was confirmed when she signalled to the Pitguards and they set off after her.

'Who was that?' he asked when she had gone.

'Ellyn, Barran's wife,' Fiarn replied, looking at him in some surprise. 'You're lucky she was here. She knows a lot about wounds.' He pulled up a chair and sat down. 'Now, young man.' He waved a hand in front of Pinnatte's face. 'Are you with us?'

Pinnatte blinked in lieu of a more hazardous nod. 'Yes, I think so,' he said. 'But I wish she'd put some of that ointment on my head.'

Fiarn laughed and slapped his shoulder, both actions shaking Pinnatte bodily and making him wince. Fiarn did not seem to notice. 'Barran was impressed by what you did – that's why he got Ellyn to look after you. I told you, you saved us all a lot of problems, and he's known for paying his debts. He's busy now, tidying up the mess, otherwise he'd have been here himself, but he'll speak to you later. In the meantime he's told me to talk to you – see whether there's anything we can do for you.'

Rinter, standing slightly behind Fiarn, gave Pinnatte a massive, knowing grimace. It was not necessary, Pinnatte was sufficiently recovered to appreciate fully the opportunity that was being presented. He opted for honesty.

'I'm a Den-Mate,' he said. 'Cutpurse, mainly – and good at it. Work on my own, or with a team, it doesn't matter.' Both men instinctively checked their belts and pockets. Pinnatte raised a hasty hand. 'I never worked the Pits, though. You can ask the Pitguards about that – the old ones, that is.' Fiarn was watching him narrowly now, but was secretly pleased that his own estimate of Pinnatte had been correct. Pinnatte looked at him squarely. 'It's not enough. I want more. Could I work for Barran?'

Even as he heard himself speaking, he could scarcely believe what he had done. So blunt, so direct. What was he doing here? How could his whole world have changed so utterly in one day? He felt suddenly disorientated, as if he might at any moment wake to find himself lying in his old room at Lassner's and this all a vivid dream.

But though looking doubtful, Fiarn was nodding. 'That, I don't know,' he said. 'Barran picks his people very carefully. But he might be able to find something for you. I'll tell him. Who's your Den Master?'

'Lassner.'

'I've heard of him. What can you do apart from steal purses?'

'What do you want?' Pinnatte put his hand to his head and frowned. His head was not hurting particularly but he contrived this small piece of theatre to distract Fiarn from answering the question.

It worked. Fiarn stood up. 'You take it easy for a while. I'll have to get back downstairs and help now you're all right. I'll ask Barran about you when I get the chance, but be prepared to ask for something else if he says he can't use you.' He leaned forward. 'And don't argue with him if that's what he says. He'll look after you for what you've done – he always looks after those who look after him – but he doesn't tolerate fools or impudence. Do you understand?'

'Yes,' Pinnatte said, with a careful nod.

When Fiarn had gone, Rinter took his chair. 'If Barran can't use you, I'll try to help you find something,' he said. He drew his hand across his mouth. 'It won't be the same, of course, but I owe you more than he does. I've never been so frightened in all my life. As soon as you'd climbed up those two in front, the whole crowd just tightened around me.' He hunched his arms tight into his sides and shivered. 'And when you dropped out of sight . . .' He hesitated. 'I thought for a minute you'd just saved yourself – run away. I'm sorry.'

Pinnatte was beginning to doze off. 'It's all right,' he mumbled. 'I don't know what I was thinking myself. Just the little lad's face . . . had to do something . . .'

He was asleep.

And he was moving through the darkness again. Only this time, it was different. This time, he was who he was, and . . . what?

Deep, animal urgings filled him as they had before, drawing

him on. They were both repellent and desirable, but where before they had been a measure of him, now something was keeping him apart from them, something cold and heavy. Yet he was bound to them. He could not escape. He must go wherever they led. Be a part of whatever happened.

On through the darkness he was carried, following the strange trails that he knew and did not know. Then there was stillness. His nostrils filled with an ancient perfume.

Prey was near, very near.

An image formed, vague and unsteady in the gloom, yet etched vividly by his other senses. It was a man, sitting on the ground, leaning with his back against a rocky wall. He was asleep.

Prey was chosen.

Something fearful was about to happen. Pinnatte began to struggle. But to no avail. He belonged here. This was his destiny.

No! he shouted out, though no sound came.

He tried again. His cry became a low rumbling growl – not a warning, but an announcement. The figure stirred and Pinnatte was aware of bleary eyes searching into the darkness. He was drawn nearer. The growl came again and something from within, something that was at the heart of his purpose, reached out and touched the man.

The bleary eyes were suddenly wide and terrified. Beneath them, a mouth formed into a gaping hole. Ancient memories consumed Pinnatte – an endless, overlapping line of such sights – filling him with desire.

Then came the screaming.

Chapter 20

Heirn woke more easily than he had anticipated after his fretful night. 'Probably feel it later,' he growled to himself, but his complaint was unconvincing. He felt good. The light coming through the open window told him that it was going to be another hot day, and while the continuing heat presented its own problems, on the whole it was preferable to the grey dampness, raw winds and driving snow that would inevitably arrive in a few months.

As he washed himself, the events of the previous day, with their fateful and fatal conclusion, rolled through his mind again. They concerned him still, concerned him greatly – a man had died and all manner of strange, frightening things had been revealed to him – but he did not feel burdened by them. It was not the response he would have expected. He paused and looked at himself in the mirror as if expecting to see some change in his appearance that might account for this calm.

Unfamiliar noises attracted his attention through the general clamour from the street. One was the rapid clicking of small feet. Atlon and Dvolci were about. Perhaps it was the presence of these two that accounted for his lack of agitation, he thought. Strange couple though they were, there was an openness, an honesty, about both of them. And a quietness. As if they had known far worse and survived it. Faced their worst fear and walked through it.

Atlon's greeting when he emerged from his room was a smile, and, 'Are you well?'

Heirn could do no other than blurt out his thoughts. 'I am,' he replied, 'but I don't know why. I was awake much of the night and I'm surprised I got any sleep at all after what happened yesterday.'

Atlon nodded sympathetically. 'Sometimes your body has more

255

sense than your mind. And there's little to be gained from trying to run away from things like this. We spent most of the night talking and thinking, deciding what to do.'

'Which was?'

'Which was that we must find out much more about the Kyrosdyn and the crystal trade. We must find out what they're doing. Are they just an old cult that's fallen into corruption, or are they something more dangerous? Are they just blundering about, dabbling with things they don't understand, or do they have a focus, a clear end they're trying to achieve?'

Heirn looked uncomfortable. He gesticulated vaguely. 'Like bringing . . . Sammrael . . . back,' he said, half-expecting to be laughed at.

Atlon turned away from him quickly. He opened his mouth to reply twice before he managed, 'No,' stammering slightly and with a weak smile. 'It couldn't be that. It wouldn't be possible, not so soon. No.' But his words carried no conviction and he moved hastily to another conclusion. 'If they're doing anything, they're probably using the crystals and their knowledge of the Power to make weapons.'

'Weapons? Hardened swords and spear – that kind of thing? There's nothing new there.'

Atlon looked straight at him. 'Don't *ever* forget the force that held you against the wall in that alley. There was nothing that you could see, or hear, or feel – yet, strong though you are, you were helpless. And that was the casual effort of a comparatively unskilled novice. And you saw the damage it did to him in the end. The hurt that the Power can do is beyond your imagining, Heirn. Swords, shields, whole armies, even castle walls, are useless against it.'

Atlon's unexpected passion took Heirn by surprise. All he could ask was, 'Why would they want such weapons?'

Atlon shrugged. 'You know your own city, your own people. You tell me.'

Heirn opened a cupboard and a small gust of cold air seeped into the room. He took out a loaf and jug of milk and various items of food then closed the door quickly. 'Most of the serious jostling for power is done quietly, behind the scenes – bribery, blackmail, assassination – that kind of thing. Those of us with any sense keep clear of it – get on with our lives. Sometimes there'll be a riot stirred up by one faction or another, but there hasn't been any serious armed conflict – a war – just to gain power, in generations.'

'Could there be?'

'No, no.' Heirn was categorical. He was rattling through a drawer in search of a knife to cut the bread. 'The city's too big, too crowded, too full of independently minded people, for any one group to hold sway over it for any length of time, if at all. History's full of failed attempts.' He began to slice the loaf.

'I can believe that from what I've seen of the place,' Atlon said. 'Even so, a weapon that used the Power would give them great sway here. It would be infinitely more powerful than any number of swords and spears. One man could hold – even destroy – whole crowds, just as the Kyrosdyn held you last night.'

Heirn frowned as he tried to reject the idea, but Atlon's reminder about the Kyrosdyn's Power held him as helpless as the Power itself had. He reverted to practicalities again. 'But why? What would be the point?'

'I've no idea,' Atlon said, shaking his head. 'But it's in the nature of powerful people always to accumulate more power. They need no reason. And, as I said, I fear they could all be slaves to the crystals – who knows where that will have led them?'

Heirn motioned Atlon to help himself to the food, then paused. 'I don't know what I'm doing, talking about such things, and eating!' he said through a mouthful of bread. He shook his head as if that might re-order his thoughts. 'All of which leaves you where?' he mumbled, spraying crumbs.

'All of which leaves us with the need to find out more about the Kyrosdyn and, specifically, what they're up to,' Atlon replied.

Heirn looked at him intently. 'And when you've found out, what're you going to do?'

'Go back home. Tell the senior Brothers of my Order.'

'What will they do?'

Atlon sensed his concern. 'It depends what we find, obviously. But they won't come marching in with a great army, if that's what you're worried about. We've neither the men nor the inclination for more war and, in any case, it's far too far away for us to be mounting a campaign.'

'But they'll do something, won't they?'

'It depends what we find,' Atlon said again. He leaned forward insistently. 'But listen, Heirn. From what I've seen so far from that one man, if he's typical – and you seem to think he is – your city's in far greater danger from the Kyrosdyn *right now* than from anything my people might do at some vague time in the future.'

Heirn let out a short sigh then looked at a timepiece on the wall. 'Do you still want a job?' he asked.

It was sufficient to end the inconclusive debate, and shortly afterwards they were heading for the forge. Heirn led them the way he normally went, keeping well away from the more secluded route they had taken the previous night.

'I'm still not happy about leaving that body, but I suppose someone will have found it by now,' he whispered to Atlon. 'We'll see if there's any gossip about it.'

And there was, though it was not much.

'Flock of crows kicking up a fuss not far from your place this morning,' one of Heirn's regular customers announced jauntily.

'Crows?' Heirn queried.

'Crows. You know – the Brothers.' He screwed up his face into a peevish mask. 'Seems one of them popped his sandals in an alley just down from where you live.'

'Kyrosdyn, you mean?' Heirn said.

The man was scornful. 'You're getting particular in your old age, aren't you? Crows is nearer the mark – "Kyrosdyn" makes them sound almost human.'

'What happened?' Heirn asked, carrying on with his work.

'I've no idea,' the man said, moving to watch Atlon who was stitching a leather purse. 'I just saw a crowd of them carrying someone out of the alley when I was going past. Apparently it was an old man – *really* old, someone said. Seemed surprised they'd let someone so frail out on his own, but you know what they're like.'

Heirn grunted indifferently.

258

'Mind you, they seemed upset about it. Milling around like frightened hens, with a deal of arm-waving and shouting. They don't normally do things like that in public. And the looks they were giving the crowd . . .' He puffed his cheeks out. 'You'd think one of us had seen the old beggar off.'

'Maybe he was a respected Higher Brother,' Heirn said. 'Not everyone has your jaundiced view of them.'

'Not everyone's had my dealings with them,' the retort bounced back. 'And since when have you had a good word for them?' He did not wait for an answer. 'I'll wager they weren't getting so excited because they loved him. He'd probably embezzled the funds and was spending them on a lady friend when time caught up with him.' He made an obscene gesture.

Heirn laughed and threw him the belt buckle he had been working on. 'Here, pay your money and clear off. It's too nice a day for your cynicism.'

When he had gone, Heirn turned to Atlon. 'Well, at least the body's been taken care of.'

Atlon looked up at him sympathetically. 'What do you think will happen next?' he asked.

Heirn shrugged. 'You tell me,' he said. 'Normally the Weartans would investigate an unexpected death, but I very much doubt the Kyrosdyn will even tell them about it. If they're asked, they'll probably say one of their older Brothers died of heart failure, or some such. Anything else would leave them with far too many bizarre questions to answer.'

The day drifted on, Heirn working at his forge, Atlon turning his hand to repairing tackle and various leather goods. 'Not my favourite work,' Heirn admitted shamefacedly as he pointed out the neglected items. 'Been putting some of it off for a long time.'

They heard the tale about the dead Kyrosdyn a few times more but nothing was added to what they already knew. They also heard about the unexpected developments at the Jyolan.

'They say Barran's taken it over – from the Kyrosdyn, no less. He'll liven it up.'

'All the balconies were open. It's a queer place that, I tell you. Tunnels and passages winding everywhere.'

'A few people killed in the crush. Could've been more but for some young lad opening the gate.'

'Never seen anything like that creature at the end. Sort of a dog of some kind, I suppose. Really fast and vicious when it got going. Bit this dog's leg clean off – threw it out of the arena. And it was frightening somehow – even when it was just sitting there.' The voice was lowered and the speaker leaned across Heirn's anvil. 'Tale is that it's something the Kyrosdyn found down below.' The last two words were mouthed rather than spoken, and a significant finger was pointed downwards.

Heirn seemed anxious to let the topic go, but Atlon intervened. 'What did it look like?'

He listened to the description interestedly, but shook his head when it was finished. Dvolci, curled up in the shade near the back of the forge, stirred uneasily.

When the two men were alone again, he joined them.

'That was a Serwulf,' he said urgently.

Heirn looked puzzled, and Atlon said unconvincingly: 'It can't be.'

'Sounded like one to me. The description – the way it moved – and frightening even when it was just sitting there.'

'It can't be,' Atlon insisted. 'It'd be from the time of the First Coming. They were all destroyed . . .' He faltered.

Dvolci was shaking his head. 'Most of His creatures were destroyed, but some fled into the deeps. *We* know that for a fact, don't we?' He turned to Heirn. 'Tell us about down below,' he said, mimicking the last customer, with a downward thrust of his paw.

'What's the matter?' Heirn said to Atlon, ignoring Dvolci.

'I'm fine,' Atlon said, though his expression said otherwise. 'Tell us about where this creature's supposed to have come from – the caves.'

'Not much to tell, really,' Heirn said, eyeing Atlon anxiously. 'There are tunnels beneath the city – man-made tunnels – very old. Supposed to be more of them down there than streets up here. Probably used for storage or as escape routes from the time of the founding of the city – no one knows.'

'People live down there?'

Heirn grimaced unhappily. 'The poor, the stupid, the vicious. "Tunnellers", we call them. Anyone who for various reasons can't or won't live up here. It's a bad, sad place.'

'And below these are caves?'

Affected by Atlon's sudden seriousness, Heirn strove for accuracy. 'Yes, well, everyone believes there are. But, to be honest, I can't say I know anyone who's actually been down there. Most people don't even go into the tunnels if they can avoid it, let alone any deeper.'

'Someone told me that the Kyrosdyn go to the caves to capture animals – strange animals – for the Pits.'

'So the tales go – the gossip. But that's all it is – gossip. I'm no lover of the Pits. As far as I'm concerned, they're an obscenity. I'd as soon see people fighting in them, as animals – at least they'd be there by choice. I don't know what goes on in them, especially the Loose Pits.'

'But some strange things appear from time to time?' Atlon pressed.

'So I've heard,' Heirn replied hastily, waving his hand as if to be free of the subject. 'I've also heard that the Kyrosdyn breed their own fighting animals; perhaps this thing was one of them. What's a Serwulf anyway?'

'Until now I'd thought it was just a memory,' Atlon replied grimly. He glanced at Dvolci. 'But we know there are creatures in the depths that have been long gone from the daylight.' He stared out at the sunlit square. 'At the time of the First Coming, when His true nature was revealed and the wars started, He had all manner of creatures fighting with His armies – creatures that he had created. The Serwulf was supposed to be one of the worst, the peak of His achievement as it were. Part wild dog, part boar, part human, part who can say what – the whole made into something unique and terrifying, totally His – an abomination. Apart from strength and speed and cunning, it's said they sent terror before them, and fed on that of their victims – tormenting them. They ran in great packs and were supposed to have scattered entire armies – broken infantry that had held firm against the finest cavalry.'

Atlon's tone seemed to darken the forge. Heirn clung to the practical.

'Surely nothing could have stayed alive down there in the darkness – breeding, hunting, not after all this time?'

'We have,' Dvolci said simply. 'My people live in the depths – there are many things that thrive there – and there are regions far deeper than we venture.'

Heirn made no reply. The noise of the square filled the forge.

When Atlon spoke, his voice was low, as if he were reluctant to hear his own words. 'If this *is* a Serwulf, then it confirms what I said earlier. The Kyrosdyn are a bigger danger to the city than any outside enemy, or any other power group within it.'

'It's a lot to assume on the strength of one freak animal in a Loose Pit,' Heirn said.

'I hope I'm wrong,' Atlon said. 'But we'll have to find out.' He stood up. 'Have you anything else that you want me to do today? I need to go to the Jyolan to find out about this creature. And I might find something out about the Kyrosdyn as well.'

Heirn stammered, 'No, no, there's nothing urgent. And what you've done is splendid – you've saved my reputation with some of my best customers.' He ran his hand admiringly down a saddle hanging nearby. 'Are you sure you want to go to the Jyolan? Whether it's being run by the Kyrosdyn or Barran's men, they won't like you prying around, asking questions.'

'Yes, I'm sure. Don't worry, I'll be careful.'

Heirn looked doubtful. 'Shall I come with you?' he asked, adding hastily, 'You might get lost. Besides, if the Kyrosdyn are as dangerous as you say, it's a city matter, isn't it? It shouldn't be up to you to sort it out.'

Atlon shook his head. 'No, you stay here. I can remember the way.' He rubbed his hands together. 'And if I get into *my* kind of difficulty there you won't be able to help.' The remark came out harsher than he had intended. He became conciliatory. 'Besides, if that happens it'll be as well if you're not associated with me. That way, they won't come after you as well.'

Heirn was not totally convinced. 'It's still a city matter.'

'True,' Atlon conceded, 'but,' he counted off the points of his argument with his fingers, 'the crystals are my affair – they've already affected my people. If the Kyrosdyn seize Arash-Felloren they'll not stop there. And *I'm* the only person who knows what to look for.' He took Heirn's arm. 'Nothing would delight me more than to ride away from here, but I can't. And you'll help me best by being here if I need you.'

Heirn straightened up and looked at him paternally. 'Very well, young man,' he said. 'But if you're not back by an hour to sunset, I'll come looking for you. I've never started a quarrel in my life, though I've finished one or two.'

'Thank you,' Dvolci said before Atlon could remonstrate further with him.

A few minutes later, Heirn was standing at the front of his forge, watching Atlon, mounted, wend his way across the busy square. He had left his long coat at the forge, but after a glance at the high sun he had donned his wide-brimmed hat. It provided a focal point for Heirn when all other details had merged into the crowd. When finally the hat had disappeared from view, Heirn turned back into the forge. It seemed very empty.

Even allowing for two or three acrimonious exchanges at certain busy junctions – all of which Dvolci both won and subsequently gloated over – the journey back to the Jyolan did not seem as long as when they had travelled the other way on the previous day.

When they arrived, a confusing swirl of activity in front of the building was spilling across the street, blocking much of it, to the noisy irritation of the general traffic. There was a constant stream of people bustling in and out, while others were generally milling around, or standing in groups, talking urgently. Still more were dragging things out and dumping them into carts with a reckless disregard for anyone standing in the way. Everyone seemed to be shouting at everyone else, not least the men precariously perched on the several ladders that were leaning against the front wall. An atmosphere of both confusion and urgency pervaded the scene.

Atlon reined his horse to a halt and stared at the building for a long time.

'Nervous?' Dvolci asked eventually.

263

Atlon took a deep breath. 'Scared stiff,' he replied. 'So much has happened these last two days. Things coming to light I'd not even dared imagine. Our simple search for the source of a few troublesome crystals is turning into a nightmare. I'd give anything to be away from here – back at the caves, studying, riding, talking . . . anything.' Reaching up, he touched the felci hesitantly. 'If anything happens to me, don't take any risks. Go back on your own. Tell the others about whatever's . . . happened. They must know.'

'I will if I have to,' Dvolci said quietly. 'Don't worry. But let's deal with the present first. Have you any idea where to start?'

Atlon dismounted. 'Not really. But for what it's worth, this place feels worse than it did yesterday – and that face on the archway is really disturbing.'

Dvolci gave a low, thoughtful whistle. 'Yes, it is,' he said. 'It's an ill-rooted place.' He began to whisper. 'Listen, if there are any of these Kyrosdyn in there, be very careful. That one last night was as taut as a bowstring. They might smell you out even if you don't use the Power. Whatever happens, whatever you see or feel, stay very calm, completely in control. You understand, don't you? You're back on the battlefield here, so be alert. I'll be watching, and if it looks as though you're slipping, I'll try to remind you, or distract matters somehow – but I won't be able to do much.'

Atlon nodded then closed his eyes and took another slow, deep breath. 'Don't be afraid to be afraid,' he said softly to himself. 'You've been in worse places.' It was only slightly convincing – he still wanted to be somewhere else.

Dvolci dropped into Atlon's pack and pulled the flap down so that only his muzzle protruded. Atlon tethered his horse loosely to a rail in front of the building next to the Jyolan, speaking to it as he did so, then, carefully keeping his gaze away from the face carved on the archway, he began pushing his way through the activity in the entrance hall.

There was even greater confusion inside than outside. The leaves of the gate that Pinnatte had unbolted the previous night had been removed from their hinges and were occupying much of the entrance hall while they were being repaired. When it had burst open, the gate had crashed back so violently that its hinges had been damaged and parts of it had buckled. Pinnatte was fortunate to have been flung clear or he would certainly have been badly injured. Braziers were crackling and throwing up sparks, adding their own heat and fumes to those of the day and the city, and several large men were levering and hammering in an attempt to straighten the buckled frames. The noise was deafening. It was not helped by everyone shouting to make themselves heard over it.

Atlon was gazing around for someone to speak to when a heavy hand was laid on his shoulder. He turned to face Fiarn. The big man was not a welcoming sight. His battered face was creased with frustration and his posture was decidedly menacing. 'You one of the painters?' he shouted.

Atlon leaned forward to catch the words. 'No,' he shouted back. Fiarn swore irritably and looked around as if searching for a place where this intruder might be placed in the confusion. 'Who the hell are you, then?' he demanded.

Atlon pulled off his hat and tried to hold Fiarn's restless gaze. He ignored the man's unpleasant tone. 'My name's Atlon,' he shouted. 'I'm looking for a man call Rinter – Irgon Rinter, I think. I was supposed to meet—'

There was a burst of frantic hammering from the men repairing the gate which made everyone in the entrance hall put their hands to their ears.

'What!' Atlon could see Fiarn's mouth saying.

'Rinter. I'm looking for a man called Rinter,' he bellowed back into what proved to be an equally sudden silence. All eyes turned to him. It was this that took the brunt of Fiarn's response. He looked around, eyes wide with disbelief. 'Get on with your work!' he roared. 'What d'you think this is – Prefect's Holiday?' The clamour returned, with increased vigour. Fiarn returned to Atlon. 'For crying out – I'm not Rinter's keeper, you know. I've got enough to do today without chasing after him.' He turned and walked away, waving vaguely in the direction of the interior of the building. 'He's knocking about somewhere. With the new one – Pinnatte. Go find him yourself.'

'Scarce commodity in this city, charm,' Dvolci muttered into

Atlon's ear. Atlon looked at the archways which opened off the entrance hall. 'I don't like the look of those,' Dvolci said.

'I don't like the whole place,' Atlon retorted. He blew out a heavy breath. 'Still, he invited us in, so let's go and see what we can find.'

It took them a little time to decide which of the arches they should try, there being no indication on any of them as to where they led. In the end they chose the one that seemed to be the busiest. It opened into a wide passageway, but they had not gone far along it when Atlon stopped.

'What's the matter?' Dvolci asked.

'Bad feelings, bad feelings, that's all,' Atlon replied. 'Like a weight on me. Somehow this place is like a travesty of the caves back home, as if it were designed to gather darkness rather than light.'

Dvolci gave a non-committal grunt. He was staring around. 'Bad feelings are appropriate, I think,' he said. 'It probably *is* the opposite of our caves. It's not been built for any good purpose, that's for sure. All these openings look wrong. It's almost as if they were Song Ways, but . . . wait a minute!'

Before Atlon could do anything, Dvolci had slithered out of the pack and disappeared down one of the holes. Self-consciously, and more than a little concerned, Atlon squatted down next to the opening, his back against the wall. He resisted the temptation to bend down and shout along the small tunnel.

'Don't let Fiarn catch you sitting around,' said a red-faced passer-by pushing a hand-cart. Atlon gave him an acknowledging wave.

Then the passage was alive with eerie, grating sounds. They set Atlon's teeth on edge and his skin started to crawl. He felt an almost overwhelming urge to flee. Everyone else in the passage seemed to be similarly affected – all of them stopping suddenly and covering their ears. Abandoned rubbish clattered to the floor and untended carts tumbled over.

Dvolci emerged from the opening at great speed and disappeared into Atlon's pack with such force that he almost knocked Atlon over. 'Move!' came a muffled but unmistakably urgent instruction.

266

As Atlon scrambled to his feet, the noises died away and, with a great deal of cursing and head-shaking, the traffic in the passage returned to normal.

'What did you do?' Atlon hissed as he set off again.

'I'm not sure.' Dvolci's head came a little way out of the top of the pack. 'I was just trying them out as Sound Ways.'

'And?'

'And they are – and they're not. Not Sound Ways as I've ever known them. They're more like a defence of some kind. Like the labyrinth protecting the Armoury at the Castle.'

'The noise out here was bad,' Atlon confirmed, sympathetically.

'You should've been in there,' came a terse and heartfelt response. Dvolci's tone indicated that he did not want to pursue the matter. Atlon was not certain, but he thought he could feel the felci shaking. In the end he decided it was his imagination; perhaps Dvolci was just scratching – but even the idea of Dvolci being afraid was unnerving.

After a while, they came to a fork in the passage. Atlon chose the busiest branch again. 'Pay attention to where we're going, in case we have to leave in a hurry,' he said, though more in an attempt to reassure himself that Dvolci was all right than anything else.

'I am, I am,' came the scornful reply. 'You see you do the same. As I remember, you're pretty poor at finding your way around underground, for one of your Learned Order.'

Atlon smiled and ignored the jibe other than to hitch his pack roughly.

As the passage wound on they passed several other junctions, each time choosing to follow that which seemed most populous. Atlon was unsure whether to feel pleased or alarmed when two people asked him where the main entrance was. He flicked a thumb vaguely backwards.

Finally they emerged on to one of the terraces surrounding the arena. The sudden opening out should have brought relief after the dingy confines of the passage but to Atlon it was as though he had stepped outside to find himself under a lowering and thunderous sky. Of its own volition, his hand came up and began circling his heart. He stopped when he realized what he was doing and returned

267

his hand to his pocket uncomfortably.

'Do it, if it'll make you feel better.' Dvolci had clambered on to his shoulder and was gazing around the huge hall, his nose twitching. 'I'm not laughing.' The gesture was gone but it had served its purpose, and Dvolci's comment helped.

'What in the name of all that's precious *is* this place?' Atlon whispered, looking up at the balconies looming overhead. The arches were like so many eyes – some dark and sightless, others squinting ominously, flickering with lamplight and shadows. They drew his gaze inexorably to the solitary crystal hanging from its barbed roots. It seemed to be pointing towards him, like an accusing finger.

'His place, that's what it is,' Dvolci replied. 'I shudder to think what it's been used for. There were terrible sounds – old, old sounds – still lingering in that tunnel I went into, and worse beyond, I'm sure. That's what made me cry out. I didn't dare go in further . . . But it's His place beyond a doubt.'

Atlon could not disagree. His throat was dry and the building seemed to be trying to crush him. He straightened up in an attempt to throw off the feeling. 'Where next?' he said hoarsely.

'Anywhere,' Dvolci replied off-handedly. He bent close to Atlon's ear. 'But be careful – *very* careful . . .'

Atlon raised a hand to silence him. 'I know,' he said. He was holding himself very still. 'The least hint of my using the Power here will make me shine like a beacon to anyone with the eyes to see it. I can feel it now. This place was built for the likes of me.' He closed his eyes. 'It's a trap.'

A hand seized his elbow.

Chapter 21

Atlon started violently. As did the person who had seized his arm.

They both hastily backed away from one another in a flurry of mutual apologizing.

Atlon snatched off his hat and peered at his assailant.

'Rinter?' he asked, as face and name came together.

'The late Rinter, nearly,' came the reply, Rinter patting his chest earnestly. 'You frightened me half to death, jumping like that.' Atlon made another apologetic gesture, but Rinter was in a beneficent mood. 'My fault, I suppose,' he conceded. 'I saw the hat and I thought, that's got to be Atlon – better late than never. I should've seen how engrossed you were.' He looked around proprietorially. 'I don't blame you. Nothing like this where you come from I'll wager. Isn't it magnificent? I always said it was worthy of better things, and now Barran's in charge, it'll get them. Great days are coming.'

A burst of abuse behind them precluded Atlon's answering and they both moved quickly to one side as three men staggered out of the passage carrying a bulky and apparently very heavy metal frame. After a brief and profane debate they disappeared into another passage. Rinter and Atlon watched them in silence.

Rinter's familiar face and agitated presence made Atlon feel less exposed, but he was still unhappy about lingering in this place and cut straight to the heart of his concern. 'I heard it was a great success last night. What was that creature they had at the end?'

'Oh, interested now, are we?' Rinter could not resist this gentle jibe in the face of Atlon's seeming enthusiasm. Atlon gave a non-committal shrug. Rinter became paternal. 'A great success indeed – a first-class Loose Pit. But it wouldn't have been suitable for your – felci, was it? I know he's a tough little character, but the least of the animals fighting last night would have seen him off in seconds.' He put an arm around Atlon's shoulder and began leading him down towards the arena. 'Still, don't worry. There'll be plenty of opportunities for you to get him earning. They won't be holding Loose Pits very often – they take a lot of organizing – and fighting these animals too much spoils the market. Scarcity always adds value, doesn't it?' He lowered his voice confidentially. 'But stick with me. There's some big game going on. When we were here yesterday morning, no one had any idea of what was going to happen. Then, when I arrive in the evening,' he gave Atlon a mildly reproachful look, 'searching for you, there it is – the place all lit up and bustling, crowds coming from everywhere. And for a Loose Pit to be set up so quickly, there've got to be considerable resources put to work.' He gave Atlon a massively knowing look.

'I've heard the Kyrosdyn had something to do with it,' Atlon said, trying to ease the conversation back to the creature.

Rinter looked rather surprised, then he became knowing again. 'That's the gossip,' he said. 'Though it's unlikely ever to be more than that. I told you yesterday, the Kyrosdyn are a strange lot. What they do is what they do, and the rest of us are best keeping away from them.'

As anxious to escape from the topic as Atlon was to pursue it, he was torn between boasting about his re-established contact with Fiarn through his friendship with Pinnatte, and straightforward curiosity about Atlon. The latter won. Despite the excitement of the last day, business was business. He still had a living to earn and he was certain that the felci could do well for him if he handled it correctly. 'Where did you get to yesterday?' he asked pleasantly. 'Did you get lost? I was quite concerned about you. The city's not the safest of places for strangers.'

'I got a job,' Atlon replied.

With commendable control, Rinter confined himself to a simple, 'Oh?' rather than, 'Not in a damned Kyrosdyn workshop, I hope,' which is what sprang immediately to mind.

'With a blacksmith – doing his leatherwork and harness repairs,' Atlon offered.

'Good, I'm glad,' Rinter lied. 'As I said, I was concerned about you. It'll help keep you going until something better comes along.'

'That's where I heard the gossip,' Atlon went on, tapping his ear. 'And when I heard about last night's performance – especially the creature at the end – I had to get along and see for myself. Is it possible to view the animal?'

The question took Rinter aback.

'No,' he replied. 'All the animals have gone now. They're usually taken away after the show – if they're fit to be moved, that is.'

Atlon looked disappointed. 'Well, tell me about it then. What did it look like? I must have had half a dozen descriptions, all different. Where did it come from? And who'd own a thing like that?'

They had reached the edge of the arena. Despite concentrating on prising information from Rinter, Atlon could feel the solitary crystal high above his head, seemingly focusing the attention of the entire hall on his unwanted and treacherous presence. Instinctively he replaced his hat. Rinter gave a cursory description of the creature which confirmed what Atlon had already heard, then ended with a short homily. 'It's not a good idea to ask who owns particular animals when it's not been announced by the Master of the Pit. Some people are very sensitive about their privacy.'

'I didn't mean to cause any offence,' Atlon said hastily.

'It's all right between you and me,' Ringer assured him. 'No harm done. But a careless question in the wrong place can land you in trouble.' He became confidential again and slipped in his boast. 'Even *I* don't know who that creature belonged to, and I was talking to Fiarn last night – Barran's second-in-command. But for what it's worth, I'd say it belonged to the Kyrosdyn.' Resting his elbow on the parapet wall at the edge of the arena, he placed his hand casually over his mouth and spoke behind it. 'And I'd say it was something they've brought up from the caves.'

'Does that happen a lot?'

'Who can say?' Rinter replied. 'As I said, Loose Pits aren't all that common – and I don't get to many of them. But I've seen some strange things come and go. Nasty things, to be honest, some of them. And I've heard of worse.'

Atlon strove to look impressed but he was disappointed by the turn in the conversation. It would be pointless pressing Rinter further about the creature and probably downright foolish to ask how he might gain access to the caves to see for himself. But Rinter was still his best hope for further information.

'I hear there were people hurt last night,' he said. 'Something to do with the gate – I saw it being repaired.'

Rinter nodded significantly, fully centre-stage now. This would enthral Atlon and keep the felci nearby. 'I was in the thick of it,' he declared. 'Thought my last moment had come at one stage. Dog escaped from the Pit, you see. Caused a panic on the terraces and a crush in the entrance hall. Only one small gate open.' He relived the moment, gesticulating. 'Then, Pinnatte – that's my friend – just reaches up, clambers on to the shoulders of the people in front, runs across the top of the crowd, squeezes over the fence and opens the gate.' He blew out a noisy breath. 'You should have heard the din when the gates flew open – I'm not surprised they got damaged. Then I was being pulled along without my feet touching the floor. Good thing I was near the edge or I'd have been carried halfway down the street before I got free, otherwise.' Unexpectedly the re-telling disturbed him, bringing back the incident to him with peculiar vividness. He drew his hand across his forehead and shivered.

'Are you all right?' Atlon asked.

'Yes, I'm fine,' Rinter replied with forced heartiness.

'Your friend was very brave. Did he get hurt at all, in the crush?'

'The gate threw him to one side, clear of the crowd. All he got was a bang on the head and a cut hand.' Rinter bore Pinnatte's injuries with great fortitude. Sensing that he had Atlon almost hooked, he tugged the line gently to draw him in further. 'He had a disturbed night though – bad dreams and all, but . . .' and, as if inspired, '. . . I'll introduce you to him if you like.'

Anxious to be away from this fearful place with its feeling of focused oppression, Atlon took the bait happily. 'Didn't you say this Barran was some kind of a bandit – a criminal?' he said as they walked along yet another winding passage. 'How's he come to be in charge of a place like this?'

Rinter looked at him sharply, then glanced around nervously, as though someone might be listening. 'No,' he said firmly. 'I think he must have misunderstood me. Barran's a businessman – a distinguished and successful businessman. He's quite . . . robust . . . in the way he works – he's known for it – but he'll have come by this place in the normal way of things. More I couldn't say. I might know Fiarn, but that doesn't make me Barran's confidant.'

Sensing his error, Atlon remained silent until eventually they came to the room in which Pinnatte had awakened after his collapse. Subsequently he had spent the night there. The door was open and Pinnatte could be seen sitting on the edge of the couch which had served him as a bed. He was gazing down at his feet. Two large, ill-favoured individuals stood by the door. They acknowledged Rinter curtly but moved to intercept Atlon.

'He's a friend,' Rinter declared confidently. The two men exchanged a glance then slowly stood aside, leaving a small gap for Atlon to pass through. As he did, smiling uncomfortably, one of them rested two fingers on his chest and said, 'Keep your hands where we can see them, *friend*.' He laid an emphasis on the last word which indicated that Rinter's intervention really counted for nothing. Atlon exuded timidity. The two men moved into the room after him and took up positions on each side of the door.

'How're you feeling now?' Rinter was asking Pinnatte. 'I see Barran's looking after you.' He nodded towards the two guards.

Atlon looked at the young man. Though he had a natural curiosity about the person whose bravery had saved so many lives, he had stayed with Rinter predominantly because he wished to remain in the building with a view to learning about the creature. When Pinnatte looked up to reply to Rinter, however, Atlon felt as though he had been struck. Instantly, he was back with his companions on the rainswept battlefield, sixteen years ago, their meagre line stretched to hitherto unknown limits, but holding at bay the awful forces whose unseen and mysterious touch would smash the ranks of the struggling army utterly if they faltered. Pinnatte seemed to be at the centre of a disturbance of a kind such as Atlon had only known on that day. He was both there and not there – of this world *and* in many others – a conjunction that should not be possible . . .

Long training held Atlon motionless – gave him a little time to absorb the shock of what he was sensing, without betraying anything to those around him. Long training too, enabled him to quell his deeper instincts which rose up screaming for him to use the Power to protect himself. Inconspicuously, he took control of his breathing, forcing himself towards calmness. After scarcely four heartbeats an incongruous frisson of pride seeped into the racing thoughts that were seeking an explanation for what was happening here. He had given not the slightest indication of his knowledge of the Power in the face of this revelation. He had survived!

It did little to lessen his terror however.

For there was no control here. Unlike the Kyrosdyn that Atlon had encountered the previous day, Pinnatte was obviously not a conscious source of the disturbance. He was more a gateway, though the word 'rent' came to him – an accidental tear.

With an effort, Atlon succeeded in easing away from his questions. Training again told him that logic alone was, for the moment, inappropriate. Now all he could do was observe. It was not easy. At one moment it seemed that he and Pinnatte were the only solid things in the room, all else becoming vague and hazy, like a hesitant sketch for a painting. At another it was Pinnatte who was unreal and distant, a thing that did not belong in this reality without great hurt being done somewhere.

He became aware of Dvolci's head by his ear, whistling urgently but very softly. Reaching up, he touched him gently, simultaneously giving assurance and taking support.

'What's that in your pack, friend?' It took Atlon a moment to realize what the words meant, they were so garbled and raucous as they crashed into his heightened awareness. It was the emphasis on *friend* that told him it was the guard who had accosted him at the door.

When he replied, he had to force out each word as though he were speaking a language totally alien to his own. 'Just a . . . travelling companion,' he managed, though his voice rang strange in his own ears. He was aware of a scornful laugh and a coarse exchange going on behind him in response, but it was as meaningless as the rattle of branches in a wind-shaken tree.

Pinnatte was speaking. 'I'm not sure how I feel,' came the words. Atlon clung to them to keep his mind clearly in this room. 'One minute I'm fine – the next, I don't know. I'm somewhere else. And I keep thinking about that dream. I . . .' He stopped and looked away, distracted. Atlon felt as though he were facing a great wind.

Rinter looked helplessly at Pinnatte. 'Have you seen Barran yet?' he asked with that concerned, patronizing tone that the uncertain well use to the bewildered sick.

Pinnatte shook his head though he did not seem to be listening.

Atlon heard himself asking, 'What kind of dream was it?'

Pinnatte turned to him, painfully slowly. To Atlon, the movement seemed to be tearing through reality itself. He offered his gaze as an anchor. Pinnatte took it. Atlon noticed that the young man's eyes were black.

'What kind of dream was it?' he asked again.

'This is Atlon,' Rinter said, glad to be free of the initiative. 'The man I was looking for last night when we met, remember? I told you – with the big hat and the felci.' He pointed to Dvolci peering out of Atlon's pack. 'That's him. A fine animal. You should've seen him sort out Ghreel's dog up at The Wyndering.'

Atlon took off his hat and held out his hand. The disturbance about Pinnatte was diminishing. He took the offered hand. Then the disturbance was almost completely gone – reduced to little more than a mildly irritating fly buzzing about the room. Pinnatte smiled.

'The dream?' Atlon reminded him.

Pinnatte frowned. 'I don't want to talk about it,' he said.

'I'm sorry. I didn't meant to intrude,' Atlon said. He searched the young man's face. 'Do you want to tell me what you meant when you said you're sometimes here, sometimes somewhere else?'

Pinnatte looked at him but did not reply.

'I've had some experience with head injuries,' Atlon said, crouching down by Pinnatte, 'and with nasty incidents such as you were involved in last night. Either on its own can prove more troublesome than you'd think; both together can be a real problem.'

Pinnatte tried to be dismissive. 'I'm fine,' he said. 'I just feel a bit . . . distant at times. Not exactly dizzy, just far away. Somewhere else.'

Atlon nodded. 'May I look at your injury?' he asked.

'I don't think there's anything to see,' Pinnatte replied, pointing to the back of his head. 'It's just a little sore to touch.'

'Remember what I said about your hands, *friend*.' It was the guard again, calling across the room. He was not concerned about Pinnatte, however, but indicating someone just beyond the door. As Atlon looked round, Ellyn came in. The guards moved with her. She nodded to Rinter then looked at Atlon, who stood up. Rinter performed a hasty introduction. Uncertain how to treat 'Barran's wife', Atlon settled for a slight bow. For the first time since he had entered the Jyolan, he felt almost at ease. This strong-looking woman with her searching but not unkind gaze seemed in some way to be immune to the building's pernicious influence. Indeed, he suspected, she was probably immune to many of life's vagaries. Words such as complete, self-sufficient, came to him.

Ellyn's eyes narrowed curiously and she tilted her head on one side, looking past him. 'What's that?' she asked, pointing to Dvolci.

Atlon gave his usual answer, 'Just company for me on my travels, ma'am.' Dvolci clambered out of the pack, jumped down to the floor and sidled over to Ellyn. One of the guards stepped forward, reaching for a knife, but Ellyn held out a hand to stop him. Dvolci sat back on his haunches and looked up at her.

Ellyn's mouth creased a little, and her eyes shone. 'Is it all right to touch him?' she asked.

'He won't bite you,' Atlon said, perpetually hesitant about giving his friend's permission for such matters, even though it was obvious what was going to happen. 'I wish I could seduce women as easily as that damned felci does,' a friend had once said to him bitterly.

Ellyn bent down and ran two fingers over Dvolci's narrow head. The felci closed his eyes ecstatically as she tickled behind his ears. Sunlight seemed to be coming into the room. 'He's delightful,' Ellyn announced. 'What is he? I've never seen anything like him before.'

'He's a felci, ma'am,' Atlon said. 'They live in the mountains in my country.' Adding caustically for Dvolci's benefit, 'They're very tame and quite intelligent.'

Still stroking Dvolci, Ellyn looked up at him. 'You're not from the city, then?'

'No,' Atlon replied. 'Just on a journey south, for a friend.'

'I thought there was something different about you.' Ellyn was attending to Dvolci again as she said this but there was a note in her voice that Atlon could not identify. Relief – surprise? No, it was something deeper than both.

Then Dvolci dropped back down on to all fours and walked over to Pinnatte. He stood up, resting his front paws on Pinnatte's knees.

'He's not usually very keen on too much company,' Atlon said, uncertain about what was to follow. Certainly, Dvolci would not have put on this performance for any slight reason.

Tentatively, Pinnatte imitated Ellyn's action, stroking Dvolci's head with his bandaged hand. It seemed to relax him and Atlon felt the disturbance emanating from him slip even further away. He reproached himself. Dvolci's judgement in these circumstances would be sounder than his. The felci never seemed to be affected by the Power or any of its manifestations; felcis never did. They were an ancient race.

Dvolci dropped back down again and, scuttling up Atlon with wilful clumsiness, ensconced himself in the pack. As he did so he whistled softly to Atlon. 'Look at his hand. Be careful – *very* careful. You won't like it. Remember where you are. The woman's interesting.'

Atlon affected a heartiness he did not feel. 'Well, that's Dvolci for you. Very much his own animal.' He spoke to Pinnatte. 'I was going to look at your head.'

Pinnatte, brighter now, turned and placed a finger on the back of his head. 'It's sore just there.'

'Are you a healer?' Ellyn asked.

'I've had some training,' Atlon said, examining Pinnatte's head. 'And I've picked up one or two things on my travels.' He patted Pinnatte on the shoulder reassuringly. 'There doesn't seem to be anything wrong there – just a bump and a little bruising. If you've come through the night without problems then you should be all right, though you'll probably have a headache for a day or so.'

Ellyn looked pleased that her own prognosis had been confirmed, but Atlon was waiting to see if Pinnatte would take the opportunity to refer to his dream again. He said nothing however. Atlon took hold of his injured hand.

'It's all right,' Pinnatte said, withdrawing it nervously. Atlon noted that Ellyn looked uneasy. 'The bandaging's well done,' he said, suspecting she feared some criticism.

'I put a drawing ointment on it,' she said. Atlon looked at her inquiringly. 'It was quite a nasty graze, and there seemed to be ...' She hesitated. 'There seemed to be a crystal stain on it.'

'What do you mean?' Atlon asked, genuinely at a loss.

Ellyn looked surprised by the question, but Atlon's open-faced expectancy left her no choice other than to answer it. 'It's something that mainly the miners do – the crystal miners.' She rubbed the back of her hand nervously. The gesture was all the more powerful because it so contrasted with her otherwise assured demeanour. 'They ... incise the skin and close the wound with crushed fragments of crystals.' The words came out quickly. Atlon drew in a sharp breath and raised a hand to spare her any further description.

'I've heard of the practice,' he said grimly. 'And I grieve for anyone misguided enough to do it. It's a sure route to destruction. It's a fundamental quality of crystals that they take more than they give. Is it a common thing here?'

'No. Not in the city. Not yet. But many miners do it. It's the nature of the work.'

'And your ointment is effective against it?'

'It helps a little, if it's not too late – if the habit's not too ingrained. But it can't do anything about the desire. It's only a wound-cleaner really.'

'Is this something you've done to yourself?' Atlon addressed Pinnatte sternly.

'No.' Pinnatte's denial was buttressed by many years of professional protestations of innocence. 'What would I do something like that for?' He grimaced. The idea was repellent.

278

'And where would I get crystals from to waste like that?'

Atlon turned back to Ellyn. 'It looked like a crystal stain,' she said with a shrug. 'I thought it odd at the time, given that he was probably only a Den-Mate. And it wasn't near one of the usual pulse nodes.' She lowered her voice. 'And the mark looked almost green.'

Atlon's eyes widened and, without further comment, he took Pinnatte's hand firmly and began unwinding the bandage. Pinnatte made only a cursory attempt to retrieve his hand. Dvolci whistled softly to Atlon. It was a timely reminder, for as the bandage fell away, the sight of the wound struck Atlon even more forcefully than had his first contact with Pinnatte. Once again, even though there was no direct threat to him, his inner self cried out to him to defend himself, and once again he had to struggle to set it aside. It was difficult.

Superficially, the wound was no more than a bad graze – raw, red, and glistening damp with healing and ointment. It was clean and seemingly free from infection, though there was a hint of darkness to one side of it which was the remains of Rostan's Anointing.

But beyond that, to Atlon's deeper sight, the edge of the darkness was a churning maelstrom of contamination, as Ellyn's simple ointment and Pinnatte's natural well-being battled against the culmination of Imorren's and the Kyrosdyn's work – against the mysterious resource in their unguent, given unholy vigour by Rostan's use of the Power, which sought to use Pinnatte for purposes unknowable even to its creators.

It was unequivocally the source of the other unease that Atlon had felt in Pinnatte. Forcing himself to stay calm, and weighing his every movement as if casual carelessness might unleash something terrible about him, he nodded slowly. 'Your ointment's been very effective,' he said. 'The wound's clean. You must show me how to make it. I'm naturally clumsy – always cutting myself.' The light-heartedness was almost choking him while the urge to ask Pinnatte how he had come by such a mark was virtually uncontrollable. He sensed however, that no answer would be forthcoming. This was no trivial thing. Even without a close study he could tell that green crystals were involved in some way, and from what he had learned from Heirn it seemed highly unlikely that this young man, with his generally unkempt appearance, would be able to afford such things. Besides, there was more at work here than just an addictive habit – much more. Green crystals alone, used thus, would almost certainly have killed the man within hours, whether they were near a pulse or not.

Ellyn was handing him a clean bandage and the jar of ointment. He took them from her absently. As he opened the jar, the smell of the ointment wrapped itself around him and drew him away from the turmoil. It was clean, sharp and deeply familiar. Immediately he was a child again, being tended by his mother, delicately dabbing at a gashed knee. All about him was the indestructible solidity of his childhood. It had an intensity that no description or deliberate memory could have captured.

'Relics of our ancient hunting days,' someone had once said to him, discussing the extraordinary power of scents to recall the past.

His vision blurred. As he lifted a hand to wipe his eyes, Ellyn caught it. 'I'm sorry,' she said. 'I should have warned you, it's very strong when it's fresh. Don't get any in your eyes.' A small white kerchief was pushed into his hand. He wiped his eyes then returned it gratefully.

As he applied the ointment to Pinnatte's wound, the memory of his mother and his childhood remained, though it was a shadow now of what it had just been. Contrasted with it was the horror of Pinnatte's hand and, suddenly highlighted, the sense of the cloying wrongness that pervaded the whole city and which seemed to be focused here, in the Jyolan. Untypically self-pitying, Atlon found himself asking, 'How did I get here, to this awful place?' But even as he asked the question, he knew the answer. It had been asked and answered many times before.

'Step by step.'

And who could say which step he might have taken differently to avoid this conclusion?

It was the only answer he would ever get, but he felt easier nevertheless.

He was about to bandage Pinnatte's hand when he changed his mind. He must get the young man out of this place. Standing, he wiped his eyes again, though this time with the side of his hand. He had to clear his throat before he spoke to Ellyn. 'I think the ointment's done all it can. The wound looks clean. It's probably best to let the fresh air get at it now – give it a chance to heal.' He looked down at Pinnatte. 'If you've been in here since last night, I think some fresh air would do *you* no harm either, not to mention a little exercise.'

Pinnatte eyed him unsurely. There was something about this stranger that disturbed him. He didn't seem to belong here. And his voice was odd. Was he really from a land beyond Arash-Felloren, or had he just misheard? His thoughts swung between extremes. This man would look after him – would take the confusion from his head – put right whatever it was that that Kyrosdyn had done – for, despite his earlier protestation, his hand *was* troubling him, albeit not in any way that he could find words to describe. Then Atlon was almost like a demon – a fearful shadow – come to obstruct him on his way to his rightful future – come to keep him from the wealth and power that would be his now that he was on the verge of leaving Lassner and working for Barran.

'Barran wants to see me,' he said eventually. 'I should wait for him.'

Ellyn intervened. 'Barran's busy now, and liable to be so for most of the day. Don't worry, he's not forgotten you – nor will he – not after what you did. He spoke about you this morning.' Briefly her gaze locked with Atlon's. 'And Rinter's friend is right. It's dismal in here. Get outside, into the light. Walk around – get something to eat. You'll feel a lot better for it.'

Pinnatte's thoughts shifted under this gentle onslaught. The room *was* gloomy, and the two guards who had been with him for most of the time were ill company, making no effort to disguise their boredom at the chore.

Atlon extended a hand and Pinnatte took it. 'You're right,' he said, pulling himself up.

'I'll tell Barran what you're doing, if he asks,' Ellyn said. She reached into her bag and produced some coins which she offered

281

to him. 'That'll get you and your friends a meal. Come back this evening and ask to see me.'

Used to stealing almost everything he needed, this unexpected generosity shook Pinnatte and left him gaping. Ellyn folded the money into his dithering hand with both of hers.

'Come back this evening,' she said again.

'I'll see he does, ma'am,' Rinter said earnestly, a little concerned that he was being left too much to one side in the developing proceedings.

As they made their way out of the Jyolan, led by one of the guards, Pinnatte once more felt himself torn by doubts about this newcomer. This was *his* place. He belonged here, wandering its complex warren of passages, searching, learning . . .

Learning what?

How to become rich and powerful by studying the ways of Barran and those who followed him? No, it was something else. Tantalizing images flitted elusively about his thought.

'Are you sure your hand isn't bothering you?' Atlon's inquiry scattered them.

'No, it's fine.' Pinnatte waved it airily.

'I'll have a proper look at it in the daylight,' Atlon persisted. 'Just to be sure.'

Pinnatte was inclined to argue but before he could speak, a dark form emerged from a side passage just ahead of them. It stopped as they did. Then it turned towards them and growled.

Chapter 22

The guard hesitated for a moment, then drew his sword and stepped between Pinnatte and the animal.

'It's that damned dog that caused the panic last night. It ran off. We couldn't find it.' He shouted this information, as much for his own reassurance as for that of the others, but unfortunately, his voice echoed the tremor visible in the extended sword.

The dog, hackles raised, stared at the group. It might have been completely outmatched in the arena the previous night, but it was a large and powerful animal and in an uncertain temper. Even in the dim light of the passage, bone-crushing teeth could be seen beneath a viciously curled upper lip. And the throaty rumble of its growl was not a sound that invited confidence.

Used mainly to dealing with people less physically able than himself, and that in the company of his own kind, the guard was uncertain what to do. He opted finally for retreat, pushing his charges into an awkward shuffle as he began moving backwards. 'We'll go out another way,' he said, mustering such command as he could. 'Then we'll get a party together and trap it.'

Abruptly, Pinnatte stepped forward. 'No!' he cried, his voice strange. 'It is prey. It is mine, it must be taken.'

Atlon seized his arm anxiously but Pinnatte shook him off, unexpectedly strong. He moved towards the dog. It redoubled its growling but made no movement. Atlon tried again. 'Leave it;' he urged Pinnatte. 'It won't attack us if we don't attack it. There are plenty of places for it to run. It's probably more frightened than we are.' The last remark was uttered more in hope than from knowledge. The dog had, after all, been trained as an attack animal, and it certainly did not give the appearance of being about to flee.

The guard recovered from Pinnatte's sudden move and now came to his side. 'He's right. We should leave it. It's—'

'It is prey.' Pinnatte cut across his appeal. 'It is mine.'

He moved forward again but this time, both Atlon and the guard seized him. Pinnatte stopped, then, letting out an eerie mewling cry, he flung off the guard as if he had been little more than a child. The big man stumbled into the wall and his sword clattered on to the floor. The sound seemed to release an endless sequence of clanging echoes.

Through the din, Atlon found himself looking into a face that was demented with rage. It bore no resemblance to the uncertain young man whose injured head and hand he had just examined. Pinnatte's voice was strained and distant, almost as though he were unfamiliar with speech.

'You do not belong. You are . . .' He faltered, then recognition came into his face. And hatred. Fear almost overwhelmed Atlon. But mingling with it came a burning rage and disgust which told him that this abomination should be destroyed now, where it stood, and without mercy. It should be obliterated utterly before it grew and gathered strength and—

Pinnatte was going to attack him! He could feel the wild precursors of the Power building in him. Yet, insofar as he was thinking at all, he knew that to defend himself in this place might have untold consequences.

But not to defend himself would surely see him destroyed!

Then it seemed that neither he nor Pinnatte nor Rinter or the guard were part of the Jyolan – or anything. They were empty mannequins in a grey nowhere that was beyond, or between, all things.

He became aware of a high-pitched, insect whine. Even as it touched him, he and all around him were whole again and the whine was a penetrating screech filling the passage. Everyone else pressed their hands to their ears. Pinnatte dropped to his knees. The dog was gone.

Atlon, recognizing the sound, was the first to recover.

'Sorry about that,' Dvolci whispered in his ear, 'but it was all I could think of.'

Atlon nodded, then knelt down by Pinnatte. The young man was himself again, his face confused and concerned. The guard was swearing violently while Rinter was pale and shaking.

'What was that?' he asked in between the guard's oaths.

'I've no idea,' Atlon lied, trembling himself from the remembered vision of Pinnatte's sudden ferocity. 'And I don't care. I'm just glad it frightened that dog off.'

He was helping Pinnatte to his feet. 'Come on, get us out of here quickly,' he said to the guard, who was having some difficulty in sheathing his shaking sword. 'Before that thing decides to come back.'

The remainder of the hurried journey was completed in comparative silence, and within a few minutes the guard was ushering them into the clamour of the main entrance hall. One of the gates had been replaced, but the hammerers were in full song on the other so Atlon only caught part of the guard's shouted remarks about 'getting a team together,' as he left them.

Pinnatte's brow furrowed at the din. Atlon took his arm and began manoeuvring him towards the street. As he did so he became aware of his name being called. Looking round he saw the bulky form of Heirn, waving to him. The big blacksmith pushed his way through the confusion.

'I didn't realize we'd been in there so long,' Atlon shouted.

Heirn did not reply, but began clearing a way through the crowd for them like a huge plough.

'You look awful,' he declared as they reached the street. 'Are you all right?'

'A bit shaken,' Atlon said. 'We just had a little excitement with the dog that escaped last night – but no harm's been done.'

He introduced Pinnatte and Rinter. Heirn eyed them both narrowly and greeted them with a courtesy that was obviously an effort. At the same time he gave Atlon a look not unlike that of a father finding his son in scapegrace company but unwilling to embarrass him publicly.

Atlon caught his mood and sought to retrieve himself. 'Rinter I met at The Wyndering. He was kind enough to bring me to the city. Pinnatte's the man who opened the gate at the Jyolan last night.'

Heirn's manner changed perceptibly – at least towards Pinnatte.

'A brave thing you did there, young man,' he said, laying a heavy hand on his shoulder. 'Mind you, if there'd been no one in there in the first place, it wouldn't have happened. Still, it was well done.'

Rinter considered an indignant retort to this but, noting Heirn's size and his obvious concern for Atlon, he thought better of it.

'Is there anywhere round here where we can just sit and relax?' Atlon asked, still anxious to get Pinnatte away from the Jyolan.

'And eat,' Rinter added.

Heirn pointed. 'There's a small park over there,' he said. 'Just a few minutes' walk.' He recollected something. 'Oh, I think there's been a little problem with your horse.'

Atlon's face darkened and, without comment, he pushed past Heirn and made towards where he had left his horse tethered. People stepped aside from his purposeful advance. The horse was standing patiently, apparently untroubled, though its tethering rope was hanging free. Atlon stroked its neck and whispered to it. Then he saw a ragged individual sitting propped against the building. He was holding a bloodstained kerchief to his face. In front of him was another man, sprawled face down. As the seated man met Atlon's gaze he began talking earnestly, if unintelligibly, into the kerchief and gesticulating towards what was apparently his fallen comrade. Atlon cast a stern eye over his horse, then, satisfied, bent down and checked the prone figure. Almost reluctantly, he manoeuvred the man's arms and legs and deftly rolled him on to his side so that he looked like a child in bed.

'What's happened?' Heirn was standing by him. The man against the wall began talking again and waving his free hand wildly at Atlon and the horse.

'They tried to steal the horse. Or from it,' Atlon said. His voice was cold.

The bloodstained man's protestations became indignant, though they were still unintelligible. Abruptly Atlon's face creased into rage. He spun round and snatched the weighted staff that hung from his saddle. It was a swift and practised gesture and Heirn stepped back in surprise, as did most of the gathered crowd. Atlon pressed the staff against the man's chest.

'Don't call my horse a liar,' he said, with a seriousness that robbed the words of any incongruity. The man stared at him wide-eyed and silent. 'Think of this as a lucky day. The horse didn't kill you for what you tried to do, and so far – *so far* – I'm not inclined to.' He drew the staff back. 'But I may be, if I see you again. Do you understand?' The man nodded his head. 'And you won't forget to explain this to your friend when he wakes up, will you?' Atlon threw the staff into the air and caught it with the other hand. The man nodded again, desperately.

As they walked away, Heirn bent forward and asked softly, 'Would it?'

'What?' Atlon said, replacing his staff.

'Would it have killed him?'

'Of course,' Atlon replied tersely. 'If I hadn't asked it just to defend itself when I left it.'

It was not an answer that Heirn had expected. 'And you?' The words were out before he could stop them.

Atlon stopped, lowered his head for a moment then looked at him. 'I understand almost nothing about this city of yours, Heirn. I'm trying to be careful all the time – making allowances – adjusting. But you can't understand about my people and horses either. In my country, stealing a horse, or from a horse, is to risk being killed. It's that simple. Always has been. It never happens. And I can't answer your question.'

'I think you just did,' Heirn said.

Atlon frowned and waved a hand to signal an end to the discussion. He did not want any reminders of his home, so starkly contrasted as it was to Arash-Felloren. 'Something bad happened in the Jyolan. I need to think about it. And I need food.' He smiled, to banish the incident further. 'Thanks for coming to look for me.'

'One hour to sunset I said, and one hour to sunset I meant.'

The park to which Heirn led them was indeed small – scarcely two hundred paces across – although, following in miniature the pattern of the city, it contrived to have no less than four small hills in this space. It was surrounded by buildings but they were substantially hidden by trees, and though much of the grass had been burned off by the prolonged summer, giving the place a worn and tired look, it still formed an unexpected haven away from the busy streets.

Today it was deserted.

As soon as the four men passed through the ornate metal gates, Dvolci jumped out of Atlon's pack and ran off at great speed, whistling noisily. Rinter twitched nervously as his fighter-to-be disappeared from view. Atlon released his horse, which trotted off after Dvolci.

In the shade of a large old tree near the centre of the park, a little grass still survived. The four men sat down on it and ate the food they had purchased from a street vendor. None spoke. Each was preoccupied with his own thoughts.

Rinter was restless, his dominant concern being the whereabouts of Dvolci and, following that, how he might set about finally luring Atlon into putting the felci in the Pits. His considerations were not made any easier by Dvolci's occasional appearances as he careered recklessly and at great speed about the park. He fought with a constant urge to pester Atlon – 'He will come back, won't he?' – but, having witnessed the scene with the two men the horse had injured, he determined that in future he should not be too sanguine about Atlon's apparent naivety.

The same incident was occupying Heirn. Atlon's anger at the men had surprised him. He had no difficult in accepting the virtues of summary justice – few in Arash-Felloren had – but he did not know what to make of the threat that Atlon had made to the injured man. It was quite different from the confrontation that had resulted in the death of the Kyrosdyn. There, Atlon's response, mysterious and frightening though it was, had been unequivocally defensive. This time he had been openly aggressive. It was difficult. Atlon did not impress him as a man who would say something he did not mean; yet equally, he did not impress him as being naturally aggressive, still less maliciously violent. Quite the reverse, in fact. Atlon almost radiated gentleness.

'You can't understand about my people and horses,' he had said.

I don't understand *anything* about you, Heirn decided resignedly.

288

Walking around with a fortune in your pocket, with strange invisible powers at your command, and a head full of terrifying tales. Not to mention a talking animal for a companion. It occurred to Heirn that he might be dreaming, or worse, going mad. But the idea did not last for long. There was a palpable solidity about everything around him and everything that had happened which denied him the luxury of such an escape. And escape, he realized suddenly, was what he wanted. But why? He wasn't bound. He could walk away from the man at any time if he so chose. Surreptitiously he glanced at Atlon, now lying flat on his back, half in the shade, half in the sunlight. His hands behind his head, he was staring up at the sky through the motionless leaves of the tree.

How far from home are you? Heirn thought. How alone in this alien place with your terrible knowledge and your deep fears?

An image formed in the wake of the questions. This seemingly ordinary and simple man was like a tiny, distant cloud, no bigger than a man's hand, that might grow to envelop and deluge the whole city, carrying all before it. Heirn felt afraid – very afraid.

Another image came, familiar and reassuring in the trembling confusion – that of iron changing its very nature as it was heated and worked. The idea seemed to possess him. Then he was the iron and the change was stirring deep inside him, deeper than could ever have been reached by any conscious decision. It was almost physical in its intensity. Whatever Atlon was, and oddly frail though he seemed to be, he was more a beacon of hope than despair. The change completed itself. Though he could have given no reason, he was resolved now to help this stranger – protect him, if he could, from the many ills that Arash-Felloren offered. Somehow he could do no other. A pledge blazed with trumpets and pageants could have been no truer.

Heirn closed his eyes and leaned back against the tree. He felt more at ease than he had for a long time.

Pinnatte, also leaning against the tree, wiped crumbs from his mouth. That the pie he had eaten had been bought by Ellyn's freely given gift gave it a peculiar savour he had never known before. He had eaten it very slowly. This stranger, Atlon, with his healer's manner had been right – the short walk, the food, and lounging idly in the sunshine had made him feel calmer, less torn.

But what was – had been – tearing him? Memories of the previous day and night were fresh and vivid, yet it was as if they had happened in another time, in another place – even to another person. The flight from the Kyrosdyn, the strange mark on his hand, the resolution to change his life, to leave Lassner. Then the many disturbing responses he had had in the Jyolan. More settled though he was now, these still troubled him. Too much excitement, he tried to convince himself, but unsuccessfully. The blood frenzy he had felt and the feeling that the place and its rituals were precious, even holy, should not have happened. They were obscene. He wasn't that kind of person – delighting in the suffering of others, even animals. Yet they had happened. And even now, part of him took relish in them. The events returned to him, unbidden, culminating in the arrival of the creature. He dared not close his eyes for fear that he would see it again, bowing in homage to him. For that is what it had done. In some way, it had known him.

And he, it.

Like a sudden bitter wind, the memory of his nightmare was all about him. He drew in a sharp breath and wrapped his arms around himself involuntarily.

Atlon noted the movement. Despite his relaxed manner, he had been watching Pinnatte constantly. So much frightening strangeness hung about this young man. He desperately wanted to question him, but that would not be possible while Rinter was with them and, in any event, it was something that would have to be approached very delicately. Through half-closed eyes, he caught a glimpse of Dvolci, brown and sinuous, tumbling down a small slope. A gleeful whistling reached him. Then his horse came in pursuit, shaking its head. The freedom of the two animals washed over him. Guilt followed it. They deserved better than being constrained in this awful city with its hard, crowded streets and abrasive, mistrustful people. He could rightly say that, like him, they were free creatures, here of their own choosing, but that would be only partly true. None of them was truly free. Knowledge would bind him the instant he tried to walk away from what he had found here. The horse was bound to him, and he to it, by ancient bonds which neither of them could, or would wish to, break. And Dvolci, the freest of them all – who could say why he was here? Had he been asked, he would probably have said it was in fulfilment of the felci's ancient duty as guardians of the less gifted species – the human race – then he would have laughed. As if echoing his thoughts, Dvolci's laughter floated across the park. The horse whinnied.

Atlon brought himself back to the present. He must concentrate on the matters in hand; the first thing to do was to get Pinnatte alone and trusting him. He levered himself up on to his elbows.

'After you've been to Jyolan tonight, where will you go?' he asked Pinnatte.

The question drew Pinnatte back from the memory of his nightmare. He shrugged. 'It depends,' he said. 'If Barran's got anything for me, he might be able to find me somewhere for the time being. If he hasn't . . . then I suppose I'll go back to Lassner's.'

Atlon looked thoughtful. 'I'd like to keep an eye on you. I don't think there should be any problem with the bang you took, but head injuries are queer things. You could get bad dreams, disorientation, dizziness. You need to be with someone who understands these things. And I'd certainly feel bad if I just walked away from you.'

Heirn, sitting behind Pinnatte, scowled but, meeting Atlon's pleading gaze, reluctantly nodded his permission. Pinnatte glanced at Rinter, who could scarcely believe his good fortune. Atlon being the keeper of Dvolci, and Pinnatte being his renewed contact with Fiarn, with perhaps the chance of meeting Barran himself, keeping them both together would be ideal. He affected a casualness he did not feel. 'Seems like a good idea to me,' he said. 'I can't invite you back to where I'm staying, it's too small. And I imagine it could be awkward if you go back to Lassner's right now, couldn't it?' He did not wait for an answer but gave his final push. 'And even if Barran can use you, he won't be too impressed if he has to start finding accommodation for you – him being so busy.'

It swayed Pinnatte enough. He had no desire to meet Lassner again until everything had been resolved. He certainly didn't want Lassner approaching Barran with a proposed Deed of Transfer in the hope of a large commission. If Barran wanted him, it was far better that his people approach Lassner about the traditional Guild formalities. And if Barran didn't want him . . . he shied away from the thought. He'd never have a better opportunity – he must make sure that Barran took him on. Rinter was right; it certainly wouldn't help if he immediately went whining to him for somewhere to stay.

The decision made, the four men left the park. Before he parted from them, Rinter, though relieved by the return of Dvolci to the safety of Atlon's pack, nevertheless confirmed several times the hour at which Pinnatte would return to the Jyolan that night. When he had gone, the others set off for Heirn's home, walking at a leisurely pace through the early evening streets, transformed into strange canyons by long, dusty shadows and hazy shafts of yellow and gold.

Reaching Heirn's, Atlon casually looked at Pinnatte's hand. He had examined it carefully in the park and pronounced it satisfactory, but that had been a lie. The graze was healing normally, but the turmoil that he saw emanating from the dark green mark, albeit less than it had been in the Jyolan, was unequivocally present, and all the more frightening for being clearly visible away from the Jyolan's pernicious influence. What it was, or how it could have come about, defied him. It took him a considerable effort not to interrogate Pinnatte immediately.

'It's all right,' Pinnatte said, tugging his hand free from Atlon's grip. It was a categorical statement, full of implications that further inspections were not only not needed, but would be refused.

'It's better,' Atlon said gently, offering no opposition. 'But let me know if it starts to trouble you.'

Pinnatte dropped down into a chair and stared into the dead fire grate. He was uncertain about Atlon again – his moods kept shifting for no apparent reason. Why this interest in his hand? It was nothing to do with him. It was only a graze. *His* graze. And why had Atlon brought him here? He seemed all right, but . . .?

He pressed his injured hand to himself.

And Heirn didn't like him, that was for sure. He glanced at the blacksmith lighting a lamp. His posture was stiff and formal. But at least he knew where he was with Heirn. He was the kind of person that he normally avoided. One who would have very little in his purse and yet be permanently on the alert for street thieves. And probably faster than his size indicated. Generally shrewd and dangerous.

'Where do you come from?' The question came out unexpectedly, surprising Pinnatte as much as it surprised Atlon and Heirn.

Heirn was on the verge of telling him to mind his own business when Atlon answered him.

'From the north,' he said, sitting down opposite him.

Dvolci clambered on to Pinnatte's lap. Atlon could see by his twitching snout that he was unhappy there.

'Some people say there's only Arash-Felloren,' Pinnatte went on. 'That there's nowhere else except perhaps the Lowe Towns and the Wilde Ports. That it goes on for ever.' There was a hint of childish petulance in his voice.

'It's big, for sure,' Atlon said. 'Bigger than any city I've ever seen.'

The petulance faded, to be replaced with pride. 'The biggest?'

Atlon smiled. 'The biggest I've seen,' he said again. 'But I haven't seen them all, by any means.'

'Why've you come here?'

'I was travelling south on a message for a friend. I stopped at The Wyndering, and met Rinter, who brought me here so that I could look for work. Heirn was kind enough to employ me and offer me shelter for a day or two.'

Pinnatte was about to ask another question but Atlon spoke first. 'Ellyn called you a Den-Mate. What's that – some kind of apprentice?'

Pinnatte stared at him blankly, then, embarrassed, looked to Heirn for assistance. 'He's an outlander. He doesn't know,' Heirn said impatiently. 'You ask him questions, he's going to ask them back.' He spoke to Atlon. 'He's an apprentice after a fashion. A Den-Mate's a thief, working for a Den Master somewhere. A member of the so-called Guild of Thieves.'

Pinnatte glowered at Heirn. He had no idea how to respond to the turn in the conversation. Such matters weren't spoken of openly.

He took a pride in his work – as much as this blacksmith, for sure. The man had no right to adopt that tone.

Atlon too, was taken aback by Heirn's stark description of his guest, albeit he was an imposed one. He opted for conciliation. 'Well, perhaps those days are behind you now, Pinnatte, if you manage to get a job with Barran.' Heirn snorted, but Atlon ignored it. 'In any case it doesn't detract from your bravery last night.' Reluctantly, Heirn had to nod in agreement to this.

Pinnatte was again looking at Atlon as a friend. He wanted to boast about what he had done – spin a fine yarn as he might have done for Lassner or the other Den-Mates, but he could not to this man. 'It didn't feel brave,' he said. 'I don't really know why I did it. I was just so frightened when that crowd closed around me. I had to get out. It was like being at the bottom of a deep pit.' He shuddered. 'I remember scrambling upwards – catching hold of anything I could. Then I was on the other side of the fence.' He gritted his teeth and reached up to massage his shoulder as he recalled the struggle with the bar that secured the gate. 'I remember trying to open the gate, then nothing else until I woke up with everyone around me.' He shook his head and words came that he had not intended to voice. 'I don't even know why I stayed – why I didn't just run off once I was safe.'

Atlon leaned forward and put a hand on his arm. 'We all do things without knowing why,' he said. 'There's no shame in that – especially when we're in danger. Our instincts are older than our thoughts – they take over. You've a better nature than I suspect you allow yourself. You did what you did, and people are alive now who might have been dead. They were lucky you were there, thief or no.'

Pinnatte had no reply, but the atmosphere in the room had eased. Heirn lowered himself into his favourite chair and the three men sat for some time in a companionable silence: Heirn carefully watching Pinnatte, Atlon waiting as patiently as he could for an opportunity to question him.

They were interrupted by a knock on the door. Both Atlon and Pinnatte started, but Heirn just smiled and made a reassuring gesture.

The callers were friends of his, pursuing an intermittent but time-honoured ritual of luring him to an ale-shop or similar, 'To settle the day's dust.'

Heirn refused but brought them in, glad to have familiar faces about him. He introduced Atlon as an outlander and 'the finest leather-worker I've ever seen – and a healer', and Pinnatte as the hero of the moment, spending a quiet evening recovering from his injuries. After congratulations that left Pinnatte feeling decidedly self-conscious, Atlon was asked about his country and his travels, though the questions had a quality of politeness about them rather than genuine interest. Most of the citizens of Arash-Felloren held, in one manner or another, to Pinnatte's idea that Arash-Felloren was all there was, though few would have admitted it quite so simply. This lack of inquiry and the newcomers' parochial manner suited Atlon, enabling him to question them in turn, under the guise of an outlander's naïveté. As a result he was able to confirm many of the conclusions that he had already formed about the place, though he learned little that was much more than long-established rumour. The Prefect and his legion of administrators probably 'meant well', but on the whole were 'useless'. The Weartans were conceded to be 'much better than they used to be, but still too corrupt for most people to rely on'. The Kyrosdyn were untrustworthy and generally disliked – they had strange powers and they dabbled in things that were 'best left alone'. They were also too secretive and too involved in the city's political and commercial life, where they didn't belong. That conclusion was unanimous. As was that about whatever it was the Kyrosdyn were doing to the Vaskyros. There was a great deal of head-shaking and silent bemusement about the endless building and rebuilding that had been the hallmark of the Vaskyros for many years now. The only people who kept the city going and who kept alight the flame of integrity and honesty were the traders and craftsmen – to which category the two visitors, like Heirn himself, belonged. In addition to this social analysis, Atlon heard three versions about the 'old man' who had been found in the alley, two versions of the founding of the city, several versions of how large it was, including almost whispered references to parts of it which came and went mysteriously, and to others where time itself seemed to be 'fractured'. He was loath to inquire about these in depth, fearing that he might inadvertently insult Heirn's friends, and he was not able to lead the conversation around to the tunnels and the caves.

When they had gone, Pinnatte, who had been fighting sleep for some time, yawned noisily. Heirn pointed to a door. 'There's a bed in there. Go and lie down. I'll wake you in an hour if you're still asleep. That should give you plenty of time to get back to the Jyolan.'

Pinnatte hesitated in the doorway as he looked into the room.

'What's the matter?' Atlon asked.

'Nothing,' Pinnatte replied, though his voice was uncertain. He went into the room.

Partly to avoid disturbing him and partly to avoid being overheard, Atlon and Heirn continued their conversation with lowered voices.

'If you want to know anything, just ask me. Don't try to wheedle it out of my friends,' Heirn said sternly and without preamble.

Atlon put his hand to his head. 'I'm sorry,' he said. 'I didn't mean to be rude. I'm floundering, Heirn. Part of me wants to head back home right away, but I can't – not until I've found out what the Kyrosdyn are up to. I'm just trying to get some kind of feel for this place – it's so bewildering. There seems to be no sense of an underlying order. I get the impression from everything I hear that those with authority hold it by virtue of treachery and strength rather than by the agreement of the people over whom it's held – or for their good.' He frowned, attempting to clarify his ideas. 'There seems to be an urge to seize power for its own sake, without realizing that that in itself provokes opposition – particularly amongst a people so strong-willed and independently-minded as most of those I've met here. It's very frightening.'

Heirn was unsure how to respond. 'Your people live in perfect peace and harmony?' he said.

Atlon laughed ruefully at his caustic manner. 'I asked for that, I suppose,' he replied. 'But, answering your question, no, my people argue and quarrel a great deal – as too do my respected and learned Brothers – a *great* deal. One thing my travels have taught me is that while customs, costumes and tongues differ, people don't.

You're not the only strong-willed and independently minded people by any means. But, on the whole, those with authority in my country are burdened by it. They're aware of where their true power comes from and they strive to use it for the general good.'

Heirn leaned back in his chair and looked at him narrowly. 'It all sounds like something concocted by a twelve-year-old.'

Atlon laughed again, loudly this time, forgetting the sleeping Pinnatte. 'That's because I said it quickly.' He threw up his hands in surrender. 'I told you I was floundering.' Then he became suddenly serious. The laughter had released tensions from him that he had not realized were there, but this only served to show him the starkness of his position. He held up his hand, his thumb and forefinger a little way apart. 'The difference between those who have power in my country and those here is perhaps only slight, but it seems to be vital. It seems to be the difference between some semblance of order, and chaos.'

'You think Arash-Felloren's chaotic?'

'I told you. I think it's frightening.'

Heirn fell silent. He stared into the cold grate. 'I think you're right on both points,' he said eventually, speaking slowly and softly. 'Though it's always been like that and I can't imagine it changing.' He paused. 'There are splendid things in the city – and good people – and honest livings to be made.'

'I'm sure there are,' Atlon said. 'You're very patient with my clumsiness. I'm an academic – a student, not a diplomat.'

'And you're floundering.' Heirn's tone was gently ironic.

'Indeed.'

Heirn turned back to him. 'I suppose I am too, now,' he said. 'I know nothing about you other than that you've brought disruption and even death in your wake, but for some reason I trust you. I decided when we were in the park that you were worth helping.' He tapped his head. 'No reason – just going with *my* instincts. Sometimes they take over, as you just said. So . . . what do we do?'

Heirn's declaration was so simple and open that Atlon was at a loss for a reply. He was spared any awkward delay however, as, from the bedroom where Pinnatte lay, came a loud and anguished cry.

Chapter 23

Imorren gazed around in wonder. This must surely have been brought about by the Anointing.

All study, all calculation, all experiment to determine the precise consequences of the Anointing foundered eventually in tangled infinities and improbabilities. More than one Higher Brother had taken refuge in insanity as a result of Imorren's relentless drive to negotiate this shrieking intellectual vortex. More than one anonymous vagrant had perished as a result of her experiments. Yet she would not even allow the whispering of that growing consensus that the consequences were, by definition, unknowable.

'You are flawed,' she would say. 'Your faith is weak. Try harder.'

All that was known for certain was that the Anointing would reach across those regions whose ultimate description defied known logic, and open Ways to the endless worlds that lay beyond and between the flickering existence of the world which held Arash-Felloren. Worlds across which He was scattered. Broken once again by cruel and treacherous enemies.

Just the prospect of this brought with it an old question. How could it have happened? How could He have been so defeated?

Imorren twitched away from it, as she did whenever it came to her. Answers to that question defied her as much as answers to the outcome of the Anointing. Not least because she could not even begin to approach them rationally with the little knowledge she had of His end. But once asked, she could do no other than wearily rehearse again the responses she had had almost from the time she first heard the news. Had she been there, would it have been different? Or would she too have been swept away by whatever Power it was that had dispatched Him? Had she been sent away to learn about the crystals because He had foreseen His destiny? Was His passing and her leaving no more than part of a deeper scheme – perhaps a re-forging of His new lieutenants? That idea had come later, and held a little more comfort. But no answer seemed wholly credible. He had been so powerful. So seemingly invincible.

Yet . . .

As it always did, the flurry of guilt and anger dwindled into a dull ache low in her stomach. And as she always did, she centred herself. There was now, and only now. What had been, what might have been, served only to cloud and obscure. She must have faith. She was here by His will and serving His ends. She it was who must open the Ways so that He might begin His return. For only in this world could He be truly whole. And only from this world could He spread forth again to take what was rightfully His.

She returned to her vigil.

She knew that she was dreaming. She had always been able to stand aside from the swirling confusion of her sleeping thoughts. Often, she was able to control them. Deep inside, where lay that hidden ache, perhaps even deeper, she believed that this was why she had been chosen, and why it was her destiny ultimately to be by His side – His powerful right hand. For had not He Himself told her of the importance of those few who could walk the dreams of others? Those who could find the Portals and Gateways that led to the worlds beyond and between, and who could move freely amongst them, guiding those who could re-shape them.

She paused and held her breath at the memory, and her dream seemed to halt with her, watching, listening. Had she imagined it, or had some subtle demon of self-deceit placed the thought in her mind subsequently? But surely there had been a hint of *envy* in that telling . . . Even now she scarcely dared consider such a thing. It was not conceivable that He, in His perfection, could be tainted with so gross a human failing.

Yet . . .

She shook the thought from her violently – the dream trembled.

To think such things was heresy! No, it was worse than heresy. Words did not exist that could adequately frame such treachery. The failing was hers. She had misunderstood Him – some subtlety in His telling. It could not be otherwise.

Yet . . .

Inexorably, other thoughts slipped in to compound her crime. Could it be that she, with her control over her dreams, was one such? Did she have, latent within her, that elusive ability to move between the worlds?

It should not be so, for she could use the Power. And it did not seem so, for He would have known it, surely? For even when He was whole and strong, with many plans afoot, and she lay at His feet, He bade his servants, above all things, to search constantly for those so gifted.

Yet . . .

The dream slipped from her, as if fearful. It drew her back from this dangerous edge and on to familiar terrain.

For the dream was both new and not new. As ever, she was amid a vision of the Vaskyros. Towers, spires, ramping walls and vaulting arches pierced and spanned a sky, black with ominous clouds. Rooms, chambers, halls, innumerable and ornate, formed the complex weave of its heart, while dark tunnels and cellars reached over downwards, like great roots, burrowing deep below the city. And Imorren, motionless, floated amongst it – became it – seeing all things at all times, marvelling at its subtle, ever more detailed symmetries, and searching always for a sign of its true purpose that she might better create its tangible counterpart. But that too eluded her. Words such as resonance, conjunction, alignment, came and went, each striking a faint spark but bringing no illumination.

Older resources came to her aid, setting aside the conjectures resolutely and turning her mind to the unfolding vision. For this dream was of extraordinary vividness. It must surely be a consequence of the Anointing! The thought became the last tremor of her inner debate. Her mind was free now, so that she would see what was there, not what she thought was there, or what she felt should be there. Now, nothing would go unmarked, unrecorded, for this would be to miss much – perhaps everything. For whatever else this was, it was a nexus, a joining – an intersection – of many places and times and, as with all else, when it must come to be made, the consequences of the least error were incalculable.

The dream was totally hers again, the jagged complexity of the changed Vaskyros embedded in her mind to be carried forward into wakefulness.

But still there lingered a hint of her old belief: that it would be she who one day would walk through the dream and into the worlds beyond, to hold out her hand to Him and draw Him forth into His true world.

Then, at once suddenly and as if it had been thus always, she was not alone. Such dreams had always carried a hovering unease that others too, somewhere, somehow, were watching – that the dream was not for her alone. But this was different.

Now, another was looking through her eyes! Fear possessed her.

Neither of these things could be! Fear such as this she had long since banished, and all here, she knew, was of her making, touched only by His will reaching out to guide her.

But the fear remained. And the other watcher.

Realization.

The fear was not hers!

'Who are you?' she demanded.

The fear grew.

'Who are you?' she demanded again. 'What are you? How did you come here?'

Then, a greater realization.

It was the Anointed!

And the Vaskyros was gone. A silent cry ringing through her, she was falling. Falling, through a darkness gibbering with a myriad sounds and images. And she was nothing. All that existed was her awareness, hard as diamond, insubstantial as an idle summer breeze.

The fear became terror, and, bound as she was, it threatened to become hers.

Imorren reached out to waken herself.

But nothing happened.

She was aware of herself, lying motionless on her bed, symmetrical and ordered even in the brief sleep she was taking before her night's work – the central flower of the elaborate patterning that dominated the room and which she must ever note. But she was here too.

She reached again. But bonds held her that nothing could break. She could not escape. An ancient will was carrying her now, and with her, the Anointed. An ancient, hunting will. It possessed her. Prey was all around, rich and bountiful. She was heady with the stink of it. Soon, she would feed again. Satiation was not possible. Her body would ring with the screeching of prey as it fought to hold to the life that was truly hers. Until the final yielding . . .

It was good.

Ecstasy suffused her.

Then an agonizing cry of denial was all around her. She tried to oppose it, but she was as nothing against such an intent.

The darkness was rent open. Mouth and eyes gaping, Imorren burst into the light.

Mouth and eyes gaping, Pinnatte burst into the light. For even the dull light seeping into Heirn's room seemed bright by comparison with where he had just been. For a moment, his eyes were like black pits.

Gasping for breath, her heart pounding and her mouth awash with saliva, Imorren sat upright and rigid. Her hands, clawed, were reaching out either to seize something or to defend herself against it. The familiar pattern of the room closed about her as her eyes focused. Teeth bared, she forced her breathing to harmonize with its undulating flow. Saliva trickled down her chin. Sucking in noisily, she leaned over and spat into a basin on a table by the bed. Snatching up a glass, she took a mouthful of water and spat again. Then, standing up unsteadily, she leaned on the table and gazed into the bowl with its streaked and frothy contents.

The movement had made her feel cold. Touching her forehead,

she found that it was wet – very wet. Then her arms were cold, and her gown was clinging to her. And inside she was aching and empty. Tentatively, she turned over a small mirror and looked into it.

Bright eyes shone from a flushed and glistening face. Hair was slicked and awry. She could not recognize herself. 'Where are you?' she asked meaninglessly. Every part of her body urged her to sit down on the edge of the bed and put her head into her hands, but the face in the mirror snarled at the image. Slowly and with great deliberation, she replaced the mirror, face downwards – mirrors were such wild and frightening things. Then, with equal deliberation, she straightened, turned, and walked towards a door at the far end of the room.

It was no easy task. She must bathe and compose herself completely before she saw anyone, but buffeting her, like an angry wind, was a grim knowledge that was stretching her self-discipline to its limits. Disorientated though she had been, she had recognized the creature carrying her from the dream, and she had recognized the Anointed. But something was amiss – grievously so. The consequences of the Anointing might be beyond calculation, but many of the things that they could *not* be, were known. And what she had felt had been one such.

All had been well when she felt his presence at the Loose Pit.

Now, there was a flaw. A flaw that jeopardized everything she had worked for and achieved.

He must be found and examined.

'You're all right. You're all right.' Atlon wrapped his arms around the struggling Pinnatte, partly in an attempt to comfort him, partly to restrain him. Heirn, better suited to such a task, stood by and watched helplessly, stunned by the terrible cry that Pinnatte had uttered.

'What's the matter?' he asked weakly as Pinnatte became quieter.

Atlon looked into the still staring eyes, bracing himself for a return of the recognition that he had seen in the Jyolan. And the hatred. But there was nothing there except fear. He relaxed. 'It was just a dream,' he said.

'Some dream,' Heirn retorted disbelievingly. He lit a lamp. Its soft light pushed aside the city's gloaming and made the room both smaller and more welcoming. 'He's whiter than my sheets and wringing wet.' He went out and returned a moment later with a cloth and a towel. Sitting on the edge of the bed, he gently displaced Atlon and began washing Pinnatte's face. The young man made no response, other than to gaze about the room.

Atlon stood back, watching the scene. For a moment he felt like an intruder. It was obvious that Heirn had performed this duty many times before, and under less than happy circumstances, he suspected.

Then Pinnatte waved him aside. This too, was something that Heirn was obviously used to. Atlon looked away as the big man hesitantly stood up. Then he turned to Pinnatte.

'Tell me what happened.'

Pinnatte hugged his hand to his body and looked back at him suspiciously. 'Tell me what happened,' Atlon said again, more forcefully this time.

'Just a dream,' Pinnatte said hurriedly. 'You said I might have dreams. It was—'

Atlon was shaking his head. 'It was the same as you had last night, wasn't it? The one you've been fretting about, on and off, all day. The one that made you hesitate when Heirn suggested you lie down for a while.' He leaned forward. 'And the reason why you tried to stay awake when you did lie down.'

Pinnatte was again oscillating between trust and distrust of this strange man. How could he know so much?

'It was just a—'

'No!' Atlon interrupted him. 'No more foolishness. Something's troubling you badly and I might be able to help you with it. But I must know what's happened to you – about your dream – about your hand. How did you get that mark?'

It was a risk, but Atlon was glad that the question was out. Pinnatte clutched his hand closer.

Atlon pressed on. 'I don't know what's happening to you, Pinnatte, but this is something you need to be free of, you must be aware of that.'

The word *free* echoed in Pinnatte's mind. But no, this stranger should be minding his own business. There was nothing wrong with his hand. The Kyrosdyn's touch, given for whatever reason, had brought him to this point where his life was going to be better, where a future existed in which real wealth, real freedom, might lie.

And it brought the nightmares.

The thought came from nowhere and made him shudder.

'I *am* free,' he said defiantly. He flaunted his injured hand, the graze now scabbed over. 'I can go anywhere I want, do anything I want . . .' He stumbled, realizing how ridiculous such words sounded coming from a mere Den-Mate. 'That is, I will when . . .' He stumbled again then raised his voice to force his conclusion out, 'When Barran takes me on. I'll have the money to do everything then.'

'Except sleep,' Atlon said quietly into the strained silence that followed.

'I'll sleep well enough,' Pinnatte retorted angrily.

Dvolci clambered on to the bed and lay across his lap. Atlon looked earnestly at Pinnatte and shook his head. The denial seemed to enrage the young man. 'The Kyrosdyn has shown me the way,' he burst out, but his voice trailed off and his arm came out as if to snatch back the words.

'So it *was* something the Kyrosdyn did to you, was it?' Atlon said sympathetically. 'I was beginning to suspect that.'

Pinnatte stammered, 'No,' and 'Yes,' a few times, ending with an uncomfortable, 'Yes.'

No sooner had he uttered the word than a wave of guilt and dismay flooded through him. This tormentor had tricked him! The guilt became suddenly a raving anger. Something in him reached out to destroy Atlon.

He had a fleeting vision of Dvolci, teeth bared, hackles raised, leaping up, and Atlon's hand being lifted in front of him, filling the world. Then there came a blow that seemed to strike every part of his body, and a suffocating darkness folded around him.

'Ye gods,' Dvolci exclaimed. He was crouching low on top of a cupboard. 'Where did that come from? What is he?'

306

'What've you done to him?' Heirn burst out. It looked to him as though Atlon had struck the young man after Dvolci had suddenly leapt away. But even as he spoke he saw that Atlon was swaying. He seized his arm.

'What's the matter? What's happening?'

Atlon waved a hand for a moment's pause. 'I'm all right – I think. But I hadn't expected that.'

'Expected what? Why did you hit him?'

Atlon gently prised Heirn's grip from his arm. Bending over Pinnatte, he began to examine him thoroughly, listening first to his breathing, then testing many pulses.

He looked only partially relieved when he stood up. Heirn noticed that his hands were shaking. 'He's all right, as well,' he said. 'Which is due more to his good fortune than my skill.' He groped backwards for a chair then sat down like an old man. 'I didn't hit him, Heirn,' he said, after a long pause. 'It was he who nearly hit me – nearly killed me – and you. I just defended myself – like I did against the Kyrosdyn yesterday.'

Heirn was about to proclaim that Pinnatte had never moved, but Atlon's pain reached into him like a revelation. 'You mean, he used this . . . Power . . . of yours?' He needed no answer, even though his own protests followed immediately. 'But he's a street thief, not a Kyrosdyn. What would he know about such things? I'll wager he's never studied anything in his life except how to cut purses. And I doubt you'll find even coins on him, let alone crystals.'

But even as he was speaking, Heirn could feel Atlon's own bewilderment and concern. It trembled through him. He motioned towards the other room. 'If he's all right, we can talk next door.'

Atlon shook his head. 'I daren't leave him. He might be quiet for the moment, but . . .' He left any conclusion unspoken. 'I need to think.' He took hold of Pinnatte's right hand and examined it closely. Dvolci came to the bedside and joined him, his snout twitching as he peered at the seemingly innocuous wound. His hackles were still raised and he seemed unusually energetic, as if keeping himself ready for another sudden flight. Atlon laid a hand on him.

'I'm sorry about before,' Dvolci said. 'I didn't mean to get in your way. I just didn't see it coming fast enough.'

'Don't distress yourself,' Atlon said. 'If you hadn't moved so quickly, I wouldn't have seen it either. We'll both of us have to be more careful in future. Heirn's hospitality has made us lax. It's as you said, we're still on the battlefield.'

He put Pinnatte's hand down. 'That's the second time,' he said. 'First the Jyolan, now here. And both times there was virtually no warning. It was almost as though he was suddenly someone else. Someone who recognized me.'

'More likely, recognized what you are.'

'Would you please tell me what's happening?' Heirn asked into the ensuing silence. He sounded almost plaintive.

Atlon tapped his hand on his knee nervously. 'I don't know. That's the problem. Something very strange has been done to this young man. Something awful. And it's to do with that mark on his hand. I'm getting responses from it and to it which I can't begin to understand.' He looked at Dvolci but the felci simply shook his head. 'He tried to attack me in the Jyolan for no apparent reason. Dvolci managed to stop him, which was fortunate, to say the least. I shudder to think what the consequences would have been if I'd had to defend myself *there*. But just now, he actually used it – used the Power – and as a weapon.' He wiped the back of his hand across his forehead and Heirn was horrified to see true despair in his eyes. 'In the name of pity, Dvolci, what have we got here?'

'An abomination.' The felci's reply was harsh.

'An ordinary young man,' Atlon said.

'He might have been ordinary once, but he isn't now,' Dvolci said, jumping on to the bed. He peered intently at the sleeping Pinnatte. 'Though he seems harmless enough now. It makes no sense.'

'But for how long will he be harmless?'

Dvolci did not reply.

Atlon straightened up and leaned back in his chair. He looked at Heirn. 'You were right before, of course. Someone like this shouldn't be able to use the Power. Even people who have a natural aptitude for it can't normally use it in any significant way – certainly not like this one just did. Long and careful training is needed to turn aptitude into ability. And great personal dedication.'

Heirn, lost, snatched at ideas. 'He says he's a Den-Mate, and he acts like one, but perhaps he's lying. Perhaps he's a Kyrosdyn novice, pretending to be a thief, for some reason.' The conclusion rang false to him even as he was speaking it. His every Arash-Felloren instinct told him that Pinnatte was what he said he was.

Atlon was shaking his head. 'He had no vestige of control, Heirn. He was like a leaking bucket.' He closed his eyes and laid his hands on Pinnatte again. 'And now there's not a vestige of Power within him, other than . . . something . . . from his hand.'

'You can tell that?' Heirn asked. 'Just by . . .' He ended with a vague wave of his hands.

'Oh, yes. And so can anyone else who knows how. That's why I wanted to keep away from that Kyrosdyn, and why the Jyolan frightened me so much.'

Heirn was determined to help. 'Has he any crystals on him? You haven't looked.'

'He wasn't using crystals.' Atlon was categorical. 'It was a natural use. Uncontrolled, but unaided.' He glanced up at Heirn and reproached himself. 'You're taking all this very well.'

'I don't seem to have a choice.' The immediate and somewhat acid response reassured Atlon. 'Things are happening in front of my eyes, and while I can't understand most of them – any of them! – I can't deny them, can I?'

Self-reproach filled Atlon's face. 'We're fortunate indeed to have met you, Heirn. And I'm sorry for burdening you like this, if I haven't apologized already.'

Heirn waved the remark aside. 'It's only a burden if I choose to make it one,' he said. 'But knowledge would help me without a doubt.'

'And me,' Atlon said ruefully, turning back to Pinnatte again. 'It's not possible, you see. The way he uses the power can't be achieved without a certain kind of control – a structure, a shape, if you like. And he has none. It's . . .' He shrugged helplessly. 'It's as though he's climbing a ladder with no rungs, or . . . melting iron without heat. It's impossible. *It just can't be.*' Angry frustration ripped into his voice. He struck his palm with his fist as if the violence would resolve the paradox.

'But it is?'

Atlon let out a loud, grating breath, which was almost a snarl. 'Yes, it is.'

'Which leaves us where?'

Atlon looked at him helplessly. 'Which leaves us with Pinnatte,' he said after a long pause. Heirn too, took some time before he spoke again. He searched Atlon's face. 'Perhaps you should just walk away from him.'

It needed no great perception to see that Atlon was sorely tempted by the suggestion. Dvolci watched the two men.

'I'd like nothing better,' Atlon said eventually. 'But I can't. I'll walk away from you any time you tell me to, but I can't walk away from this young man. I wish I could. I don't know what I expected to find when I set out on this journey, but it was nothing like this nightmare. But having found it, I've no choice other than to find out more about it. Something terrible's happening here.' He pointed at Pinnatte. 'And he's near the heart of it, I'm sure. He's admitted that the Kyrosdyn are involved . . . that they've done something to him.' He fell silent, his face distressed. When he spoke again, he echoed his last phrase slowly, as if hasty speech might scatter the pieces of a delicate puzzle. 'They've done something to him . . . and it's gone wrong. That must be it. He's an accident.'

He stood up. 'What could they have been trying to do? And why?' He tapped a finger towards Pinnatte. 'Nothing for his benefit, for sure. And it wasn't this – not what he's turned into. Nothing could be gained by making someone able to use the Power as he does without the discipline that's intrinsic to it. Nothing. It's like loosing a stampede into a crowded square. Like making a weapon which is as likely to kill its user as his enemy. Perhaps even more so.' He nodded, satisfied with this conclusion, but little wiser. 'Yes. They've tried some obscene experiment on him, and it's gone wrong. It's not remotely conceivable that he was ever meant to be like this.'

He took Pinnatte's hand again. 'Probably this open cut and Ellyn's drawing ointment have conspired to play havoc with their scheme. Incredible.'

Heirn frowned at his tone. 'You sound almost regretful,' he said.

Atlon looked a little guilty. 'No, not really,' he replied. 'Not at all, actually. But . . .' He seemed reluctant to voice what he was thinking for fear it might give the lie to this denial. 'To have done something like this deliberately would have been a staggering achievement, requiring remarkable knowledge and skill.' He shook his head, an admiring academic, despite himself. 'There's knowledge here that would have even the most sedate of my elderly brethren skipping like children. Knowledge that reaches into the profoundest depths of what we think of as our world, our reality.'

He released Pinnatte's hand. 'But it's also an obscenity. An appalling and dangerous obscenity, with profound consequences for us here, now. Perhaps even for the whole city. They've been meddling near the heart of a region where infinite possibilities jostle incessantly, dabbling with a swirling dynamic equilibrium which is beyond any understanding. Even to approach it they must have known the risks they were running. And it's gone wrong. It's unforgivable.' Anger lit his face briefly, then faded. 'So, being honest, yes, perhaps part of me *is* regretful – but it's a very tiny part. Mainly I'm frightened. Though if it weren't so tragic and so dangerous, I'd also be darkly amused that Ellyn's simple ointment has so disturbed such a sophisticated venture.'

Heirn could offer nothing against this confession. As ever, he clung to the practical. 'What are we going to do with him, then?'

Atlon, who had begun to pace up and down, stopped. 'Ideally, what I'd like to do is take him back with me so that my Elders could find out what's happened to him and help him.'

'No chance of that,' Heirn said conclusively. 'He's a bonded Den-Mate for one thing, and, you heard him, he's got aspirations to further himself as a result of his escapade last night – with Barran, no less. From the melting pot into the forge as far as I can see, but that's what he wants. He's a young man who could use

311

some guidance, without a doubt, but there's nothing you can do about that – the city's full of the likes of him. I'll tell you this – even your horse would be hard-pressed to drag him away from the city and what he imagines to be his future prospects.'

'I was only ordering my thoughts,' Atlon said. 'I wouldn't attempt to take him away. Not least because there's no saying how dangerous he's liable to become, nor how soon.'

Heirn looked at the slight figure on the bed. Atlon anticipated his question. 'He mightn't look dangerous, but he is, believe me. If he'd released the Power he intended for me just now, you'd have been killed as well, and this room would have been wrecked.'

Heirn's doubts flared. 'I'm doing my best with what you're telling me, but he's not the size of two good nails, for pity's sake. What could he possibly—'

'Have you forgotten how casually you were pinned against that wall, so soon?' Atlon cut across his outburst. 'And that Kyrosdyn was little larger than Pinnatte here.'

Pinnatte stirred. Despite his protestations about Pinnatte's size, Heirn jumped back. Atlon took a deep breath and moved to the side of the bed.

'You feeling better now?' he asked, as Pinnatte's eyes opened.

Pinnatte levered himself upright. 'Yes. Did I fall asleep in the middle of something?' He started and turned anxiously to Heirn. 'The time, the time. I mustn't be late to see Barran. He'll forget me for sure if I keep him waiting.'

Without waiting for a reply, he swung off the bed.

'It's all right,' Heirn replied, taking note of Atlon's studied calmness, and trying to copy it. 'You just nodded off. There's plenty of time. I wouldn't let you miss your appointment.' He was not entirely successful in keeping an edge from his voice.

'Do you remember what you just did?' Atlon asked.

Pinnatte looked at him, automatically assuming a puzzled and innocent expression, and preparing to reach for one of his extensive collection of well-rehearsed excuses. He hadn't taken anything here, he knew. Oddly enough, the idea had not even occurred to him while he had been with these people.

312

'Don't you remember getting angry with me, a moment ago?' Atlon pressed.

Pinnatte became genuinely puzzled. Then the memory of the nightmare crashed in on him with a force that was almost physical – the scents, the screams, the emotions, the helplessness. He gasped and lifted his hands as if to fend them off.

Heirn took another pace backwards. Dvolci planted his front legs on the side of the bed opposite Atlon, his eyes flicking intently between him and Pinnatte. Atlon managed to remain outwardly calm, but his mind was racing. The disturbance about Pinnatte that he had felt before had returned strongly, and though it lacked the power and vividness that it had had when first he encountered it in the Jyolan, it nevertheless confirmed that Pinnatte's condition was not improving. If he let him return to the Jyolan, who could say what the consequences would be in that awful place? Another thought came – startling him with its obviousness. Why was Pinnatte wandering loose? It did not seem probable that the Kyrosdyn would have performed their experiment and simply let him walk away. Were they even now watching him? A great many responses arose in the wake of this but he hastily set them aside for consideration later. The other possibility was that the Kyrosdyn did not know what had happened to Pinnatte subsequently. Both options alarmed him. Despite the risks, he had no alternative but to try to win the confidence of this young man. At least this time he would be ready for a violent reaction. Reaching the decision calmed him, and his voice was soft and encouraging when he spoke.

'If that dream's still troubling you, you'd be best advised to spit it out. Many night-time monsters shrivel at the touch of the light.'

Once again, Pinnatte shot him a look full of doubt and suspicion, and for an instant Atlon sensed the antagonism that he had faced before, though this time it was distant and weak.

'I don't understand,' Pinnatte blurted out. 'I don't have dreams. At least, I don't think I do. I've never remembered one, ever.'

'Some people don't,' Atlon said, heartened by this first response.

Restraints suddenly broke in Pinnatte. 'It's the creature,' he said. 'I know it is. I didn't realize until just now. It looked at me

313

last night. Looked up at me – *me*. Singled me out of the entire crowd and bowed to me. It wants me for something.'

Atlon said nothing but motioned him to continue. Pinnatte's voice fell to a whisper. He was almost a child now. 'It's joined to me in some way. It reached into my mind last night – took me hunting.' He shuddered.

'I don't understand. What do you mean?'

Briefly the antagonism flared again, but it could not survive against the torrent of fears that Pinnatte had released. 'I was there with it. No, I *was* it. I could hear prey screaming.' There was cold resonance about the word *prey*. 'I was making them scream. I was feeding on their screaming – their terror.' Pinnatte shuddered again, but this time the shudder turned into an uncontrollable shivering. Though he did not move, Atlon braced himself inwardly, for he could feel a maelstrom of conflicting forces struggling for supremacy within the young man's tortured frame. Carefully he held out a hand to prevent Heirn from stepping forward to help.

Pinnatte's shivering showed no sign of abating, and indeed, Atlon could feel his inner struggle worsening. He could not sit by and watch idly. But in such confusion there was no saying what the results would be of anything that he did.

His every instinct was to put his arms around the young man again and offer him some comfort in his pain. But he knew enough to be aware that Pinnatte had probably never had such treatment and that its unfamiliarity might be more disturbing than calming. Instead he risked an approach he thought Pinnatte might well have encountered. He took him by the arms and shook him firmly.

'Enough!' he shouted. 'All you've had is a nightmare – a bad dream. It's out in the open now, and it's gone. There's nothing to be frightened about. Besides, do you think Barran would be interested in someone who trembles at his dreams?'

Almost immediately, Pinnatte became calmer. Atlon felt the darkness within him slip away.

Then it was back again, taking him completely unawares.

Pinnatte's hand shot out and struck him in the chest, hurling him against the wall. The same fate befell Heirn who reached forward to seize him. 'No!' Pinnatte bellowed at Atlon, even as he

314

was brushing Heirn aside. 'I know what you are, warlock. The time is coming. You too will be prey soon.'

Then the room was echoing to the sounds of his fleeing footsteps.

Chapter 24

Rostan was unashamedly afraid. Twice now he had explained in great detail what he had done to Pinnatte, and the circumstances that led to it. Such few lies as he had told at his first confession he had reiterated so often to himself subsequently that they had now become the truth for him, but that gave him little comfort. Imorren's manner was glacial as she probed relentlessly into every nuance of the event, peeling back layer after layer, cruelly dissecting his actions. He had not seen her like this often, but he recognized the mood. Something was appallingly wrong. So wrong that someone could die for it – and very unpleasantly. Already he had a list of scapegoats to hand.

Then there had come this silence, with Imorren sitting motionless and unreadable, and a sense of oppression so filling the small room that it threatened to choke him. In the end, he could do no other than speak.

'Ailad, may I ask what has happened?'

The question released Imorren from her circling thoughts. Such that Rostan had done he had done correctly – or in accordance with what had been decided for the Anointing. That he was lying about the circumstances she knew and accepted. It was of no importance. For even had he Anointed the wrong person, the consequences could not have been what she had felt when she was so violently torn from her dream. And it had *not* been the wrong person. Rostan must indeed have been moved by His will to do what he did, for there was nothing amiss about the Anointed when she had felt his presence at the Jyolan the previous night. All then had been well. A feeling of wholeness, of the coming together of many disparate threads, had pervaded her, almost ecstatically.

But now?

The bonding of the Anointed to her and the creature, in some region beyond the dream had been a strange and unexpected experience, yet there was an order to it that did not seem untoward and which doubtless would yield its secrets to careful study later. But the Anointed's terror, his violent severing of the bond when he should have plunged with her into the creature's offering, was deeply disturbing. Even worse however, was the fleeting glimpse she had had as she tumbled back into wakefulness: the Anointed had acquired the ability to use the Power. Just as Rostan was endlessly repeating his encounter with Pinnatte, so Imorren returned to this revelation over and over. It was an impossibility – but she had felt it, surely? Or had she misunderstood, misinterpreted? No, she had felt what she had felt. It had been the Power. But wild and uncontrolled – another impossibility. But . . .

Round and round.

Something had happened to the Anointed since last night.

'Tell me about the dead novice,' she said.

Rostan started at this sudden departure from the intense scrutiny of the Anointing. Imorren herself was surprised by it, coming to her unbidden as it had.

'There's little to tell, Ailad,' Rostan said, tentatively relaxing. 'He left on a routine task – alone – then he was found this morning by a passer-by who reported it to us in the hope of a reward. I sent some Lesser Brothers to pick him up. He was . . .' He hesitated. 'Badly spent. So much so that the crowd who gathered just presumed that he was one of our older Brothers who had simply collapsed and died.'

'How badly spent was he?'

'Completely, Ailad,' Rostan said. 'Although I only discovered that myself a little while ago when I examined him personally.'

Imorren touched her throat. 'And his crystals were gone, you said?'

Rostan nodded. 'Stolen, presumably. They'd have been transmuted completely. Worth a fortune.'

Imorren became practical. 'And they're still ours. Contact Barran. Tell him that first-water greens – worked greens – have

318

been stolen, and to detain anyone trying to sell them. We may as well put our novice's contribution to some use. Crystals of that quality aren't easily come by.'

Rostan made to stand up. Imorren waved him back to his seat. 'Later,' she said.

She became thoughtful. 'It's a long time since anything like this has happened. What do you know about this novice?'

Rostan gave a dismissive shrug. 'Nothing much. He was competent, conscientious. He'd have made steady progress, quite probably to the Higher Brotherhood eventually.'

'And his sensitivity?'

'Better than average, his Teaching Brother said.'

Imorren frowned slightly. 'Temperament, control?'

'His control was appropriate to his sensitivity – above average – more than adequate for his normal duties. As for temperament, who can say? Apparently he wasn't someone that this would have been expected of.'

Imorren turned to him, cold again. 'You haven't thought about this, have you?' she said.

Rostan, suddenly afraid again, opted for honesty without a moment's consideration. 'No, Ailad. Not at all. I've had little time with all that's been happening.'

'Think about it now.'

Rostan bowed slightly. 'I imagine he'd been experimenting in some way,' he said casually. 'That's the way these things usually happen.' A flicker of movement in Imorren focused his concentration with brutal swiftness. He rejected his remark before she did. 'But in an alley far from his own cell? And on his own?' He stopped as the implication of the novice's death unfurled with stark clarity. How could he have missed it? He added quickly to his list of scapegoats even as he put his hand to his head and voiced the inevitable conclusion. '*And completely spent?*' He paused significantly. 'Unless he accidentally stumbled on a more advanced technique – which is unlikely, to say the least – he couldn't possibly have taken the crystals through the phases like that on his own.' It was not necessary to say more. He cursed inwardly. As if there wasn't enough happening at the moment. Someone – another

Brother – had murdered the wretched man! But why? For some petty slight? Novices could become dangerously intense, but that was always watched for. Or perhaps it was a jockeying for position. Or a woman? He blurted out excuses before they were sought.

'But there's not been even a hint of trouble amongst the novices. There hasn't been in years, not since your re-ordering of their duties. And they're watched constantly for signs of instability.'

Imorren nodded slowly. 'Nor would I expect one of them to resort to such sophistication to murder someone. Especially when by doing so they'd only point towards themselves. It's not as if there aren't assassins enough to be hired in the city.'

'It might have been a sudden quarrel.'

Imorren's hand dismissed the idea. 'A novice who had done this would almost certainly fall victim to the crystals himself. And who else amongst us would bother killing a novice thus?'

The analysis was accurate and Rostan, with nothing to add, remained silent. Something was pending.

'Which leaves us with the possibility that someone other than one of our own did this.'

Rostan's eyes widened and, in spite of himself, he ventured to argue with his Ailad. 'But that's not possible! There've been no users of the Power other than ourselves in generations. Our control's been absolute. No one could suddenly appear with the ability to use the Power – especially like that.'

'I did.'

The reply cut through Rostan. He stammered before lapsing into an uncomfortable silence.

'Yes . . . but . . . you were . . .'

'I was not from this city.' Imorren's tone told him nothing, but when she turned to him, he sat very still. 'In common with most of the people who are Arash-Felloren born, you make the mistake of imagining it to be the whole world. Many things it is – more than you know. But, everything, it is not. There are powerful lands far from here which eventually, when the city is wholly ours, we will have to deal with. And in these lands are people who study the Power as we do – quite openly – though they have neither the crystals nor our knowledge. They should not, however, be underestimated. It is possible that someone has come as I did. Perhaps a passing traveller, perhaps someone with a more sinister intention. Such a person could well have been challenged by our novice and done this as a result.'

'But . . .?'

'I am speculating, Highest,' Imorren said. 'Speculating that this is what could have happened. To speculate further would be pointless, but it's an alternative that mustn't be ignored.' She became brusque. 'Discreetly examine the novices, of course – by way of trying to discover how the poor man might have come to be where he was. Did he experiment, talk of experimenting, was he concerned about anything . . . you need no counselling from me about how to deal with this.' Then she was thoughtful again. 'But tell everyone to be watchful when they're out in the city. On the pretext of looking for the stolen crystals, tell them to report any unusual manifestations of the Power that they encounter.'

Rostan bowed again. 'I will, Ailad,' he said. He carefully adjusted his robe preparatory to a formal leave-taking.

'The Anointing has been marred.'

Imorren's words jolted Rostan back to the condition he had been in before she digressed on to the subject of the dead novice. His mouth opened to echo her last word, but no sound came.

'I don't understand, Ailad,' he managed to say, eventually.

'It is marred – flawed – not as it should be.'

Imorren did not need to look at him to feel his terror. It gave her some pleasure, but she needed him and she needed him alert, not paralysed with fear. Unusually and reluctantly, she released him.

'The fault is not yours, Highest. What you did, you did well. But while all was satisfactory last night, now it is not.'

Out of immediate danger, Rostan risked a question. 'How has this made itself known to you, Ailad?'

'That is of no import.' She stared at him, grey eyes piercing. 'Gariak lost track of him at the Jyolan, you said?'

'Do you wish him punished, Ailad?'

Imorren shook her head. 'Give the Anointed's sign to the Lesser and Higher Brothers and tell them he's to be found and brought to me. But *gently*. He must not be harmed. He must not even be frightened. Make that clear on pain of my gravest displeasure. His role is too uncertain at the moment for any rashness. But he *must* be found, and found soon. See to it.'

By the time Atlon and Heirn had reached the door, Pinnatte was nowhere to be seen. Atlon, rubbing his bruised chest, glanced up and down the busy street. 'That way,' he and Dvolci said simultaneously. Heirn put a restraining hand on Atlon's shoulder as he made to set off.

'Where are you going?'

'After him, of course.'

'He's a street thief, Atlon. He'll run three paces for every one of yours, weave through a crowd you couldn't charge a horse through, and climb walls you wouldn't tackle with a ladder. Not to mention the fact that he knows the city and you'd be lost two streets from here.'

'Don't worry, Dvolci and I can track him.'

Heirn released him. 'Maybe so, maybe so. But when you've tracked and caught him, what're you going to do then?' He acknowledged a greeting from a passer-by.

Atlon sagged. He looked up and down the street again then at the surrounding buildings. Despite the solidity of Heirn's presence, the city was a deeply alien place to him.

'I don't know,' he admitted. 'But I can't just let him wander free. He's dangerous, for one thing.'

Heirn was sympathetic. 'The city's full of dangerous people,' he said. 'Always has been. What's one more?'

'In Pinnatte's case, it's one too many,' Atlon replied.

Heirn did not speak for a moment. 'You can't sandbag him and hurl him across your saddle, can you? You can't do anything about him if he doesn't want you to. And I think, on reflection, you'd be well advised not even to try.'

There was a note in Heirn's voice that sharpened Atlon's attention. 'What do you mean?'

Heirn looked uncomfortable. 'This . . . Power . . . of yours – and Pinnatte's. I've seen you use it – experienced it myself. But I don't think you realize how disturbing it is. Even now I have to

322

make an effort to accept it.' His voice fell, and he glanced significantly at the late evening traffic. 'But there's a lot here likely to be considerably less understanding.' He produced a key and locked the door then motioned Atlon to accompany him along the street. 'It's only just dawned on me, but what you call the Power, is called "Kyroscreft" here. And it's greatly feared. In fact, even a hint of it is likely to start a riot.'

'I don't understand,' Atlon said.

Heirn turned a corner into a steeply sloping street. 'You know already that the Kyrosdyn are intensely disliked by most of the people.' Atlon nodded. 'Well, it's more than just their political meddling. It's something that's come down through the ages. A fear. Fear that they can do strange – forbidden – things. That they can move objects without touching them, control people, see through walls, hear people's thoughts . . . all sorts of things.'

'How can any kind of knowledge be forbidden?' Atlon interrupted scornfully. 'That's like forbidding the wind.' He became both passionate and withering. 'The Power's no more a "forbidden" thing than the opening of a flower. It's true nature isn't understood, granted, but that's the case with most things if you think deeply enough – not least ourselves. And you wouldn't deny that it's in *our* nature to inquire into such things endlessly, would you? Forbidden indeed!'

Heirn made to speak but Atlon pressed on earnestly. 'The effects of the normal use of the Power are understood perfectly. They're calculable and consistent. They obey rules of logic and reason. Seeing through walls and hearing people's thoughts with it is just plain foolishness – wild ignorance.'

Heirn adopted a schoolmasterly manner which left Atlon looking at him self-consciously when he had finished.

'Logic and reason aren't common commodities in Arash-Felloren, outlander,' Heirn continued, as if he had never been interrupted. 'Ignorance is. Very common. And, as I'm sure *you* know, ignorance breeds fear. And, right or wrong, like it or not, fear of what the Kyrosdyn are *believed* to be able to do has caused serious trouble in the past. Trouble that's resulted in people being killed – hundreds of people. Take it from me, Pinnatte's Power – if

323

he uses it – is a greater danger to him than it is to anyone else.'

'How?' Atlon asked, incredulous.

Heirn became wilfully patient again. 'If he uses it conspicuously – perhaps to attack someone like he did you, or to stick someone to a wall like that Kyrosdyn did to me, or even to move a horseshoe, he'll bring the City – the mob – down on him like a rockfall. He'll be lynched.'

Atlon stopped and looked at him. The smith's manner was assured and straightforward.

'The mob?'

Heirn gave him a quizzical look then indicated the people passing by. 'Them – *me*, I suppose. I've followed the Cry after some thief before now, when I was young.' There was a defensive note in his last remark. He did not seem to be proud of the memory. 'You behave differently in a crowd.'

'Yes,' Atlon said thoughtfully. 'That I understand. But they'd *kill* him for using the Power – even innocuously? Just like that?'

'Just like that,' Heirn confirmed. 'It's happened times beyond counting when the Cry goes up.'

Atlon stood for some time assimilating this before starting up the hill again.

'All the more reason we find him and . . . do something about him,' he said after they had gone a little way.

Heirn maintained his patient tone, but the effort showed. 'Atlon, you said yourself that he has no control over what he can do. Believe me, if he uses the Power and the word "Kyroscreft" goes up, he'll almost certainly be killed.'

'I might be able to protect him.'

'No. If you're with him, you'll be killed with him.'

Heirn's voice was as matter-of-fact as his conclusion was harsh. It allowed no further appeal.

They walked on in silence for a while. As they were approaching what Atlon took to be another bridge passing over the street, a brilliant array of glittering lights emerged from one end and began moving slowly across it. Its progress was hypnotically smooth.

He stopped to gaze at it.

'It's only a drinking barge,' Heirn said.

'An aqueduct,' Atlon said, smiling. 'I thought it was just another road.'

'The city's full of aqueducts, canals, culverts, streams, rivers,' Heirn said. 'Don't you have them where you come from?'

'Not aqueducts like that – not in the middle of our cities, anyway,' Atlon replied. 'They're very flat compared with here.'

'Flat,' Heirn mused. 'I find it difficult to imagine a city without hills.'

Atlon made no comment, he was entranced by the barge. Decorated with flickering lights which were brighter by far than the subdued street lighting, it looked like a dazzling constellation of stars drifting through the night sky. As he watched it however, the noise of the passengers reached him. Though full of laughter, it was violent and raucous, a sobering contrast to the almost serene impression that the lights gave. The contrast seemed to typify this confusing and frightening city for him. Nevertheless, he watched the barge until it was out of sight.

Heirn shook his head. 'You're making me look at things I've been seeing all my life,' he said.

'We all wear blinkers,' Atlon replied as they set off again. 'I don't think I could have imagined a city with so many hills a week ago, but I'm getting used to it already. And it never occurred to me that a city without hills would present anyone with a problem.'

Atlon found himself looking upwards at each bridge they passed under before they eventually emerged into a broad well-lit street. Following so soon after their conversation, Atlon appreciated the irony that, for Arash-Felloren, it was unusually straight and level. Typical of Arash-Felloren however, it was busy. Carts and carriages of all kinds were lumbering and trotting by, as were a great many riders, and the whole was set in a matrix of bustling pedestrians. Somehow, everyone seemed to be making progress, but, as Atlon had noted before, there was little order in the traffic and the general clamour was punctuated constantly by shouts and curses. He pursed his lips disapprovingly, but kept his peace.

Brightly lit arcades and open basements lined the street while stalls and carts spilled out on to it confusingly. Even at a casual

325

glance, Atlon could see all manner of places offering opportunities to eat, drink, gamble, watch this, watch that, even pray. And there were many others which he could not immediately identify save that they were obviously offering opportunities to part with money. There were also more than a few establishments advertising entertainments which left him blushing. Almost every place had people standing outside, vying noisily with one another for the attention of passers-by, most of whom were walking past without paying the slightest heed. Street traders were everywhere. Atlon found it at once exciting and disturbing. Dvolci, sitting on his shoulder, confined himself to muttering darkly under his breath.

'Where are you going?' Atlon asked, glad for the moment to be free of the topic of Pinnatte. A group of children dashed past them at great speed, looking backwards and laughing unpleasantly. To Atlon, it was not a sound that children should have been making. It was followed by angry cursing and a heavy, flustered individual waving a large stick menacingly. Neither Heirn nor anyone else paid any attention to him other than to step aside.

'Nowhere special,' Heirn replied. 'It's a warm evening and I didn't want to sit inside brooding about everything that's happened over the past two days.'

'It won't go away,' Atlon replied, regretting it immediately.

'It might have already gone,' Heirn retorted, fending off a street trader. 'Gone from anything we can do about it anyway. If I'm any judge, Pinnatte'll be at the Jyolan by now, looking to see Barran. And if Barran takes him on – and he could well do so – he'll be moving with people that you don't want to have any dealings with. Besides, let's be honest, whatever's happened to him, he reacts very badly to you. If you find him he might attack you again, and who can say where that'll lead?' He became conciliatory. 'Maybe if he's left to his own devices, this . . . trouble . . . he's having will fade away, as his hand heals. Perhaps Ellyn's ointment might do what you couldn't.'

There was a robust commonsense in Heirn's remarks which tempted Atlon. He was at a loss to know what to do. What had happened to Pinnatte was something quite beyond him. Yet Heirn was right. If they met again, Pinnatte or whatever was infecting him – would probably react badly to him. It was unlikely he would be able to question him without risking some serious consequence. And there was no chance of taking him from the city back to his Elders. But he was clear about one thing.

'It's not a temporary effect, Heirn,' he said. 'The Kyrosdyn have done something profound to him, and even though it's been affected by his injury, or Ellyn's ointment, for him to be able to use the Power the way he does, something's spread deep into him.'

Heirn shrugged regretfully but dismissively. 'It makes no difference, does it? I think you've learned all you're going to learn. Meeting Pinnatte again is too risky, as is going to the Jyolan, so you tell me. It could be you're at your journey's end, Atlon. Maybe home is your next destination.' He placed a heavy hand on his shoulder. 'Come on. You are hungry, aren't you?'

Heirn's invitation took Atlon under a gaudy red canopy, through a small iron gate, and down a flight of steps. At the bottom, a glass door led them into a low-ceilinged room filled with tables at which people were eating. The din from the street stopped abruptly as the door closed softly behind them. On a counter to their right, perched on a branch, a raven spread its wings and croaked, 'Welcome,' in a rich, deep voice. Both Atlon and Dvolci started at the sound and then peered at it intently, as if recognizing it.

'Clever, isn't it?' Heirn said. 'Elda made it.'

'Made it?' Atlon and Dvolci said together.

'Yes, watch.' Heirn opened and closed the door again. The raven repeated its performance. 'See, it's a toy.' He prodded it. The bird swayed slightly but made no other response.

'I'll give you toy, smith. That's a life-size representation, accurate in every detail. And don't poke it.'

The speaker was a red-haired woman who had appeared through a door behind the counter. She was about Atlon's height, with a full figure and a round face which, though it was smiling, struck Atlon as being capable of expressing considerable determination. She was jabbing a finger into Heirn by way of retaliation for his assault on the raven.

'This is my friend, Elda,' Heirn said, rather gauchely. He

327

introduced both Atlon and Dvolci. Atlon received a firm handshake and a pleasant smile, but Dvolci brought Elda around the counter in unstoppable delight. 'Isn't he lovely. May I?'

The question was as cursory as it was unnecessary, as Dvolci slithered down off Atlon's shoulder and into Elda's voluminous embrace. Atlon caught Heirn's eye and raised a cynical eyebrow. Dvolci closed his eyes rapturously.

'Atlon's an outlander,' Heirn said gruffly. 'He's finding the city a bit difficult, so he's helping me at the forge while he gets used to the place. I thought he'd enjoy your cooking.' He leaned forward. Elda, still attending to Dvolci, kissed him casually on the cheek and pointed to an empty table at the far end of the room.

'I'll take him off you, if you like,' Atlon said, holding out his hand to receive Dvolci. 'He can be quite a burden.' The felci opened one eye and gave him a baleful look as, with a final stroke, Elda parted with him.

'I've not much money,' Atlon said.

Heirn looked at him and shook his head. 'You're a strange one, Atlon,' he said. 'Scarcely two days in the city and you've killed one man – or made him kill himself,' he added hastily, 'threatened another with the same fate simply for meddling with your horse, got yourself involved with a demented street thief and a third-rate trainer for the Fighting Pits, not to mention meeting that murderous bastard Fiarn, and Barran's wife, no less. Anyone would think you'd lived here all your life! Yet you've got the way of a teacher about you – a quiet student – and a naivety that's positively staggering.' He leaned forward. 'I *know* you've not much money – I'll make no mention of the wealth beyond imagining that you've got casually bouncing around in your pockets. But you've not much money because you didn't even discuss payment with me when I offered you a job. Nor have you demanded any wages since.' He tapped the table vigorously. '*I'm* going to pay for this meal. I invited you, didn't I? Then, when we get back home, I'll pay you for what you've done today and we'll discuss what I should pay you tomorrow.'

Atlon sat wide-eyed and motionless as he listened, then said blandly, 'I *am* a teacher, and a student. And I knew you'd pay me

328

what you could afford when you'd had a chance to look at my work.'

Heirn put his hand to his head. Atlon looked concerned. 'I'm not *that* naïve, Heirn,' he said. 'It's just that I don't confront things in the way that everyone seems to do around here. You neglected to mention, for example, that I also got involved with you, who's been a fund of guidance and support without whom I'd have been in serious trouble.'

Heirn coloured and made to reply, but could not.

'I think that's a draw,' Dvolci said.

Elda came to the table and ended any further discussion. She placed a hand on Heirn's shoulder and sat down beside him. 'Your food will be here shortly.' She looked squarely at Atlon. 'Heirn said you're a stranger to the city. I've never met an outlander before. Where do you come from?'

Atlon however, did not answer the question. Instead, he pointed to the raven by the door and asked his own. 'You made that yourself?'

'I made all these,' Elda replied, gesturing around the room. There were alcoves and shelves along every wall, each filled with models of birds and animals and small figurines.

'She's the best toymaker in Arash-Felloren,' Heirn announced.

'Most of these are life-size representations,' Atlon said, using Elda's own words, to her obvious delight. 'How did you manage to make the raven speak?' he continued.

Elda smiled then reached across and tapped his nose with a delicate finger. 'With great difficulty,' she said. Heirn laughed.

'I'm being naïve again, am I?' Atlon asked.

'A little, if you think that any craftsman round here is going to give away their hard-won secrets,' Heirn replied.

Atlon made an apologetic gesture. 'It's just that I'm intrigued by it. It's a splendid piece of work. Would it be foolish of me to ask where you got the idea from?'

'Who knows where ideas come from?' Elda replied. 'But this one, as it happens, was given to me by a man in a dream.'

Atlon cocked his head on one side. 'You're teasing me,' he

said. 'I'm asking something I shouldn't again, aren't I?'

'No and no,' Elda said. 'I'm not teasing you, and the idea did come from a man in a dream.' Her face became thoughtful. 'He played a flute and told me a story about a raven that talked, and a marvellous castle. It was the strangest dream I've ever had – very vivid, as if I was really there. Never had one like it before or since, but sometimes, when I'm neither properly asleep nor properly awake, I'm sure I hear a flute playing in the distance.' She pulled a wry face that dismissed the idea as foolishness, then turned to Dvolci. 'I'll make a model of you, next, you're gorgeous.' Dvolci sat up very straight and preened himself.

'I might be naïve, but I'm not vain,' Atlon said when Elda had left.

'That's because you've nothing to be vain about, dear boy,' Dvolci said, mimicking the raven's rich voice.

Atlon's mind had been far from food when they entered but the pleasant atmosphere gradually relaxed him and the food, when it arrived, won him over completely.

After they had eaten, Heirn, replete, sat back and rested his hands across his stomach. 'I thought coming here would do you good,' he said. 'I know you perhaps don't think so, but there are more civilized places than uncivilized ones in the city – and more decent people than scoundrels. It's just that they're quieter – less conspicuous.'

'I understand,' Atlon said, mirroring his actions and stretching in his chair. 'I'd no real doubts about it. So large a city couldn't survive if it were otherwise. But it's still a difficult place for me to come to terms with.'

His eyes drifted idly around the many models decorating the room. Then they narrowed. He gestured towards the model of a small brown bird. 'May I look at that?'

'You can look at anything you like,' Heirn replied without looking. 'So long as it doesn't involve me in moving.'

However, when Atlon returned with the model, Heirn's manner changed. 'Oh, that thing's still here, is it?'

'Not your favourite piece?'

Heirn took the bird from him and examined it distastefully. He shook his head. 'No, it's not. It's accurate though – very accurate. I wasn't just being biased when I said she was the best toymaker in the city, she really is very good.' He put the model down with a grimace. 'Look at its eyes. They're awful.'

Atlon grunted, noncommittally. 'Have you ever seen any birds like that around here?' His casualness sounded forced, but Heirn was too sated to notice it.

'Ten, fifteen years ago – I can't remember – there were quite common, round the Vaskyros mainly. Then they suddenly disappeared. Never seen any since, I'm glad to say. Nasty little things – I never liked them. They used to fly like arrows – dead straight, very fast, almost as if they had some purpose in mind. And those bright yellow eyes seemed to look right through you. I'm not surprised no one wants to buy this.' He pushed the model away. Atlon returned it to the shelf, turning its face to the wall as he did so. He looked relieved.

'I've been thinking about what you said while we ate. About this perhaps being my journey's end. I'm torn. One minute I think, yes, there's nothing else I can do. Pinnatte's undoubtedly near the heart of something awful, something I'm sure will spread far beyond Arash-Felloren, even if the Kyrosdyn themselves don't seem to realize it yet. But he's gone beyond where I can reach him, in almost every sense. Then I hear my companions – my Elders – questioning me, and I hear myself blabbering: "I don't know this, I don't know that." And while they wouldn't reproach me, I'd know I was letting them down – letting many people down – people who might have to go out and face whatever it is the Kyrosdyn are intending.'

Heirn looked at him sympathetically. 'I can see your problem,' he said. 'But I honestly don't know what else you can do. If you talked to the Prefect's people about it, they'd probably lock you up as a lunatic. Of course you'd be able to walk away while they were looking for forms to complete, but that's beside the point. And the Weartans wouldn't do anything, except perhaps make inquiries into the death of the Novice, and that would only bring you to the attention of the Kyrosdyn, which is precisely what you don't want. And as for me helping you, I'm just a smith trying to earn a living, but board, lodge and wages are yours for as long as you want to work.'

Atlon looked at him guiltily. 'I'm very grateful for everything you've done for us. I shudder to think what predicaments I'd have landed myself in by now if I hadn't met you. But I can't allow you to become too closely involved with me. I could be dangerous.'

Heirn raised a hand to stop him. 'Have you had enough to eat?' he demanded.

Atlon slapped his stomach and puffed out his cheeks by way of reply. Then he put his elbows on the table and rested his head in his hands thoughtfully. 'I don't have any choice about this,' he said. 'Your advice is sound. This should be the end of my journey. It's a logical conclusion, given the facts. But something bad is happening here – something that could well overtake me before I get home. I *can't* walk away from it.'

'But . . .'

'No choice, Heirn. No choice. I've had none since I first came here. Somehow I have to find out what's happened to Pinnatte and what the Kyrosdyn are up to, no matter what it costs. It's just unfortunate that it's going to be harder now. If the worst comes to the worst, Dvolci will get a message back home.'

Heirn frowned. 'We've discussed this. How are you going to deal with Pinnatte? Not only will he not want you there, but he'll probably be surrounded by Barran's people. I really don't know how dangerous the Kyrosdyn are with their crystals and Power, but Barran's people are dangerous in the good old-fashioned way. They'd slit your throat and drop you in an alley as soon as look at you.' He jabbed his forefinger into the table for emphasis.

'I thought that would be the case from what I've heard of Barran, so I'll go straight to the Vaskyros.'

As Heirn's mouth dropped open there was a crash at the other end of the room, and a wild-eyed figure burst through the door.

Chapter 25

'Welcome,' the raven said. The man started away from it violently then, crouching low, he stared blearily round at the watching diners.

'Just a drunk,' Heirn said casually, but nevertheless pushing his chair back so that he would be able to move quickly if necessary as Elda began to speak to the newcomer.

'I'm not sure,' Atlon said. 'He looks more petrified than drunk.'

Then, Elda was leaning over the counter, shouting and pointing towards the door.

'Go on, man, go on,' Heirn muttered softly. 'You're making a mistake.' He was narrowing his eyes as if in anticipation. Suddenly the man lunged threateningly towards Elda. As he reached the counter, Elda leaned backwards, then her right hand described a wide vertical circle and an incongruous bell-like sound filled the room as a large pan struck the man on the head. He slithered to the floor. Atlon cringed in response, as did most of the spectators, though their recovery was quite rapid and Elda was almost immediately regaled with an enthusiastic burst of applause. She raised the pan in triumphant acknowledgement.

'Excuse me a moment,' Heirn said to Atlon.

'Come on,' Dvolci said excitedly, clambering roughly over Atlon's lap and running after the smith as he threaded his way through the tables. With some reluctance, Atlon followed him.

'Look at this.' Elda was waving the pan at Heirn indignantly. 'You're making them too thin.'

Glancing down as he stepped over the fallen figure, Heirn took the pan and examined it. He shook his head. 'If I made them any thicker, you'd kill someone,' he said firmly.

Elda's mouth moued into a denial but she confined herself to a grunt and a scowl.

'He's all right.' It was Atlon. During the exchange about the pan, he had been examining Elda's victim. 'But Heirn's right – your pans are thick enough.' The man confirmed Atlon's diagnosis by groaning.

Elda nodded to Heirn who bent down and, wrinkling his nose, seized the man by the scruff of the neck. 'Come on, my lad,' he said, dragging him upright. 'Out you go. And don't pick on a defenceless woman next time.'

As he opened the door to eject the man, the noise that washed into the room was no longer that of the usual clamour of a busy street; now there was uproar. Still supporting the intruder, Heirn cautiously moved up the steps until he could see what was happening. Atlon and several of the other diners followed him.

The traffic in the street was in even greater confusion than before, for running through it, regardless of riders, vehicles, and pedestrians, were men and women as ragged and unkempt as the one that Elda had just felled. And the warm night air was full of angry voices. From where he was standing, Atlon could see a score of violent arguments, several loose horses, and at least two carriages resting on their sides.

'What's happening?' he gasped. 'Who are these people?'

Heirn shook his head. 'I've no idea,' he replied, adding softly, 'but can you use that sword you're wearing?' He withdrew his free hand from his pocket. It was decorated with a heavy set of iron knuckles.

Atlon looked alarmed. 'I can use it after a fashion, if I have to, but what's going on?'

'They look like Tunnellers,' Heirn said. He wrinkled his nose again. 'They *smell* like Tunnellers.' He shook Elda's victim. 'What're you all doing up here?' he demanded.

The man, recovered now, though holding his head, yanked himself free. His eyes were wide with fear. 'We're not hurting anyone. Leave us alone! We don't want to be here, but we can't stay down there.'

'He's terrified,' Atlon said. 'He's trembling from head to foot.

334

Do they normally come out on to the streets like this?'

Heirn shook his head. 'They come up to beg now and then, and they can be a nuisance. But I've never seen anything like this.' He made to interrogate the man again, but Atlon laid a restraining hand on his arm.

The noise from the crowd rose and Atlon had to shout to make himself heard as he addressed the man directly. 'What's happened? What's frightened you? Why've so many of you left your . . . homes . . . to come out on to the streets?'

The man opened his mouth several times before he managed to speak. 'There's something down there. Something awful. In the shadows. It's killing people. Killing and killing.' He clamped his hands to his ears. 'The screaming. I can still hear it – echoing and echoing. It's everywhere. You can't tell where it's coming from. Is it ahead – or behind?' He clutched at Heirn. 'There's nowhere to hide. Then it howls. Whatever it is, it howls.' He began swinging his head from side to side frantically. 'It's not something anyone should hear. It's something out of a nightmare.' Then, with two sudden strides, he was gone, lost in the confusion.

Heirn and Atlon exchanged a look but did not speak.

'What was he talking about?' It was Elda, standing just below Heirn on the stairs. She was hefting her bent pan.

'I've no idea,' Heirn replied. 'It's probably a . . . flood, or . . . foul air.'

'A flood! After *this* summer?'

'I don't know,' Heirn insisted, though with a hint of irritability that he did not intend. 'Who knows how these people think – how they live.' He put an apologetic arm on her shoulder. 'Don't worry, there can't be all that many of them. Atlon and I will stay here until things quieten down. You look after your customers.'

Temporarily mollified, Elda descended the stairs ushering everyone vigorously before her. As they disappeared behind the glass doors the faint sound of 'Welcome' drifted up through the general din.

But Heirn was wrong. Although the first rush of people gradually dissipated, carriages were righted, horses recovered, and fights and quarrels were noisily abandoned, more and more Tunnellers kept moving along the street. Their presence became like a miasma, muffling and subduing the bustling liveliness that had previously marked the scene. After watching them for only a short time, Atlon was appalled. Though he had seen many things that distressed him in the short time since he had arrived in Arash-Felloren, nothing had prepared him for the sight of so many wretched individuals. Some were obviously strutting thugs, but it needed no skilled healer's eye to measure the pervasive weakness that typified most of them: the blank, frightened and lost expressions, and, for many of them, malnutrition verging on starvation.

'This is awful, Heirn,' he said soberly. 'How can people be allowed to live like this?'

Heirn did not reply for a long time, and his voice was unsteady when he did. 'They choose it,' he said, but everything about him told Atlon that the comment was at best a half-truth and that Heirn knew it.

'I'm sorry,' Atlon said. 'It's not my place to offer reproach.'

Heirn's jawline was set. 'Yes, it is,' he said very softly. 'It's everyone's place.'

They stood in the silence for some time, then Dvolci gently whistled in Atlon's ear. Atlon shook himself out of his dark reverie.

He was already facing tasks that were probably beyond him. Fretting about the lot of the Tunnellers when he could do nothing about it was a self-indulgence he could not afford. He must concentrate on those matters which he *could* do something about. The decision hurt him however.

Looking around to ensure that no one in the immediate vicinity might overhear him, he said, 'It must be that creature – the Serwulf. The damned thing's loose.'

'"It took me hunting. I could hear prey screaming".' Heirn's voice was flat as he echoed Pinnatte's words. 'I didn't really know what to think about your creature before but, bad or not, the Tunnellers make their own lives and they don't come out except when need drives them. It must be something truly awful down there for this to happen. What can we do?'

'I don't know,' Atlon said. 'With each turn of events, things seem to get worse.' He straightened up. 'But they also become clearer. I can't reach Pinnatte, and even if I could find the Serwulf and kill it – which is debatable, to say the least – what end would it serve? None. The heart of the troubles here lies with the Kyrosdyn and, thrash about as I might, that's where I'll have to seek an answer.'

Heirn turned to him sharply and pointed to the door below. 'I'd forgotten in all this confusion. Did you really say you were going to the Vaskyros?' He did not wait for an answer. 'Are you mad? Didn't you say they'd know about your . . . abilities . . . with the Power? Sense it in you in some way?'

'It's a risk,' Atlon replied, feigning a casualness he did not feel. 'But I should be able to hide it from them. I've faced worse by far. And I'm not without resources.'

Heirn looked extremely doubtful. 'But you still can't just walk up to the gate and start asking questions.'

Atlon thought for a moment. 'Why not?' he decided. 'What else would a traveller from another land do – a traveller who was interested in the working of crystals as part of his trade, and who'd heard of the famous Kyrosdyn from far away?'

'You're crazy.'

Atlon's fear balled up and threatened to overwhelm him. When he spoke his voice was hoarse with it. 'Don't, Heirn, please. I'm frightened enough. Just help me to do what I've got to do.'

'Help you to commit suicide, you mean.'

'No, damn it. I've every intention of staying alive.' Atlon paused. 'But just be here for Dvolci if something goes wrong. Take him – and my horse – to the road north of The Wyndering. They'll be all right from there. Then keep an eye on what's happening in the city and help my friends if they come looking for me.' He gazed at Heirn earnestly. 'Will you do that for me?'

Heirn met his gaze unhappily. 'Of course I will, but—'

'No buts, Heirn. Nothing that'll weaken my resolve.' He stared into the crowds passing by, larded now with Tunnellers, wandering aimlessly, like terrified grey ghosts. 'I think I'd like to go back to your home now and rest. I'll need to prepare myself before . . .' His voice tailed off.

Heirn nodded. 'Let me say good night to Elda then we'll get back,' he said.

When he came back they passed a great many Tunnellers. Some of them were begging and of a vicious demeanour, but Heirn's size and determined stride kept them at bay. The majority, however, were as Atlon had noted before, sad and weary creatures, most of them looking for a dark corner to lie down in. Fear radiated from all of them.

'A long way from their homes,' Atlon said, half to himself.

Heirn ignored the remark. 'There'll be trouble if they're still wandering the streets tomorrow,' he said.

'Then there'll be trouble,' Atlon said resignedly. 'If that is a Serwulf loose in the tunnels, and everything we've heard indicates that it is, it'll be getting stronger by the minute. No one will go back down there.'

'They'll get no choice,' Heirn replied. 'The Prefect will set the Weartans on them to make sure they do, because if he doesn't, there's a score of merchants that'll turn their own mercenaries on to them once they look like affecting trade. And past experience shows that it's difficult to confine mercenaries to what they're supposed to be doing once they've banded together.'

'From what I know about the Serwulf, I think you'll find all these people will die where they stand before they'll risk facing one again.'

Heirn was openly disparaging. 'It's only an animal,' he said. 'You want to see a Weartan Renewal Squadron in action. *That's* something that no one'll stand against. The Tunnellers will be scuttling back at the first hint of one of those being let loose.'

'I don't know whether to hope you're right or wrong,' Atlon said. 'But I fear you're wrong. I fear you're going to have trouble on your streets soon.'

Heirn shrugged. 'There's always trouble on the streets. Why do you think I carry these?' He thrust his iron-clad knuckles in front of Atlon's face. 'But it's not worth worrying about. Generally speaking, so long as you can hear it coming, you can run away from it.'

The observation brought Atlon back to his own dark concerns

338

and the two men made the rest of the journey in silence.

That same night, with Rinter left to hover outside a closed and guarded door, a breathless Pinnatte finally met Barran. The preliminaries to the encounter were comparatively brief, Barran still being occupied with the take-over of the Jyolan and the consideration of its future. Almost all the provisional plans he had made for it in the past were being dashed aside by what he was discovering about the place, not least the Mirror Room. Though he was not by nature given to idle speculation, it still both puzzled and troubled him to learn that the Kyrosdyn had not used such a remarkable asset. As it was, he had spent more time than he knew he properly should, just sitting in the room and thinking, sifting through the innumerable possibilities that it offered for the further advancement of his power and influence within the city.

He was only a little taller than Pinnatte but his heavier and more muscular presence made him seem much taller to the young street thief. 'You're one of Lassner's, are you?' Barran began.

Pinnatte remembered what Ellyn had whispered to him just minutes earlier. 'You'd be best advised to run away to another part of the city and find honest work for yourself, young man. But I can see you're not going to pay any heed to that advice, so if you're bent on being bound to my husband rather than being free, stand up straight and answer clearly when he speaks to you. Don't be insolent, but do try, at least, to look him in the eye.'

Pinnatte found the latter very difficult – Barran's gaze had crushed stronger by far than he – but he did manage to stand straight and answer promptly.

'Yes, I am, sir.'

Barran maintained his stare, looking up and down Pinnatte as though he were a piece of furniture he was contemplating buying. Then he sat down behind a desk and, after a brisk but impatient search, retrieved something from one of the drawers. He dropped it on to the top of the desk. It was a small money bag. Without lifting his wrist from the desk, he unlaced the bag with one hand and emptied out the contents. It was an unexpectedly dextrous movement and particularly caught Pinnatte's attention. Coins glittered in the lamplight, one of them rolling a little way, another spinning on its edge. Barran casually stopped the rolling coin but let the other spin. Pinnatte watched as the coin turned imperceptibly from a spinning sphere into a quivering disc which seemed to stretch time itself as it gradually rattled into a distant silence. A silence which filled the room.

'You did well yesterday, Pinnatte,' Barran said, breaking it. He leaned forward and began pushing the coins around idly while still watching Pinnatte. 'Apart from saving me a great deal of difficulty with the Prefect's people and the families of those who'd have been killed, there were friends of mine in that crowd.'

He turned one of the coins over. Though he had been trying to meet Barran's gaze, Pinnatte had been unable to keep his eyes from the money. The coins were large and he knew exactly what they were, even though he had never actually handled one. Despite trying to concentrate on what Barran was saying, he had done a quick calculation and worked out that there was more money on the desk than he could look to earn in three of four years – good years at that.

'I won't ask you why you did it – I shouldn't think you know, really. It's enough for me that you acted when everyone else was panicking. It's a trait I value in my people. A good battlefield trait.'

Pinnatte started at the word 'my' and remembered to stand straight again. With a swift gesture, Barran spread out the coins. There were nine in all. Pinnatte increased his estimate to five or six years. 'I can give you these now and you can go on your way with my thanks,' Barran said off-handedly. He threw a smaller coin on to the desk. 'Or you can work for me and get one of these a month.'

'I'll work for you, sir,' Pinnatte said, without calculating and without hesitation, though he added quickly, 'If Lassner will release me.'

Barran's expression was unreadable.

'I've little call for street thieves, Pinnatte. What else can you do?'

Suddenly on the point of tumbling into abject panic, Pinnatte was rescued by an inspiration. 'I can learn, sir.'

Barran looked down at the coins, then swept them up and, again using only one hand, dropped them back into the bag and tightened the lace. He stood up. 'You enjoyed the Loose Pit last night?'

It took Pinnatte a moment to register the question. 'Very much, sir. Exciting. I've never seen anything like it before.'

'And the Jyolan – what do you think of that?'

Pinnatte's eyes lit up. 'I'd never seen anything like that either. It used to be . . . just another hall – dismal really. But last night it was alive.' The elation he had felt the previous night began to return.

Barran looked at him intently. 'Would you like to work here?'

Something leapt inside Pinnatte. He was filled with a sense of something growing, blooming. 'Yes,' he said eagerly.

Barran continued looking at him, then reached a decision. 'Come with me,' he said.

Pinnatte was vaguely aware of Rinter trying to catch his attention as he followed Barran out of the room, but he could only keep his eyes fixed on his new master. As they walked along, Pinnatte wanted to dance and shout, to seize Barran's hand and thank him profusely. At the same time he was castigating himself for such folly, reminding himself that Barran had not actually said he would employ him yet, and that he was a dangerous and much-feared man who must be watched and listened to very carefully at all times. He reminded himself also, to mention his bond with Lassner again. Too open a disloyalty to a previous master was unlikely to endear him to the next one.

Eventually they arrived at the door to the Mirror Room. Barran unlocked it and ushered Pinnatte inside. For the first time since he had rushed, gasping for breath, into the Jyolan, he felt a frisson of alarm as Barran followed him and closed the door. He had been alone with this powerful man at their first meeting, but there had been guards by the door and he had been aware of people moving to and fro outside. There had been no safety in that, he knew, but here there were no guards, no people pursuing their business – no one. Indeed, Pinnatte realized, he had not seen anyone for the past few minutes. This entire part of the Jyolan seemed to be deserted.

'Push that panel to one side.'

Barran's businesslike voice cut across Pinnatte's half-formed fears. At first he did not understand the command, then Barran motioned him towards the decorated timber panel and indicated what he wanted with a wave of his hand. It took Pinnatte some effort, but after a brief struggle the panel creaked aside to reveal the mysterious mirrors.

Pinnatte took a step back and looked at the uneven rows uncomprehendingly. Then be bent forward and examined one closely. 'That's a picture of the arena,' he said. He made to wipe the dust from the mirror, but a sharp 'Don't touch' from Barran snatched his hand away and made him turn to see what wrath he might have brought down on himself with the carelessness. Barran however, impassively indicated that he look at the mirror again. As he did so, two figures moved across the scene.

Pinnatte gasped and stepped back in alarm. Barran's hand arrested him.

'These are the Eyes of the Jyolan, Pinnatte,' he said, maintaining his grip. 'This is an ancient building, full of things that perhaps couldn't even be built today. Precious things, that must be tended carefully. Tending these will be your task until I get to know you better.'

'I'll do whatever you ask, sir,' Pinnatte said, trying to affect a man-to-man attitude, but failing. The sudden movement in what he had taken to be nothing more than a picture had shaken him badly. Only Barran's grip on his shoulder had stopped his hand from circling his heart in the old sign of protection. The grip tightened. It was not painful, but Barran's hand felt heavy and immovable – it was not something to be disputed with.

'Clean this room, make it more comfortable. Then polish each of these mirrors. I'll show you how to do it – it needs care. Each morning, come to me, wherever I am, for the key. See that all's well here, and return the key to me. No one else is to enter this room under any circumstances. No one is to be told about it, it is no one else's concern. Should anyone ask you about it, you will tell them to speak to me.'

The hand became heavier and Barran's voice became softer. 'Understand, Pinnatte. This is no slight thing. The trust I'm placing in you is greater than you know. How well you do this task will decide what happens to you next. If you do well, there's a good fortune waiting for you. Should you disappoint me . . .'

The conclusion was unspoken and the grip was gone. A reassuring pat replaced it briefly but there was a menace in it that no amount of threatening and abuse could have conveyed. It brought home to Pinnatte what he already knew about Barran, albeit only by repute. Now, as the soft impact of the pat on his shoulder vibrated through him, he *felt* it. He had developed ways of coping with Lassner over the years, but even he could present problems – and Barran was no Lassner. Barran would support and protect him, but he would also kill him – or have him killed – without a moment's hesitation if he offended or disobeyed. He must cling to this knowledge at all times. He must watch and listen and learn as never before. It was a frightening and cruel lesson, but Pinnatte learned it instantly. Indeed, it seemed to resonate with something deep in his own nature, giving him a fleeting vision of himself in Barran's position passing down the instruction to some young hopeful. He cradled his injured hand and, turning, for the first time he looked his new master squarely in the eye. 'I won't disappoint you, sir,' he said. 'I gave Lassner good service and, if he'll release me, I'll give you the same.'

There was a brief flicker of something in Barran's eyes but his usual impassivity closed over it before Pinnatte could interpret it. 'Lassner will release you, Pinnatte,' Barran said. 'He's a reasonable man.'

As they were walking away from the Mirror Room, Pinnatte noticed several other rooms, apparently empty. Though he was elated at the prospect of working for Barran, the problem of accommodation was troubling him. He could no longer stay at Lassner's Den, he had no desire to return to Heirn's to face Atlon's relentless prying and, fine weather or not, the street was no place for him. Better Lassner than that. He'd have to risk it.

'Can I use one of these for a while?' he asked. 'I'll have nowhere to stay if I'm leaving Lassner.'

Barran stopped and looked at him, then at the open door he was pointing to. He took a lamp from the wall and peered into the room. It was bare and empty like most of the others he had bothered to examine. And the Jyolan seemed to be full of rooms and halls. He sniffed. 'Better than nothing, I suppose,' he replied. 'Pick whichever you want – there doesn't seem to be much to choose between any of them.' He pursed his lips and nodded as if warming to the idea. 'Yes, make the place yours. I'll tell Fiarn you'll be staying here for the time being. I doubt we'll be able to find a bed for you tonight, but we should be able to manage some blankets. Will that be all right?'

Pinnatte nodded an awkward, 'Fine, thank you.' The sudden note in Barran's voice of concern for his personal comfort had taken him by surprise. As it had many before him. For Barran was far too subtle a leader to motivate solely by fear. He constantly showed an interest in the well-being of his followers, some of it quite genuine, some contrived, but all of it effective. It bred strong loyalty, and when it was necessary to deal harshly with someone, that, and his invariably swift and ruthless action, usually brought condemnation on the victim rather than himself.

Later, Pinnatte related the news of his acceptance by Barran to Rinter. The animal trainer was scarcely less elated, seeing what he perceived to be a continuing improvement in his own prospects. First had come his encounter with Atlon and the felci and the possibilities that stemmed from the quietly ferocious little animal. Then, his random meeting with this young street thief which, having started by saving him money at the Loose Pit, had ended with him having a contact direct to Barran himself.

'Such is the way of Arash-Felloren, eh Pinnatte?' he said expansively as they walked idly along the busy night street. 'One moment a bound Den-Mate, the next a hero and working for one of the richest and most powerful men in the city. What'll you be doing for him?'

The memory of Barran's hand on his shoulder returned to Pinnatte. 'I don't know yet,' he replied. 'I'll find out tomorrow.' He looked earnestly at Rinter. 'But I mightn't be allowed to talk about it,' he said.

Rinter nodded knowingly. 'I understand,' he said. 'Besides . . .' He lowered his voice. 'I don't think it would be in my interests to know anything of Barran's business that I wasn't supposed to.' He drew a finger across his throat. Pinnatte did not respond.

'Are you going back to Heirn's tonight?' Rinter asked as casually as he could, anxious, despite his euphoria, not to lose his contact with Atlon.

'No, I've got a place in the Jyolan,' Pinnatte replied. 'Well, a room and three blankets at the moment, until I can get a bed and some bits of furniture.'

Rinter tried to look pleased but it was not easy and he stammered a little when he spoke. 'Oh. That's lucky. Are you going to tell Heirn and Atlon about your good fortune?'

Pinnatte hesitated. The blacksmith had been decent enough to him – offered him a home, albeit temporary, and a bed – and kindness was not a common thing in his life. But his thoughts about Atlon were buffeting to and fro. He too had been kind and helpful, yet he had also been intrusive – prying into matters that did not concern him. Why did he want to know what the Kyrosdyn had done to him? Why did he want to know about the dream?

He prevaricated. 'Not tonight. I told them I mightn't be back, depending on what happened.' But mention of Atlon and the memory of his dream had unsettled him again. What would happen tonight when he went to sleep in his spartan new quarters? Would he wake covered in sweat, perhaps crying out? It was a disturbing thought – the new boy having bad dreams like some hapless child, shouting for his mother. Hardly something to make a good impression on Barran's men. Yet even as it occurred to him, he realized that he was no longer really concerned. As soon as he had entered the Jyolan, the aura of the place had wrapped itself about him – steadied him – told him that here was his true home. And when Barran had asked him about the Jyolan, he had answered truthfully. He wanted to be there desperately, wanted to see the animals fighting again, wanted to feel the deep reverence for the happenings in the arena that he had felt the previous night . . .

Wanted to feel himself part of the creature again – hunting prey, lusting for the terror and the screaming . . .

He wiped his hand across his forehead. The prospect was making him sweat.

'It is warm, isn't it?' Rinter said, misinterpreting the movement. 'Makes you think that the winds and the rain and the snows we had only a few months ago will never come again.'

Pinnatte nodded absently. He should be rid of this jabbering oaf. He should be back at the Jyolan, learning about it, communing with its ancient secrets. His life as a Den-Mate – a thing of the streets – was now over. He did not belong here any more. It was surely no mere chance that he had fallen in with the man who now owned the Jyolan. No mere chance that he was actually staying there. Powers were conspiring to bring him where he should be – in his rightful place – the place from which his influence would spread forth, carrying with it the majesty of the Jyolan and the sacred events that happened there. He would . . .

Someone bumped into him, jolting him from his vaulting fantasy.

'Watch where you're going, you dozy sod.' The rebuke cut through Pinnatte. Furiously he lashed out. His blow struck the offender in the chest with such force that two other passers-by were knocked to the ground before he finally crashed into a street-trader's cart and overturned it. Rinter gaped, but moved immediately when it seemed that Pinnatte was going to pursue the man further.

'Come on,' he said urgently, taking Pinnatte's arm. 'A certain person wouldn't like you being involved in a street brawl, would he?'

Pinnatte had taken two steps forward, almost dragging Rinter, before the words sank in. He did not speak but levelled a menacing finger at the fallen man, now being disentangled from the remains of the cart by its cursing owner, then turned away.

'You don't know your own strength,' Rinter said, looking nervously over his shoulder to make sure that no irate pursuit was under way.

'He should have been more respectful,' Pinnatte said. Rinter frowned. Respectful was an odd word for a street thief to use – even one who was going up in the world. He was about to remind Pinnatte that it was he who had bumped into the man, wandering along in a trance, but he decided against it. If Barran had decided he could use this young man, it was highly likely that there was more to him than met the eye. Perhaps he had just seen an indication of it.

The outburst however, had caused Pinnatte's mood to shift again. Generally, a quick kick or punch to startle rather than injure, followed by flight, had been the most violence he had ever had to use. The punch he had just delivered he would not have thought himself capable of, either physically or emotionally. The power of it seemed to have come from some hitherto hidden well within him. It had surged up along with his rage and simply burst out of him. He had felt the harm it had done even as he struck. The man's entire frame had shuddered with the impact and he knew that he had broken bones and hurt him badly.

Part of him revelled in the thought. Such would be the fact of those who opposed him; they must learn their place, learn respect. Yet another part of him was sickened. The violence had been unnecessary. Taking purses was one thing, but damaging people, perhaps depriving them of their livelihood, throwing them into the hands of healers and physicians and all that that could lead to, was another entirely. It broke the rules he had always lived by. He shouldn't have done it.

The inner conflict brought him to a halt, swaying and wide-eyed. His whole body was shaking.

'You really don't look well,' Rinter said, greatly alarmed by Pinnatte's increasingly strange behaviour.

For a moment, such was the turmoil inside him that Pinnatte thought he was going to vomit, but then came the feeling that should he do so, he would never stop; his entire insides would burst forth in a scalding stream, leaving him an empty shell filled with darkness. Desperately he reached out and seized Rinter. The animal trainer yanked his arm free from the powerful grip, but put a supporting arm around Pinnatte.

'Shall I take you to Heirn's? Perhaps Atlon can help. He seemed to know what he was doing.'

The mention of Atlon redoubled Pinnate's conflict. Atlon's presence returned to him. It was full of deep and genuine concern,

347

and a willingness to enter into his pain and tear out the torment that had come into his life. Ellyn's words hovered in the background: he should run away from all this, and find an honest life somewhere in this vast city. There would be such a place, surely – everything was possible in Arash-Felloren. This was the way he must go. The rightness of it was beyond any dispute. Yet at the same time, the Jyolan was all about him, dark and blood-streaked, infinitely alluring – redolent with power, and the satisfying of desires he had no names for. A myriad tiny barbs tore at him. Then Atlon and Ellyn were gone, swept away by the Jyolan's ancient lure. The inner wracking faded rapidly to become little more than a vague unease. Carefully, Pinnatte breathed out, and the street formed itself around him again.

'No,' he said hoarsely. 'I'll go back to the Jyolan. I'm just tired, that's all.'

Rinter made one or two half-hearted attempts at conversation as they returned, but they all foundered on Pinnatte's preoccupation.

That night, Pinnatte left the lamp burning in his new room. He lay for a long time staring up at the dust-stained ceiling, uncertain about what might greet him should he fall asleep, yet knowing that he could not avoid it.

Then he was sitting upright, wide awake and alert. It took him a moment to remember where he was then he lay back in relief. He was safe at the Jyolan, away from Lassner, away from his old life, and under the protection of Barran. And whatever had wakened him, it was no dream. He had no recollection of falling asleep or being asleep, which was the way it normally was for him – night and morning separated only by the blink of an eye.

Yet something had wakened him. He looked around, puzzled. The door was bolted and he could hear nothing from the passageway outside. Then he became aware of a faint, high-pitched sound, like a small, irritating fly. But it was not a fly. There was a persistence to it – an urgency – that caught his attention. Quietly he stood up and began moving about the room, listening intently. It was some time before he discovered the source of the noise. It was coming from one of the small openings that pocked the walls of his room, as seemingly they did in every part of the Jyolan. It was barely the width of two fingers. Hesitantly he bent forward and placed his ear by it.

The whining became clearer. It was coming from far away. As he listened, though he could not identify any part of it, he knew what it was.

It was screaming.

Many people.

Screaming.

It was good.

Chapter 26

The next morning, the atmosphere at Heirn's was strained. Atlon was still set on his intention of going to the Vaskyros, though sufficiently unhappy about the prospect to be unable to eat anything save a little bread. Heirn was still anxious to prevent him, though loath to press his objections knowing the dilemma that Atlon was facing. Even Dvolci was subdued.

Atlon took refuge in stern practicalities. Dvolci was to accompany him and, should things go badly, he was to retreat to Heirn's. The blacksmith would take him and the horse to the road that led north from The Wyndering, from where both would make their own way home. Heirn was then to do nothing except watch whatever events unfolded. Atlon gave him a simple phrase that would identify any of his colleagues should they feel it necessary to come to the city themselves. Heirn too, was to look after the crystals.

Unable to dissuade Atlon, Heirn accepted these conditions, though he was uneasy about keeping the crystals and positively unhappy when Atlon said he could sell any of them if he needed the money. He did however, make a personal resolution to discover the fate of his new friend should need arise, though he kept this to himself, knowing that it would serve no useful purpose save to disturb Atlon further.

One thing he was insistent upon. 'I'll come with you as far as the Vaskyros. It's a long and complicated journey.'

'Well, it will save me getting lost, I suppose,' Atlon rationalized gratefully. 'But you're to come only as far as the street, or the square, wherever this place is. Under no circumstances must the Kyrosdyn associate you with me.' He looked at Heirn squarely. 'I stand a chance in there if I'm careful, but you'd be snuffed out like a candle.' He rolled his thumb and fingers in imitation of the act.

There was no hint of drama or foreboding in his voice, and the very calmness unnerved Heirn. He nodded his immediate agreement. 'I'll watch from nearby.'

The first part of the journey took them along the streets they had walked the previous night. Atlon looked up at the aqueduct as they approached it. It was a robust, well-made stone structure typical of the area, simple in line and undecorated save for what the birds had contributed. In a tawdry echo of the vivid image he had seen before, a dirty, ramshackle barge eased into sight. An equally dirty, ramshackle individual was leaning over the side. As the barge reached the middle of the span, the man sniffed then spat, lifting his head back so that his offering would land in the road below rather than the canal.

Noting the action, and already unsettled by what he was doing, Heirn's response was uncharacteristic. He raised a clenched fist and regaled the man with a series of well-chosen oaths. The man made an obscene gesture and spat again as he slid from view.

'Sorry,' Heirn said uncomfortably as they continued on their way. 'I'm just a bit . . .' He did not finish.

'It's all right,' Atlon said. 'Better out than in, I'd say. And I don't think you did him any lasting damage.'

Despite his anxiety, Heirn chuckled at the remark.

Shortly after passing the aqueduct, Heirn turned off the route they had taken the night before and Atlon found himself in a street that, no different from many others he had seen, was lined with an arbitrary assortment of dwellings and businesses. Quite different from anything he *had* yet seen was the other side – which crumbled into a wide open space littered with rubble and the remains of derelict buildings. Trees, bushes, and generally dense undergrowth indicated that the area had been in this condition for a long time.

Atlon was too preoccupied to be particularly curious; though it did occur to him briefly to ask what had happened here, he did not speak. Heirn however, unusually sensitive to his companion's actions, followed his gaze. Then he stopped and frowned. This did prompt a question.

'What's the matter?'

'Those people,' Heirn answered. He strode across the street. Atlon followed him. As he reached the edge of the abandoned area he saw that much of it was below street level. The overgrown remains of tumbled arches and shattered walls indicated that there had once been cellars there. And streets, he realized, noting expanses of buckled pavements. Then he saw what Heirn was looking at. At first he thought there were only two or three people wandering about, but as he looked, he saw many more, almost indistinguishable against the mottled background of the ruins and the deep-rooted and still green vegetation. There were also a great many temporary shelters.

'Tunnellers?' Atlon asked, recalling the generally wretched appearance of those he had seen the previous night.

'They certainly look like it,' Heirn confirmed. 'But what the devil are they up to, camping here? They must know the Weartans will shift them.'

'Why?'

Heirn looked at him. 'They just will. They even clear parts of the Spills from time to time. You said yourself you'd seen a "renewed" area when that idiot of an animal trainer took you into one. Ostensibly it's at the behest of the local businesses, or the residents, *or anyone*, to stop the Spills from becoming too established, but if you ask me, they just enjoy it.'

'But this place must have been abandoned for years – look at it.' Atlon swept an arm across the site. 'Surely they're not doing any harm just staying there.'

Heirn was both angry and fatalistic. 'Probably not. But the Weartans will still shift them as soon as they hear about it. They've even less love for Tunnellers than Spill-dwellers.'

Atlon had to force himself not to inquire further. He knew by now that Arash-Felloren would provoke at least two more questions for every one he had answered, and he must concentrate on the task ahead of him, much as he would have preferred not to. It gave him a little comfort that what he was intending to do would quite probably relate to the fate of the Tunnellers, for he had no doubt that they were emerging from their chosen habitats because of the

353

Serwulf, and that was surely linked to the Kyrosdyn and their schemes.

He was about to move away when he noticed a group emerging through the bushes which fringed the wall that marked the far boundary of the site.

'Where are they coming from?' he asked.

'There'll be an entrance over there.'

'Are there many entrances?' Atlon knew that he was merely postponing what he had to do rather than seeking information.

'They're everywhere,' Heirn replied with a rueful look. 'Almost every cellar in the city has got a bricked-up opening. There's one in Elda's building, and two in mine.'

A shout drew their attention back to the Tunnellers. They were gathering around someone.

'Come on,' Heirn said. 'I've no idea what they're up to, but we don't want to be around if the Weartans come.'

As they set off however, it became apparent that it would be no easy task to be clear of the Tunnellers, for groups of them were emerging on to the road further along. Then the casual traffic became a steady stream. Moreover, they were heading in the same direction as Atlon and Heirn.

Heirn quickened his pace. Atlon looked at the Tunnellers. Dirty and unkempt, and far from sweet-smelling, they were an intimidating sight, far more so than they had been in the garish night-time streets. The intimidation lay mainly in their appearance, which was in sharp contrast to most of the other good citizens of Arash-Felloren pursuing their business in that street. Certainly they were offering no one any actual threat. Their dominant mood seemed to be anxiety to be away from this place, and they were paying little heed to anyone else. The converse was not the case however. Passers-by were paying them considerable heed and were looking distinctly alarmed. Like Heirn, most were beginning to hurry along, although some of them were taking shelter in doorways until the growing flood might pass. The response puzzled Atlon at first, then it occurred to him that, amongst other things, the Tunnellers were walking reminders of the fate that lay in store for those who faltered before the city's relentless challenge. Like I'm faltering before mine, he thought guiltily.

Heirn stepped closer to Atlon and took his arm protectively. Atlon noted him reaching into his pocket with his free hand. 'I don't think you're going to need your knuckles,' he said. 'Not with these people. Look at them – they're scared out of their wits, and there's as many women and children as there are men.'

Heirn grunted an uneasy acceptance of Atlon's comments and his hand emerged from his pocket empty. But he did not relinquish his hold on Atlon's arm, not lessen his increased pace.

'If you hear horses coming, speak up, and get ready to run for it,' he said.

'Why?'

There was some impatience in Heirn's reply. 'Because it'll be the Weartans, that's why. Trust me, they'll just ride into this lot regardless. And they'll not pick and choose targets once they start swinging their damned cudgels.'

Atlon's eyes narrowed angrily but he only asked, 'Where do you think these people are going?'

'If you're lucky, they'll be going to the Vaskyros,' Heirn replied, though without humour. 'But it looks as if they might be going to the Prefect's Palace.' Anxiety broke through on to his face. 'They must be crazy! I've never seen anything like this. Whatever's driving them, they'll get no help up here, least of all from the Prefect. There's going to be bad trouble sooner rather than later. We must get away from them.'

Dvolci whistled softly in Atlon's ear. Atlon grimaced then said, 'I was just thinking the same.' Gently he pulled himself free from Heirn and, after a brief hesitation, ran forward to catch the arm of a large man who had just passed him, striding out purposefully.

'What are you doing? What's made you all leave the tunnels?' he said, quickly releasing the man's arm as he turned with a start. He repeated the question before the man could speak, adding, 'I don't come from this city but my friend tells me it's very dangerous for you up here – especially for women and children.' The man stared at him uncertainly. His eyes were a mixture of fear and anger. 'He says they'll turn horsemen on you. Did you now that? People will be hurt?'

'Hurt?' The man echoed the word scornfully. Then he gave a cold laugh and his face was suddenly alive with despair. 'Better hurt than dead! We can't stay down there. Not while that thing's loose.' The despair became anger and he raised his voice. 'If the Prefect doesn't want us here, he'll have to go down there and kill the thing himself. Or send his precious horsemen, if they're feeling brave. If he sends them after us they'll get more than they bargained for, I'll tell you. I'll face a score of mounted Weartans before I'd risk coming within a thousand paces of that thing. Eh, lads?'

Voices rose up in support and Atlon found that he was becoming the mobile centre of a growing group. He was aware of Heirn close by him again, trying to catch his attention.

He lifted his hands in surrender. 'You're risking facing the Weartans because of an animal?' He kept his voice balanced between surprise and incredulity. 'It must be something particularly nasty. What's it look like? Can't you trap it? I've seen some strange creatures on my travels, but I've never seen anything that couldn't be brought down with a little determination or cunning. Nothing that's worth facing a cavalry charge for, believe me.' Heirn's estimation of Atlon rose once again. Somehow his tone had robbed the words of any hint of challenge. Nevertheless, he kept his hand through his iron knuckles.

'Then you've never seen anything like this,' the man replied, stopping to face Atlon. The crowd came to a ragged halt with them. The man grimaced. 'And you've certainly never *heard* anything like it.' There was a chorus of agreement. 'When it howls, the sound's like *nothing* you've ever heard. It's something out of your worst nightmare. It goes right through you, churns your insides – turns your stomach and your legs into water. You daren't move. You can't move.' The man had lowered his voice, almost as though talking about the creature might in some way bring it down on them.

Atlon wondered what kind of a person he was talking to. An inadequate presumably, to have been driven beneath the city, but there was a power in his simple telling that would have eluded many a learned man. The crowd around him was still and silent, and he could feel the dank presence of the tunnels hanging in the

356

air despite the bright sunlight warming the street.

'It came barely a day ago, but it feels as though it's been there for ever. There's dead everywhere.' The man slumped a little and his eyes became distant. 'When I was . . .' He faltered. 'Before the tunnels, I had a growing plot – nothing much, but enough. One night a fox got into the chicken coop. Killed them all. Didn't eat them – just killed them.' Atlon was looking once again into terror. 'That's what we are down there – chickens. Squawking and helpless. We could no more hunt that creature than my chickens could've hunted that fox.' He bent close to Atlon, a prodding finger raised. 'I saw it open a man up with a single blow.' He made a cutting gesture from his shoulder to his groin. 'Lift up another, half as big again as me, and shake him like rat. His arm was torn clean off – it flew fifty paces and landed at my feet. Then the thing was gone. So fast.' He clapped his hands explosively. Then he began shaking. Hands reached out to comfort him.

'It's just killing for killing's sake,' someone said. 'And it doesn't stop. It doesn't even seem to get tired.' He put his hands to his ears. 'Everywhere you turn, you can hear it howling and people screaming. Far away one minute, close by the next. And all the time you're thinking: What's that in the shadows? Is it my turn? Will it be me making that awful noise?' He shook his head violently. 'I'll take my chance with a Weartan truncheon, but I'm not going back down there.'

'The Prefect'll have to do something about it. We can't,' someone else cried out, to a clamour of agreement. 'We're staying here till he does.'

Atlon reverted to his first question. 'What does it look like, this creature?'

Several garbled descriptions were given simultaneously. It was bigger than a man, smaller than a man. It was like a large dog, it was like a large cat. Its eyes were red – green – yellow. It ran in a strange way – on two legs, on four legs – but it was very fast. That, everyone agreed upon. It was *very* fast.

Atlon looked down, his vision filled with the ragged trousers and worn shoes of the Tunnellers gathered around him, and the dusty jointed stones that formed the road. What he was about to do disturbed him profoundly. He had no right to use people in such a way, especially the weak and the vulnerable. That these people were almost certainly destined for a bloody confrontation, that he was telling them the truth, gave him little consolation. But throughout, he had not lost sight of the terrifying problem posed by what had happened to Pinnatte. If that were not resolved, then the Serwulf loose in the tunnels would be as nothing to the carnage that might follow. For an instant, the shoes and the stones vanished to become a vision of the victorious battlefield he had stood on. All around him were sights that should not be seen. Sights which could not be seen without embedding themselves in the memory for ever and changing the direction of the life of the observer. He drove his fingernails into his palms until the pain returned him to the street.

'The other night,' he said, 'there was a Loose Pit at the Jyolan. I didn't see it myself, but the last animal to fight sounds like the one that's killing your people.'

He was suddenly aware that the group had fallen silent. All eyes were on him.

'No one knows who owns it, but the rumour is that it belongs to the Kyrosdyn.'

The mood about him changed perceptibly. The words 'Kyrosdyn' hissed all about him like a living echo as it passed through the crowd.

Atlon saw realization come into the eyes of the man he had first confronted. 'Of course,' he said softly, 'who else? They're always sneaking about down there – going below into the depths – into the caves themselves. Going into places where people aren't meant to go.'

Then the whispered 'Kyrosdyn' was being replaced by 'Vaskyros'. It soon rose to a shout and, abruptly, the crowd was moving away.

Atlon had difficulty meeting Heirn's look. 'I hope somebody, somewhere, will forgive me for that,' he said.

Heirn looked round at the passing stream of Tunnellers. His face was pained. Honest and straightforward, what he had heard Atlon do appalled him. He wanted to walk away – return to his forge – forget everything he had seen and heard over the past two days. He half-turned. Yet he could feel Atlon's own pain and desperation. He could not perceive this newcomer as a gratuitous manipulator of other people for sinister ends of his own. Nor could he leave him.

His voice was gruff when he forced his words out. 'You told them the truth. They're destined for bad trouble anyway. Better it be at the Vaskyros where it belongs than at the Prefect's Palace for nothing.'

Heirn's analysis chiming with his own, barely heartened Atlon. Somehow he would have felt better receiving an angry remonstrance. He gritted his teeth. He had seen others take decisions far more terrible. He would survive it, just as they did – he supposed.

But the pit of his stomach felt cold and hard.

As he and Heirn set off again, he consoled himself as best he could. Circumstances were allowing him few choices against fearful odds. There was no saying in what way directing the Tunnellers against the true cause of their trouble would change these choices, but change them it would, and where there was change, there would be opportunity.

'Well done,' Dvolci said to him quietly and very gently. 'It's at times like this that I'm particularly glad that I'm not a human.' It was a remark that Dvolci frequently used, but this time its usually biting tone was replaced with genuine compassion. Atlon felt a little easier.

As they walked along, Heirn kept looking nervously over his shoulder.

'Don't worry about the Weartans,' Atlon said. 'Listening for horses is something I've been doing all my life and I'm good at it. I'll tell you when they're coming.'

Heirn gave him a nod of acceptance, then automatically looked over his shoulder again.

As Heirn had declared, it was indeed a long and complicated journey to the Vaskyros. Most journeys tended to be thus in Arash-Felloren, with its endlessly winding streets, its complicated and confusing junctions and its rambling, open spaces. From time to time, Atlon thought that he sensed some kind of pattern to the

359

whole, but it defied easy discovery and he did not pursue it. Nevertheless, he studied the route that they were following with great care, frequently, like Heirn, though for different reasons, looking back at where they had just come from. It could be that he might have to travel it again and at speed. Each time he did this, thoughts of his horse came to him and he had constantly to set aside regrets at having to leave it at Heirn's. It was a pain he had not anticipated.

Gradually, he was becoming accustomed to the hectic activity that typified most of the city; under other circumstances, he would have welcomed an opportunity to study this remarkable place and its people. Now he was in a street like a deep canyon, hemmed in by high soaring buildings which darkened the sun and directed the flow of the people and traffic below like ominous shepherds. Then he was looking over the parapet of a bridge, flying high above level upon level of streets and buildings far below, and offering a panorama of at least part of the city. Confusion was everywhere: bustling alleyways, high galleries, arcades, the derelict and the decaying shouldering equally the new and flamboyant and the old and sedate. And there was the occasional, almost incongruous burst of greenery, where some parkland or growing plot was being assiduously protected from the withering sun.

But these were impressions that Atlon registered only in passing. His brief vision of the old battlefield had focused his resolve and he clung to it, grim though it was. With each step he used this and the disciplines of his training to prepare himself. Whenever he felt his concentration drifting he intoned inwardly: 'This is not a bright and sunny day in a strange and fascinating place. It is still the battlefield – His battlefield.' The absence of smoking entrails spilt from hacked bodies, the awful sounds of the wounded, the stink – of terror, of voided colons, of burning flesh, of earth churned with feet and hooves and rain and blood – did not change this. *His* presence was everywhere – faint and tenuous, but real nevertheless. And such havoc would always be His legacy.

Seeking other sources of courage in his inner trial, Atlon returned to the short time he had spent with the Queen's élite troops. He had learned little from them in the way of fighting skills, save that he was no warrior, but he had picked up a simple directness of thinking that had stood him in good stead many times since in arenas not associated with combat. Above all, they had taught him that he should not be afraid to be afraid – that fear was a necessary thing for him if he was to survive any threat.

'Mind you, nobody says you have to enjoy it.' The long-forgotten memory of this rueful observation, uttered as he had crouched trembling behind someone's shield, floated up into his mind and made him smile.

'How are you feeling?' Dvolci asked, sensing his mood.

'Bad, but I think I'll be ready,' Atlon replied.

'Good,' Dvolci said. 'You *can* do this, Atlon. Don't let the natural uncertainty of your inquiring nature cloud your measure of your true ability.' He was unusually serious. 'When you stood with the others that day, you faced a power and a will far beyond anything these people can offer. It forged you into someone stronger by far. You take no pride in this, but you *do* know it! And all the years since have strengthened you further. The Atlon before that day could not have contained that novice, or what Pinnatte did, could he?'

Atlon did not reply but could do no other than ask, 'There *is* no other way, is there?'

'No.' Dvolci's reply came without hesitation. 'Whatever's been done to Pinnatte is turning him into something that shouldn't be possible, according to everything we know. Perhaps these Kyrosdyn, these . . . crystal meddlers . . . hoped to control him in some way, but I agree with you. I think they don't know what they've done. I can't conceive of anyone – not even humans – doing such a thing deliberately. Such a . . . creation . . . could no more be controlled than the turning of the globe. He's already wildly dangerous and he must surely get worse. And rapidly at that. We've no time to go home. We have to go to the heart of this – and that's the Kyrosdyn. They mightn't know what's happened at the moment, but they will soon enough. And at least they know what they did to him.'

Atlon reached up and touched the felci's head. Dvolci's use of the word 'we' cut into him. 'A very human trait, selfishness,' he said. 'I'm sorry. How are *you*?'

Dvolci grunted. 'Ready enough, you know me.'

'Bad taste in your mouth again?'

'Afraid so.' Dvolci shook his head noisily.

They fell silent and the clamour of the city closed about them as they continued on their way.

After their encounter with the Tunnellers, it seemed to Atlon that they had all disappeared, merging into the bustling morning. Slowly however, he became aware of an increasing tension in the air. Heirn, more used to the nuances of the city's moods, had already noticed it – and its cause.

'There are Tunnellers all over the place,' he said quietly, as though afraid some might overhear him.

Looking round, Atlon began to notice them. Their characteristic shabbiness was to be seen everywhere. A tide of ragged greyness was gradually pervading the street, draining the colour from the city and its inhabitants like the touch of a baleful sun.

'Is it true there are more people below the city than actually in it?' Atlon asked. In their short acquaintance, he had never seen Heirn look so uncertain when he replied.

'So it's always been said. But then we say all manner of things without thinking about them, don't we? Now you ask me, I have to say I don't know. I doubt anybody does. There are whole areas of the city above ground that no one knows anything about, let alone underneath it. Oh!'

They had turned a corner into yet another square. Diagonally opposite them was a broad avenue which rose up and curved out of sight to the left. Rising above the buildings Atlon saw the towers and spires of the Vaskyros. He knew it for what it was immediately, its jagged outline impinging on him almost physically with its strangely violent symmetry.

The cause of Heirn's exclamation however, was not the building, but the straggling crowd of Tunnellers wandering along the avenue. He was about to say, 'Your troops, General', but even as the jibe came to him its injustice repelled him and he thought about shaping it into a dark joke. Finally, he left it unsaid.

Instead, Atlon said it for him, though his mouth was dry when he spoke. 'Did just those few words do this?'

'It would seem so,' Heirn said, inadequately.

As the initial impact of the sight faded, practical considerations returned. Heirn was looking around again. 'I'll hear the horses,' Atlon repeated reassuringly.

'I'm surprised there are none here already,' Heirn said. 'They must know what's going on by now.'

'Unless there are just too many Tunnellers in other parts of the city.' It was Dvolci. 'There are far more here than we saw. They must be coming out all over the place.'

'Could be,' Heirn agreed. 'Could be a host of things, not least some political quarrel between the Weartans and the Kyrosdyn, but whatever it is, it's not good.'

'Explain,' Atlon said tersely, his eyes fixed almost hypnotically on the Vaskyros.

'Rightly or wrongly, people just don't like Tunnellers,' Heirn replied. He gave an encompassing wave towards the distant crowd. 'This isn't going to be tolerated for long. If the Weartans can't or won't deal with it, then the Trading Combines, the Guilds, the Noble Houses, any of them and a score of other groups, will send in their own mercenaries sooner or later. And they're even less disciplined than the Weartans.'

Atlon nodded, recalling the same observation from the previous night. 'And if we get caught up in any of it, we're just as likely to be victims as any of these.'

'We are indeed,' Heirn confirmed.

Atlon's eyes narrowed. 'If they come on foot, you protect me. If they come on horseback, I'll unseat one and protect you. Is there another way to this place?' He flicked his hand towards the Vaskyros, as though reluctant to mention it by name.

Heirn looked at him sharply, involuntarily answering his question before asking one of his own. 'Yes, I think so. What do you mean, you'll unseat one and protect me?' His tone was incredulous.

'Precisely that,' Atlon replied, motioning Heirn to lead on. 'I've seen plenty of people on horseback since I arrived, but I haven't seen a single rider so far. The majority don't ride much better than Dvolci here. There'll be no difficulty unseating someone. It's

363

verging on the miraculous that most of them manage to stay in the saddle at all.'

There was an undemonstrative but absolute confidence about Atlon's manner that left Heirn with nothing to say, though the remains of his jibe leaked into his acknowledgement. 'On foot I look after you, on horseback you look after me? Fine, General.'

The square too was cluttered with Tunnellers, all unknowingly following Atlon's guidance which had spread through them like a virulent disease. While they all seemed to be intent on reaching the Vaskyros, their presence was being loudly resented by the locals, particularly the small traders who littered this square as they did every other in the city. As he followed Heirn, Atlon heard the angry voices that he had heard in the street the previous night. Noisy, vicious quarrels were springing up everywhere.

'Just keep moving,' Heirn said.

Atlon felt a sense of relief after they passed the avenue and the Vaskyros disappeared behind the buildings fringing the square but, as they came to the next junction, Heirn paused. Five roads came together in a typically confused fashion, and Atlon could see that some way along, each one branched into several other roads.

'This way,' Heirn said, after some thought. 'I'm not too familiar with all the streets around here. This isn't an area I've had cause to visit all that often. The difficulty is that the Vaskyros is built into the side of a hill. One side's a sheer drop, and there's a whole maze of little roads round here that just peter out into nothing.'

The street was narrow and dusty, constructed of smaller, more uneven stone blocks than most of the others Atlon had seen. Grasses and weeds were growing between joints, restrained only by the effects of the long hot summer. The road was obviously very old, and little used, though ruts running along it indicated that once, at least, it had frequently been used by heavy carts. The houses on one side stopped abruptly as a rocky outcrop intruded. Those on the other side changed suddenly after this point, becoming smaller, simpler and more functional in appearance. Atlon could see no sign of any gratuitous decoration. Save for the variations made necessary by the sloping ground, they were also identical. Built from a stone similar to that of the road they too, were obviously old. Some were still occupied, some were empty, and one or two were patently decaying. At regular intervals, equally narrow streets turned off at right angles to reveal rows of other identical houses. The whole made an oddly dismal impression despite the bright sunshine. The thought came to Atlon that they were servants' quarters, or perhaps accommodation for low-ranking Army officers or civilian employees.

He turned away from their dun monotony and looked up at the rugged rockface which now formed the opposite side of the road. He could see nothing, but he knew that on top of it would be the looming bulk of the Vaskyros. And even as he thought this, the rockface began to fall away to be replaced by a high wall. Atlon walked over to it and examined it closely. The stones that formed it were very large, and the joints between them were so tight that it would have been difficult to insert even a fine blade. No grasses and weeds found haven here.

Looking up, he saw that the wall curved outwards. It was giddying perspective and it made him step back.

'Fine workmanship,' he said to Heirn.

'I've never really looked,' Heirn replied.

'Military engineers built this,' Atlon went on. 'Good ones at that. I'll wager there are ramparts with anchorages for all manner of siege defence devices up there.'

Heirn could not work up any enthusiasm. 'I thought you were a scholar, not a soldier.'

'I've had cause to study wars and fighting, amongst other things. Tragically, many great achievements have come about through war. People's minds are uniquely focused when their survival is at risk. Failure to learn from their suffering is to make their battle doubly futile and to risk having to fight it again.'

Heirn followed his gaze and stared up at the wall. 'I suppose you're right,' he said, still unenthusiastic. Then he frowned. 'You really make me look at my city through a stranger's eyes. Some of it's been a revelation, but I'm not totally sure I like some of the things you see.'

Despite his preoccupation, Atlon smiled. 'The greatest protection you can ever have is to see things the way they are, rather than as you think they are, or as you think they ought to be.'

Heirn gave a non-committal grunt.

The street grew steadily steeper, making the two men slow down. They had passed no one since they entered it, though now, occasionally, someone would peer through a window and stare at them curiously as they plodded by. As they neared what appeared to be the top of the slope, the sound of an angry crowd reached them.

Chapter 27

On the edge of panic, he lay for a long time staring up at the ceiling before he slowly began to remember who he was. The panic receded only partly as it took him almost as long to remember *where* he was.

The night had been a black and turbulent torrent, buffeting him between stark horror and manic elation. The high-pitched whine that had drawn him to the small opening in the wall had held him there, immobile, while it coiled itself through and around him until it was all he was. What he had been, all that had brought him to this point, was gone as if it had never happened. There was just the flickering darkness through which he was plunging, filled with the rich heady scent of prey. And their song – long and irresistibly alluring. Thoughts pervaded him that were incoherent and alien, save that they were alternately terrifying and rapturous, though there were faint remembrances among them that told him of a great loss, and a flight from a terrible, glittering foe. Dominating these however, was the dull ache of an endless empty exile in the barren darkness.

Pinnatte screwed up his eyes then opened them wide, as though trying to force the light of the solitary lamp into the lingering remains of that darkness. He was trembling. The events of the night, jumbling and fragmenting now at the touch of his wakening mind, were already slipping away from him. But events they had been. It had been no dream. Not only did he never dream, there was an undeniable reality about what had happened. For at times he had drifted apart from the will that had held him and drawn him into its killing frenzy. He had been briefly himself, aware of the horror of what was happening, aware of people – men, women, children – fleeing terrified and screaming through the darkness. The recollection sent a spasm through him. Waves of both delight and appalled disgust washed through him.

Shocked, he struggled into a sitting position, each movement helping to distance him from this unwanted flood. He looked round at the room, forcing himself to think of other things. This was his room now, chosen by him but given to him by Barran, no less. Yet even as he looked at the age-stained walls, he knew that terrible things had been done beyond them, terrible things that he had been party to. And too, he knew that they were continuing . . .

Still, it was of no account – for what was a little bloodshed along the way of his unfolding future?

The callousness of the thought jolted him again, and accusing echoes of the terror and the screaming cascaded into his mind. Yet even as they did, he realized that they were *only* of his mind. His body felt no such repulsion, no shame at what had happened. Deep inside, his body had relished what was happening. Even now, it longed – desired – for . . .

For what?

He pressed his hands to his temples as his inner conflict washed to and fro.

Slowly, a clinging presence slipped away from him. As it did so, the longing began to fade. And thoughts came to calm his mind. What had happened had been beyond his control. He had neither sought nor encouraged it. It wasn't his fault! There was a feebleness about these that reduced them to the level of mere excuses, but they sufficed to make him feel more whole again, all turmoil sunk below his awareness.

It had been the creature, he knew, as the reality of the room finally closed about him, banishing the last of the shadows. Its touch was unmistakable. It had bent its knee in obeisance to him when it entered the arena and, once again, it had reached out and drawn him into its awful hunt. How such a thing could be was beyond him. As was the question *why*? But it had been so, nevertheless.

What would happen the next time he went to sleep? The thought did not carry the fear that it had done previously, but he still let it go quickly. This was the beginning of more than a new day, and sleep was a long way off. Plenty of time to worry about that later. He paid no heed to the hint of anticipation that fluttered in the wake of the thought.

He stood up, rubbing his hand. It was itching a little. Holding it up to catch the light, he saw that the remnant of the mark left by the Kyrosdyn was unchanged. It ended abruptly where the graze from his fall cut across it, a hint of its greenness colouring the edge of the dark red scab. He ran a finger around the mark. He could feel nothing. No pain, no swelling. What was it? What had the man done? Had he in reality done anything, or had it all been, as Lassner had said, a malicious trick to frighten him for his impertinence?

He smiled. It didn't matter. Whatever the man's intention had been, the mark had done him no harm, and while it had alarmed him at first, it had also brought him here – free of Lassner and the Den, and working for Barran. He clenched his fists in delight and offered the anonymous Kyrosdyn a caustic thank you.

The thought of Barran however, galvanized him. 'If you do well, there's a good fortune waiting for you,' he had said. And all that was to be done, to start with, was the cleaning of a few mirrors – or whatever they were. But, dashing this excitement to one side, came Barran's other words: 'Come to me each morning.'

A different kind of panic took hold of Pinnatte. What time was it? Probably just after dawn, he hoped. That was when he normally woke. But after a night like the one he had just spent, who could say? And there was no hint of either light or noise from the outside to help him.

He left his room at considerable speed but slithered to a flailing halt as he came to the first branch in the passageway. He could well be late already, but if he got lost, rambling about this place . . .

He felt his future slipping away, like water through his fingers. 'Slow down,' he muttered grimly to himself, successfully invoking the habit that had saved him from many a pursuit.

Immediately, another old habit asserted itself and he began to search his various pockets for a piece of chalk. The street thieves of Arash-Felloren had a considerable repertoire of signs and symbols with which they adorned walls to communicate to their fellows – such and such a trader had employed new guards, or got a new dog, So and So would be away from his house for so many days, the Weartans were purging a particular area, and so on. Finding one, Pinnatte headed back towards his room, still forcing himself to walk calmly. It became increasingly difficult as he opened each of three identical doors unsuccessfully before he found the correct one, and he let out a breath of considerable relief as he finally made a slight mark on the frame of the door.

That had been a timely lesson. He laid an affectionate hand on the wall. It felt familiar to him. The Jyolan was where he wanted to be, and he must not only learn such lessons if he was to have a future here, he must anticipate them. He looked up and down the passage and made a determined resolution. Notwithstanding any tasks that Barran gave him, he would learn about this place until he knew every last stone. The intimate knowledge he had of the many alleys, lanes, run-throughs, sewers and general escape routes in the part of the city where he worked, had been acquired over many years, partly by accident, partly deliberately, under Lassner's tuition. Now he must start again. Exhilarated though he was at being accepted by Barran, he was not so naive as to imagine that the road to wealth which he saw lying before him would be free from difficulty. Apart from falling foul of Barran himself, if he wanted to make progress, then, as in the Den, he would have to compete with others, and the kind of people who worked for Barran would be different by far from his old Den-Mates. Violence would be lying in wait for him if he misjudged his step. For a moment, his face hardened as part of him looked forward to such a challenge. It was a response that would have surprised him only days earlier, but now it seemed quite normal.

Thus, in addition to ingratiating himself with Barran – as he had with Lassner – it was imperative that he explore this new terrain he found himself in. Here there were no walls to be nimbly scaled, no narrow openings that led into open cellars, no drops into the sewers. Here there were only interminable passages, twisting, turning, narrowing, widening, rising, falling, like the streets of the city itself writ small. And knowledge of these might one day save his life.

His new home duly marked, and his new resolution firmly made, Pinnatte decided first to find the Mirror Room before seeking out Barran. This proved to be comparatively simple, the route being still fairly fresh in his mind from the previous evening, and the room standing alone at the end of a long passage. Nevertheless, he marked the way.

Having found it, he stood for a while staring at the door before tentatively reaching out to try the handle. Then he hesitated and knocked gently, three times. The soft sounds sank into the dead air of the passage. He was reaching for the handle again when it turned. He had taken a swift pace backwards and was trying to look casual when the door opened to reveal Barran. His new master had a bundle of papers in one hand while the other was out of sight behind the door. Though he looked both tired and suspicious, Pinnatte could sense an aura of suppressed excitement about him. He could also sense danger in the hidden hand.

'You asked me to come to you for the key, sir,' he said quickly, with an extravagant gesture which enabled him to take another discreet pace backwards in preparation for flight.

Recognition came into Barran's eyes and he opened the door fully. The hidden hand was adjusting something behind his back. When it emerged, it was empty.

'How did you know I was here?' he asked.

Pinnatte chose the truth. 'I didn't, sir,' he replied. 'I was just finding my way around and I thought I'd see if you were here first. You did say it was an important place.'

Barran nodded then stepped out of the room and closed the door behind him.

'You look tired, sir,' Pinnatte risked.

'That's because I am,' Barran replied tersely. 'It's been a busy time.' He looked at Pinnatte narrowly. 'You're looking little better yourself, young man. Are you all right?'

'Bit restless last night, sir. New master, new place.' Pinnatte smiled broadly. 'And I'm hungry now. I was going to find you, then try to get some food somewhere.'

Barran continued his inspection of his new charge for a moment, then, seemingly satisfied, opened the door again and motioned Pinnatte into the room. A table and two chairs had been added since he was there last, and the wooden panel was already pushed back to reveal the mirrors. The Eyes of the Jyolan, Pinnatte remembered Barran calling these strange objects. He thought of them as mirrors, accepting the word used by Barran, but they were not like any mirrors he had ever seen. All he could see of his reflection was the faintest hint, and that only when he searched for it. What he could see was what he had seen the night before: different parts of the Jyolan – with figures moving about most of them. The sight did not startle him as much as it had previously, but it still unsettled him. How could such a thing be? He was tempted to ask what the mirrors were used for, but they were so strong that he could think of no clear question. Besides, he sensed that Barran was in no mood for casual chatter.

'You'll need some rags and a bucket of water.' Barran's voice yanked Pinnatte back to the present. 'And I think Ellyn's got something she uses for cleaning glass.'

Pinnatte bent forward and listened intently as Barran explained how the mirrors were to be held and supported while they were being cleaned.

'You must be very careful until we know more about how these things work.'

There was an ominous emphasis on the word 'very' that sharpened Pinnatte's attention even further. Notwithstanding that however, once or twice he found his mind wandering. Having one of the most ruthless and powerful men in the city talking to him about such matters as dusting and cleaning, like a fussy old maid, was oddly disorientating. When he had finished, Barran put his hand on Pinnatte's shoulder. Pinnatte remembered the weight of it from the previous evening and concentrated again.

'You will take great care with this job, won't you, Pinnatte?'

It was not a question, it was an order.

Later, Pinnatte sat in the room alone, the door locked behind him. Barran had taken him to the rooms he was using as temporary living quarters while work at the Jyolan was under way. Ellyn had

372

given him a long look when he demanded, 'That stuff for cleaning glass', obliging him to repeat the question. She said nothing, but raised an ironic eyebrow when she finally gave him an earthenware bottle unearthed from one of several wooden crates. Pinnatte wilfully avoided looking directly at either of them during this exchange. Then Ellyn wrinkled her nose slightly and with a nod of her head towards Pinnatte gave Barran a significant look. He sniffed conspicuously and nodded in agreement. 'Show him where he can get cleaned up, get him some decent clothes and feed him,' he said brusquely.

It was thus an unusual Pinnatte who eventually sat staring at the Eyes of the Jyolan. He was cleaner, smarter, and easier on the nose than he had been for a long time. Rearranged dirt being one of his disguises, his erstwhile Den-Mates would have found him almost unrecognizable with a clean face. Occasionally he preened himself, and moved his head this way and that in an attempt to see his faint reflection in one of the mirrors, though generally with little success. In addition to being clean, he was also replete, Ellyn having fed him quite handsomely.

On his return to the Mirror Room, he had pursued his allotted task as bidden. At first he was extremely careful, holding the thick mirrors very firmly and applying his rag very hesitantly. However, after a few heart-stopping fumblings which left mirrors vibrating, their images streaked and blurred, he realized that they were far more robust than Barran had imagined. For in each case, the mirror settled back into its original position, its image unimpaired.

Cleaning them proved to be a harder task than he had anticipated. The dust on them had been there a long time and was stiff and reluctant to move, as were his fingers after he had been working for a while. Nevertheless, he pressed on, engrossed, for as each mirror was cleaned, its surface had a quality of perfection about it, displaying an image with a clarity the like of which he had never seen in an ordinary mirror. So vivid were the sights he could see that he felt as though he should be able to reach out and actually touch them. And even though he began to grow used to the strangeness of what he was seeing, he found it difficult at times not to just sit and stare.

Eventually he pushed his chair back, stretched himself noisily and then flexed his fingers energetically in an attempt to ease the stiffness in them. It did not work. He was going to have to pace himself better. So far he had cleaned only one row and his arms and shoulders were aching, as well as his hands. It was going to take him a long time to finish them all. And some of the higher mirrors would be extremely difficult to reach even standing on the table.

Still, it did not matter. If Barran was unhappy about the progress he was making, he would be able to demonstrate both the intransigence of the grime coating the mirrors and the care he was taking. He decided not to mention, for the moment, how robust the mirrors actually were – that might prove to be a useful 'discovery' on some future occasion. For the time being, while he was doing this job, he would have legitimate opportunity to wander about the Jyolan – to fetch clean water, to find more rags, perhaps locate a ladder – all of which would enable him to find his way about the place. Something dark turned over luxuriously inside him at the prospect and the mirrors seemed to shimmer. He shook his head. He'd been here too long, he decided. And been working too intensely, just like when he'd been an apprentice thief, learning to pick pockets. Now was as good a time as any to start his exploration of the Jyolan.

Rooting under his jacket he retrieved the key, soundly secured in a hidden pocket next to his skin. Experienced in such matters, Pinnatte knew how to carry things safe from the sly touch of such as himself. As he stood up, a movement in one of the mirrors caught his eye. It was one of the mirrors that normally showed no activity. Pinnatte peered at it closely, resisting the temptation to rub the dust away with his hand. He found himself looking along a dimly-lit and seemingly empty passage – one of many such. But there was something there, he was sure. Something hiding, low and skulking. A shadow in the shadows.

A shape flitted by a lamp.

Though the movement was too quick for him to see any details, he knew immediately that it was the fighting dog which had escaped the arena at the Loose Pit. Instantly he was back with Rinter and

Atlon and the guard in the passage where they had encountered the same dog. As then, powerful emotions surged through him, possessing him, dismissing all reason. This thing was prey! It had escaped once and, in so doing, had left a pain that could be healed only by its death. It must be taken now! Almost as if it had felt his presence, the dog froze, then suddenly dashed around a corner. Pinnatte felt something in him leap after it. He stepped back quickly, scanning the mirrors for other signs of the fleeing animal. It flickered past one and was gone again. Spinning round, he dashed for the door. His thigh struck the corner of the table with considerable force.

The pain scattered all other responses and he cried out and dropped on to one knee, massaging his leg frantically and cursing. Even as he did so he became aware of a clattering sound. It was the key! He saw it bouncing on the stone floor. The implications of losing the key flashed before him, stark and uncompromising, dismissing in its turn the pain in his leg. Quite unnecessarily, for the key had stopped moving, he lunged after it, sending himself sprawling full length across the floor as he slapped his hand down on it.

He lay there for a moment, breathing heavily, before curling his fingers tightly around the key. His leg began to hurt again. Slowly he sat up and began rubbing it with the hand clenched around the key. As the worst of the discomfort left him, he levered himself on to the chair and carefully put the key back in its special pocket.

Still rubbing his leg, he cursed himself for a profound fool. What had he been thinking about, crashing around like that? The table had been knocked clear across the room, so violently had he struck it. What if the key had bounced into one of those damned grilles? He went cold. He did not want to think about it. The only solution to that would have been to take Ellyn's advice and flee this part of the city completely – and very quickly at that!

As he became calmer, he asked the question again. What *had* he been thinking about? What had possessed him to behave with such folly? But he knew the answer. Indeed, as his thoughts turned again to the escaped dog, he could feel the presence bubbling inside him, threatening to burst out again. It was the creature. Some remnant of its night-time joining with him still lingered. But as the realization came to him, so did another, leaking up in some subtle way from the creature itself. This time, he was in control of it. *He* was master here. It would bend to his will, just as it had bowed to him in the arena. He knew now that it had drawn him into its killing spree because he was unprepared for it and because it was long starved of its true sustenance and near-frantic with excitement at finding him. Now however, the true balance of their relationship was established. A thrill passed through him.

Feed, he heard himself saying to it. Take your fill, I need you strong. Come to me when I call.

Then the presence was gone and he was more himself again. A little breathless, and with an extremely painful leg, he was Pinnatte, the one-time street thief on the way up. The joining with the creature no longer disturbed him; nor what it was doing. It was the way things were, the way they had to be. It was the inevitable working out of his destiny. Calmly, he picked up his buckets and rags and, carefully removing the key from its pocket again, left the room.

The area around the Mirror Room was, as usual, deserted, but he was soon part of the bustling activity that marked Barran's intention of developing the Jyolan to its full. He noticed with some amusement that many of the people he was encountering appeared to be lost. He noticed too that he was barely using the marks he had made for himself. It was as though he had some natural affinity for the place. Almost as though he already knew it.

He made a few such journeys that morning, deliberately taking a different route each time, fulfilling his promise to himself to learn his way about the place as quickly as possible. With each excursion he became more at ease. While being lost in the Jyolan would be a legitimate source of panic for most people, it held no terrors for Pinnatte – it was more of an amusing challenge. There was an order here which he sensed and worked to, even though he could not have explained it to anyone or marked it on a paper. Once or twice he sensed the nearness of the escaped dog, and it gave him some pleasure to deny the will of the creature as it responded to him.

Returning again to the Mirror Room he put down the buckets

and inserted the key in the lock. To his horror it did not turn. As he twisted it the other way, the door locked. His hands began to shake. He must have left the room unlocked! Surely not. He'd been as meticulous about locking the door as he had been about securing the key. He cursed himself even more roundly than he had when he banged into the table. He must concentrate on everything he did here. This was no Den, full of petty thieves. This was a place full of dangerous people, not the least of whom was Barran. He unlocked the door and pushed it open with his knee as he picked up the buckets. The image of a raging Barran filling his mind, coincided with that immediately in front of him and it was a tribute to his quick-wittedness that he did not cry out and drop both buckets. The Barran waiting for him however, was not raging, but actually looked rather amused by the flustered appearance. For Pinnatte was not quick-witted enough to prevent his mouth from dropping open.

'I thought I'd left the door unlocked when the key didn't turn,' he blurted out, wide-eyed.

Barran shook his head and held out his hand. 'Yours isn't the only key,' he said casually. 'But give it to me now and come back in a couple of hours. I need to be in here for a while.' He looked at the mirrors. Pinnatte had cleaned four rows.

'You're not working very quickly,' he said with a frown. 'I'd like this finished today.'

Pinnatte performed the demonstration he had prepared earlier, showing conclusively the difficulties he was dealing with and eventually wringing a grunt of acceptance and approval from Barran. He decided to risk taking advantage of it and pointed to the ring on which Barran had put the key.

'That's not a good idea,' he said.

Barran looked at him quizzically. Pinnatte stepped close to him, pointed to one of the mirrors and said, 'Look.'

'What?' Barran demanded irritably as he glanced at the mirror and back again.

'This,' Pinnatte replied, handing him the ring of keys. Before Barran could respond, Pinnatte was giving him sterling advice about how he should best carry the keys, and anything else that he valued, so that they would be safe from such as himself.

As he finished his lecture, Barran nodded knowingly. Then he snapped his fingers and said, 'Look.'

Pinnatte started and turned even as he realized he was being caught by his own trick. Except that Barran's trick was different, for as Pinnatte turned, it was into the edge of a knife against his throat. 'Good advice for good advice, Pinnatte,' Barran said quietly, bringing his face close. 'I like your enthusiasm and your ideas. Don't be afraid to tell me about them. But tell me softly and more circumspectly. And be very careful how close you come to people around here.' He nodded towards the door. 'Two hours,' he said.

Pinnatte leaned against the door after he had closed it, breathed out noisily and put his hand on his chest as though to stop his heart pounding. Not for the first time, Barran's simple purposefulness had terrified him, more by its mundane ordinariness than by any overt menace. He could see that he had indeed been given good advice for good advice, and it had taught him several lessons about life in this new world, not the least of which was to be more careful with his new master. But something else had happened, for even as Barran had released him, a manic rage had welled up inside him – a rage that had almost made him lash out at Barran for his insolence in handling him thus. It was unlike anything he had ever felt before, and it terrified him to think how close to being expressed it had come.

He moved unsteadily away from the Mirror Room. Cold thoughts formed to quell the heat of the rage as he walked, though they were no less alien to him. Some other time, they said. Patience is everything. Great forces are gathering within you.

With nothing specific to do, he began occupying himself by continuing to find his way about the Jyolan. In the course of this he succeeded in finding a bed and a couple of chairs which he dragged to his room. He also found a better room, nearer to both the Mirror Room and Barran's quarters – the Jyolan was awash with vacant rooms – but he made no attempt to occupy it. It would be better to wait until a suitable opportunity presented itself for him to ask for it. He had no desire to walk inadvertently into any more 'lessons'.

After a while, his room ordered to his satisfaction, he headed for the entrance with a view to buying food from one of the street traders. As he entered the main entrance hall, the scene of the events which had so advanced his fortunes, he began to feel uneasy. The feeling grew as he passed through the gates and moved towards the arch which opened on to the street. He lifted his hand to shield his eyes.

When he reached the arch, the light became intolerable and the heat struck him like a physical force. He could not move out into the street. Every part of him cried out for the subdued lighting of the Jyolan passages and its cold, enclosing stonework. If he moved forward, he knew the sunlight would burst into him, searing through to his very heart. And the air would be torn from his lungs, escaping into the vast, unbearable open sky – the sky which would ring mockingly with the echoes of his dying cries. As he stood there trembling, he sensed the creature somewhere, howling, lost.

Someone bumped into him. 'Come on, shift yourself, there's people with work to do here.'

The impact propelled him out into the street. He tried to cry out, but no sound came. Someone else bumped into him and cursed him. Then something made him open his eyes despite the awful daylight. The face carved into the keystone of the arch met his gaze, calm and serene, yet full of terrible power and purpose. His trembling began to fade. The Jyolan was his place, but then so was the whole city. From the Jyolan he would derive his strength so that, in the fullness of time, he would remake the whole city in its image. And until that time, he must walk in it, in its flawed, imperfect state. He had nothing to fear. He was awakening. Power was growing within him.

Slowly his breathing grew quieter and the street – his street – formed itself about him.

A hand took his elbow.

He spun round angrily, his hand raised to strike.

A Kyrosdyn stood in front of him. At his back were three bodyguards. Pinnatte held the man's gaze and did not lower his hand. The Kyrosdyn faltered, as did the bodyguards before they remembered their duty. When they moved forward however, the

Kyrosdyn raised his own hand to stop them.

Pinnatte felt the other man's fear and his weakness. It both surprised and did not surprise him.

Then he recognized the Kyrosdyn who had placed the mark on his hand.

Chapter 28

Rostan felt as though all life had been suddenly emptied from him and that he was now nothing more than an ice statue awaiting the sun's deathly kiss. What was standing in front of him, what appeared to be the young man that he had Anointed, was an abomination. There was Power coiling within him unlike anything he had ever encountered, Power which was without any of the form or control which, by everything he knew, was intrinsic to its existence. Such a thing was not possible. Yet it was there. And it was about to be released at him.

Harsh experience gained over the years he had spent with Imorren rose up to tell him that he must stand firm here, that to flee would be certain to bring destruction down upon himself. But the warnings were unnecessary, he could not have fled even if he had wanted to, so terrified was he.

Yet even through the terror, questions clamoured at him. How could such an impossibility have come about? What could have gone wrong? Nothing he had done by that fountain should have produced this, even if Pinnatte had been totally unsuitable for the Anointing. He might have gone mad, and probably died, but no calculation, no theory, nothing in the long history of the Kyrosdyn's searching and experimenting could have foretold this!

The anticipated blow did not come, but Pinnatte's gaze was relentless.

What was this creature seeing, with those wide, angry, black eyes? No more than he could flee, could Rostan tear his eyes away from Pinnatte's. It seemed to him that he was looking into the shifting, empty void in which this and all other worlds flickered endlessly in and out of existence. Vertigo mingled with his terror, telling him that should he move or speak, those black pools would expand until they encompassed him utterly and he would be lost for ever, tumbling through the dark nothingness where even time did not exist and where lay creatures and powers beyond any imagining.

Pinnatte lowered his hand and turned away slowly to look at the face on the arch. When he turned back, the brief release had given Rostan some of his wits back. He forced his mouth into an apologetic smile.

'I'm sorry,' he said, suddenly grateful that his many years serving Imorren had given him some control over his voice. 'I startled you.'

He felt the strange Power in Pinnatte retreating. It gave him only slight encouragement however. The Power had appeared as suddenly as though a curtain had been flung aside, and it might well do so again. His mind was racing. Since Imorren's command, he and the Lesser and Higher Brothers had been searching for this man. It had not taken him long to detect the sign of the Anointed – it had grown markedly – but that had given him no inkling of what he was going to face. And now that he had found him he realized that he had walked blithely to the edge of a precipice. To use the Power in such a public place, even subtly, would have been a great risk at any time, but it was completely out of the question now. Who knew what response this thing might make? As for getting the mercenaries to capture him, that would be even more foolish. Imorren's statement that this man's role was too uncertain for any rashness had proved to be both a timely warning and a considerable understatement. Nevertheless, he would still have to be taken back to her somehow.

Even as he was thinking, he was aware of Pinnatte's Power continuing to recede. It gave him the opportunity to look at his erstwhile victim with calmer eyes. What he saw puzzled him. Had it not been for the sign of the Anointed which surrounded him, he doubted he would have recognized the man. He had been a scruffy street thief only days before; now he was clean, and though his clothes were ill-fitting, comparatively well dressed. Some change in his fortunes had occurred other than the Anointing. Rostan gathered enough resources to resort to normal diplomacy.

'I'm sorry,' he said again. 'I didn't mean to startle you.'

Pinnatte cocked his head on one side, as if Rostan were speaking an unknown language. The Kyrosdyn, in his formal robes, was obviously a high-ranking Brother of some kind and, with the three mercenaries at his back, he should have been an intimidating sight – someone whom, under normal circumstances, he would have diligently avoided. Yet now, though elements of his former existence tugged at him anxiously, he felt at ease and in command of affairs. The Kyrosdyn was nothing. In fact, for some reason, the man was afraid. And Pinnatte knew that this was how it should be – that, if necessary, he could dispatch this irritation into oblivion at a mere touch. The thought made no sense to him, a small voice somewhere crying out that he was being a fool and that he should not trifle with such people, but he knew it to be true nonetheless.

And now the Kyrosdyn was being polite. This was something Pinnatte was not used to, and to receive it from a Kyrosdyn both stilled such doubts as he had and triggered a feeling of dark amusement. He did not reply, but continued staring at Rostan.

Rostan shifted uncomfortably, then held out his hand and introduced himself. Pinnatte looked down at the hand and then back at Rostan, without taking it. One of the mercenaries, Gariak, who had been at the fountain, made to step forward, eyes narrowed, but a slight gesture from Rostan stopped him.

Though far from being relaxed, Rostan was feeling easier now. No blow had been struck and the strange Power seemed to have faded almost completely. What it had been, whether it might erupt again, were questions which along with many others he set firmly aside. All that mattered now was that this man be kept at his ease and lured to the Vaskyros. He brought his hands together in an attitude of prayer and affected a look of contrition. 'I understand,' he said, lowering his eyes. 'Our meeting the other day was . . . ' He shrugged regretfully, 'Ill-judged, to say the least.' Pinnatte making no response, he pressed on, mustering all the sincerity he could find. 'I'm afraid you caught me at a particularly difficult time and sadly, my temper got the better of me. I can assure you I regretted my behaviour almost immediately. In fact I've been looking for you ever since so that I could apologize.' He became fatherly. 'I

383

appreciate that you didn't realize who I was when you took my purse. I know the Guild of Thieves has great respect for our Order. It was my fault for walking the streets in ordinary clothes. It's not something I'll do again quickly.'

Pinnatte was beginning to feel awkward. This Rostan seemed quite different from the angry individual who had confronted him the other day. Indeed, he seemed to be genuinely upset at the trouble he had caused. And, after all, not only had no harm come of it, but a great deal of good. Had it not been for that stormy encounter, he would not now be working for Barran nor have discovered the Jyolan. The thought of the Jyolan made him feel good. At the same time, Rostan seemed to shrink into a cringing underling. Pinnatte looked at him. The man deserved something for what he had inadvertently wrought. He thrust out his hand. 'A misunderstanding,' he said. 'You needn't have concerned yourself, but I thank you.'

Rostan took the hand hesitantly. The strange Power had returned, suddenly and without warning, and even though he felt no threat in it this time, it was still frightening. As he touched Pinnatte, it seemed momentarily to swarm through him, possessing him utterly, then just as suddenly withdrawing. He pulled his hand away as quickly as he dared. Again he wanted to flee, but again he knew he could not. While the Power did not actually threaten him he must continue to try to lure this abomination back to the Vaskyros where Imorren could deal with him. *If* she could deal with him, he thought heretically.

'You're very generous,' he said. 'Imorren will be most relieved.'

'Imorren?' Pinnatte echoed, suddenly curious. 'The Ailad? The head of your Order?'

'Yes.'

Pinnatte frowned. 'Why would she be relieved? Why would she know anything about me?'

Rostan noted the response. It showed him the way. So Imorren was the bait that would reel this one in. Bite, little fish, he thought.

'I told her about it,' he said. 'She saw I was upset about something and, being the person she is, she asked me about it. It was her suggestion I should look for you and apologize if I was to have any peace. She said she was sure you'd understand if I found you. And she was right, wasn't she? She usually is. She takes a great interest in everything that happens in the city. And she has such wisdom. It's an honour just to be near her.' He became wilfully hesitant. 'I'm uncertain about how to ask this – you've been very kind already – but I'm sure she'd like to meet you.' He leaned forward confidentially. 'She was quite angry at me in her way. She's very concerned about how the people think of us. There's a great deal of misunderstanding about. It would be a kindness both to her and me if she could hear from you herself that all's well.' He held out an arm as if they might leave right away.

Pinnatte looked at him uncertainly. In two days, he had been released from Lassner and placed with Barran, fulfilling an ambition he scarcely knew he had. Now chance was offering him the opportunity to meet with another of the city's most powerful figures. Who knew what might come of such a meeting? Just to have it known that he had caught the attention of Imorren would make him someone to be feared, to be respected. It would be folly to refuse such an opportunity. But old cautions caught up with his bounding thoughts. The Kyrosdyn weren't to be trusted. Imorren was even more powerful and ruthless than Barran. He should keep away from her, and the Vaskyros. It was an article of faith amongst Den-Mates that no one went into the Vaskyros voluntarily; 'things' happened to people there – no one ever came out. But that was part of his old life. He wasn't a mere street thief any more. Scorn crept into his thinking. What would any Den-Mate know about the Kyrosdyn? Nothing, other than idle gossip. He, for one, had never even met a Kyrosdyn until the other day, and now here was this Rostan seeking him out and apologizing for what had happened, and offering him an opportunity to meet Imorren. It was time for him to set his old ways aside. There would be many other things to learn in his new life than just finding his way about the Jyolan.

Yet, the caution lingered. A lifetime of distrust, misplaced or not, was not to be set aside lightly. 'I'm one of Barran's men now,' he said, indicating the Jyolan. 'I have to be back in a few minutes. He'll be waiting for me.'

385

Rostan could not keep the surprise from his face, but he managed to make it look appreciative. Barran had little use for street thieves; why would he take this one on? And 'He'll be waiting for me' no less, so he was working directly for Barran. He must be special in some way, was the obvious answer. It was another puzzle hanging about the shoulders of this slight figure. A small conundrum, compared with that of the seemingly flawed Anointing, but one not to be ignored. Still, he could not allow it to deflect him from fetching this man to the Vaskyros.

'Your star is rising, young man,' he said heartily. 'Imorren will be even more pleased to hear of that.' He risked laying a hand on Pinnatte's shoulder. 'I know Barran very well. I can have a word with him, if you like. I'm sure there'll be no problem – he values Imorren's good opinion.' He considered shepherding Pinnatte towards the Jyolan, then thought better of it. Instead, he released him and stepped back a little to give him a sense of freedom.

Pinnatte's uncertainties dwindled under the combination of Rostan's affable assault and his own rekindled, if vague, ambition. He smiled. 'I think I know where he is,' he said, and motioned Rostan to follow him.

As they neared the main arch, it was Rostan who began to be uncertain. The Jyolan was an unsettling place for those who could use the Power. He had been there many times, discreetly, to watch the Fighting Pits, as had most of the Kyrosdyn, but there always seemed to be an unspoken consent amongst them not to speak about what they felt – that the building itself was aware of them, watching, waiting.

The origins of the Jyolan were long-lost, though the Kyrosdyn believed it had been built at the behest of Sammrael Himself at the very beginnings of Arash-Felloren. Nothing was known of its purpose, although ancient writings held by the Kyrosdyn referred to it as being built upon one of the Places of Great Power, though what this meant, none now knew. What *was* known was that the Jyolan had existed before the Order of the Kyrosdyn, and it had always been in their hands. Yet it, too, had always been an uncomfortable possession, with successive Ailads reluctant to use it for anything of consequence and frequently letting it to others.

Though there had been surprise expressed at Imorren's releasing it almost unconditionally to Barran, there had also been a general feeling of relief, albeit, as ever, largely unspoken.

Rostan felt what he thought of as the will of the building close about him as soon as he passed under the arch. But it was different today – very different. Whereas normally it was little more than a frisson of unease, it was now almost palpable. Rostan seemed to sense countless eyes watching him, even studying him. More alarmingly, he noted, there was an marked aura of danger about Pinnatte. For a moment he thought that it was the strange Power returned, but it was not emanating from Pinnatte. Rather it was as though the building was reaching out to protect him.

Questions about the Anointing returned, demanding attention, but a deeper instinct told Rostan simply that he must concentrate on carefully handling Pinnatte. And he must get out of here as soon as possible.

Pinnatte was striding out confidently. People stepped out of his way. Rostan noted that he did not hesitate as he negotiated the many junctions and branches that they passed. Though he knew the building quite well, he could not have walked through it so purposefully, yet this man – this abomination – who had been here only two days at the most seemed to know the place as if he had been born here. It reinforced Rostan's growing feeling that Pinnatte and the building were connected in some way.

Then, an unexpected concern began to make itself felt. The route they were following was vaguely familiar though he knew it was one which he had not taken for a long time. As he began to remember it, the knot of fear which had tangled in his stomach as soon as he had confronted Pinnatte, tightened. Somewhere around here was the accursed heart of this place: the room whose purpose both mystified and terrified the Kyrosdyn: the Mirror Room. Rostan's mouth went dry. He was about to touch the crystals at his neck for sustenance, when an inner voice warned him against it.

'The Room and all the Mirror Ways that feed it should be destroyed,' had been the common cry raised by Kyrosdyn through the ages. But what if its creator had indeed been Sammrael? Who could say what purpose such a place would serve? And who would

387

perform such a task? And how? What might happen if the intricate pathways of the endlessly reflecting images were disturbed? What chance scatterings, refractions, splittings might occur, what terrible conjunctions and resonances might come together to slice through this reality and open uncontrollable gateways into . . .?

Despite himself, Rostan ran his hand across his forehead. This was no time to be bothering about that intractable dilemma.

In the end, just as they had vaguely allowed the Jyolan to become a rather tawdry asset far from the centre of their main concerns, the Kyrosdyn, as much by default as any conscious decision, had opted for ignoring the Mirror Room. It was something that someone else could deal with – at some unspecified time in the future.

The nearer they drew to it, the more uneasy Rostan became.

Ironically, it was Pinnatte who spared him any further torment. Coming to the last junction before the passage that led to the Mirror Room, he stopped the small procession. The Mirror Room was obviously of importance to Barran, and Pinnatte was still sufficiently in command of his thoughts to realize that he would probably not appreciate that interest being casually exposed to anyone else, specially the Kyrosdyn.

'Wait here,' he said. 'If he's where I think he is, he mightn't want to be disturbed, but I'll tell him you're here.'

Barran looked surprised when he opened the door in response to Pinnatte's knock. 'You're early,' he said.

Too flustered to be tactful, Pinnatte flatly contradicted him, then blurted out his tale, almost incoherently. 'No, I'm late, I'm afraid. I'm sorry. But some Kyrosdyn Brother stopped me in the street. He's waiting along the passage. He wants me to go to the Vaskyros to see Imorren. I told him I'd have to ask you first. He says he knows you. He—'

Barran blinked owlishly and lifted a hand to stop him. 'Some Kyrosdyn says he wants to take you to *Imorren*?' he said with amused disbelief. 'He has a name does he, this Brother?'

'Rostan.'

Barran's manner changed abruptly and the amusement vanished. He hissed something under his breath, then took Pinnatte's arm in a powerful grip. 'I'll tell you this once, Pinnatte. Learn it! I've little sense of humour at the best of times, and *none* at the moment. Whatever you're—'

Alarmed, Pinnatte pointed with his free arm. 'He told me he was called Rostan. He's back there – go and see. I told him to wait. I didn't think you'd want him to know where you were.'

Barran hesitated, darker thoughts forming. Pinnatte didn't seem to be lying, but was he perhaps being used unknowingly by others? Others, taking advantage of the confusion surrounding the transfer of the Jyolan to catch him unawares?

Discreetly he checked his various knives, then he dismissed all other concerns from his mind. Had he made a mistake? He was alone in this part of the building and, even if he were loyal, this street thief would be no use if assassins had come. 'Do you know who Rostan is?' he asked. Pinnatte shook his head. 'He's the Highest of the Order – second only to Imorren herself. Now why would such a man want anything to do with you?'

His alarm now turned to fear by the subtle changes in Barran's demeanour, Pinnatte told him a modified version of his encounter with Rostan. 'I took his purse by mistake the other day, and his bodyguard knocked me about a bit even though I gave it back. He just met me in the street to apologize. Said he'd been looking for me. Said Imorren wanted to make sure I was all right, as well.'

Barran shook his head as if he had just found himself in the middle of a strange dream. Rostan, apologize! Imorren concerned for a street thief! It was impossible. But it was also too ludicrous a tale to be used as a lure to draw him into an ambush. And still nothing about Pinnatte indicated that he was lying. What had this Den-Mate been up to? Had he really done something to attract the attention of Rostan and Imorren? If so, it couldn't be anything trivial, yet, equally, it couldn't be too serious, or he'd have quietly disappeared by now. He set the questions aside, took a deep breath, and shook his shoulders to loosen them. When he spoke to Pinnatte he was a mercenary again, looking to make the most of an inadequate ally.

'I think someone's deceiving you, Pinnatte, but come with me. If there's trouble, keep out of it, you'll get in my way. Just run for help. Do you understand?'

Pinnatte nodded. 'Run for help,' he echoed.

'Now, tell me exactly where this . . . Rostan is.'

Pinnatte told him, volunteering, 'There's three bodyguards with him.'

Barran cursed silently. In the confusion of taking over this place he'd let basic precautions slip away. That would end today – if he lived! But, too, Pinnatte's information was odd. Four men would simply have followed him and struck as soon as the door had been opened.

He patted Pinnatte's arm reassuringly then motioned him to lead on.

As they neared the waiting group, Barran called out, almost jovially, 'Step more into the light, Rostan.'

Rostan raised his hands in an apologetic gesture and did as he was asked, at the same time telling his bodyguards to move well back.

'Wait here,' Barran said to Pinnatte in a reciprocal gesture.

Reaching Rostan, Barran greeted him with heavily feigned warmth, but made no attempt to disguise his genuine surprise. 'What's this Pinnatte tells me?' he began. 'The Ailad sends the Highest to seek out our hero?'

'Hero?' Rostan queried, obviously at a loss.

Barran looked at him intently. 'He's the one who opened the gate the other night. Saved us a lot of problems, not to mention the lives of some of my friends.'

He gave some significance to the last remark to announce that Pinnatte was under his protection.

Still unsettled by what he had found in Pinnatte and by the heightened aura of the Jyolan, Rostan found himself unable even to make an attempt at diplomacy other than to glance round to ensure that Pinnatte and the bodyguards were out of earshot. 'I know nothing about that,' he said coldly. 'This man is needed by Imorren on a Kyrosdyn matter. A serious matter. It's in your best interests to tell him he can come with us, now.'

Barran was surprised at this bluntness, but he was in no mood to be addressed thus and he replied in like manner. 'What possible Kyrosdyn matter could a street thief be involved in? He told me some wild tale about being beaten after taking your purse and you wanting to apologize. If he's still got something of yours I'll get it for you, but I'm obligated to him and he's doing important work for me. He goes nowhere until I know what's going on.'

Barran's manner forced Rostan to compose himself. He tried to retreat into reasonableness, giving an elaborate shrug and becoming confidential. 'It's to do with that incident, Barran,' he said. 'You see, it was witnessed by a lot of people – including some of the Prefect's agents.' He lowered his voice to a whisper. 'And, unfortunately, someone in the crowd saw fit to . . . air . . . the word *Kyroscreft*.' He coughed uncomfortably. 'The difficulty is, we're involved in some delicate negotiations with the Prefect at the moment, and the incident's causing us . . . problems.' He fell silent and met Barran's searching gaze with a look of his own appealing for understanding, one businessman to another. 'So we need the young man just to confirm that nothing untoward happened and that it was merely a . . . typical street quarrel.'

Barran did not reply immediately. Rostan's tale chimed with Pinnatte's and had a convincing air about it. The Kyrosdyn were always negotiating with someone – as was he – and the consequences of the cry 'Kyroscreft!' going up would indeed be a problem for them – and many others as well. Nevertheless, he was fairly certain that Rostan was lying. The spectacular ineptitude of his initial approach had given that away. What Pinnatte could have done to bring the likes of Rostan and Imorren down on him, he could not imagine, but he knew he was not going to find out unless Rostan specifically wanted him to know. And, given such an appeal, it was virtually impossible for him to refuse Rostan's request. However, he was growing to like the young thief and he was genuinely indebted to him for his actions at the Loose Pit.

He signalled Pinnatte to come forward. Putting a protective arm around his shoulders he said, 'I want you to go with Rostan, Pinnatte. The Kyrosdyn need our help with something and we always look to help one another whenever possible. It shouldn't take long.' He looked at Rostan. 'Make sure he's back before sunset. Apart from the work he's doing for me, the Prefect's insisted we hold a celebration for what he did. He's hoping to be here himself.'

He became proprietorial. 'Pinnatte's the talk of the Noble Houses and the Trading Combines already. He's become very famous. People are queuing up to meet him.'

There was a little truth in what he was saying, but with no idea what the Kyrosdyn really wanted of Pinnatte, it was the only protection he could offer him. It was also probably the best, openness and public knowledge being the biggest hindrances to the compulsively secret dealings of the Kyrosdyn – as they were to his own.

Reassured, Pinnatte left the Jyolan with Rostan. Throughout the incident he had been suffering conflicting emotions. Beneath his alarm at Barran's first response, and the general uncertainty about Rostan, there had been bubbling a monstrous anger. It was not right that he be treated so. Those who offended thus should be struck down without pity. And more than once he had felt the blow forming within him.

Even as he reflected on these responses, he knew they were still there, an almost continuous undertow to everything he did now.

And Rostan felt something too. The Pinnatte whom he had encountered in the street had been frightening enough, but the brief sojourn in the Jyolan seemed to have made him even more disturbing; the strange power in him washed to and fro without any semblance of reason or order. It occurred to him, very strongly, that the Kyrosdyn's neglect of the Jyolan over the years might have been a serious mistake, and he resolved to speak to Imorren about it as soon as an opportunity presented itself.

They walked on in silence for a long time, Pinnatte and Rostan wrapped in thought, and the bodyguards forming a discreet triangle about them. It was Pinnatte however, who came out of his reverie first, as years on the street told him something was amiss. He looked round quickly, but could see nothing. The bodyguard Gariak picked up his movement.

'What's the matter?' he asked, stepping alongside him.

Even as he spoke, Pinnatte saw the cause. 'Tunnellers,' he said. 'Everywhere.' As he recognized them, deep inside he felt the angry cry, 'Prey!' and a sense of raging frustration. It took him a conscious effort to still it and as he did so he realized where his night-time hunting with the creature had occurred. His two selves became momentarily one. He turned to Rostan. 'Nothing to concern us,' he said quietly, so that the bodyguards could not hear. 'Merely our creature feasting down there.' He smiled darkly. 'They think they can escape.'

Our creature! The knot in Rostan's stomach tightened again, partly at this first outward acceptance by the Anointed of what he was, and partly because the strange Power was all about him again. He had been right. Whatever Pinnatte had been before he returned to the Jyolan, he was worse now. And even more frightening. Whatever the flaw was in the Anointing, it was spreading, and Pinnatte's Power was growing rapidly both in intensity and instability. Would even Imorren be able to cope with this?

And, if she couldn't, would they be able to kill him?

A deep chill of denial filled him by way of reply.

Without realizing it, he began to walk a little quicker. They were not far from the Vaskyros now. All he had to do was stay calm and get this abomination there.

Suddenly Gariak grabbed his arm and dragged him into a side street. The other two bodyguards followed his lead and ushered Pinnatte after him. Before either of them could speak the bodyguards were obliging them almost to run.

Encumbered by his robes and unused to any form of vigorous exercise, Rostan was soon suffering. He pressed his hand to his collar and recovered a little. 'What's the matter?' he gasped. Without breaking his pace, Gariak glanced backwards by way of answer.

Rostan turned to see a group of about twenty Tunnellers following them. Most of them were carrying sticks or swords and their manner bore none of the vagueness that usually hallmarked their kind. As soon he turned, there was a cry and the crowd began to run towards them. Something dark flared up within Pinnatte demanding that he reach out and destroy the pursuers, but a long-imbued instinct of flight overrode it.

'This way,' he shouted, turning into a narrow alley. Gariak hesitated for a moment then bundled Rostan after him. Glancing round, he shouted something to the other guards that Pinnatte did not understand. Halfway along the alley, another intercepted it. Reaching the junction, Pinnatte turned to look back. Rostan was some way behind him, being supported by Gariak, but he could not see the other two bodyguards. The crowd had reached the alley and were milling about in some confusion as they struggled to enter it. This was as he had expected, and he knew too that the crowd would soon lose its momentum in this confined space. Almost wholly street thief for the moment, he was considering whether to flee and save himself or to risk helping Rostan and thus perhaps ingratiating himself further with Imorren. He was still debating when the two bodyguards suddenly jumped up. They had been crouching low amongst the rubbish near the entrance.

There was as brief spasm of violent activity – swords rising and falling repeatedly and rapidly, though to Pinnatte, gaping horrified, it seemed they were moving with intolerable slowness. Tangled skeins of . . . something . . . arched through the air, silhouetted against the sunlight beyond. Then high-pitched screams, scarcely human, were echoing frantically along the alley, racing after the two bodyguards. Pinnatte could not move. Mingling with his horror at what he had seen was the darkness within him, rejoicing. This was the way things should be. This was the way they *would* be.

'Which way?' Gariak demanded, as the two bodyguards reached them. Pinnatte started, then moved without thinking. The sight he had just witnessed, dark shadow-play against the bright mouth of the alley, and his response to it, had torn away a veil. Hitherto he had been a passive victim of events, looking only to win wealth for himself in this city where wealth was everything. But he had relished the carnage of the Loose Pit and he had accepted the joining with the creature and wallowed with it in its terrible hunting. Now he saw that there had been throughout, some small part of him which rebelled against this metamorphosis. A frail green shoot amid the blood mire of a battlefield. It began to bloom now, though a gale of excuses bowed it low: the changes were beyond his control, he must tread this path to reach his chosen goal, the events were happening anyway, why should he not benefit from them? Yet they did not destroy it. And now the last excuse, the faintest but the most persistent – that perhaps none of the events had been truly real, but had existed merely in his imagination – had been hacked away by the slashing swords of the bodyguards. The awful cries of the wounded and dying had wrapped themselves around him. These were *real* people, inadequate people for the most part, driven from their sorry homes by a monster which he, above all, knew could not be faced by *anyone*. For whatever reason they had been following Rostan, escape from them was a comparatively simple matter and the slaughter had been as unnecessary as it was brutal.

It sickened him. He did not want this! The realization was vivid and absolute. Wealth and power he wanted, yes, but not at this price.

It must be so. It will be so.

The rebuttal filled him. Its certainty was terrifying and, briefly, as he ran along the alley, Pinnatte thought he was going to vomit under its impact. Tears filled his eyes, blurring his vision.

How could he oppose such an urging? How could he oppose something that came so clearly from within himself? He clung to a simple inner cry of, 'No!'

'Which way?'

Gariak's cry reached through his turmoil. They had reached another junction. He picked another alley at random. He had no idea where he was, but he knew the crowd would not be following them now, and they would come to safety eventually.

'Wait. I need a moment.'

It was Rostan. He was leaning on Gariak and was breathing heavily. Pinnatte looked at him. He rubbed the mark on the back of his hand. It was hurting him now. All that had happened to him had happened since his encounter with this wretched, gasping man. It came to him clearly. He was the victim of one of the experiments that the Kyrosdyn were notorious for and, notwithstanding Barran's protection, he would not emerge from the Vaskyros once he entered it. A terrible anger welled up inside him.

Rostan looked up sharply, his eyes wide with fear. Pinnatte's anger became something else at the sight, something ancient and predatory. It drew in Rostan's fear like the scent of a luscious bloom. When it breathed out, the Power went with it and Rostan was hurled twenty paces along the alley to crash into a wall. He had scarcely time to form the word, 'No,' still less use his own Power to defend himself, between sensing Pinnatte's intent and dying.

Gariak and the other bodyguards stared from Pinnatte to Rostan, stunned by what they had witnessed, but seeing no cause. Gariak's hand hovered about his sword-hilt for a moment then he extended both hands in hesitant surrender and began cautiously backing away. The others joined him.

Pinnatte remembered the hand that had pushed his head under the water, and the Tunnellers who had been so casually and callously slaughtered.

It was the merest wave of his hand that brought down a section of wall and crushed the three offenders.

As he studied the results of his endeavour, a slight noise behind him made him turn.

Emerging from a basement doorway, eyes bright yellow even in the dull light of the alley, was the Serwulf.

Chapter 29

As the noise reached them, Atlon and Heirn stopped and listened. Dvolci ran up the road and disappeared into the grassy verge fringing the rocky outcrop that marked the end of the monotonous houses. Atlon signalled Heirn to remain where he was. After a little while, there was a low whistle.

'Come on,' Atlon said, setting off again up the slope.

Dvolci was standing in the middle of the road when they reached him. 'Not good,' he said.

Just beyond the rocky outcrop, the road petered out abruptly and untidily into a narrow path which vanished into a jumble of rocks that skirted the dominating wall of the Vaskyros. Atlon had anticipated some semblance of a panorama of the city, but he was disappointed again as the rocks obscured his view. Nor was there any sign of a crowd, though the noise was still all about them, echoing off the rocks and the great wall which curved in a contour of its own around the hillside.

'Further round,' Dvolci said, answering Atlon's question before it was asked. 'The road starts again. This path will take you.' And he was gone again.

The path followed the line of the wall and, as Dvolci had said, brought the two men quite quickly to the ragged end of another road, which had obviously once been part of the one they had just left. This time however, there were no ranks of dismal houses to greet them, but a steep rocky slope on one side, the bottom of which was out of sight.

Atlon half-ran, half-walked down the road, fearful about what he would see when he found the source of the noise. The first bend revealed it to him, bringing him to the top of an incline which overlooked the square in front of the Vaskyros. Though a few traders' stands and wagons added random splashes of colour to the scene, the predominant impression was of a dull, seething greyness, for the square was full of Tunnellers.

Heirn drew in an alarmed breath. 'Well, good idea or not, you'll not be getting into the Vaskyros while this lot's here,' he said.

Atlon did not reply immediately. He was looking around the square. Though the crowd was noisy, it seemed to have no single intent. Little groups formed and dispersed at random, like eddies in a boisterous stream, and more Tunnellers were arriving along every street that he could see. The first sound of the crowd that he had heard had alarmed him, but the sight redoubled his concern.

'Straw waiting for the flame,' he said.

Heirn looked distressed at the image. It had not been addressed to him, but it chimed uncomfortably with his own thoughts.

'This is not a good place to be,' he said.

Atlon nodded, but replied enigmatically, 'There's nowhere else.'

Heirn took his arm urgently. 'I don't know what they think they're going to do, but there's going to be bad trouble down there, and soon. Trust me, we should get well away before it starts. Trouble here has a habit of spreading very quickly.'

Atlon stepped forward a little, drawing the big man after him. To the right he could see the entrance to the Vaskyros. The wall swept up over it in a graceful curve which was markedly at odds with the barbed and thorny structure of the Vaskyros tearing at the sky behind it. At its crown was a carved head, its mouth gaping, its eyes staring. From where he stood, Atlon could not decide whether it was human or animal, but, whatever it was, it disturbed him even more than had the face above the entrance to the Jyolan. Two great sloping abutments jutted out on either side of the gate and curved round into the square like embracing arms.

Again taking Heirn with him, he moved forward until he could see through the entrance. 'The gate's open,' he said, in considerable surprise.

'I've never seen it closed,' Heirn replied off-handedly. He was still watching the crowd anxiously. 'I'm not even sure it does. There's a constant stream of traffic in and out of the place. They've been building and rebuilding bits of it for years now. I wouldn't be surprised if the gates hinges were rusted solid. Besides,' he looked at Atlon significantly, 'no one wants to sneak into the Vaskyros. No one goes in there at all, unless they have to. Apart from the reputation of the Kyrosdyn, they've got some of the nastiest mercenaries in the city protecting them.'

'Like those,' Atlon said, pointing. Heirn followed his extended arm.

Across the front of the entrance, joining the two abutments, were several rows of grim-faced individuals dressed in what Atlon took to be chainmail. The first two rows were standing shoulder to shoulder with rectangular shields held in front of them, keeping the so far unresisting crowd at bay. Behind them was a clear area back to the open gateway where stood several other rows of guards, disappearing into the Vaskyros. These were carrying long pikes topped with narrow, slightly curved blades.

'Yes,' Heirn said, 'exactly so. Come on, let's get away from here. We can come back some other time.'

Atlon's posture rejected the advice. His voice was flat and cold. 'I've seen their like before. If that crowd starts to move forward, the shield line will retreat and those pikes will come down in staggered rows. Whoever's at the front of the crowd will find themselves being pushed on to a serrated rows of points and edges. It's a fearful thing.'

'I . . . I suppose so,' Heirn stammered unhappily. 'It's not something I've ever thought about.' Then, despite himself, he was drawn into Atlon's tactical analysis. 'You could duck underneath, I suppose.'

'Those guards look as if they've done this before. If they really know what they're doing, the back ranks will attend to anyone who tries that,' Atlon rebutted. 'And I'd be surprised if they haven't deployed archers. Probably up on the wall somewhere.' He bared his teeth and clenched his fists. 'Look at the way the square's filling up. People are going to be killed here if something isn't done soon to disperse them peacefully.'

Heirn looked at him, wondering again what sights this stranger had seen, what terrible lessons he had learned, before he came to

Arash-Felloren. 'Maybe,' he said, trying to pull his mind away from Atlon's cruel assessment. Traditional city opinions found voice in justification. 'But everyone's got a right – a duty – to defend himself and his property – even the Kyrosdyn – especially against a mob. You can't ask anyone else to do it, can you? And you went for that man who meddled with your horse. Those people might be Tunnellers, but they know this – everyone does. If they choose to attack the Vaskyros that's their problem.' His voice faltered as he recalled that it was probably Atlon's remarks that had brought the Tunnellers here. Atlon spoke the reproach.

'They're here because of me,' he said. 'I can't walk away. And whatever happens, I've still got to get into that place and find out what they've done to Pinnatte.' His jawline stiffened and he took a deep breath. He could scarcely bear to listen to what he was saying. 'If I don't do that, then far more than these people here are going to be hurt.'

Heirn could see his distress, but the sight of the crowd below left him feeling impotent. He had a momentary vision of Atlon, on his fine horse, galloping across his own land – wide and empty and lush underneath a vast, sunlit cloudscape. Arash-Felloren must be an appalling place to him. The image renewed his sense of protection to this stranger.

'Have you ever been in a crowd like that?' he asked. He did not wait for an answer. 'It's something you don't want to do twice. It closes around you so you can hardly breathe. You're nothing. You go where it goes. People you're holding get torn away from you, no matter how tight your grip. If you stumble, it walks over you. And it can get into your head. Make you do things you—' He stopped, disturbed for a moment, then dragged his attention back to his charge. 'You won't even be able to walk through that crowd. And if you could, how would you get past those guards?'

'I need your help, Heirn, not this,' Atlon said tensely. 'Is there any other way into this place?'

Heirn shook his head. 'Not that I know of.'

Dvolci reappeared. 'I've got to go down into that lot,' Atlon said to him. 'Do you want to come or would you rather stay with Heirn and keep an eye on me from up here?'

Heirn intervened. 'If I can't stop you doing this, I can at least come with you. I've more chance than you of keeping us both safe.'

Atlon shook his head. 'Our arrangement was that you keep away from me once we reached the Vaskyros.' He became very serious. 'Nothing's changed that. It's imperative that if anything happens to me, you help Dvolci get back home.' He raised a hand to forestall Heirn's opposition. 'This isn't open to debate,' he said. 'You might well be better equipped than me to survive that crowd, but if I get in trouble with the Kyrosdyn, you won't survive what *they* can do, and I won't be able to protect you. You might even burden me. Please stay here.' The combination of authority and pleading in his voice left Heirn no reply.

Atlon turned to Dvolci, who was scratching himself vigorously. 'So many human beings in one place isn't a happy prospect, but I'll come with you. I'd be interested to find out what these Kyrosdyn have been up to.' He trotted off.

Atlon held out his hand to Heirn. 'Thank you for everything you've done for us, Heirn. I'm sorry I've brought trouble into your life. Don't run any risks by staying here. We'll find our own way back to the forge. I think I can remember it.'

Heirn put on as brave a front as he could manage. 'I'll be waiting for you,' he said. 'You've still got some leatherwork to finish as I recall.'

Halfway down the hill, Atlon turned to give Heirn a final wave. The blacksmith had gone.

'We'd have been lost without him,' Dvolci said, clambering into Atlon's pack.

'You don't think he's going to do anything foolish, do you?' Atlon asked anxiously.

'I don't see why he shouldn't,' Dvolci replied. 'We are.'

Atlon glowered at him. 'No,' Dvolci agreed reluctantly. 'He's probably just keeping a crafty eye on us somewhere. Don't worry. I think he understands how important it is that he be there if needed.' Atlon seemed less certain, but made no reply.

Since they had first come in sight of the square, more Tunnellers had been arriving. The isolated eddies of people had gradually faded away and become broader, slower sweeps as the density of the crowd grew. Waves of movement rippled across them, giving the square the eerie appearance of a field of grey corn swaying in the wind.

Suddenly a faint sound caught Atlon's attention through the general hubbub. A sound that he had been attuned to listen for since birth. 'Muster,' he muttered to himself. It was an echo of the much louder cry that rang in his head and which took him to his own land again. He clambered on to a rock to improve his view and saw the horsemen almost immediately. They were spread out across the full width of the broad avenue that was the main entrance to the square, and there were at least six ranks.

'Weartans,' Dvolci said. 'This must be what Heirn was expecting.'

Atlon watched them for a moment, then shook his head in disbelief. 'What are they doing? They're just pushing people into the square. They should come through to the gate in slow file and then form ranks to ease them out. They're going to provoke trouble, not prevent it.' His first reaction was to run down into the crowd to warn them, but the futility of such an act was immediately apparent. The effect of the approaching horsemen was already being felt. The gentle cornfield rippling was becoming erratic, and angry cries were beginning to be heard above the general din. His practised ears noted a change in the pace of the horses. Heirn's comments about the Weartans enjoying such work came back to him.

'This is going to be awful,' Dvolci said, voicing Atlon's own thoughts. Both of them were trembling.

Even as Dvolci spoke, Atlon saw Weartan batons begin rising and falling. Then, horrifically, the whole crowd seemed to move away from the Weartans as one, surging like a great tide against the walls of the Vaskyros. The line of guards in front of the open gate buckled under the impact, but, with the assistance of the second rank, held. Then those in the second rank were lunging and striking at the crowd with batons wherever space permitted. The noise of the crowd became one furious roar, so loud that Atlon felt it encasing him, crushing him.

The onslaught of the guards on the crowd made those at the front falter momentarily and, very swiftly, the shield guards retreated and passed back through the ranks of the pikemen. It was a practised and well-timed manoeuvre, as was that which brought down the pikes to form the staggered rows of points which but moments previously Atlon had described to Heirn. Despite himself, Atlon thrilled at the sight – it had the dark beauty that has always lured men to war before betraying and breaking them.

A fearful dance began as the crowd became a thing of its own, caught between the advancing Weartans, batons flailing wildly and indiscriminately, the unyielding wall of the Vaskyros, and the murderous points of the pike line. Atlon watched in silence, a numbness creeping over him as he saw the consequences of his remarks to the Tunnellers unfold. Somewhere he heard himself saying that he could not have foreseen these consequences, that Arash-Felloren being what it was, this conflict would have happened somewhere, anyway, but this gave him little consolation.

He could see people trying to flee along the narrower streets that opened into the square, but they were moving against the continuing inflow of new arrivals and there was swirling congestion at the head of each street that allowed too few to escape to ease the increasing press in the square.

He drove his fingernails into his palms as he saw bodies beginning to accumulate in front of the pikes. Looking up, he saw that there were indeed archers on the top of the wall, though they were not shooting yet. Such Tunnellers who were reasoning as Heirn had, and trying to escape underneath the pikes, were being caught by the rear ranks as he had predicted. And had any succeeded in passing through unscathed, the shield guards were reformed and waiting.

Atlon found himself walking towards the fray. He clung desperately to what he had told Heirn. If he did not find out what had happened to Pinnatte, then far more than the people massed in this square were going to die. That was still true and he must not let it slip away in the pain of the moment.

As he moved down the uneven old road, he encountered Tunnellers running up it. Men, women, children – some bleeding, some leaning on their companions, some hysterical, some raging, but all of them with glazed, shocked eyes.

'Go along the path at the top and down the other side,' he shouted. None of them gave any sign of hearing him and the sound of the urgent helpfulness in his voice seemed to mock him.

But he had no time for self-reproach. More and more Tunnellers were escaping from the square along the road which narrowed drastically at the bottom where once again houses lined the left-hand side. None of the escapees paid any heed to Atlon, and he was constantly obliged to dodge and weave to avoid being knocked over by their relentless progress.

Then there was a strange, dreamlike lull. The road turned and dipped sharply, taking him out of sight of the square. The terrible clamour faded and, for some reason, there was a halt to the fleeing Tunnellers. In the unnatural silence, Atlon was drawn to look up at the wall of the Vaskyros. Its looming dominance overawed him. He was nothing. This was surely His place. What had possessed him to think that he could storm such a fortress single-handed?

'Never underestimate the value of the small deed.' The thought made him start. It was a remark often quoted within the Order, a matter of both commonsense and the sternly tested logic that guided their studies into the nature and use of, amongst many other things, the Power. Consequences rippled outwards, for ever, and to unforeseeable ends. An intuitive corollary – an article of faith held by many in the Order, though by no means universally – was that good deeds generally produced good consequences, while bad ones generally produced bad consequences.

Then the chaos of Arash-Felloren was about him again. Tunnellers were running up the road, forcing him to take shelter in the doorway of a house, and the noise was even louder. It was also different. As the initial rush died away, he left the doorway and battled his way through the crowd until he could see the square again. For a moment he could not understand what had happened, then he saw that the line of pikemen was gone. The pressure from those Tunnellers escaping the advancing Weartans had pushed their compatriots relentlessly into the cruel edges and points and finally overwhelmed them. Now, where the pikemen had stood, there was a mêlée of screaming people surging through the gateway and into the Vaskyros. It was a fearful sight and Atlon could only watch it in mounting horror.

A swift movement at the edge of his vision made him look up. It was an arrow streaking into the crowd. Another followed it. The archers on top of the wall were shooting at random. He could feel the panic of the Kyrosdyn guards. Whatever discipline they had seemed to have evaporated utterly, but that merely heightened his anger at this senseless act. His anger was as nothing compared with that of the crowd surging through the gate, and even as he watched, a high-pitched scream gave him the measure of this as one of the archers crashed on to the rocks at the base of the wall. The sight and the sickening sound reached him through the din and jolted him back to his present needs.

Looking round he saw that the Weartans had reached the square and were fanning out into a ragged line. He could not forebear sneering. 'I've seen cows ridden better,' he muttered.

'At least they've stopped herding the Tunnellers,' Dvolci said. 'Presumably someone's had the wit to see what they've actually achieved.'

With the end of the Weartans' advance and the clearing of the gateway, the press in the square had eased a little and fewer Tunnellers were now running past Atlon. Indeed, some of them were beginning to do as Atlon was – watch. Then they were running back down the road towards the crowd.

Atlon gritted his teeth. 'Go back to Heirn,' he said to Dvolci. 'I'm going to try to get in.'

High on a narrow balcony, Imorren looked down on the developing conflict in the square. With each movement of the crowd she could sense years of carefully garnered control slipping relentlessly away from her. How could such a thing have come about so suddenly? An actual assault on the Vaskyros was beyond the memory of anyone living, and when one had occurred in the past, it had invariably been preceded by a long period of growing tension between the Kyrosdyn and some other power in the city. But this . . .! And from Tunnellers! It made no sense.

Yet her anger was tempered by other considerations. That it was the Tunnellers acting thus, indicated that it was not part of some more serious plot she had failed to detect. And too, Tunnellers generally regarded as being less than human, whatever justification they had to offer would not be listened to, and whatever action the Kyrosdyn took against them would go substantially unremarked. Also, in the confusion that must inevitably follow such an event, she, as the injured party and by virtue of her talent for such matters, would be better placed than anyone else to make political gains. She would certainly extract a great deal from the Prefect about the Weartans whose conduct had provoked the breach of the main gate.

For a moment she allowed herself to relax and savour the bloodletting that was going on far below. There was little danger that the Tunnellers would get too far into the Vaskyros. It was a complex building seemingly designed for dealing with such an assault, and she had kept under constant review the plans that the Kyrosdyn had always had for its defence: plans which assumed the attackers would be professional soldiers, not a mindless mob. It was irksome that good guards would be lost in the fray, but Arash-Felloren was never short of such people and it would be a salutary lesson in the virtues of discipline for those who survived.

A crash brought her out of her reverie. She leaned forward to see that a large scaffolding tower had been knocked over by the crowd surging around the outer courtyard. Several people had been hurt. Her anger returned, or rather her irritation – her usual mood when dealing with anything that involved the builders and artisans who were needed to service her plans for the Vaskyros. She would have to intervene before even more damage was done.

'Where is the Highest?' she demanded as she strode into the Audience Hall. The Acolytes and Novices abandoned the windows around which they were gathered and, after some brief but frantic confusion, lined up in front of her, their heads bowed.

'He's in the city, Ailad,' one of the replied. 'With Gariak and two other guards.'

Imorren nodded. That was not good. Whatever had disturbed the Tunnellers it would be naive to imagine that their anger would be confined to the Vaskyros. And most of the Lesser and Higher

406

Brothers were out looking for the Anointed. There was no saying what the consequence would be if one of them were attacked and had to use the Power to defend himself.

Damn those Weartans!

This must be ended, and quickly.

'Find the Captain of the Guards,' she snapped. 'And have one of the Tunnellers brought to me immediately.

Imorren made her way to the seat from which she conducted much of the Order's daily business. She knew that the performance of so simple and familiar an act would reassure the others. She looked at them and allowed herself a slight smile, as if the turmoil surrounding the building was nothing unusual and not worthy of any other acknowledgement. With a kindly gesture she singled out four Acolytes, and said quietly, 'Stay with me. I will need you to carry messages. The rest of you continue with your normal duties.'

They had scarcely left when a Novice returned with the Captain of the Guards dragging a bloodstained figure. Imorren beckoned him forward and motioned the others away, out of earshot.

'I was bringing this one to you, Ailad,' the Captain said, bowing. He kicked the Tunneller brutally behind the knees, making him drop to the floor. A powerful hand bent the man's head forward. 'Show some respect for the Ailad, worm.'

Imorren had read the Tunneller's face as soon as he came into the hall. Stupidity riven with terror. Pushed too far, he probably wouldn't be able to remember his own name, still less explain what was happening.

'Gently, Captain,' she said. Her tone was mildly reproachful but her look made the Captain step back smartly. 'These people obviously have some serious complaint to attack us like this. We must hear it.' She bent forward. 'Please, look at me, sir,' she said coaxingly. 'No one's going to hurt you. You're safe here. You must tell us what's brought all this about.'

Slowly the man looked up. As he met her gaze, she smiled radiantly and gave an encouraging nod. It was a look that had destroyed the will of sterner men than the wretch now before her. 'Why are your people doing this?' she asked, her voice soft and a little tremulous.

The man, transfixed, did not appear to hear. The Captain raised a hand to strike him but a gesture from Imorren stopped him. She repeated the question, adding, 'We've done you no wrong, surely? You must tell me what's happened so that we can talk about it properly. People are being terribly hurt. Do you understand me?'

The man licked his lips several times, then swallowed and nodded. 'It's that thing – that animal – whatever it is,' he whispered hoarsely. 'The one you brought up from the caves for the Pit.' He began to plead. 'It's killing everyone. Just killing them. On and on. It . . .'

Imorren had heard enough. Her smile vanished and she was again cold-faced and upright in the chair. The man reached out to her. 'Ailad . . .' He fell suddenly silent and began clawing at his throat and gasping, as though there was a band tightening about it. The four watching Acolytes each took an instinctive pace backwards, as did the Captain. Though she had given no outward sign, they knew she was using the Power against the man.

Imorren was satisfied. The actions of the Tunnellers were now clear to her. She even conceded that the assault was probably her own fault. Flush from the slaughter in the Loose Pit and the contact she had had with the Anointed at the Jyolan, she had sent the creature to feed. But she had forgotten its true nature, the nature that He had so assiduously bred into its original sires countless millennia ago. Forgotten or underestimated. It seemed that its appetite for the terror it caused in its victims was truly without limit, as it was meant to be. Unlike any other animal, it would kill and kill without pause unless controlled.

A noise disturbed her reflection. It was the Tunneller. He was on all fours, retching as he struggled for breath. Imorren cast an irritable glance at him, then as suddenly as he had been attacked, he was released. He collapsed on to the floor, gasping and twitching. 'Get him out of here,' she said to the Acolytes. 'Take him to the dungeons.'

As the man was being dragged from the hall, Imorren moved to the window. It overlooked the main courtyard which was filled with struggling Tunnellers. 'Your men can hold the second gate?' she asked the Captain without looking at him.

'No,' the Captain replied. 'We lost several in that first rush, and we've got too many out in the city on personal escort duties. But we'll hold the third. They'll soon get tired of dying in front of that, then we can start getting them out without too much trouble.'

'They'll do a great deal of damage if they get past the second gate.'

The Captain could read nothing in her tone or her posture. That was normal. He put his faith in the estimate of his worth to her that he had formed long ago – she needed the benefit of his fighting experience. That and that alone, clearly stated. 'We can't hold it,' he confirmed unhesitatingly. 'There's too many of them and too many ladders and platforms lying about there. If we make a stand, they'll outflank us and move directly to the third gate.'

Imorren nodded. 'I have complete faith in your judgement, Captain. Do what you must to get rid of them. Keep me advised of events.' She turned and looked at him. He met her grey-eyed gaze. Like most in the higher ranks of the guards, he was tied to her by bonds he could not begin to understand. 'Take as many prisoners as you can. We'll have need of them later.' The Captain bowed and left.

Imorren looked down into the courtyard again. Who'd have thought the Tunnellers had such spirit in them? Suddenly, she felt good. The damage that they might do would be an inconvenience, no more. In return she would have captives whose life energies could be taken without question. No one was going to ask questions about missing Tunnellers. And the creature – the Serwulf – His blessed harbinger – was indeed as powerful as the old writings had said. What an asset it would be. It could perhaps even be used to track down others of its own kind – for there must be others for this one to have survived. A pack could be bred. They would be trained and ready for when He returned, perhaps even improved upon, if that were not a heresy. Then an idea came to her. It amused her. If the creature had driven these people from the tunnels, then it could be used to drive them back – or at least out of the Vaskyros. She would enjoy watching it work, and in the panic it induced there would surely be many wounded to be taken as prisoners. She must find the Keeper and have it recalled.

Faint echoes of the conflict outside followed Imorren as she descended into the lower depths, but she scarcely heard them. Her mind had leapt beyond the disturbances of the present and was vaulting into a new future.

She came eventually to the cages and stalls which held the strange and tortured creatures that the Kyrosdyn had bred or captured in the depths, for experiments and use in the Loose Pits. As it always did, the feral stink pervading the place roused her, touching the deep hatreds that sustained her. She bared her teeth in response to the cacophony of barkings and mewlings that greeted her, but walked on without pause.

Coming to a small circular cellar, she called out, 'Keeper!'

Her voice echoed several times, and the lamps lighting the place seemed to waver at its touch, but there was no reply. Puzzled, she looked into a small antechamber which served as the Keeper's living quarters. It was empty.

Slowly she began walking around the circular room. Except when at the Loose Pits or guiding an expedition into the caves, the Keeper never strayed from either here or the animal pens. A rare survivor of an early experiment with the Anointing, he had emerged from it silent and enigmatic, but with a strange ability to control the Kyrosdyn's grotesque menagerie. He it was who had found the Serwulf. It had always quailed before Imorren's power, but it responded to the Keeper like a fawning dog. Though she would not have admitted it, his dark presence was almost as solid and reliable as the memory of the One she served. He was an unknown pillar in her life. Even less would she have admitted that she had an affection for him, but that he was not here disturbed her.

Then she found him. He was lying across the threshold of one of the doors that led down into the tunnels. His eyes were wide with surprise when they met hers. Normally focused on some place that he alone could see, their expression startled her more than the gaping wound across his body which had killed him.

She knelt beside him, partly out of some long-forgotten habit of concern and partly to avoid acknowledging to herself that her legs were buckling. The scent of the Serwulf rose up from the Keeper's body, filling her with those overpowering responses that only scents can evoke, and darkness and pain closed over her. Not since the news of His cruel defeat had she felt anything like such distress.

She remained thus for a long time, giving no outward sign of her pain other than her hand resting on the Keeper's – cold now. It was as well none of her many enemies came upon her, so defenceless was she.

But the old shadows of her former self could not survive in the cold glare of the woman she had become, and gradually they faded. As she recovered, she crushed the remains of her feelings and turned to matters of the present. The death of the Keeper had implications far more serious than a crowd of Tunnellers assailing the Vaskyros, though it took her longer than usual to order her thoughts.

Then, a terrible realization exploded in her mind, and threatened to take her legs from under her again. If the Serwulf had killed the Keeper, it must have found a new master. And only one could fulfil such a role. *It had joined itself to the Anointed.*

Long-laid plans and schemes wavered like reflections in a wind-stirred pool under the impact of this revelation. The Anointed was to have opened the Ways by which He would return, but what had been created was an abomination, a thing that should not be, a thing unfettered that both used the Power and opened the Ways. And now it was joined to a Serwulf rapidly coming to the height of its own powers. Who could say what awful Ways would be opened across the worlds, what chaos and anarchy would come from this fearful coupling?

And who was there who could stop it?

Chapter 30

Heirn had been horrifically correct, Atlon freely conceded. He had followed a small group of Tunnellers returning to the square and had almost immediately been sucked into the crowd's fearful tide. A lifetime of riding enabled him to keep his balance and to avoid the temptation of opposing the forces that were moving him, but to be so out of control had frightened him badly. Far worse however, had been the panic and mindless anger of the crowd which threatened constantly to overwhelm and possess him. That had been truly terrifying.

He was swept through the main gate to find himself in a spacious courtyard. Builders' materials and equipment lay all about and those Tunnellers who were not already armed were improvising with whatever they could lay their hands on. The mood of the crowd was becoming increasingly violent.

The crush lessened in the wider space, but still Atlon could do no other than yield to the crowd's momentum. He was drawn on through a second open gate. Though there was no opposition there was a ripple in the crowd as bodies were tripped over, telling Atlon that there had been some fierce fighting before the gate was yielded. When he himself nearly stumbled, it was over the body of a guard, though such others as he encountered were all Tunnellers.

Then, like a wave striking a rocky shore, the rush foundered. Unlike the first gate, the second opened on to a semi-circular court which led the crowd into a confusing array of covered passages, the collective will of the crowd was broken also, with individual voices, shrill and forced, being more clearly heard. Several of the passages swung round, returning to the courtyard, causing groups to collide in the near darkness and resulting in many Tunnellers

413

being injured by their own kind in the consequent fighting. Others were joined together confusingly, causing similar problems, while a few became increasingly narrow and dark, eventually bringing all progress to a halt and forcing people to turn about – very much nervous individuals again.

When eventually, Atlon was carried through to the far side of this maze, he found himself in a narrow, gloomy chasm, bounded claustrophobically by high, menacing walls. The pressure behind carried him across to the inner wall, where he managed to manoeuvre himself into the lee of one of the buttresses that protruded from it at regular intervals. He slumped against the wall and, gasping for breath, closed his eyes for a moment. Immediately, disorienting impressions swept over him. This was a terrible place he had come to. The wall at his back was older by far than the outer one, and an ancient malignity pervaded it. He could feel its roots plunging deep into the rocky heart of the hills over which, much later, Arash-Felloren had sprawled. They went far below anything that was needed for stability or for the frustrating of burrowing sappers. The image reversed itself. It seemed to tell him that the wall had not been thrust into the rock, but drawn up from it.

A spasm of vertigo jerked open his eyes. He shook his head to clear the images from his mind. This was neither the time nor the place to ponder such things, however vivid and powerful. He looked up at the narrow strip of bleached sky high above. It was perforated by the black silhouettes of carved creatures jutting out from both walls. Though he had never seen such a place before, he had studied warfare enough to know what it was. It was a killing ground. Anything could happen here. It could be flooded, hot coals and blazing oils could be dropped into it, archers and spearmen could make sport from high windows and balconies, wild animals could be released into it. And anyone who retreated into the passages would find them sealed or filled with cruel-eyed soldiers and waiting steel. Whatever it had been once – and that was no thing of light – the Vaskyros had become, and was now, a fortress designed to keep out the most determined of enemies.

Many fears began to make themselves felt. Underscoring all of them was the dark nature of the whole place, but more pressing were those concerned with his immediate fate. Surely even in Arash-Felloren a massacre such as he had just envisaged would not go unremarked? But little he had learned so far about the city made him confident of a hopeful reply to this. Coming in the wake of this was another fear. So far he had managed to keep himself safe by his own wits, but if some atrocity threatened, then he would surely use the Power to protect himself, if only out of instinct – and who could say what the effects of that would be in this place?

He looked around for inspiration. Buttresses lined both walls and, between them, as well as the exits from the maze of passages, there were many small doors. Groups of Tunnellers were beating loudly on some of them, but they were made of iron and set deep into the walls in such a way that no bars could be inserted nor leverage applied. He noted too that he was now near the edge of the crowd. Most of the Tunnellers had moved some distance away. Stepping out from his shelter, he saw that they were gathered about a large gate in the inner wall. Some of them had managed to drag a substantial baulk of timber through the passages and were using it as a battering ram. It made a resounding noise as it struck the gate, and a great deal of shouting accompanied each blow, but there was too little space to move it properly, and their effort was as fruitless as those who were banging on the doors.

And all the time, more Tunnellers were pouring into the narrow space.

Increasingly concerned about the outcome of this venture, Atlon decided that he would be best advised to move still further away from the crowd and await events. He slipped back behind the buttress. As he did so, he saw one of the doors in the wall opposite open. Before he realized what was happening, four guards had rushed out, seized the two nearest Tunnellers, and dragged them back through the door. Their action was so swift and silent that no one other than Atlon noticed what had happened.

Shaken by the speed and determination of the seizure, Atlon instinctively took a step backwards, into one of the deep-set doorways. Just as he realized where he was, a hand closed over his mouth. The gloomy daylight of the chasm abruptly became darkness as he was dragged roughly through the door – and then he was aware only of violent hands moving him and keeping him too unbalanced to resist. Finally there was a jarring impact as he was slammed into a wall.

'Keep quiet, Tunneller, and don't move or you'll get this.'

Atlon's eyes slowly focused on a mailed fist immediately in front of his face. He nodded. The fist moved away but its owner still kept a hand firmly against his chest, ensuring that the command would be obeyed. Atlon risked a quick glance to each side. He was in a dimly lit passageway busy with guards running to and fro. The sound of the crowd outside was barely perceptible, though occasionally there was a dull thud which Atlon identified as the improvised battering ram.

'Another one here,' his captor called out. There was a shouted exchange full of both anger and cruel laughter, then Atlon was being kicked and prodded along the passage. He emerged into a room in the middle of which stood a group of sullen Tunnellers. Several guards were lounging around the walls, watching them indifferently.

Despite his confusion and alarm he wondered why the guards were taking prisoners. The hand that had clamped across his mouth could just as well have cut his throat for all he had been able to do about it. Further, there was no real need for anyone to venture beyond the wall. From what he had seen, the assault was losing its impetus and it was only a matter of time before it was completely spent and the crowd dissipated naturally. Ironically it made him feel easier. Perhaps somewhere in this benighted city there *was* some legal authority and individuals were being seized to be taken before it as token ringleaders.

A powerful hand propelled him into the Tunnellers, ending his conjecture. As he recovered his balance he became aware of a sudden angry commotion amongst the guards.

'You idiot, that one's still got a sword!'

Seeing two guards suddenly moving towards him, weapons drawn, Atlon raised his hands and, with as much authority as he could muster, voiced the excuse he had prepared for this or some similar contingency.

416

'I'm not one of these people. I got caught up in the crowd. I'm a traveller here to see the Ailad on a crystal matter.'

The advancing guards paused but did not lower their swords. A third guard stepped between them and looked at Atlon closer. His manner, as much as the different insignia on his uniform, identified him as an officer of some kind.

'Well, you don't look like a Tunneller, for sure,' he conceded eventually. 'Watch him,' he said to the guards, then to Atlon, 'Keep your hands up.' The swords came forward with him as he intensified his scrutiny. 'Not at all like a Tunneller, now I look at you. Where are you from?'

'From a land to the north. Far away.'

'Outlander?' Surprise and suspicion.

'If that's what you call people from outside the city, yes.'

'What are you doing with this lot?'

Atlon met the officer's gaze squarely and risked a hint of anger and a lie. 'I told you. I got caught up in the crowd and couldn't get away. It was dreadful. Is this a regular thing here? My companions were going to the Prefect's Palace. Do you think this trouble has spread there as well?'

The officer faltered slightly, quickly disguising the response by half-turning to one of the guards. 'Fetch the Captain.'

'My arms are getting stiff, may I put them down?'

A combination of politeness and command in this request unsettled the officer further. 'Yes,' he replied curtly, after a brief hesitation. 'Wait over there.' He indicated a bench at the far end of the room then whispered something to the other guard who immediately moved to accompany Atlon.

In the interval that followed, Atlon took firm control of his breathing and waited as patiently as he could for the trembling in his arms and legs to pass. He knew enough about himself not to argue with this response, even though he did not like it. His body was readying itself for conflict and it was in his best interests to trust it. The trembling would relax him more than any of his formal exercises. Don't be afraid to be afraid, he reminded himself, several times. Look squarely at what you've done. You've committed yourself now. The only steps you can take are forward. He had no

417

desire to face any Kyrosdyn skilled in the use of the Power and aided by crystals, but circumstances had left him no alternative; he must pursue his search into what had happened to Pinnatte and his connection with the Serwulf no matter where it led.

Gradually the trembling faded, seeming to diffuse itself through his entire body.

He was fully in command of himself when the Captain of the Guard arrived. Again, it was the man's demeanour that identified him as he entered the room. As the guard standing next to him jumped to attention, Atlon used the opportunity to stand up confidently and offer his hand.

The Captain's position as protector of the Kyrosdyn made him as much a schemer as most of them, and far more of a diplomat, and habit made him take the hand before he realized fully what he was doing. Seeing his momentary discomposure, Atlon pressed home his advantage. He would have to strike for the centre now. 'Your men rescued me from the crowd, Captain,' he said, with just a hint of being someone used to talking down to senior officers. 'They were a little rough, but it was bravely done and I'm grateful. I'll see that the Ailad hears of it.'

The Captain tried to assess this strange individual but found that he could not. The man was a little dishevelled but he was obviously not a Tunneller and he had a presence which marked him as being above the common crowd. Particularly disturbing however, was the fact that he spoke with an unusual accent – an accent which had hints of the Ailad's own in it. Caution raised its banner.

'The Ailad is busy with many things,' he said, taking Atlon's arm and directing him towards the door. As he reached it, he turned and looked at the Tunnellers gathered in the middle of the room. 'The Ailad will want more than this,' he said to the guards. 'A lot more. See to it.' He signalled one of the guards to follow him.

'Looking for the ringleaders, Captain?' Atlon asked.

The question caught the Captain by surprise and he stammered slightly as he said, 'Yes . . . Of course.' He picked up his previous remark and made to reassert his authority. 'The Ailad's very busy, as you'll appreciate. She cannot give Audiences to everyone who arrives at the gate.'

Atlon plunged on into the darkness. 'I understand, Captain. But perhaps you would tell her that I am here and that we have two serious problems in common – the Serwulf, and a man abroad in the city whose wild Power could destroy us all.'

The Captain stood and stared at him then, still cautious about this stranger's status; he motioned the guard to step back so that he would not hear the rebuke that he was going to have to deliver before they went a single step further. Before he could speak however, Atlon laid a hand on his shoulder.

'Do it,' he said. 'Tell the Ailad I left you no choice.' For an instant, the Captain felt himself pinioned. Something was binding his every muscle. He knew the touch. This man could use the Power. But only the Kyrosdyn could use the Power. Who was . . .?'

Almost immediately he was free, but the shock of the revelation made him stagger. Atlon's hand sustained him.

'Take me to the Ailad now,' he said.

Struggling just to contain his shock, the Captain nodded and motioned Atlon to follow him.

Atlon felt no triumph at what he had done. Indeed, he was trying to feel nothing at all. He knew that he must concentrate absolutely on things as they happened, seeing them for what they were and not allowing his responses to be clouded by what should have been, what might have been, what might yet be, and all other imponderables. Though he had used the Power only slightly and very briefly, it had been a frightening risk and he was well aware that he was forcing events.

The long corridors of the Vaskyros both heartened and repelled him. Pictures, statues, elaborate carvings were everywhere, brilliant crystal designs swept over ceilings, walls and floors. All of them demonstrated workmanship of a high order and, even to Atlon's eyes, they gave a clear measure of the Kyrosdyn's great wealth and power in Arash-Felloren. But the ornate and complex symmetries also distributed him in ways which he could not clearly define. The whole seemed to be the work of a cold and deeply obsessive intellect – at once inhuman and all too human. Abruptly, the images around him became one with his memory of the outside appearance of the Vaskyros. The entire building had a purpose beyond that of a mere dwelling place or citadel for the Kyrosdyn. Just as crystals could draw in and transmute the Power, so too, this edifice had some similar function. The realization shook him profoundly, and though no logic or reason guided him, he knew that the Vaskyros was intended to be the focal point, the key, the bridge to the Ways that would return Him to this world! Knowingly or unknowingly, the Kyrosdyn were working to draw together the scattered shards of His being, spread now across a myriad other worlds.

I must survive this! The inner cry rose out of the turmoil which followed this revelation. No matter what the cost, others must know what was happening here. At the very least he had to get back to Dvolci and tell him what the Kyrosdyn were doing so that the message could be carried home.

For a moment, he was on the battlefield again, shoulder to shoulder with his Brothers, facing the power of His lieutenants. Deflecting it, returning it, to protect the hastily gathered army from certain annihilation, thus leaving the conflict to sword against sword, resolve against resolve, courage against courage.

Scarcely a day passed but what he remembered some part of that scene.

It must never happen again.

He had walked barely two paces in the course of this learning, but he walked in another world now. One of clear needs and desperate urgencies.

Yet he knew too, that albeit strong and vigorous, the Kyrosdyn's intent was only a continuation of the ancient purpose of this building. The events of the present were different. Pinnatte, the Serwulf – the reasons why he was here – did not belong in this scheme. They were an unexpected and unknowable threat – a great boulder loosed finally by the least of breezes and crashing down through forests and villages, threatening all alike.

Against them, both he and the Kyrosdyn had common cause!

'This is the Audience Hall, sir. Would you wait here, please. I must announce you properly.'

The Captain's now-deferential voice cut across Atlon's shock at his conclusion. He gathered himself together sufficiently to manage a nod.

As the Captain leaned forward to open the double doors of the Audience Hall, they opened in front of him, leaving him gaping awkwardly into the face of Imorren.

'Catch as many as you can, then get the rest of that vermin away from here,' she said, walking past him. The tone of her voice and a slight gesture were sufficient to send the Captain running down the corridor, all concerns about Atlon dismissed.

Atlon stared into Imorren's face. She was very beautiful. He had not expected that. He flushed slightly.

Imorren noted the signal, but she sensed his knowledge of the Power also and the shock overrode her judgement. 'Who are you?' she demanded, coldly. Atlon held her gaze and she cursed herself inwardly as she saw the magic slipping from his face. A different tone, a hint in the eyes and this man, whoever he was, would have been hers so easily. Now it must be handled another way.

'My name is Atlon.'

'I mean, who are you? What are you? Where are you from?'

'From the same land as you, by the sound of it.'

Imorren did not respond, though her eyes narrowed. 'Did you think to hide your paltry skill from *me*? In this, of all places?'

Atlon's fear threatened to overwhelm him. This woman was so dangerous. But his resolve sustained him. He must survive. And while he might perish facing this woman, he certainly would if he tried to fly from her.

He reached two conclusions. He must try no deceit against her, she would smell it and it would weaken him. And he must keep her unsettled, emotional. In calmness she would gather resources beyond him for sure. He sneered. 'Do you think to frighten me with yours?'

Imorren's eyes widened. She lifted her hand. Atlon copied the gesture. 'It's possible you might destroy me with the bloated perversion you've made of your gift, but you know nothing of me. Take care. The consequences may not be what you expect.'

Unused for many years to anything other than abject obedience, Imorren's control evaporated. Her eyes blazed and her mouth drew back into a snarl. Atlon felt the hairs on his neck rising, but he braced himself and continued to hold her gaze.

'Who are you!' she hissed.

'Someone looking to undo the harm that you and your minions have let loose. Tell me about Pinnatte before this entire city and perhaps the whole land is engulfed by what you've made of him. Perhaps together we can stop him, and deal with that damned Serwulf you've released.'

His voice was shriller than he had intended, but the content of his words was sufficient to steady Imorren.

'Pinnatte?' she echoed.

'The man you experimented on. The man you've made into something that cannot be. What in the name of sanity were you thinking of?'

'The Anointed,' Imorren whispered softly.

'The abomination.' Atlon's voice was full of a terrible menace now. It jolted Imorren.

'It shouldn't have happened,' she said abruptly defensive. 'Nothing indicated such an outcome.'

'Nothing indicated!' Atlon burst out. 'You've mastered the mathematics of infinities, have you? You can peer into the heart of such wild extremes – such instabilities – and predict? You must have known the risks you ran.'

'They were not this,' Imorren protested, still defensive. 'They were calculated, tested, known. The crystals, the formulations, the pulse meridians, the energy, the manner of the Anointing. All were . . .'

Her voice faded. For a moment, Atlon felt the awful doubts of a fellow student. Someone who had done everything thoroughly and conscientiously and yet found herself facing an outcome that could not be, but which perhaps might have been anticipated had the obsession been less, the vision broader. But how? He could feel her mind rolling endlessly backwards and forwards over everything that had been done and still finding nothing wanting. Despite himself he wanted to reach out and comfort her – tell her that incalculable chance had taken its toll – that it was Pinnatte's injury and Ellyn's simple drawing ointments that had marred her work. He crushed the impulse. The truth would ease Imorren's burden, enable her to still the turmoil of her mind, help make her whole and balanced again – and unbelievably dangerous.

She must remain as she was if he was to stand any chance of dealing with Pinnatte, the Serwulf and her, and surviving.

'Where is he?' he demanded. 'You can tell me what you did while we go to him.'

Imorren did not reply.

'Where is he?' Atlon repeated, fiercely.

Imorren looked at him. Her expression filled him with both terror and pity. He wanted both to embrace her and to draw his sword and strike her down.

'The Serwulf has taken him as its master,' she said simply. 'It is one with him now.'

Silence floated into the glittering corridor. There was not the faintest suggestion of the fighting beyond the walls. Two frightened people stared at one another.

'Where is . . . where are they?' Atlon said, very softly.

Imorren shook her head.

Atlon closed his eyes. What was he doing in this awful place? He should just turn and walk away – let the Vaskyros, the whole of Arash-Felloren burn in whatever damnation Pinnatte and the Serwulf would unleash. It would be an end to the threat that the Kyrosdyn posed, at least.

But it was not an alternative. Countless tiny bonds held him to what he must do. Heirn and the thousands like him, who asked no more than the right to pursue their own lives, seeking their own quiet ways, burdening no one. That they offered this right to others less benignly disposed to their fellows, and then found themselves trapped as helpless observers, was a failing shared by most people. It was its own punishment, but it did not warrant death.

Or whatever else might emerge from the pending chaos.

A face came into his mind. He shivered. It was the head graven into the arch over the entrance to the Jyolan. *He* would surely revel in what was to happen. Mutual killing was His way when all else was lost. Thus had ended the First Coming with the death of the Great Alliance's leader. Was it to be so again, an awful vengeance reaped so many years after He had been dispatched for the second time from this world?

423

Yet it was inconceivable that He could have brought this about. Even if He had had the Power and the insight to do so, He would not. Such a creation could destroy Him along with everything else.

Atlon pondered the image.

Why should that awful face come to him now? What was his deeper knowledge trying to tell him?

He looked at Imorren.

'There are ways to the Jyolan from here other than the streets?'

Imorren nodded uncertainly. 'Through the tunnels.'

'We must go there. That is where they are.'

Chapter 31

Pinnatte sat back and looked at his work. All the mirrors were bright and clear. It had taken him less time than he would have thought, but he seemed to be tireless now. He felt as though he could run and run for ever, down street after endless street, climbing walls, vaulting obstacles, dodging and weaving effortlessly through the thickest of crowds. Why he had cleaned the mirrors he did not know. Why he had come back to the Jyolan he did not know. Perhaps it was some remnant of his commitment to Barran, though he no longer needed the goodwill of such people.

He sought no further explanation. Thoughts, ideas, images were pouring through his mind in such a torrent that he could not pause to pursue any of them. He leapt from conclusion to conclusion – momentary stepping stones in the flood. It was sufficient explanation for his actions that he could choose to follow such whims now. Now he could do anything he wanted. For none would be able to oppose the Power that he could feel relentlessly growing within him, a constant in the swirling confusion.

Such progress he had made these last few days since his fateful contact with Rostan! Had not Barran himself stepped aside, wide-eyed with fear, and then fled, after he had opened the door of the Mirror Room to confront him, with the creature at his side?

As he looked at the mirrors, Pinnatte was taken by the frantic activity in different parts of the Jyolan – it echoed his own inner confusion. The sounds of it too, washed over him for, in his haste, Barran had left the key that operated the grilles by each mirror. Now they were all open, filling the Mirror Room with their clamour.

Barran was gathering armed men for what was obviously to be a determined assault on the Mirror Room. He had tried earlier, sending half a dozen of his men to deal with, 'that crazy street thief and his . . . *dog*' – Pinnatte smiled at the word – but the Serwulf had burst out and killed two of them before they were within a dozen paces of the door and the others had scattered, screaming. They too would have died had not Pinnatte imposed his will on the animal and made it return.

The Serwulf was a bloody streak winding through Pinnatte's confusion. Since it had come to him in the alley, after the death of Rostan and his guards, it had been communicating with him in some way. Some of the images and sensations he was feeling belonged to it, he knew. They were alien, feral and awful, and though he could not understand most of them, two things were dominant. One was a seemingly limitless urge to kill and feed, though on what, Pinnatte could not properly grasp, save that the thought of it chilled him. The other was a cringing fear of Pinnatte himself – or someone, something, that had a shimmering likeness to him. His linkage with the creature both thrilled and disgusted him, but gradually the former was growing in dominance.

Pinnatte watched Barran's efforts with the outward air of a disinterested spectator. Whatever he did, Barran was doomed to failure. If he succeeded in injuring the Serwulf, Pinnatte knew it well enough now to know that the consequences would be appalling. And if it were somehow drawn away, so that he himself was apparently defenceless, they would find that he was not. Indeed, he was beginning to realize that, if he wished, he could scatter this earnest and noisy gathering just by reaching out through the images in front of him. Yet he had some liking for Barran – and what he was doing was . . . interesting.

Men were being dressed in chainmail, and given brief but effective instruction in how to fight from behind a shield wall in the narrow confines of the Jyolan's passages with swords and short spears. There were archers there too. It might have been a long time since Barran had fought on a battlefield, but he had forgotten none of his old ways, and his rage at being so ignominiously dispossessed of this most precious of places, keenly focused his intentions. Pinnatte watched and listened avidly. Oddly, he felt a twinge of disappointment at what he knew would be the outcome.

Such talents deserved better. Very distantly, he thought he heard something inside him saying, 'Keep this man alive,' but such a thing could not be. If Barran opposed him, Barran would die. That was to be the way of things.

Pinnatte pressed his hands to his temples. Thoughts like that weren't his. Barran had helped him – had been honourable to him.

The creature whined uncertainly. Pinnatte snarled at it and it cowered.

He pushed his chair back angrily, wiping his arm across his forehead. As he did so, the many images in the mirrors became one. The many sounds too, became coherent.

He froze.

He was at the heart of the Jyolan.

He *was* the Jyolan!

And the Jyolan was . . .?

For an instant there was a pause in the torrent of thoughts and sensations that were possessing him. A solitary voice pierced the silence. The voice of Pinnatte the street thief. This was not what he wanted! Something terrible was coming. Something that would come from him – through him – pour through him – bringing only destruction.

'No!'

All movement in the mirrors stopped. Even through his pain and fear, Pinnatte sensed the stillness. And he knew its cause. From here, his voice, his *will*, was that of the Jyolan, of Arash-Felloren itself. Nothing could happen that he was not aware of. Nothing could happen that he could not reach out and change.

Then the creature was howling. Its awful lusting voice echoing through the Jyolan and beyond. He felt it spreading over the city, through the tunnels, deep, deep into the ancient caves far below. Calling to its own.

Some part of Pinnatte reached out to deny it. He would not be responsible for the horror that this thing would bring.

The creature turned towards him, its mouth gaping, livid red, its eyes burning yellow like diseased suns. Its desires washed over him, re-awakening those he had felt at the Loose Pit. This was the way things should be. This was the way he *must* be. All power must be his. All people should bow before him.

Still a part of him denied it. Confused images of Ellyn and Atlon and Heirn floated around him. The mirrors became blurred and indistinct. He was only vaguely aware of the creature pacing the room.

And there was escape, clear and hopeful before him!

He was a mote – the least of things – separate from his body, tumbling through a swirling darkness, countless sounds and images all about him, mindless and meaningless, yet significant. He was moving and not moving, aware that he was both here and in the Mirror Room. As was the creature. It was hunting now, but not as it wanted to. It was hunting in another place, another way, because its deep bond with Pinnatte gave it no choice but to obey him.

Then, without transition, he was whole again, looking at a bright sunlit sky marred by gathering thunder clouds. There was a great crowd in the distance. Pennants and flags were waving, ranks of horsemen were galloping around it. It took Pinnatte a little time to realize that he was watching a battle. A movement to one side caught his eye. He turned to see two men in the distance. They were watching an old man, running and looking repeatedly over his shoulder. Something hissed past Pinnatte to thud into the grass by his feet. Looking down, he saw that it was an arrow. He stepped backwards with a cry.

As if he had always been there, he was on a grassy soft-scented hillside in the fading evening sun, strange foot-tapping music all about him. Then he was in the streets of a strange city. Only his thief's footwork kept him from being trampled by the crowd among which he found himself, for his mind was reeling at what was happening. Mainly women and children, he could see they were fleeing in awful panic. And they were crying out in a language he could not understand. Bright lights caught his eye through the dusty air. There were riders in the distance, sunlight flickering from the rising and falling of their swords.

Somewhere he could feel the Serwulf trying to reach him. And there were other animals howling, far away. Wolves, he sensed, though he had never heard wolves howling before. Their song reached out to ease him in some way.

428

An impact jarred him. He had been falling for ever. Faster and faster. And now he had stopped. All that had happened seemed to have taken but a single heartbeat, but now there was a pause. His every instinct held him still and silent. Wherever this place was, he did not belong. *No one* belonged. The sights about him now were not sights that eyes could see. He was aware of worlds within worlds, between worlds, shifting and shimmering in and out of existence, rich with life and dancing to rhythms unknowable. He was aware too of many eyes turned to him. And terrible fear, all around.

For this place, this eerie vantage, could not exist. It stood outside that which was without bounds. His touch had the power to change all things. Yet his least action might disturb this dynamic equilibrium beyond all recovering.

As might perhaps, his inaction.

He dared not move.

There was an awful, lingering moment, in this place where Time did not exist.

Then uproar.

Barran, encouraged by the silence that had followed Pinnatte's cry and the creature's howl, had managed to rouse his men sufficiently to have them storm the Mirror Room.

It was a mistake.

Bursting through the door, the attackers found themselves staring not at one of the dismal rooms typical of the Jyolan, but at a vast and shapeless greyness devoid of all perspective and points of reference, save for the seated figure of Pinnatte watching them from some indeterminate distance.

And the Serwulf.

Which was upon them instantly. Hard fighting men all of them, not one managed a stroke against it, and all died. For a moment the greyness became tinged with red.

A second team of men waiting along the passage, listened hesitantly to their friends screaming and the Serwulf roaring, then turned and fled as the last victim crashed out of the room, his head almost severed. The Serwulf's howl sped them on their way. Barran was sufficiently experienced to know when men could be rallied and when they could not. He made no effort to stop them.

Fury filled him but it could not overcome his terror.

'Let us through.'

The cold voice pierced Barran's silent rage. He spun round to see Imorren and Atlon. Atlon was flushed and a little out of breath from a hasty stumbling journey through the tunnels, but Imorren was as immaculate and calm as ever. Atlon had noticed her hand going to her throat and her wrists at times and knew that she was sustaining herself with crystals. Though such a use of the crystals was abhorrent to him, he had thought to tell her to conserve her energies against what they might find at the Jyolan, but her actions were obviously those of habit, and paradoxically he also found himself thinking that, perhaps, the weaker she was, the better.

Barran's throat was too dry for him to speak, but he had nothing to say anyway. The creature was hers, let her deal with it.

Pinnatte felt the approach of Atlon and Imorren. The event was at once trivial and profoundly significant. Trivial in that both of them could be expunged at a thought, significant in that the consequences of such an act were unforeseeable.

As they entered the door, both of them stopped. Imorren's face twitched slightly before the training of years stilled it. Atlon was openly afraid. Where Barran's men had seen a textureless greyness, both Atlon and Imorren saw a swirling ferment of the Power, restrained only by the presence of Pinnatte – or some part of Pinnatte – a shimmering likeness pervading him. Neither understood what they saw, save that such a thing should not be possible and was dangerous beyond imagining.

The Serwulf crouched as if to spring. Imorren gestured towards it and it hesitated. Then it opened its mouth and screamed at them. It was an appalling sound, but the two figures did not yield. The scream subsided into a rumbling growl and the Serwulf made no attempt to attack.

At a loss to know what to do, Atlon stepped forward slowly to speak to Pinnatte.

Coils of the Power wrapped themselves around him. Despair and self-reproach welled up like vomit inside him. Imorren had bound him. He had thought that she was cowed for the moment,

430

that she had recognized the danger and, albeit reluctantly, was working with him in the hope of dealing with it. Given a fraction of warning he might have defended himself, but now he was helpless.

'Do not struggle, Atlon,' Imorren said. 'You know I can destroy you, but who can say what events will be set in motion if we try our strengths here – at so delicate a balancing.' There was a mocking note in her voice that redoubled Atlon's rage at his folly. 'Besides, if you live, I'd like to talk with you further when this is over.'

Then she was kneeling before the motionless Pinnatte. Though ignorant of what had happened to him she had determined to act as had always been envisaged should the Anointing prove successful.

'Great Guardian of the Ways, I offer you this man, who would have sought to destroy you. Do with him as you will. Bring to this place, I beg you, the True Lord of this world so that He too might bow down before you in gratitude for His release from the unjust bondage that has so long held Him.'

Pinnatte heard the lies in Imorren's words, but just as a Kyrosdyn act had brought him here, so part of him was bound to them and must obey. Across countless worlds he felt a gathering, a coming together. It was his doing, he knew, but it was beyond him to prevent it.

A myriad whispering voices soughed through the dancing vista and, somewhere far away, he felt them shift and change, and re-form until they were bright and piercing, like the light of a single silver star. But it was no joyous event. At the touch of such a light, the whole world would become like the Jyolan until it was shaped in the bleak and barren image of its new Lord.

Drawn by him and to him, the light came nearer.

Yet there was fear and uncertainty in it. There was great danger for it here.

Pinnatte the street thief turned his eyes in appeal to Atlon, as bound and helpless as he was.

This thing must not be.

The despair in Pinnatte's gaze drove the self-reproach from

Atlon. Die he might, but fail he must not. Cautiously he tested the bonds about him. Each of them tightened. So near to the culmination of her life's work, Imorren's awareness was at its manic height and, assisted by the crystals, her considerable ability with the Power was enhanced beyond anything Atlon could oppose from such a position.

He sensed the approach of something through the skeins of the Power winding about Pinnatte. Something awful.

Imorren's eyes shone, wild and exhilarated.

Then a high-pitched shrieking pierced the whirling silence and a sinuous brown form darted into the greyness. A cruel claw slashed across Imorren's back.

Atlon was free.

And so was the Serwulf.

'Kill her!' Dvolci roared to Atlon, leaping high in the air to avoid the Serwulf's charge, and landing on its back. Trembling, Atlon drew his sword and raised it to strike the stricken Imorren, her hand clutching futilely at the bleeding gash across her back. Their eyes met and he hesitated as he saw into the heart of the young girl cruelly used by others.

Then the pitiful mask was gone and he was hurled across the room. The sword clattered from his hand as he struck the wall. Imorren's Power tightened about him pitilessly and would have crushed him utterly had not the Serwulf collided with her in its frantic attempt to free itself from the clawing form of Dvolci clinging to its back.

Atlon slid to the floor. Too shaken to stand, he rolled toward Pinnatte. Reaching him, his head spinning and his body screaming in protest, he dragged himself upright. All about him he could feel the clamouring realities that were so unnaturally focused around Pinnatte. And he could see the gathering light being drawn inexorably nearer.

Then, to his horror, though he saw the pain and the plea in Pinnatte's eyes, he did not know what to do. Nothing in his experience or his learning had equipped him for this.

Desperately, he reached out to take Pinnatte's hand. He was no great healer, but healing was all he could offer. As he reached out

432

he saw Imorren, her hand about her throat, preparing to strike him again.

The frenzy of the combat between Dvolci and the Serwulf filled his ears. Dvolci would never give up – not ever. The Brothers he had stood with on the battle field, the armies he had watched, none of them would yield. *He* must not yield. But he was too spent, and she too powerful, to defend himself.

Yet he would give what he could to Pinnatte, and he would give this fearful woman nothing but his contempt.

He clutched at his own throat mockingly and returned Imorren's triumphant sneer. 'Do your worst, crone. Do you think I'd come amongst such as you unprotected? Know this: I was one of those who helped send your erstwhile Lord to His deserved oblivion, who scattered His screaming will across the worlds beyond.'

Imorren hesitated, then her face became a mixture of fear and rage. The hand about her throat tightened, whitening her knuckles, and she levelled the other at Atlon. He straightened up and held out his arms scornfully to receive the blow. But no blow came. Instead, Imorren faltered, a terrible realization coming into her eyes. Just as the Novice had done when he attacked Atlon, so now, lured on by Atlon's taunts and threats, she had done the same. The crystals that sustained her had been stressed too far. Where they had given, now they were taking.

But Imorren was no Novice and, at this extremity, she was deadlier than any man, drawing on resources that only a woman possesses. Tearing open the neck of her gown, she wrenched the crystals from her throat with a terrible cry.

It was too late. But the approaching light lit her face like a benediction and she found the strength for a final effort.

Atlon quailed before the hatred in her face, but her final use of the Power was not against him. It was a subtle use which gave Atlon a measure of her true ability. What Power she had left, she gave to the furious Serwulf, with a simple command.

'Kill him,' she said, as she died.

Suddenly oblivious to the awful damage being done to it by the elusive Dvolci's claws and teeth, the Serwulf leapt at Atlon. So fast was it that Atlon did not even have time to raise an arm to protect himself.

As the gasping maw filled his vision, a denying hand was thrust in front of him.

It was Pinnatte's.

The Serwulf's jaw closed upon it.

There was a brief and terrible silence, then the Serwulf released the hand and reared up on its hind legs, letting out a scream that passed through every part of the Jyolan and into the city beyond. For an instant, the yellow light of its eyes seemed to fill its entire body, then it fell to the floor, twitching uncontrollably.

Dvolci killed it with a single blow, and roared at it triumphantly.

Atlon found himself holding the body of Pinnatte. The flickering aura that had surrounded him hovered on its own for a moment, shifting and changing. Through it shone a cold silver light. Briefly it took on human form again, and an awful presence filled the room. Atlon held Pinnatte tightly, terrified, but opposing.

Then, silently, the aura was gone.

Falling after it, with a noise like the rending of tortured metal, went the clamouring anomalies that it had created as the Portals to the worlds beyond vanished.

The Mirror Room was itself again. But it was carrying the echoing consequences of the collapse through the Jyolan. There was a lull, then an ominous rumbling began to build.

'Run for it!'

Dvolci's command was unequivocal. Atlon cast a brief glance at the shrivelled bodies of Imorren and the Serwulf, then throwing Pinnatte over his shoulder, he followed Dvolci.

He had little recollection of the remainder of that journey through the Jyolan, save that of constant pain, Dvolci's constant urging and the all-pervading rumbling. When he emerged into the street, a powerful arm seized both him and his burden and ploughed a ruthless way through the gathering crowd.

It was Heirn.

'We heard the noise,' Dvolci said, by way of explanation. 'Most of Arash-Felloren did.'

Unceremoniously, Heirn negotiated with a carter on the edge of the crowd for assistance in getting the casualties home.

As Atlon recovered his breath in the cart, his first thought was for Pinnatte. To his surprise and relief, the young thief was only unconscious, though he had a terrible would on his hand.

'He's normal again,' Dvolci said excitedly. 'It's gone.'

Atlon nodded, then grimaced as he glanced at the bloodstained felci. 'I'll have a look at you when I've bound his hand.'

Dvolci chuckled, then shook himself vigorously, splattering blood all over the cart. 'Don't worry,' he said. 'None of it's mine.'

A dull roar made Atlon look up.

He was just in time to see the Jyolan collapsing.

A great cloud of dust rose up into the red evening light and engulfed the crowd.

'Take us home, Heirn,' he said.

Chapter 32

Insofar as anyone cared, the collapse of the Jyolan was generally attributed to fundamental instability in its ancient and intricate structure. Ale-shop worthies nodded sagely over their jugs to confirm their surprise that it had not happened long ago. No one attempted to explain the noises that had come from it. They were left to colour the nightmares of those who had heard them.

Miraculously, no one else was killed. All except Barran had left when the sounds of the fighting began to resonate through the building, and he had escaped very quickly when the shaking began.

Barran was more than a little disappointed. The building had cost him a great deal, and the loss of the Mirror Room in particular grieved him deeply. It took him several hours to recover, then he was making plans about what he could use the site for, and to whom he could sell a considerable amount of rubble. He consoled himself also with the knowledge that he would be able to use the loss very effectively when dealing with the Kyrosdyn in future.

The Kyrosdyn themselves were however, much reduced as a force in Arash-Felloren. The loss of both Imorren and Rostan, together with the collapse of the plan for the Anointing, left them with little choice but to revert to their nominal calling as simple crystal-workers.

The Tunnellers who had assaulted the Vaskyros faded away.

Arash-Felloren continued as normal. Only the gossip changed.

Atlon was exhausted and badly bruised, but otherwise uninjured. Such discomfort as he felt, he forced himself to ignore as he worked to help Pinnatte, for the erstwhile street thief's need was

437

considerable. The wound made by the Serwulf festered badly and gave him great pain. It taxed Atlon's skills to the full, though after a few grim days it began to heal. His inner wounds were even less amenable, and for some time he would not speak and had to be encouraged even to eat. For a long time he would wake each night, wide-eyed, his mouth gaping in a silent scream.

'He's seen things that people aren't supposed to see,' Atlon said. 'When he's well enough, he'll have to come back with me. He's beyond anything I can do, but I know a healer who'll be able to help him.' Heirn offered no objection. There was nothing for someone in Pinnatte's condition in Arash-Felloren.

Ghreel recognized Atlon immediately.

'Don't expect any money back for the nights you didn't sleep here. I had to keep your room empty.'

Atlon ignored the greeting and moved to a table. Heirn followed him, leading Pinnatte. Dvolci trotted behind them. They ate a meal in silence.

When they had finished, Heirn leaned back. 'Miserable old devil is Ghreel, but he's not a bad cook.'

Atlon nodded.

'Will you come back again?' Heirn asked.

Atlon looked at him pensively. 'It's not a nice place.'

'It's better now, with the Jyolan gone and the Kyrosdyn chastened.'

'True,' Atlon conceded. He took a small box from his pocket. 'These are the crystals from the poor Novice. Take them.' He held up a hand to forestall Heirn's protest. 'Use them to make the place better still.' He placed the box on the table. 'I'll be back,' he said unequivocally. 'We need to know much more about these things.' He shook his head thoughtfully. 'I can't see how they can be natural. They have all the characteristics of a made thing. And something made for weapons at that.' He thrust the box towards Heirn. 'Still, that's for another time, isn't it? My immediate concern is to get Pinnatte home safely and in the hands of someone who can help him properly. And my people need to know all that happened.' His face darkened and his voice fell. 'I felt His presence in that awful light, Heirn. As clearly as I felt it all those years ago. He was nearly here. We know beyond any doubt now that he's struggling to return. It would be foolish of us indeed to imagine that Arash-Felloren was the only place where His followers are working to help Him.'

Heirn laid a hand on Atlon's arm. 'But He didn't return, did He? And you and your Brothers will be watching for Him now.'

'And there's one other person who knows about Him now, isn't there?' Atlon said, looking at him significantly.

Heirn returned the look then picked up the box. 'Never underestimate the value of the small action?' he said. Atlon nodded.

Then they were leaving. Heirn went first, helping Pinnatte. As he walked past Ghreel, scowling over the counter, Dvolci could not resist. He stood on his hind legs and looked at him squarely.

'Jolly nice meal, landlord,' he said loudly, and as if to a slow child. 'Jolly nice. I'll be sure to recommend you to all my friends.' He was laughing as he trotted off after Heirn.

Ghreel was still gaping as Atlon, silhouetted in the doorway, gave him a parting wave then quietly closed the door.

Desmodus

Melanie Tem

'[Her] writing is a cry from the very heart of
darkness' Dan Simmons

*My mother did not like men. Most women I knew didn't. Her
attitude toward us was more contempt than hatred, more
disappointment and disgust than dislike.*

Joel Desmodus is a male vampire living in a community
dominated by female vampires. Unlike the humans who
live in the surrounding towns Joel's species is totally
matriarchal – from the powerfully mysterious and
frightening Old Women to Joel's own fourteen-year-old
niece who, despite her youth, is seen to be better equipped to make decisions than he is.

Because of the excessive demands placed upon them all,
the women need the winter season to hibernate, leaving
the men to indulge in orgies and any other hedonistic
activities denied them during the rest of the year. And
this particular winter Joel is given the unnatural task of
managing his younger sister's weird family while she is
asleep.

When he inadvertently stumbles on a horrific secret
which has remained hidden for generations – a secret
which, if revealed, would threaten the very structure of
the vampire society – Joel is forced to kidnap his niece's
newborn baby boy, and in doing so face his own com-
plicity in the fearsome legacy of his people.

0 7472 4888 5

HYPERION

**THE STUNNING HUGO AWARD WINNING
SCIENCE FICTION NOVEL**

Dan Simmons

It is the twenty-ninth century and the universe of
the Human Hegemony is under threat. Invasion
by the warlike rebel Ousters looms, and the
mysterious schemes of the secessionist AI
TechnoCore bring chaos even closer.

On the eve of disaster, with the entire galaxy at
war, seven pilgrims set forth on a final voyage to
the fabled Time Tombs on Hyperion, home to
the Shrike, a lethal creature, part god and part
killing machine, whose powers transcend the
limits of time and space. Like another fabled
group of pilgrims, each traveller shares his story
with his fellows, seeking answers to the unsolved
riddles of all their lives. And they have resolved
to die before discovering anything less than the
secrets of the universe itself.

HYPERION is a brilliant tapestry, a superb
vision of future technology and ancient religions,
of scientific revelation and timeless mystery, of
transcendent joy and mind-bending horror. It is a
landmark in modern science fiction.

SCIENCE FICTION 0 7472 3482 5

A selection of bestsellers from Headline